# Chaos

Nights of Shadow

Lianne Miller

Lianne Miller
publisher@liannemiller.com
www.liannemiller.com

Publisher's Note: This is a work of fiction. Names, characters, places, and incidents are a product of the author's imagination. Locales and public names are sometimes used for atmospheric purposes. Any resemblance to actual people, living or dead, or to businesses, companies, events, institutions, or locales is completely coincidental.

Edited by Christina M. Frey, Page Two Editing
Cover Design by Steven Novak, Illustrator

Chaos–Nights of Shadow (Book Three)/ Lianne Miller—1st ed.
ISBN 0-9963768-5-2
ISBN 978-0-9963768-5-3

# TABLE OF CONTENTS

# Dedication

There is no greater loss in life than that of one's soul mate. But there is no greater redemption than the reunion between souls, whether in this life or the next. Only one thing separates the two—the chaos that comes in between.

This novel is dedicated to those who endure the tumult of living after such loss or while still searching for one another in this life.

In memoriam ...

For a man who left me with many great memories—childhood, school, logging, trucking, and dancing—and found our friendship so meaningful that he couldn't say good-bye. I'll never forget all the great times we shared: the ways I embarrassed you by being me or when I deliberately teased you just to see you blush; the countless times we danced; the endless days together on logging sites or in the logging camps; the precious hours we spent visiting while sitting in the cab of a truck at a truck stop. I valued the friendship we shared, as well as the friendship between you and my husband. Thank you for adding to the inspiration for the character Matt Wolfe.

Rest in peace, Dennis Sheets (9/25/2015). Have fun dancing with the angels, and remember to save a spot for me on your dance card. I don't regret that we never said good-bye, but I will miss you always. Until we meet again ...

# PROLOGUE

## *Vengeance*

"Where am I?" She rubs her eyes and tries to get her bearings, scanning the shadows in the dimly lit room. She's lying on a large canopied bed with sheer white curtains draped over a dark mahogany frame. The tall ceiling and ornate molding on the walls complement the elegant furniture—they are far grander than the simple straw-tick mattress on the floor of her attic room.

"You're home."

She startles at the deep male voice, and her head whips toward the corner of the room. "Home?" Her pulse races. *Home?*

"Yes, you're home, and you're safe now."

"Safe?" She feels stupid repeating everything he says, but none of this makes sense to her. The last memory she has is being at the table with her parents for dinner.

The man walks across the room and sits on the edge of the bed. "Yes, safe ... no one can hurt you here."

"I don't understand. Where are my parents?" She has

never seen this man before. He's tall and slender, with a narrow, angular face and light-brown hair, and his eyes are an unnatural shade of green—so dark they almost look black. For a moment his eyes shift to a lighter bright green, then back again. A chill races over her skin. There's something about him that unnerves her. "Who are you?"

Pity and sorrow chase fear and anger across the softer lines of his face. "Your uncle will talk to you about your parents. As for me ..." His hand moves as if to take hers, but then he withdraws it to his lap. "I've been assigned to protect you ... to keep you safe."

*Why do I need a protector?* "Who are you?" The look she gives him is hard, scrutinizing. It doesn't sound as if he's lying, but what he's saying doesn't seem right either. Instinct tells her that if anything, she needs protection from him.

"Dahliorn."

She raises an eyebrow. "Dahliorn ... what?"

"Just Dahliorn."

*Strange.* Her eyes dart from the man's face to the shadows in the unfamiliar room. Then another thought creeps in, and her frantic heart drives ice through her veins. Something about being here, in this place. It reeks of evil— she can smell it.

He places a hand on hers. "Easy, Ramira. There's no reason to become alarmed."

"Where are we?"

"At your uncle's estate on Rathlin Island." He seems to realize the answer confuses her, and he adds, "Off the coast of northern Ireland."

*How did I get here?*

The hinges creak as the bedroom door opens, and Dahliorn scrambles to his feet, scuttling away from her bed. Ramira doesn't miss the terror that flashes in his eyes. She turns her attention to the older man in the doorway—like her father, he's tall and thin, with black hair, dark eyes, and an olive complexion. *Uncle?* His teeth are clenched, and rage unlike any she's seen before flares in his eyes. "I told you not to touch her. Get out!"

Dahliorn bows his head and lowers his eyes as he scurries into the hall. Intense fear and anger sweep through Ramira—she hasn't seen her uncle since she was a small child, but she remembers her mother saying that he's very powerful and dangerous. One look at him now tells her it is true.

*Where are my parents? Are they ...* She tries to move off the bed, but a twinge of pain in her shoulder pushes above the sharp throbbing in her head. The presence of her uncle has always triggered a headache, but this pain is unexpected.

Her uncle walks toward her. "Lie down and relax, Ramira. You're still healing."

It's then that she looks down—a thick, blood-soaked bandage covers her upper chest below her collarbone. The dressing is saturated, and the amount of blood seeping through it terrifies her. *Am I going to die?* "What happened to me, Uncle?"

His long fingers gently pull away the bandage, giving her a glimpse of a deep, jagged wound. "I need to do another healing spell. Try to stay still."

Her uncle puts a poultice on the wound, muttering an incantation, and Ramira winces as the heat of his hand over the injury blends with the numbing effect of the poultice. "How did this happen?" she says.

He places a new bandage over the injury and pulls her bedcover up. The look in his eyes turns cold. "I don't know. Your father alerted me that they were under attack by vampires. By the time I arrived to help, your parents were dead, and you were badly injured."

Tears well in her eyes, and she swallows against the burst of grief shredding her heart. Her uncle awkwardly pulls her into a hug. "It will be all right, little one. We will have our vengeance against them someday. One day you will be the one who brings an end to the vampire realm." The suggestion weaves through her shock and grief, and as tears pour over her cheeks, a seed of hatred takes root. Through choking sobs Ramira says, "Uncle Guillermo, I will destroy them all."

# CHAPTER 1: DMITRI

## Tipping Point

*Delay, hurry, wait ... delay, delay, delay. They don't want me to find her—they only want the spoils of war.*

Dmitri Markov has no patience for these cleanup efforts or the fallout from their success, or any other damnable excuse to prevent him from getting Elizabetta back. Each Belyakov estate they take should bring him another step closer to celebrating the end of Shashenka and the terror his former master inflicted on the world. Instead it's a reminder, a distraction—an attempt to shift his focus from hunting Guillermo. It leaves a bitterness inside, knowing that it took centuries to reach this point, but their victory, their time to savor the moment, was stolen from them so soon after they achieved it.

His body trembles with the insatiable need to kill anything standing between him and his wife, but he fights to contain the urge to act; Maria will interfere again. He's already losing count of the number of times the witch has incapacitated him by way of immobility spells or potions that leave him unable to move even one muscle in his body. Just thinking about the ways he's been thwarted by her and his so-called friends sends another spike of rage rippling through him. *If anything happens to Elizabetta, I will make that wizard regret ever knowing me.*

Dmitri's vision turns red as the bloodlust thrums inside him. Images flash through his mind: bodies torn limb from limb, blood spilling on the ground. Elizabetta with the sorcerer's staff run through her. The fire of vengeance races up his spine as his muscles coil and demand the release that he knows can only be found in destroying everyone around him ... unless he finds her first.

More images assault him. Traitors, enemies—Milo, Teresina, Guillermo. *They will pay for their treachery.* Stonewalling from Maria, Vladimir, Matt, Jacques. His nostrils flare; his body longs to quench his thirst for revenge. He needs his enemies' blood ... their deaths. *I will drain every last one who stands in my way.*

Rage sends more tremors through Dmitri as Matt Wolfe returns his stare—the hazel green of the wolf's eyes slowly lifts the red haze shrouding his. An unspoken pledge passes between them—they will find her. *Matt cares ... the mongrel wants her back almost as much as I do.* But it's not good enough, not fast enough. Dmitri searches for a way to escape and flinches when a hand clamps down on his shoulder.

"Ease up, keep fighting it. We're going to finish taking care of this shit, and then we are going to get her back. Stay with me on this—I'll be right by your side." Matt shifts his gaze to the Druzhinas standing near them and folds his arms across his chest as he gives them a defiant glare.

*He's fed up with the delays too.* The mongrel's loyalty to Elizabetta is proving to be quite an asset. "I wouldn't expect you to be anywhere else." Dmitri blinks rapidly to clear his vision and glances at those around him; somehow he must finish this without giving in to the dark urges screaming to be set free. He knows Matt won't abandon the obligation to finish the war against Belyakov's lackeys, and he's smart enough to realize that Matt's resources and connections will help him find Elizabetta faster.

"Come on, buddy, I can't do this alone ... baby vamp would want us to get this done first." Matt places a hand on his shoulder again, gives him a sharp nod, and says, "Time to finish kicking some vamp ass. Let's go."

*The mongrel is right. I have to beat this ... I can't lose Elizabetta.* Dmitri takes a few deep breaths in an attempt to calm himself and can feel the rage simmer down to a mad boil.

His eyes roam over those gathered near him on the primary piano nobile. At least La Perfezione and most of the remaining Belyakov properties have been secured; there are only two left to take, Prague and Novgorod, and within minutes they will arrive in Prague to reclaim that one.

The stragglers they were waiting for finally arrive and form a circle around a young maxian with an EPM—an enhanced portable mutaport, a smaller version of the full-size device—strapped to his back. Swirls of different colors pulse over the surface of the wide ring. Dmitri notices it's dim in the standby state compared with the bright colors he saw when it was activated at Machu Picchu. The power for the portable device comes from direct contact with its bearer, which allows it to tap into the body's electrical currents as well as the maxian's magic. Because of that they are seldom used; those who carry an EPM are at constant risk of death, as the device can drain their magic and cause their vital organs to explode.

The young maxian doesn't show any signs that he fears the potential danger, but the nervous tension Dmitri can feel from those around him is palpable. *Not sure I want to use their method of transportation anymore.* It's a risk he must take if they're going to finish this and begin the search for Elizabetta.

Dmitri moves alongside Matt, joining the others lined up back to back; they're ready to fight the moment they arrive in Prague, and he is anxious for the chance to unleash some of his pent-up rage. As far as he's concerned, none are more deserving of it than Shashenka's lackeys. *Top of my list— Teresina, Milo, Guillermo. Let them be there so I can end them.*

Understanding the necessity of finishing what they started doesn't erase the fact that with each passing minute, the trail for those three grows cold. If it weren't for Matt's constant encouragement or the ever-present threat of being magically bound and left behind, Dmitri would already be scouring the world for them. A new swell of rage narrows his eyes as he says, "We will take the two remaining estates together, but as soon as we are done, I will start looking for Elizabetta. Mark my words, I will destroy this world if that's what it takes to find her and get her back. None of you will stop me."

High Warlock Jacques Boucher moves alongside him. Dmitri, wary of his presence, waits for the man to say or do something—it wouldn't surprise him if the warlock placed him under a spell, just like Maria has done more than once already.

Instead Jacques speaks in an unexpectedly reassuring tone. "I once told your wife that you didn't choose a lesser mate, but a true equal—a leader within her own right. One who can lead with or without you by her side. The same is true in reverse. You must be willing to face what lies ahead, even to rule alone if that is what fate decides."

Dmitri glares at the warlock, but Jacques ignores his pointed look. "Mrs. Markov accepted that burden, and with sorrow in her heart she rose to the challenge to lead us in battle. She would expect no less of you. If her life is to be sacrificed, don't let it be in vain."

## CHAPTER 2: ELIZABETTA

# *Divisions*

Elizabetta lies on a cot in a dark room that seems little better than the cells found at a Belyakov estate. For the hundredth time her mind races over the events that led her here. The false life and name—Eliza Ross—she was living under ended the minute the battle was won. In that moment she fully reclaimed her identity: Elizabetta Rossellini Markov, mate and wife of Dmitri Markov, and co-leader of the elite Druzhina. *I never got the chance to tell the others.* The last she remembers is watching with pride as Maria held Dmitri and Matt's hands and cast the protection spell to safeguard their allies from their enemies. The long-overdue victory had finally come—the devil vamp was dead. Their new lives were about to start. But in the next moment Guillermo appeared out of nowhere, and before she could move, his staff thrust forward and pierced her body just as her gaze met Dmitri's horrified expression—then everything went black.

*Will I ever see Dmitri again?* Her eyes fill with tears as

she probes the gaping hole near her navel. Her body is mending; the wound is now about half the size it was when Guillermo first brought her here. *Wherever here is.* Elizabetta still doesn't know what the evil sorcerer wants with her, though, and fear creeps in as she considers the possibilities. He hasn't been back to this room or even spoken to her since he snatched her away from Machu Picchu. *What is he going to do to me? I've got to get out of here.* Her pulse races. Her eyes sweep the small room again. There are no windows, only a single door, and the cot is the sole furnishing—if she can even call it that. She tries to rise from the cot, but a white-hot bolt of pain bursts through her, and she lies back to catch her breath.

She startles when the door opens and Guillermo's body fills its frame. He steps inside, followed by two others: a young woman with shoulder-length brown hair and a tall, well-built man. The man's features are stunning. *Too beautiful to be human.* Both look to be in their twenties, but Elizabetta suspects they are much older; the odds favor that they too are maxians.

The younger man carries another cot, and no one speaks as he sets it alongside Elizabetta's. The woman, likely a witch, lies down on it and turns her face toward Elizabetta. For a brief moment the woman's gaze locks on to hers— then the woman looks up at the ceiling and closes her eyes. Elizabetta shifts her focus to Guillermo and the unknown man, who is standing back against the wall, watching the three of them with an intensity that makes her feel uncomfortable. *Definitely maxian, but what are they up to?*

Guillermo steps forward and peers at her wound. He

snorts as if he's disappointed to see any improvement. "Are you ready, Ramira?"

"Yes, Uncle."

"Wait. What are you going to do to me?" Elizabetta darts a glance between the three.

The wicked way Guillermo's eyes shimmer tells her that he is insane. The sorcerer laughs as he conjures a stool out of thin air and sits next to her. "I know you're thinking that you'll be able to resist me, but as you already know, I don't fight fair." *Something tells me this won't end well for me.*

The sorcerer sneers; his hand clamps over her mouth to prevent her protests. "The time has come to destroy the most powerful of your kind, and the only way to do that is with one of the most powerful vampires remaining. It's clear you've risen to that rank since Shashenka's defeat."

*If he thinks he's going to use me to do that, he's in for a rude awakening.*

"The woman lying next to you is my niece, Ramira. Hundreds of years ago vampires killed her parents and left her for dead. She's waited centuries for someone like you to come along and help her set things right."

Elizabetta has no idea what he's talking about; his claims are proof that he's beyond crazy. *Go screw yourself. Ain't happening. I won't help you.*

"Are you ready, Ramira?" He looks at his niece and waits for her reply.

"Yes."

Guillermo begins to chant, and Elizabetta looks over the three maxians again. The sorcerer's fierce glare never leaves her face. His niece lies still with her eyes closed. The other man, still standing against the wall behind Guillermo, seems to be muttering something, but he's not making a sound. His penetrating gaze captures hers; she can't look away from his dark-green eyes. There's something odd about him, and she's trying to puzzle it out, but then the younger man's eyes flash red—and a second later Elizabetta feels something within her mind and body tear apart.

What starts as hot pain turns into a frenzied ripping sensation, as if every inch of her flesh and bones is being stripped away. Layer after layer peels apart until it seems that her body must be left in a heaping mass of blood, raw nerves, and tissue. In the next instant a sense of not being within herself, at least not fully, leaves her perplexed. More than that—it's as if her brain has been plucked out of her skull and is swirling alone within a torrent of icy wind, isolated from the heat destroying her body. The eerie similarity to the merging spell when she had her memories restored is not lost on her, and yet this is nothing like it. *What did he just do to me?*

"Ramira?" Guillermo's voice is soft. "Can you hear me?"

Elizabetta begins to shake, unable to control the violent quaking.

When the young witch fails to answer, Guillermo's tone becomes urgent. "Ramira! Answer me." The sorcerer mutters under his breath as he moves closer to his niece's side.

Horror seeps through Elizabetta's bones, and tremors rock her body. Something isn't right—she can't move enough to even protect herself or fight back. She doesn't understand what is going on or what the spell the sorcerer cast has done to her. Panic infuses itself into her marrow, but she can't force a scream out of her traumatized body.

She's trying to look at the man with the strange eyes when a gasp pulls her attention back to Guillermo, who is staring down at the prone body of his niece. Elizabetta follows his line of sight and sees blood soaking the witch's shirt near her belly. The sorcerer tugs the shirt up out of the way, and a disturbing, almost bewildered look settles over his face.

Through chattering teeth Elizabetta whispers, "W-what d-did you do? What's hap-happening t-to me?"

Guillermo ignores her and looks at the other man. "Something's wrong. Get her out of here and up to her room ... watch her until I finish here. And I mean watch her—I don't want to find a single trace of your magic on her."

Without a word the man steps forward and lifts Ramira's body from the cot. Whatever happened has the woman out cold; she lies limp in his arms as he leaves the room.

Uncontrollable shivers burst through Elizabetta again. Something is not right—in fact, something is horribly wrong. The separation she felt earlier seems to be growing, as if a huge part of herself is no longer there. Her hands shake, barely able to move, as she feels along her body; the wound in her belly is still there, but no other injuries explain the painful sensations ripping through her. It's as though her body is there and intact, but each second that races by snatches another piece of her.

Guillermo stares at her as if he's in shock.

"W-hat-t d-did you d-do t-to me?" she chokes out.

Her question seems to jar him out of whatever stupefied state he is in. He bends over and clasps her face in his hands. For several minutes the sorcerer's gaze pins her to the cot, but inside, Elizabetta's body continues to tremble and fall apart; she can feel herself slipping away. Then the chasm opens further, and in its expansive wake she knows she is losing something she may never get back. *Am I dying?* Elizabetta struggles to keep her eyes open, but it becomes too much, and her eyelids droop and slam shut. Unable to fight it any longer, she lets go, drifting into darkness.

# CHAPTER 3: DMITRI

## Unleashed in Prague

The once-immaculate Prague ballroom now bears little resemblance to its normal ostentatious state; broken and overturned furniture is scattered about, and pools of blood surround piles of disintegrated vampire bodies. There are a few burnt heads too, but unrecognizable, with no way to discern if the fallen were female or male, let alone friend or foe. Nor is there sign of the maxian who was supposed to be here helping their allies, and Dmitri wonders if she's elsewhere on the estate or if she's dead. *If she's dead, we will make them pay for this—the brutality of Shashenka's goons ends now!*

Rage seeps to the surface, and a wicked smile crosses his face as the bloodlust percolates within. He'll have an outlet for it now. The flavor of it on his tongue is tantalizing, and with little to hold the darkness at bay, he prepares to unleash the wrath it brings with it. It's just a small taste of what he's capable of, and he knows it.

Dmitri's eyebrows pull up as he meets Matt's gaze. Snout

wrinkled into a double grin, the wolf gives him a curt nod. They're both going to have a little fun. But before they launch into battle, another unspoken agreement is reached between the two—they will not leave each other's side. *Indeed, a guard-wolf.* There's no one else Dmitri would rather have fighting next to him as they wreak hell upon their enemies.

The Druzhinas disperse, pushing their way through Shashenka's remaining fighters, and the sight that greets Dmitri outside the ballroom is something he never imagined seeing in a Belyakov mansion: besides Matt, a dozen other werewolves fight next to vampires as they clash with about two dozen locals and Druzhinnikis intent on keeping control of the Prague villa. He has no idea where they came from, but they're clearly on the right side. *Hmm, even match ... well, it was until we showed up.*

Dmitri and Matt work as a team—one grabs an adversary while the other severs the head, and then they move on to the next. The wolf seems just as hungry to kill their opponents, but even Dmitri can tell the mongrel is being more rational about it. More than once the wolf nudges Dmitri off a downed foe, meeting Vladimir's silent nod of approval. When the fighting slows, Matt pushes Dmitri into a room and slams the door shut, shifting into human form. "Get ahold of yourself. If Maria sees you all wild eyed, she's going to bench you again."

Dmitri nods, blinking to clear his mind and refocus. Matt's steady tone weaves through him as he breathes deeply through his nose and stuffs the raw anger far beneath the surface. His fists clench and unclench with the effort to rein in the bloodlust, but he keeps his gaze locked on Matt's face, drawing strength from the wolf to pull harder against the baser urges telling him to kill everyone in sight. His eyes close, remaining shut for another long moment before he opens them slowly and gives Matt a hard but controlled look.

Matt says, "Are we good?"

"Yeah, we're good." He resists the urge to brush the mongrel's hands away.

They briefly regroup with the others at the top of the stairs before resuming their assault on the main level. Stephan and Victoria drop back to help the maxians execute those they incapacitate along the way, while the rest of the allies split into two teams to end the battle. They rejoin the fray, but only a few enemies are left on the lower level, and together Dmitri and Matt take them down with ease. When it's over, only a handful of neutralized vampires guarded by two locals remain to be dealt with.

The maxians, to Dmitri's surprise, have put their magic to work by obliterating what is left of the fallen and casting spells to right the disarray inside the mansion. He finds it both disappointing and satisfying—he doesn't want to stop killing, but he's ready to move on. It's another step nearer to going after Elizabetta.

"Dmitri, what shall we do with these?" Stephan says. He and Victoria are holding the two locals they found guarding the enemy outdoors.

Alexander says, "They seem to be the only ones who fought on our side and survived the battle here."

Dmitri shrugs, but everyone turns to him as if the decision is his alone to make. *They're trying to keep me distracted.* And, whether he wants to admit or accept it, they are pushing him back into leading the Druzhina—a position he hasn't held in over five centuries. He grimaces. All he desires is to find Elizabetta, and then they'll decide on their future and whether they'll even remain with the Druzhina at all. He rakes a hand through his hair as he looks around the room; there's no one else here but the locals and those who came from La Perfezione.

The disposition of the Belyakov estates was decided before they ended Shashenka's reign; this villa now belongs to Vladimir and Anna, and Dmitri insists it's their decision, not his. Vladimir nods and gives the men the choice of staying on to serve or making their own way now that they're free of Shashenka. Both locals agree to stay and lock down the estate until Vladimir returns from the Druzhinas' next task, taking the castle at Novgorod. *There will be no more delays after we capture it, or I will kill everyone who stands in my way.*

Katherine's voice pulls Dmitri back to the present. None of Shashenka's top Druzhinnikis have been found yet; they weren't at Machu Picchu but haven't been sighted at any of the estates either. Speculation on their whereabouts begins, and Dmitri reaches his own conclusion. *Novgorod. They're holding the castle.*

Kees's gaze stays on Dmitri as he says, "It's logical that Shashenka was aware that we planned to take over the estates—he likely sent them forward to ensure that his castle in Novgorod remained in his control."

Victoria nods in agreement, detailing Shashenka's last

briefing in Xi'an, before he sent his maxian allies to Machu Picchu. Peter, Leonard, and Charles were to meet other Druzhinnikis at the airport, and while their destination wasn't revealed, Shashenka's final command to them made it clear that they knew what they had to do.

"So in other words, your devil vamp was cocky enough to hope he had brute force over us, but prepared a contingency in case he failed." A lopsided grin spreads across Matt's face. "Underestimated ... sweet!"

Katherine says, "Yes, I think it's likely that, although he was prepared for a battle, he was less confident than he let on."

*So what did Teresina tell him?* Dmitri's aware that the rogue knew their plans and the danger she was putting them in, but something seems off. "Why wouldn't that bitch Teresina have told him everything?"

Justin clears his throat; hurt is evident in his eyes. "I don't know what's going on with her or why she did what she did. I ..." He draws a deep breath. "It ... something is missing here. We were talking about a life together when this was done."

The betrayal Justin must be feeling is unfathomable to Dmitri—he's never heard of a potential mate turning against the other. The devastation to the young Druzhina shows in the slump of his shoulders and the ever-present pain in his eyes. It makes Dmitri loathe Teresina all the more. He turns to Matt. "You worked with her the longest and knew she was a risk, but do you know her well enough to make any guesses about this?"

"I don't have a clue. There was never a hint that she was

unhappy, and she never hit me up for more money either. We paid her a rather hefty sum—it should have been enough to guarantee her loyalty."

*And yet she still turned against us.* A memory of Teresina flashes before him: the rogue standing next to Milo when Dmitri was transported from the cell in Xi'an to Machu Picchu. Hatred fans his bloodlust, but the wolf clamps a hand on his neck—a subtle reminder to hold himself in check. Dmitri's hands curl into fists, and he can feel the tips of his claws cut into his palms as he takes a few steadying breaths.

"These are things we can get answers to after we find her." Vladimir gives Dmitri a pointed look. "First we need to take Novgorod. If Peter, Charles, and Leonard are there, we need them taken alive for interrogation."

"Jacques, can you check with your maxian at Novgorod for an update? I'd like to know what we're walking into." Kees looks at the high warlock.

A redecrystapiezo is in Jacques's hand before Kees finishes speaking. The call goes unanswered. Dmitri asks Matt to make contact with their werewolf allies there; again, no answer. Desperate, Dmitri takes out his phone and calls Janek Novak.

"Business or pleasure?" the vampire answers in his usual manner.

"It's Dmitri. Do you have any contacts near Belyakov's estate in Novgorod?"

"A couple, why?"

"Shashenka has been eliminated, but we've lost contact with our forces at the castle—we've taken all the other estates."

Janek gives a low whistle, then laughs. "I was wondering when this was going down. I'm a little surprised none of you called me to have me help take the villa here. Congratulations, by the way—I'm happy to hear that corrupt son of a bitch is dead."

Dmitri interrupts him. "We don't have time for this ... all has not gone well since the fight." An image of Elizabetta impaled on Guillermo's staff flashes through his mind again, and his heart constricts in pain—another blast of bloodlust scorches its way to the surface. Holding Matt's gaze, he speaks curtly. "We need an outside assessment— yesterday—for what we can expect." *That mongrel is the only thing keeping my sanity grounded. I don't know if I can keep doing this.*

"Let me make a couple quick calls and get back to you."

When Janek calls back, he has unsettling news. There are possibly one hundred Druzhinnikis guarding the castle, many of whom are on its perimeter, waiting for an attack. Janek's contact doesn't know how many may be inside. Worse is that it sounds as if their werewolf and vampire allies may have met a grisly end. The lone maxian sent to help them is dead; his body was seen hanging off the top of one of the guard towers.

*I'm glad the other estates didn't turn into this type of nightmare.* "Shit! This isn't good." Dmitri swipes a hand through his hair twice and leaves it at the crown of his head. His patience is wearing thin—he just needs this mess to be over. "Kees?"

Nine Druzhinas, one werewolf, and a dozen maxians is

not enough to launch a successful assault, and they all know it. "Can you get more of your people here?" Kees asks Jacques.

Jacques agrees to send Henri, the young warlock tasked with bearing the EPM, to the other estates to recall their fighters, working his way back from the furthest estate. The high warlock cautions him not to transport more than two dozen at a time. Doing so will overload Henri's abilities and cause the EPM to become unstable—it could kill him and injure those he's transporting.

A sudden spark lights Maria's eyes; she claims to know instinctually how to boost his power and prevent the device from harming him. This is something Dmitri's noticed more and more. Since Maria learned she's a wizard and particularly since she's broken free from Shashenka's control, her instincts seem to propel her toward new, untried magic that she is capable of wielding, even if she doesn't understand or know where the insight comes from. Without hesitation Maria selects three other maxians. She believes they can enhance Henri's power to transfer at least a dozen more in each group. Granted, she hasn't been wrong yet when she's tried new spells, but Dmitri still worries what it will mean for them if she's mistaken and they can't rejoin the group at Prague.

The high warlock nods in approval, and Henri transports Maria and the other three maxians away. No one knows how many they will return with, but a nerve-wracking half hour passes before the first group arrives. Dmitri breathes a sigh of relief. The wizard was correct about her abilities; thirty-six allies arrive with her transporting group of maxians. His mind works through the possibilities for their unfinished mission. *I'll have to be patient—it will take a day or two for hundreds of allies to be brought forward.* But this will tip the balance in their favor; while they must sacrifice time staging the assault, it will mean a quicker end to the battle once they invade the enemy stronghold. His confidence rises over top of the bloodlust. *This will be the last delay, and then I can find her.*

A long hour and two transports later, ninety-six additional allies have joined their ranks. *What? That's it?* His frustration and anger boil to the surface. There were hundreds of fighters at Machu Picchu, but Maria claims these are the only ones willing to come. Some are still healing from the wounds they received, and others feel they are not qualified to fight against Shashenka's best Druzhinnikis, even though his top goons were expected at Machu Picchu. *Cowards.* It's clear that many now think the unresolved matters are a vampire realm problem and no longer concern them.

Vladimir looks over the crowd. "It will have to do. Kees, what's our best option with these numbers?"

Once Kees lays out the logistics of moving their fighters and analyzes what they may face at Novgorod, the maxians and Druzhinas agree that their best chance lies in launching a surprise attack from the inside. The biggest issue is transporting the just shy of one hundred and twenty of them to the castle. Maria and the other three maxians will need to shuttle back and forth with Henri to get everyone there, and that makes their insertion point critical if they are going to keep the enemy ignorant of their arrival.

Maria says, "The Druzhinnikis will believe the dungeon is secure, and the only guards, if any, will be few and posted at the doors on the ground floor. Arriving there may bolster our numbers. Knowing Shashenka, it's reasonable to believe that he demanded any captured allies be kept alive until he could make a spectacle of their executions."

She has a point. Dmitri, more than most, understands how Shashenka controlled his dungeon cells and torture rooms in the lower levels of the castle. Images of the horrors he endured flood his mind, and he shudders at the thought of returning there. Decades of imprisonment, torture, beatings, near starvation, and isolation ... tormented and insufferable hours he held on for the sake of Elizabetta ... bleak moments when desperation and pain had him begging for death. He tries to shake off the dark thoughts and refocus on what lies ahead. The only positive aspect of going back is the knowledge that Shashenka will never return.

*I endured and survived all of that for Elizabetta—I can hold on again. I can wait a bit longer for her.*

## CHAPTER 4: ELIZABETTA

# Mirror, Mirror

Sounds trickle into Elizabetta's awareness. It feels as if her mind is now completely disconnected from her body, or her body has ceased to exist altogether. *Am I dead?* Mocking minutes skip by as she makes futile attempts to move a hand, flutter an eyelash, or push a single noise from her mouth. Unlike with Maria's immobility spell, though, there is no underlying sense of her body's will to move being suppressed. *Did that demented psycho damage my brain? Why can't I open my eyes or get my body to work?*

Despite her confusion and panic, Elizabetta realizes people are talking—she recognizes Guillermo's voice, but not the other man's. She wonders if it's the same man who stood silently behind the sorcerer earlier. Unable to do anything but listen, she struggles to make sense of their conversation, hoping it may shed light on what is going on.

"Have you ever heard of this happening before?" Guillermo's tone carries a hint of anger.

The mystery man says, "You know this level of magic is

beyond me."

"She's been out this whole time?"

"She hasn't stirred since you cast the spell."

Guillermo curses under his breath. "What about her wound? How is that possible?"

*Are you kidding me? You freaking ran a staff clean through me. Oh yeah, he's nuts.*

"I have no answers for you."

A growl rumbles from the sorcerer. "So help me, Dahliorn, if you're withholding information that will fix this mess, I will punish you."

*Punish him? Not cohorts? Interesting.* If it's the same guy, at least she has a name for him now: Dahliorn. *What an unusual name.*

"I'm mindful of the power you hold over me. I've told you that I've never seen this before, and you know that I never practice this type of dark magic."

*What the hell?* She can't feel it, but she's certain her heart is ticking faster. "Stay with her, guard her, and be prepared for anything if she awakes. I need to do some research to figure out what went wrong." A door slams, and Elizabetta hears footsteps fade.

A silent beat of unknown minutes and hours pass her by. This is even worse than the centuries of lying in a catatonic state—at least then she knew she was in her body. Now Elizabetta isn't sure if she even exists anymore. She makes one desperate attempt after another to will any single part of her body to make the slightest motion, and she fails. *Am I a ghost?* Fear ping-pongs inside her. If she is, she may never see Dmitri, Matt, or any of her other friends again.

Then she hears what she assumes are Dahliorn's footsteps approach.

"Earth to wind, fire to water, merge, form, unite. Mix within a flash of pixies and a pinch of sprites to preserve the night child to her core. Imprint the mimic, bind them now and until released upon my command." Dahliorn draws a breath. "A fracture of my soul is recompense to save the one within, as the elements protect the night child until severed halves are made whole again."

*What kind of voodoo shit are these guys up to? Mimic? Severed halves? Is he as crazy as Guillermo?* Elizabetta's mind is racing in so many directions at once that it takes her a moment to realize her fingers can move. She opens her eyes, expecting to see Dahliorn standing nearby, but she's alone in the small dark room again. *What is going on with me?* She never heard Dahliorn leave.

She lies there for a few minutes, then moves her trembling fingers over the wound in her midriff and discovers smooth skin without the raised edges of a scar. *Well, maybe one of their screwed-up spells healed me.* She sits up, her hands patting everywhere she can reach, but she feels no pain or other injuries anywhere on her body.

She drops her legs over the edge of the cot as she looks around the dark room. Nothing has changed—gray walls, no window, single cot, locked door—except that she's alone. Then just as she rises to stand, her head swims, and she can feel herself falling back into the disconnected state she was in moments ago. There's a brief awareness that her body hits the floor, and in the next moment she again hears voices.

"Did you find anything?" Dahliorn sounds as if he's standing near her.

It takes a monumental effort to pay attention to what is going on around her.

Guillermo says, "No, and as long as Ramira remains unconscious, I won't be able to figure out what went wrong."

*Great. That twisted psycho screwed up, and now we're paying the price for it.* Elizabetta needs to know what he did to her, but she can't voice a single question.

A throat clears. "Perhaps you should remove the spell." *Dahliorn.*

"I don't dare lift it without knowing what happened or what condition this has left Ramira in. It could kill her and the vampire. I need them both."

Fear and curiosity kick Elizabetta's brain into gear. She takes quick note of everything that has happened—the witch on the cot next to her, Guillermo casting a spell, the younger man's eyes flashing red, the witch being carried away by the unknown man—possibly Dahliorn—and the odd sensation of being ripped away from herself. *What kind of spell can affect two people or keep one knocked out when it's not meant to do that? And what did Dahliorn mean about dark magic?*

Her mind drifts back over the spells that Maria has cast upon her. The only one that produced a similar, albeit brief, sensation of being outside herself was the unlocking spell that merged her suppressed memories with her present life. Aside from that, there are no similarities between the spell Maria cast and this one—isolated versus disconnected, body feeling everything versus feeling as if it isn't there, no bodily control during the spell versus intermittent body control—and whatever Guillermo did seems to have had unintended consequences for both her and Ramira. But what are those consequences, and what is considered normal about the state she's in?

Elizabetta is so lost in thought that she mentally flinches when Dahliorn whispers, "Can you hear me, little dove?"

*Little dove? Who's he talking to?* Trapped in the darkness behind closed eyes, unable to move or speak, she can't answer him regardless. Then she hears a moan. *Someone else is in this room?* Dahliorn's footsteps move away.

Her eyelids open, she can see that, but she knows this isn't right or normal. It strikes Elizabetta as odd that she can't feel their movement, and when she tries to squeeze them shut, they don't. *What the hell? I have no control ... I have no control!*

A woman, possibly Ramira, says, "Where am I?"

As Dahliorn starts to answer, the darkness crashes over Elizabetta, and she doesn't hear his reply. Moments later she can feel her body again. Slowly, cautiously, she lifts her head. She's lying on the floor of the small dark room. No one is here with her.

*Am I losing my mind?* She pushes against the cool concrete and crawls back onto the cot. This is beyond bizarre—unless whole blocks of time are escaping her or this is how it feels to be a ghost, there is no explanation for the way the others keep coming and going with each shift of the darkness that clouds her mind.

Afraid to get off the cot again, Elizabetta lies there with

her thoughts going in circles. Exhaustion pulls her into a fitful sleep. Then the nightmares begin, images of people she doesn't know mixing with emotions that range from sorrow to joy.

When Guillermo's shout wakes her, she's once more trapped inside the darkness and unable to move her body or even open her eyes.

"What do you mean, she changed?" The sorcerer roars at someone.

There is a gulp, and Dahliorn says with an underlying hint of fear, "I was watching her as you instructed, and she had a nightmare. She sat up and hissed at me, and there were fangs in her mouth."

"That's not possible."

*Guillermo knows I'm a vampire, and he should know I have fangs. Are they talking about someone else?*

The sorcerer's voice booms out, "Are you sure that you never left her and that no one was in here?"

"Yes."

"Go down and check on Elizabetta—make sure that damn vampire is still locked in her room."

*Hello? I'm lying right here. He should be in a loony bin.*

As the sound of Dahliorn running from the room fades, the darkness flickers, and Elizabetta is able to open her eyes again. There is no one in the room with her—but she didn't hear Guillermo leave. *What is happening to me?*

A key rattles in the lock, and the door swings open. The same young man she saw before is in the doorway. He seems surprised to see her staring back at him—he shakes his head and starts to pull the door shut.

"No, wait!" Elizabetta sucks in a sharp breath, unsure what to say next.

He darts a quick glance down the hall and back to her. "I have to go."

"Dahliorn?"

Color washes from his face, and a nervous twitch pulls his lips into a grimace. "You know my name."

*Okay, face and name together now.* "I heard you and Guillermo talking. Tell me what is going on, please."

"I have to go." He slams the door shut and locks it again.

The darkness pulses once, and again Elizabetta hears Guillermo speaking. *What the hell? This is going to drive me flipping insane.*

"That vampire was awake?"

"Yes." Again she detects a hint of fear in Dahliorn's voice.

"Did you speak with her?"

"I shut the door and left."

He's being evasive, but she's not sure why he dodged the question.

Guillermo groans. "Stay here with her. I don't understand what went wrong—it shouldn't be possible for her to wake up. Ramira should be awake instead of that damn vampire."

A door opens and closes, possibly Guillermo leaving. Then Elizabetta hears Dahliorn whisper, "I have to put you to sleep, little dove, but I will wake you soon."

The strange darkness surges, and Elizabetta can feel herself drift off. *He means me?* She sleeps then, but this time there are no strange nightmares with unknown people.

Instead she sees Dmitri, and her heart aches at the sadness in his eyes; it's as if he doesn't recognize her. She starts to run toward him, but his face contorts in rage, and with fangs bared he lunges at her, his dagger ready to strike. Instead of waking up, Elizabetta shifts into other dreams— some she recognizes as her own, but others feel as if they don't belong to her.

When her eyes open next, Elizabetta finds that she is still in the small dark room—alone. Her head pounds, and she's not sure if it's because of the series of disjointed dreams or if it's from whatever Guillermo did to her. *It's like he scrambled my brain.*

The dim light of her cell shimmers, and once more the blackness takes her to the disembodied state. It's quiet—no voices this time. But minutes, possibly hours later, she hears someone crying, and it seems like it's coming from her, but that doesn't make sense—she doesn't think she's crying. *Am I?* She recognizes the sensation of her chest heaving with sobs—she can't see it with her closed eyes, but she feels it—yet she doesn't have the emotion that matches what her body seems to be doing. There are warm tears running down her face, too. *Just how badly did that superfreak screw up my mind and body?*

Then she hears a door open, and a moment later Dahliorn says, "Oh, you're awake. I'd ask if you're feeling better, but you look quite upset."

*I'm getting there.*

A woman shrieks, "I don't know what you've done to me. Why are you holding me here? Who are you people?"

*That sounds like Ramira. Must have scrambled her brain*

*too.* The door opens and closes again, and for some reason it makes Elizabetta sob harder. She can't seem to stop this inappropriate reaction. It's really starting to freak her out; she was put through worse with Shashenka and never cried once. None of this makes sense to her now.

A few minutes pass before someone enters the room again. "Ramira?" Guillermo's voice sounds cautious.

There's no reply, and the sorcerer mutters some kind of spell. Elizabetta is certain that whatever he just cast was against Ramira, not her—she feels no different from before. But Guillermo leaves without a word, and the room remains silent for what seems like hours. Unable to do anything but linger in the darkness, Elizabetta drifts off to sleep.

"Little dove, are you there?" Dahliorn's voice startles her awake.

Elizabetta is still in the darkness—she struggles to open her eyes, and the moment she succeeds she hears Ramira say, "Where am I? Who are you?" She waits for Dahliorn to say something else, but he remains quiet.

*Is she talking to me? Was he?* She tries to answer, but it seems her mouth is still disconnected from her brain. It doesn't stop Ramira from lobbing a dozen questions. Once more there are sounds of someone leaving and then entering the room. Guillermo looms over her suddenly; he recites the same spell he used earlier, and Ramira falls silent. *Well, at least he shut her up.* The thought is barely out when Elizabetta's eyelids close again—she tries to resist, and fails.

She needs to see what is going on—needs to figure out what is happening to her. *What if I never get out of this mess? I don't understand ... need to fight back. How?* She knows that's the big question—how—but the answer seems content to wait to reveal itself until she completely loses her mind.

"This should not be possible." Guillermo sounds as if he's talking to himself, but Dahliorn replies.

"Can you undo it, remove the spell?"

"No." A hint of anger colors the sorcerer's voice. "There's already too much damage. Somehow I have to salvage this mess, or centuries of preparation will be lost."

"What are you going to do about Ramira's memory? She seems too confused to be useful now."

*Great! I'm not the only one with a scrambled brain. Thank you very much, jackwagon.*

"I'll have to plant a new one—that's the only way I can see this working. We have to get Ramira back on track."

Dahliorn clears his throat. "Will that work, given the condition she's in?"

"It will if I base it on her true memories, and it may even allow her to bridge some gaps on her own. Whatever memory she's lost because of the fault in the unity spell is likely permanent."

*Will I lose my mind, my memories? Again. What if I never regain full control of my body?* Elizabetta misses what Dahliorn says next. She feels as if she should be hyperventilating, but her body doesn't respond. The absurdity threatens to unhinge her; right now she needs a good meltdown, if for no other reason than to know her body is there.

Guillermo's brusque tone brings her back to the conversation. "Belyakov's downfall has set the stage for what we need to do, and I don't want to lose the opportunity. With or without the vampire's help, we will proceed with our plans; Ramira will be trained and ready to fight. But if there's any way to fix this, I'll need that vampire alive to do her part. The root of the main spell will eventually destroy their minds."

*Oh my God, what has he done to us?*

"This will kill her," Dahliorn says in a flat tone.

"She is the putrid spawn of my bastard brother and his witch wife! One of my father's mistakes that I have taken care of. My brother, a mere warlock ..." The sound of glass breaking follows a loud crash; the sorcerer's heavy breathing suggests he's responsible for the noise. "I took Ramira in retribution of what he cost me, and you know that if it weren't for the role she must serve, I'd have killed her centuries ago. If she survives her assignment now, it will be a mercy on both of us that she won't last long afterward."

*So much for being the loving uncle. I wonder if I can make her an ally, tell her the truth? Maybe Maria can fix this if we get out of here before it's too late.*

Guillermo casts another spell and begins to plant details for Ramira's memory. An internal shudder rips through Elizabetta, leaving a ghost of a chill in her unresponsive body—she recalls her own mind reset and how well she believed her false life. Yet in some ways this is different. The sorcerer isn't wiping and resetting the mind as a whole;

he's simply meddling with a specific memory. Elizabetta wonders what purpose that serves in the long run and how many times this has been done to the witch already.

She listens carefully as Guillermo provides the information about Ramira's past—but she has no idea which details are true or false. It shocks her to hear him say that the Druzhina killed her parents and that Elizabetta turned her into a vampire. *Well, that last bit is a lie—I haven't touched her.* Still, she understands what the sorcerer is doing; he is sowing the seeds of hatred and revenge. It firms her resolve to somehow make contact with Ramira and convince her that she's on the wrong side, that her uncle is pure evil and must be destroyed.

When Guillermo finishes and the men leave the room, Elizabetta lies there in the darkness and considers what little she's learned. It's clear that Guillermo intends to use Ramira as a weapon, seemingly against the Druzhina, but Elizabetta still has no clue as to her own role in his plan. *I have to figure this out before it's too late.* Her mind skips across all the planning she did with Matt to take Shashenka down. It took months for those preparations to come together; she can only hope it takes the sorcerer a while too.

"What are you doing here?" The sudden sound of Ramira's voice startles Elizabetta. *I must have fallen asleep.*

"I'm your bodyguard—your uncle pays me to keep an eye on you." Dahliorn's reply, Elizabetta notices, is in line with the information Guillermo planted earlier. *Was he there the whole time? I thought he left with Guillermo.*

Ramira snarls, "Get out."

"I see that you're still upset."

"Yes, I'm upset. Wouldn't you be if you lost your powers because some demented vampire turned you? You'd be an even bigger freak of nature than you are now."

*Lost her powers? How long was I out, and what did I miss?* A light turns on, and suddenly she sees Dahliorn standing in front of her. *I'm standing too.* She never felt her body move and doesn't know when or how she stood up. Dahliorn steps forward, then seems to change his mind and backs away. "I'm sorry; this must be terribly confusing for you."

She wants to retort with a snarky "Gee, ya think," but she's still unable to push any words to her tongue. New panic grows; she must regain control before this perilous situation becomes worse.

At the same moment Ramira screeches, "Confusing? I am not confused, but I am very angry. Thanks to Uncle Guillermo screwing up his foolproof plan, I'll have no inside information like he promised me to exact the revenge I'm long overdue against the Druzhina."

*It sure didn't take much for those lies to take root.*

"Ramira, calm down." Dahliorn again moves toward Elizabetta. The expression on his face seems both curious and hard. She sees him place his hands on her arms, but it's as if her senses are dulled—she can barely feel his grasp. "This may just take some time to fix, Ramira. You need to be patient."

"Get away from me," Ramira roars.

*Jeez, he's not even touching her. I'm thinking insanity runs deep in their family tree.*

"I didn't mean to upset you further."

Ramira snorts—it sounds as if the witch is right next to her, but Elizabetta doesn't see her and can't turn her head to look.

"Upset? You think I'm upset, really? If it weren't for my uncle, I'd kill you for touching me. If I had my way, I'd never have to look at your creepy, ugly hide again."

*Creepy ... ugly? Wow, she has no taste in men.*

As Dahliorn backs away and sits in a chair in the corner of the room, Elizabetta realizes that she's not in her tiny dark cell anymore, but in what appears to be a lavishly decorated bedroom. She'd like to look around, but her disconnected eyes hold Dahliorn's gaze, and it's beyond her ability to break it. His hostile look, at the least, should send a shiver up her spine, but her body isn't reacting to what may be a threat. Elizabetta can't even gulp down the lump of fear that must be growing in her throat right now.

Then without her conscious will, Elizabetta's body begins to pace. Every few seconds her head turns to look at Dahliorn. She has no control over what her body is doing, and a mix of frustration and the ever-present panic swells within her. *What is wrong with me? How am I going to fix this?* What's worse is that Ramira seems to be deliberately staying behind her. *Why doesn't she want me to see her? Is she afraid I'll attack her, or is she using me to shield herself from Dahliorn?* Granted, Elizabetta would love to turn around and slap the woman—Ramira hasn't stopped droning on about the injustice of losing her powers, her desire for revenge against the Druzhina, and her apparent dislike of Dahliorn.

*What a whiny bitch.* Elizabetta finds herself approaching

a vanity, and she sits in the chair, but her gaze remains on Dahliorn seated in the corner of the room. He's watching every move she makes. *Why?* She picks up a brush, though she can't feel it in her fingers—more troubling proof of her disconnected state. As the bristles move through her hair, she turns toward the vanity's mirror.

There, staring back at her, is the face of Ramira.

## CHAPTER 5: DMITRI

# The Last to Fall

They arrive at Novgorod, standing back to back and ready for battle, but no guards are in sight. The second sublevel of the castle is bathed in its usual gloom; the only light is near the bottom of the stairs, leaving most of the corridor in darkness. Dmitri's breath hitches. He never expected to see this dungeon again, and its putrid stench brings back the far too many years he spent locked in these cells, tortured in these rooms. Still, his bittersweet attachment to the last cell at the end of the corridor propels him forward. The final moments he spent there with Elizabetta after their failed rebellion were in some ways less cruel than the aftermath of their victory at Machu Picchu. At least then they shared hope of being together again. This time they're at the mercy of fate—and what little Dmitri can do to give them a future together.

They check the cells while the maxians return to Prague for the next group of fighters. During Shashenka's rule it was rare that more than a few cells were occupied, but as they open the doors they discover there are as many as three or four vampires and werewolves shoved inside each cell. Forty-two fighters are added to their ranks by the time they are ready to move up to the next level.

After Vladimir briefs the freed allies, doing his best to keep his voice down—they still don't know if the floor above is more heavily guarded—Dmitri leads them up the stairs to the first sublevel to wait for the others from Prague.

It's a relief to find this floor no more guarded than the last. Once more they move along the corridor and free their allies, adding another thirty-seven fighters to their numbers. When the last group from Prague arrives, he asks the freed fighters to brief them on what happened here at Novgorod.

A werewolf steps forward, and Dmitri hisses in displeasure. There is no love lost between them. Grigori's pack lives closest to the castle, and they collected the reward Matt paid to find Elizabetta after she was reintegrated into the coven and brought to Novgorod. They threatened him, Elizabetta, and Sally the night he gave the horse-head dagger to Elizabetta, and his ire over the encounter hasn't diminished. The vampires were outnumbered then, but they're not now, and Dmitri swore he'd make Grigori pay for it someday.

His disdain for the wolf hangs off each word. "There's no bounty in it for you this time. Why do you fight for us?"

"Ah, Dmitri. So good to see you again," Grigori says in a tone suggesting he is anything but thrilled. "My pack has lived under the oppression of Belyakov's vampires for decades. I'm more than happy to bring an end to that. My kind, as much as yours, deserves to be free."

Dmitri can't fault the werewolf for desiring to be out from under Shashenka's thumb, but that is as far as he'll go. He has no use for the mutt or his pack beyond their help to take back this estate.

Grigori shifts his gaze to Matt as he tells them that the castle was a trap. The gates were left open and unguarded, allowing the one-hundred and fifty-some allies to enter without resistance. Once all were inside the outer walls, the Belyakov fighters closed the gates and attacked, killing over one-third of their number. The rest were captured and taken to the dungeons, and Peter informed them that Shashenka planned a public execution.

"No one made it inside the castle?" Kees asks in an incredulous tone.

"No, they held us back." Grigori points in the direction of the guard tower where the maxian's body is hanging. "They took down the magic wielder pretty fast, cut off his hands, nearly drained him dry, and hung him there to finish bleeding out. After that we were marched inside and down to the cells. We thought you failed too ... we weren't sure anyone was coming to our rescue. We expected Shashenka to execute us after he returned."

Dmitri is brusque. "He's dead."

Grigori and some of the others look surprised. "It's not just a rumor?"

"We killed him—he's not coming back." Maria's fierce tone removes their doubt; Dmitri can see it in the way their stunned expressions turn to relief, hope, and even renewed determination.

"Well then, it's time to finish this," Grigori says as he gathers his remaining pack members around him.

Dmitri couldn't agree more; every minute they spend dealing with Belyakov loyalists is another delay in his search for Elizabetta. He can't deny, though, that the distraction keeps him from fixating on her whereabouts, while the darkness inside him can find a needed outlet through the fighting. The latter, ironically, is a safety valve that is helping him manage the frightening desires straining to be free. Without it, the bloodlust might take complete control.

Over the next several minutes a hasty strategy is outlined as their allies are broken into groups. At least one hundred enemy fighters guard the perimeter walls, they know, and an unknown number may be roaming inside the castle. Once those outside become aware of the battle, they will rally and join the fight. The best way to counter whatever awaits them is to form a spear with their strongest in the lead—but still, Dmitri doesn't expect to be thrust to the front with Matt and Maria while the Druzhinas line up behind them. Looking back over his shoulder, he surveys the packed corridor: just under two hundred fighters stand eager and ready to engage their enemies. *I hope it's enough to offset what we're about to encounter on the other side of this door.*

Dmitri's group will make their way to the great hall, where they expect Shashenka's top Druzhinnikis to be. The other mixed group of fighters will both take the exit points of the castle and begin a floor-by-floor sweep. They will disable the Belyakov vampires and wait to carry out their executions until the fight is over. Peter, Leonard, and

Charles are to be captured alive and interrogated—they may know where Milo Kohler and Teresina De Luca are hiding, if the two are not already here.

To emphasize his point, Dmitri claims the right of blood justice against Milo; Justin will be the one to decide Teresina's fate. Justin grimaces, but nods his agreement, and Dmitri hopes leaving him that decision is a kindness and not a cruelty. While there have been no mating signs, Dmitri has no doubt that Justin's feelings are deeply entwined with the rogue who betrayed them. If their roles were reversed, he'd want the ultimate say in how Elizabetta should be punished.

Matt, in wolf form, stands on one side of Dmitri and Maria stands on the other. He looks briefly at each of them. "Are you ready?"

Maria flashes a lethal smile. "Fág an Bealach."

With a hard push, Dmitri swings the dungeon's door wide open.

The initial push into the castle's interior meets minimal resistance as the allies move quickly to the areas they need to take and secure. Dmitri and Matt become briefly separated from the Druzhinas while incapacitating several foe, but they rejoin their group in the great hall in time to see Maria unleash a volley of magic at a quartet of fighters near the quasi-throne that Shashenka used to sit upon. Two of the enemy collapse on the floor, but Dmitri's eyes narrow in recognition of the other two. *Peter and Charles ... their judgment day has come.*

Whatever magic Maria lobs at them seems to miss; each bolt or orb of magic falls short and erupts with a near-deafening bang. Dmitri veers in their direction, slowing as he draws near the men. His eyes flash in anger. Charles and Peter stand shoulder to shoulder in a defensive crouch. These two more than any others enjoyed doing Shashenka's bidding—Dmitri recalls their laughter as they tortured him ... their boastfulness as they physically and sexually abused the concubines ... the joy they took in Shashenka's weekly slaughter of humans ... their bizarre competition to gain their master's favor. But beyond all of that, he most remembers their twisted delight as they groped Elizabetta in front of him, knowing he was power-less to stop it.

*They defiled my mate!*

Centuries of hatred roll off Dmitri—he knows he must divert his attention or he will kill them before either takes another breath. *I'm going to relish showing them no mercy when I deliver their final death.* "Surrender now so we may take you into custody." His gaze sweeps the great hall in one swift motion. Maria holds her hands up, a glowing red ball of energy hovering between them. She seems content to hold on to it until it's needed, but the look on her face suggests she'd rather hit them in the privates. His comrades among the Druzhina form an arc around them, creating a barrier against Peter and Charles. The two men back up a few more steps—they have nowhere to go.

"Go to hell, Markov," Peter roars.

"I've done my time there. It's your turn. Hit them, Maria." Dmitri's muscles tense with barely contained bloodlust rippling under the surface, and the urge to viciously mangle this vampire races through him. *I won't be like Shashenka.* His mind replays the abuse Elizabetta suffered at Peter's hands—broken bones, sucker punches. The way he unshackled her and dropped her to the floor. Desire for retribution becomes a new flavor on his tongue.

Maria finally unleashes the red ball of energy, and it strikes Peter in the chest; he cries out, stumbles, and falls onto Shashenka's chair. Dmitri bellows, "Surrender." Rage ties another knot into his heart.

"Master will kill us if we don't fight." Panic and terror accentuate Charles's plea.

"Your master is dead."

"That's not possible." Peter's eyes grow wide as he darts a sideways glance at Charles.

The most wicked smile Dmitri has ever seen spreads across Maria's face. "Trust me, Peter, it is, and I had the privilege of helping the Markovs kill him."

Dmitri turns away—he doesn't want the others to see he needs a few seconds to regain control. "They're wasting our time. Bind them, Maria."

Charles blurts out, "No, wait ... I'll surrender."

"Bind Peter." *I'm better than this ... I can hold on.* Dmitri doesn't look back until he hears Maria cast the immobility spell. Charles stands with his hands in the air, fear frozen on his expression, but Peter has a murderous glare etched across his face. *When the moment arrives, he is mine.*

"Alexander, Kees, and Katherine, help me take these two to the first sublevel and lock them in separate cells,"

Vladimir says as he moves forward and forces Peter's hands down and behind his back.

The sound of bones breaking brings a smile to Dmitri's face. The other four Druzhinas look between Dmitri and Vladimir, waiting for their orders. It's a clear reminder that they expect Dmitri to reprise his leadership role, but he inclines his head, signaling Vladimir to continue. He's still too far over the edge to think rationally.

Vladimir says, "Go with Dmitri's team to sweep the castle for those still fighting. We'll find you after we have these two locked up."

Grateful for the distraction, Dmitri takes the lead—Matt still by his side as they sprint from the great hall into the corridor that leads to the salon, the kitchen, and the inner hall with the grand staircase. He can hear the sounds of battle in other areas, but they meet no resistance themselves. *I need someone to fight.* When they reach the inner hall, he asks everyone to be quiet. "Matt, where's the heaviest fighting taking place?"

The wolf cocks his head from side to side and lifts his nose at the grand staircase. They're about to dash up the stairs when running footsteps echo in the rear passageway behind the staircase. It's too many and too soon to be the other Druzhinas. There's only one explanation: the Druzhinnikis are making an attempt to flank and pincer them between those rushing toward them and those beyond the top of the stairs.

Stephan says, "Anyone want to wager those guarding the outside wall realized we're here?"

Dmitri grimaces—the Druzhinnikis were certainly thorough in their preparations for this fight. "Defensive formation, now." He adds for Matt's benefit, "We'll form another arc, fight head on. Don't let them draw you out of line—they'll pick us off one by one."

Matt's snout twists into a grin, and he bares his teeth and rumbles a deep growl in anticipation and warning as he moves forward to attack. Dmitri snatches him by the scruff of the neck and pulls him back in line, leaving his hand fisted in the wolf's fur. *Instinct? Can werewolves feel bloodlust too?* "Let them come to us."

The wolf licks both sides of his blood-soaked muzzle and snaps his teeth.

Maria chants under her breath. Dmitri crouches into an attack stance—all three are prepared and ready to fight as their foes close the distance between them.

The wizard is the first to engage. She tosses a bolt of white light that splinters and crackles as it strikes several of their enemies. "There's too many to freeze at once. Maxians, we need to keep hitting them while the vampires fight. I'll cast the immobility spell as soon as their numbers are down far enough."

Dmitri nods in understanding. They may be badly outnumbered, but their fighting skills are unmatched—the very reason the Druzhina is the elite force among their kind. Now it's time to prove it. He chances a quick glance at their arc formation. He's at the center of it, with Matt and Maria at his sides. Justin, Anna, and a maxian are to Maria's right. Victoria, Stephan, and Jacques are to the left of Matt. In front of Dmitri, more vampires are pouring into the inner hall; he estimates there's a little more than a half-dozen stunned enemy fighters lying on the floor, and at least three dozen Druzhinnikis are coming right at them, fangs and claws ready to strike. *This isn't going to be good or easy.*

The maxians unleash volleys of magical bolts and balls. Not all of it is hitting its mark—there are too many fighters to blast all at once. The enemy surges forward, and individual battles begin. Dmitri fights off two foes, but two more jump forward to take their place the moment they fall. Their adversaries are relentless. Some are already dragging bodies out of the way as other fighters engage Dmitri's group.

A commotion from the rear passageway behind the staircase catches Dmitri's attention; the other Druzhinas have rejoined them. Alexander waves and shouts, "There's more coming behind us! Regroup—center point, regroup."

Dmitri understands, but there's no time to explain to Maria, the other maxians, or Matt what needs to be done, and he trusts that they'll follow the Druzhinas' lead. "Center point ... follow on my mark. Ready? Now!"

From the other end of the inner hall he hears Vladimir echo, "Now." Dmitri shoves back the two men he's fighting and launches into a run, veering past any attempts to grab or stop him. He catches a glimpse of Matt as the mongrel weaves around the other fighters, both allies and foes. *Shit. The maxians don't have our speed—we just left them behind.* It's too late to turn back, and Dmitri hopes they can hold their own. He'd never forgive himself if Maria were killed.

The two groups of Druzhinas reach the middle of the

room within seconds of each other. In a quick procession they form a ring and face out toward their enemies. A knot twists in Dmitri's gut—across the room, Maria, Jacques, and the other maxian have been backed against a wall, though the trio continues lobbing their magic. *Perhaps they can at least defend themselves until—*

The Druzhinnikis begin their attack. One after another the fighters keep coming, and Dmitri realizes that additional vampires—likely those who were guarding the outer walls—continue to arrive at the inner hall. He sees Justin go down with a deep wound across his throat. The young Druzhina clamps a hand over it to stem the flow of blood. Before Dmitri can move to cover the gap, he hears Matt yelp and then howl in pain; a Druzhinniki has managed to jump on his back and is biting his neck. *Damn it, I can't get to either of them.*

Concern for his friends distracts Dmitri, and he doesn't see the vampire coming from the right side in time to avoid a hard blow that almost sends him sprawling. He quickly recovers his balance and pivots to face his attacker. Even with the bloodlust enhancing his ability to fight, Dmitri senses pending defeat—there are simply too many enemies and not enough allies here. He sees the same frantic assessment in Vladimir's eyes when their gazes meet, but if this is where they will fall, then they will go down fighting as hard as they can together.

Dmitri's about to incapacitate another adversary when a blinding white light bursts through the room, knocking him off his feet. *Elizabetta ... I can't stop, we have to win.* Then his head hits the floor, and blackness overtakes him.

## CHAPTER 6: ELIZABETTA

# Things That Go Bump in the Night

*What did Guillermo do to me?* It's Ramira's reflection looking out from the mirror as Elizabetta stares back in muted horror. Somehow she is seeing through Ramira's eyes, but the witch seems ignorant of her presence. If Elizabetta were in her own body, she'd be hyperventilating now. *Breathe, breathe ... I don't understand.*

She watches Ramira put the brush down, and then the witch turns from the mirror back to Dahliorn. He draws and holds a breath, contempt creeping into his return gaze.

"Get out! I don't want you in my room," Ramira shouts at him.

His tone remains smooth, but there's an edge to it that Elizabetta can't quite peg. "Your uncle ordered me to remain here."

Ramira picks up the brush again and throws it at him. "I said, get out of my room!"

*That's real mature.*

He ducks the brush but remains in his chair. His fingers

dig into the armrest. "You should know by now, Ramira, that I follow your uncle's orders, not yours."

Elizabetta watches their spat, but she wants to squeeze her eyes shut, turn away, or do anything that will pull her from the room and from Ramira. *How is this even possible? I've got to be hallucinating. Brain damage, that's it ... he scrambled and fried my brain.* What she sees mocks her thoughts—she's lying to herself. Somehow she's ended up with the ability to see through the witch's eyes.

One key detail rises above the others: every shift in the blackness seems to move her between Ramira and her own body, and she's lingering longer each time she's inside the witch. *Oh my God, what happens if I get trapped? Is it possible for me to will myself back to my body?*

Ramira and Dahliorn continue to argue. Elizabetta ignores them. *Body, body, body.* Nothing happens. *Shit, shinola.*

Then her attention reverts to the other two as Ramira screams, "Get away from me, you freak."

Dahliorn flies out of the chair and stops right in front of the witch. The look on his face makes Elizabetta cringe inwardly—anger mixed with disgust, sadness, and death lurks in his eyes. "Your uncle made me what I am. If I could leave and never see either of you again, I would do it."

*Made him that way? What are they talking about here ... like Frankenstein's monster?*

The bedroom door bangs open, and Guillermo throws his hands out. Ramira is lifted from the floor and lands on the bed. Panic blooms as Elizabetta sees Dahliorn's body hit the wall near the corner and slump to the floor. She winces inside; echoes of pain swarm through her as she recalls experiencing the same assault at the sorcerer's hand.

Guillermo bellows, "I've had enough of both of you." He storms over to the bed, uttering some kind of spell, and Ramira quits moving. Then his head whips toward Dahliorn. "How many times do I have to tell you not to talk to or touch my niece?"

Dahliorn hangs his head, but he doesn't answer as he rises to his feet. Guillermo flies across the room and punches the younger man in the face. "I will not tell you again. You are here to watch and protect her—period. I don't care if she speaks to you; you are not to engage her in conversation. We have enough of a mess on our hands, and I'll be damned if I will allow you to make matters worse."

"Yes, Guillermo, I understand." Dahliorn focuses on the floor, and blood drips from his nose—he won't meet the sorcerer's gaze. His defeated posture reminds Elizabetta of Dmitri and the way Shashenka used torture and fear to control those around him. In that moment she feels a measure of empathy for Dahliorn. *I need to figure him out too, gain his confidence and support.* But she's trapped here—it's impossible to interact with Dahliorn when she's in Ramira's mind, and when she returns to her own body she is always alone. *How can I do this? How do I reach out to him?*

Guillermo is still shouting at Dahliorn. "I think you've upset my niece quite enough for one day. I'll sit with her for a while and let you know when I'm ready for you to come back and resume your post."

Dahliorn nods and leaves the room. For several minutes

Ramira rants about Dahliorn being anywhere near her, and then she resumes complaining about the loss of her powers. *She's a sniveling, spoiled brat. Grow up already.* Guillermo seems to tire of her incessant grousing too and tells her that she'll begin her training the next day. Since his spell didn't go as planned, he asserts, Ramira must learn actual fighting techniques rather than borrow them.

*Borrow fighting skills?* Elizabetta listens closely as Guillermo explains, and a few minutes further into the conversation she realizes that the psycho sorcerer intended for Ramira to use Elizabetta's skills—that is why she is in the witch's body. *But he said it didn't work. They must not know I'm in here.* Elizabetta can't wrap her mind around this—or the fact that she is listening to the conversation through Ramira's ears. An internal shudder runs through her, and to her surprise, Ramira shivers at the same moment. *Whoa ... did she react to me?*

Guillermo turns the conversation to their desire to end the Druzhina, intel she may be able to use, but to Elizabetta's disappointment the darkness pulses through her and she shifts back to her own body again. Her fists slam down on the cot. *Damn it. Is there any way to control this? When I want to be there, I can't stay, and when I want to leave, I can't go.*

Her body feels stiff from lying still so long, and she wonders if it moves at all when she's inside Ramira. *How long do I have this time?* Elizabetta stands and stretches, and an idea sparks—Guillermo said he'd be sitting with Ramira for a while, which means this may be the perfect opportunity for her to escape. Perhaps she can stay in her own body if she puts enough distance between herself and the witch.

She walks over and tests the door. It's locked, but it's a standard household doorknob that doesn't appear to be spelled. Elizabetta tightens her grip around it and forces the knob to turn. As expected, the mechanism in the handle breaks and she's able to pull the knob off. She extends a claw to pop the latch and opens the door into a long, dark hallway.

*Is it in the Evil Man's Handbook that if you're bad you must have a creepy dungeon?* She isn't sure which way to go but after a moment's consideration turns left, running as quickly and quietly as she can. At the *T* intersection at the end of the hall, she turns left once again. There appears to be a better-lit corridor in the distance ahead.

A sudden *click-click* chattering noise from somewhere in the darkness sends a shiver down her spine. Elizabetta slows and approaches the next corridor with caution. Unlike the last intersection, the one ahead is directional—she can go back, go straight, or turn left or right. Whatever made the sound seems to be in the hall on the right, where there is more lighting. She flattens herself against the wall and inches forward, taking a deep breath as she looks around the corner.

Disappointment rocks her. The hall on the right isn't better lit after all—there's a single lightbulb just off the intersection, but everything after it is dark like the rest of the corridors. Elizabetta can't see what's in the shadows, and for a moment she hesitates. It's too quiet—the lack of sound disturbs her more than the absence of light. Deciding to take a chance, she darts straight across the hallway.

Another hall intersection comes into view further down the corridor. *Jeez, how big is this place?* She's almost to the next junction when she hears a noise behind her. *Shit! It's quiet, too quiet, said every idiot right before something bad happened. Way to jinx yourself.* She casts a glance over her shoulder but can't make out what it is—in the faint light from the last intersection, she can see a shape, but its outline baffles her. Slowing down, she turns to look. It isn't a man or an animal, but ... *No, it can't be! What the hell is that thing?*

Fear thrusts her adrenaline into hypersonic mode, and Elizabetta backs away from the creature. But her reaction sets it in motion—it advances toward her—and a prickle crawls up her spine. Even her scalp tingles. Habit propels her hand to her waist, and then she remembers that she's unarmed. *Shit, not good.* Her fangs slide down and her claws extend as she keeps moving away from the thing in front of her. Then the creature's pace quickens, and Elizabetta can't resist the flight instinct any longer. Her heart pounding a frenetic rhythm against her chest, she pivots midstride and races away as fast as she can.

She's almost to the next hall intersection when something hits her from behind. Elizabetta loses her balance and tumbles to the floor, then pushes herself up, terrified, looking over her shoulder. The hall appears clear. The creature—her mind is in full denial of what she saw—isn't behind her anymore. *Where did it go?* Elizabetta scrambles to her feet. Her eyes focus on where the creature was, and she takes a couple of tentative steps backward.

*Run. Get the hell out of here. Run!* Her head whips around as she breaks into a sprint, and then she freezes—four pairs of glowing green eyes of varying sizes sit deep in the shadows ahead of her.

A sick knot writhes in her stomach. *Did they push me into a trap?* Instinct tells her she won't survive this encounter, but once more she backs away. The luminous green eyes come closer—the faster Elizabetta moves, the quicker the eyes stalk her. She keeps edging backward, crossing the four-way intersection with the single lightbulb nearby. The shadows recede as shapes form around the green eyes following her. *How many of these monsters are there?* She swallows hard against the tidal wave of fear and panic claiming her, and screams, "What are you?"

It responds with a series of clicking sounds—and then the creature comes into full view under the light cast by the single bulb. *Oh my God. Pluck a duck—I'm dead! It's going to kill me, and it's going to eat me. Jeez, that thing can't be real.* Terror roots her to the floor. Her mind keeps arguing that her eyes are lying, but her gaze rakes over the creature and reaffirms what she sees. In front of her is an enormous and hideous spider.

Logic tells her there is no place in the world where spiders grow this large. But she can't deny the hairy creature's legs are twice as long as her own. Its head is about the size of a basketball, and two long fangs hang parallel below its huge mandibles. The eyes are in three rows: two medium-sized eyes at the top of its head, the two largest eyes below that, and a row of four small eyes on the bottom. The short leg-like appendages above its fangs move as if motioning her to come forward. *Oh, hell no!* Horror chomps at the last thread of her bravery, and Elizabetta screams and finally turns and flees. She races past the *T* intersection, her mind whirling with grotesque images of the spider behind her. Halfway down the current hall, she's hit from behind and is sent sprawling on the floor again. This time she looks all the way around before she stands up. The spider is blocking her path in the direction she was running. She shrieks at it, "What are you? What do you want with me?"

The spider makes more clicking noises. *Great, I don't freaking speak spider. In fact, I hate spiders.* Elizabetta backs away from the mutant beast and toward the hall intersection, already planning to go straight through it instead of retreating in the direction of her cell. *There has to be a way out.* When she reaches the intersection, the creature lunges at her, but she's ready for it and ducks to avoid being knocked down again.

Elizabetta spins around to face the spider. Once more she crosses the intersection, but the moment she reaches the other side of the *T,* the spider again leaps toward her. This time she doesn't dodge fast enough, and the creature's front legs grab her as it sails over her—it keeps her from falling, but the monster is even more frightening up close. The contact makes her skin crawl. Her breaths are short, and her body trembles with waves of shudders.

Elizabetta pulls her head back, trying to put as much distance between herself and the spider as possible. Its fangs—her own are a miniscule joke by comparison—are tucked toward its body, almost as if it is making the choice not to use them on her. She flinches and screams again as the monster rises up to use its next set of legs to hold on to her, then sets her on her feet and turns her around, facing away from its mandibles. An image of fangs the length of her forearm sends her pulse pounding so hard that it deafens her. *Is it going to kill me now?*

She closes her eyes, waiting for the strike she's certain is coming, but instead the spider lets go with one set of legs while the other pair grips her sides. The monster pushes, forcing her to walk forward. She has no idea where it's taking her, but given its strength, size, and speed, she has no choice but to comply. No vampire is a match for this spider. She feels its short appendages—pedipalps, her mind tells her—stroke her hair, and bile rises, sending a shudder through her. *I'm going to be sick. If I throw up on it, will it let me go?*

When they reach the hall intersection, the creature turns her down the corridor that leads to the cell she was in. To her amazement, it stops at her open door and pushes her inside. *What the hell?* She turns and scrambles out of reach of its legs. The largest of its shiny green eyes seem to scrutinize the door. It emits more clicking sounds, and Elizabetta backs further into her cell until she bumps against the far wall. *I'm trapped ... there's no way out.* Tremors surge through her, but she stands there frozen, unwilling to move.

Spreading its legs, the spider lifts its body to cover the open doorway. At first Elizabetta thinks that it intends to stay there, but then its abdomen moves, and its spinnerets attach the first strands of silk to the doorjamb. *Damn you, freakish spider!* She needs to act, to defeat it somehow—it must have a weakness. She scans its body for vulnerabilities, and her attention is drawn to a silver band etched with symbols that's fastened around the narrow segment above the spider's abdomen. *What is that for?*

With sick fascination she watches, contemplating the belt's purpose, for almost an hour as the spider weaves a tightly knit web across the entire door opening. Small gaps—too narrow for her to crawl through—allow her to see into the hall. She isn't sure if she should feel relieved or more terrified. The silken barrier separates her from the spider, but it also leaves her trapped and at its mercy.

When the spider finishes and drops to the floor in the hall, it stares at her through the web for several interminable minutes, then makes a few more clicking sounds and leaves. *At least it didn't kill me—yet.*

Elizabetta's adrenaline crashes, and the trembling in her legs becomes too much. Slowly she slides down the wall to the floor. *That mutant spider must be something Guillermo supersized ... it's just not possible, not natural.* No matter how she tries to process it, Elizabetta can't reconcile what she saw with what she knows to be true about arachnids. Nausea rolls through her. It had her in its legs, close enough for its fangs to strike a fatal blow. Instead of having her doorway blocked off in a silken web, she should be wrapped in a cocoon while the spider's digestive enzymes liquefy her insides.

She's still struggling with her thoughts when Dahliorn appears on the other side of her webbed doorway. For a long moment he gives her a cold look. He's holding a small bag and what appears to be a walking stick in one hand and a knife in the other. Without a word he lays the bag on the floor and cuts away the web, using the stick to gather the broken strands so it looks like a huge spool of thread when he's finished. He sets the stick aside and pulls a new doorknob out of the bag.

Enough courage returns for her to whisper, "Dahliorn, what was that thing?"

"An abomination of nature." Disgust grinds through each word.

"But ... but it was a spider, right?" Elizabetta feels stupid for seeking confirmation of what she already knows—but she still needs to hear someone say it.

His posture stiffens, but he removes the old latch mechanism and begins to install the new doorknob. "Yes."

"Is it poisonous?"

His reply comes through clenched teeth. "Yes, he's deadly."

"He?"

Dahliorn nods. Elizabetta gulps, her heart racing faster. "Can you get me out of here? I'm afraid that thing is going to come back and kill me. It's freaking huge ... hideous, terrifying."

Dahliorn tightens the screws on the new handle and looks up at her finally—his eyes flash red. "I know well what he looks like. I promise you, he will not harm you." Acid corrodes the inflection of his voice, but Elizabetta ignores it.

"How can you promise that?"

He ignores her question and starts to pull the door

closed. *No! He can't leave me here alone.* She jumps to her feet and bolts across the cell, sliding her foot between the door and the jamb as she grabs the edge of the door. "Please don't go. I-I'm terrified it's going to come back and attack me."

A pained expression contorts his face, and she sees shame reflected in his eyes. Dahliorn mutters something under his breath, but he pushes the door open and steps into the room. "Lie down." He takes her hand and leads her over to the cot.

Elizabetta has a death grip on his hand and doesn't release him even after she complies. He kneels next to the cot, his fingers stroking her long hair away from her face. Her eyes plead for the truth. "What if that monster comes back? How do you know it won't hurt me?"

"I'd never allow him to hurt you." Dahliorn grimaces and looks away, and she has to strain to hear what he says next. "I'm going to put you to sleep now, little dove. I will make it so you won't have nightmares."

Elizabetta squeezes his hand tighter—she doesn't want to let go. She doesn't want to be alone in this place anymore. It's terrifying to think of her body lying here vulnerable if that spider comes back when she is in Ramira.

Against her protests Dahliorn says, "Sleep, little dove. I will wake you soon."

Her eyelids grow heavy and close; she doesn't have the will or strength to keep them open. She's nearly asleep when Dahliorn kisses her temple and whispers, "Sweet dreams."

# CHAPTER 7: DMITRI
# An Era Ends

Dmitri's ears ring as he comes to, blinking to focus his vision. *What happened?* Maria is bent over Matt, performing what looks like a healing spell. Dmitri's head swims for a moment, and he takes a couple of deep breaths to help steady it. Slowly he sits up. The battle appears to be over; there is no sound of fighting anywhere. But with the exception of the vampires who were already neutralized, he can't tell the extent of injuries to their enemies—or to the Druzhinas, aside from Justin. Dmitri appears to be one of the first to recover from the blast.

"Maria, what happened?" He looks across at the wizard as he tries to stand. There are bodies everywhere around the room. Jacques is next to Justin, casting a mending spell.

Her head whips toward him. The urgency in her voice is out of character; something is very wrong. "Give me a minute to finish one more spell, and I'll tell you."

Dmitri stumbles over and kneels by the wolf. When Maria stops the incantation, she looks up, anger and worry chasing fear across her face. A muscle twitches below her left eye just before her lower lip trembles. "It's bad," she says. "That gobshite injected venom into him. I don't know how much was expressed, but Matt's in grave condition." Her words seem to leave something unspoken, but the possibility of losing Matt pushes it to the forefront of Dmitri's thoughts.

*Shit. Elizabetta will never forgive me if he dies.* His rational side tells him there was nothing he could have done differently, but Dmitri still feels as though it's in part his fault both Matt and Justin were wounded. After losing Sofia, it would be too much to bear to lose these two as well. Worse is that if the others had let him and Matt leave before they ever came to Prague or Novgorod, the mongrel's life wouldn't be hanging by a thread. *What kind of leader am I when I abandon my allies and fail to protect my friends?* His gaze shifts to the shivering werewolf lying between them. "Is there anything I can do?"

"As soon as some of the others come around, we need to move him to a bed. I'll continue experimenting with healing potions and spells. If I can pull him past the worst of this, there's a chance his immune system may be able to fight the venom." She glances at the carnage—the dead, the incapacitated, and those still knocked out by the blast—looking for something.

"I'll find a blanket," Dmitri says. Maria nods, confirming his assumption. He runs toward the hall where his and Elizabetta's bedrooms once were. Dozens of vampires and werewolves—friends and foes—lie unconscious on the floor as he maneuvers through the corridors and great hall to his old room. He strips a blanket from the bed. Then the thought occurs to him that he passed other bedrooms on his way here, and he's not sure why he felt compelled to come this far. Then it makes sense. Elizabetta said they'd slept in this room together on their last night here—it's the closest he can get to her at the moment.

But he doesn't allow himself the luxury of lingering to reminisce. When Dmitri returns to the inner hall, he finds most of the Druzhinas either just sitting up or already standing near Maria and Matt. He drapes the blanket across Matt's body. The wolf's skin is pale and bathed in sweat, and unease takes up residency in Dmitri's bones. "Is he ready to move?"

"Yes." Maria looks up, tears welling in her eyes.

*Have Matt and Maria grown that close?* The wizard may be as upset as Elizabetta if something happens to this former nemesis he's since come to respect. "Vladimir, will you help me pack him back to Elizabetta's old room?" There might be a hint of her scent lingering there; it may help the wolf somehow.

Vladimir commands the other Druzhinas to go through the castle and finish executing the last of the Belyakov fighters. Unlike at Machu Picchu, the enemy within these walls are Belyakov's most hardcore loyalists—none will be spared.

As Dmitri and Vladimir carry Matt to Elizabetta's old room, followed by Maria, Dmitri again asks the wizard what happened.

"As we were fighting, I suddenly had a notion for a spell that would create a concussion blast. I've never done one

before, and when I saw that vamp attacking Matt, I may
have panicked and put a little too much magic into it. I was
getting concerned with the length of time it took for
everyone to come out of it."

Dmitri frowns; it carried beyond the inner hall, at least.
"I don't know how far it went out, but it seems to have
ended the battle."

Maria opens the bedroom door. "The only ones it didn't
affect were the maxians. That type of blast may knock us
off our feet if we're caught unaware, but something in our
magic prevents us from losing consciousness."

Vladimir and Dmitri set the werewolf in the middle of
the bed, and Maria sits on the edge of the mattress and
murmurs another incantation. When she finishes, Vladimir
looks at Dmitri and says, "We need to start our interrogations." His tone is somber. "I know the werewolf is
injured, but we may still have enemies among us who aided
Teresina or Milo in giving information to Shashenka."

Dmitri tenses at the reminder, but when he looks at Matt
and Maria, there's a slight pull against his desire to find
another foe to kill. *I can't leave him to fate—I want him
with me when the time comes.* But he knows the wizard
won't leave the wolf's side, and they need answers if Dmitri
is ever to start the search for Elizabetta.

Maria explains that the other maxians have subdued the
remaining enemies and put them into a deep sleep. "We can
revive any you wish to speak to, but I'll leave it up to you
whether you want them awake for their executions."

The maxians found Leonard disabled among the throng
of downed vampires, but as far as Dmitri is concerned, it's

Peter and Charles who will need reviving. He moves toward the door. "Stay with him, Maria ... we'll find Jacques or one of the other maxians to wake any we need to talk to."

Dmitri and Vladimir agree that Charles may be more forthcoming with the truth than Peter and decide to start with him. Charles doesn't resist when they place him in shackles inside a torture room, but Dmitri and Vladimir have already decided they'll only resort to methodical violence if their other tactics fail; neither wants to be as cruel as Shashenka. Dmitri also understands that his friend is trying to help constrain the raging darkness inside him. If Vladimir allowed the slightest bit of hostile aggression to flow forth, there'd be no stopping Dmitri, and they both know it.

Once Charles realizes that they have no intention of torturing him, he's emboldened in his refusal to provide answers—his pat reply is "I don't know—they never told me." The repetition drives Dmitri's frustration into danger-ous territory. *I don't know how much more of this crap I can put up with.* When the other Druzhinas arrive to an-nounce that the executions are finished, Dmitri leaves Stephan and Kees to continue with Charles while he and Vladimir go to interrogate Peter instead.

This time Vladimir begins—they'll take turns asking questions. *If he parrots Charles, I'm going to lose control.* "How much did Shashenka know about the revolt before he left for Machu Picchu?"

"He never told me."

Dmitri scowls. "Bullshit. You were in lockstep with him for years."

Peter shrugs as much as the shackles will allow. "I ran the inner lair. Our discussions were mainly about those living and working there."

"I doubt that." Vladimir glares at the vampire. "You were up to your neck in almost everything Shashenka did. We know that you were given information others weren't privy to."

"That may be, but I'm not telling you."

Dmitri snarls—pitch-black wrath heats the marrow in his bones. Fists clenched, he says, "You will tell us what we need to know." The only thing holding him back from killing Peter outright is the possibility of a clue that will lead them to Elizabetta.

"Go to hell!" Peter spits at Dmitri.

Dmitri wipes the saliva off his cheek and punches Peter in the face. "If you do that again, I will cut your tongue out."

"This is getting us nowhere. We'll leave him here to ponder what's left of his life." Vladimir grabs Dmitri's arm and starts for the door. "Come on, Dmitri, I think that we can find a better way to get what we want."

Peter laughs as they shut the torture room door behind them. *Arrogant prick.* Dmitri aches to turn back and remove the smug smile from Peter's face, but Vladimir's truculent scowl is proof enough that he'd be thwarted.

They return to Elizabetta's old room and find Maria still sitting on the edge of the bed, holding Matt's hand. There doesn't appear to be any improvement. The wolf is drenched in sweat—Dmitri has never seen him look so pale.

"He's stable," Maria says, but she sounds as if she's

trying to reassure herself more than them that Matt is holding on. Her biggest concern is the fever, and the fact that there is no known antidote for vampire venom. The wizard's words aren't saying what her body is—Dmitri can smell the fear coming off her. *How afraid is she that Matt won't make it? What does she know?*

That is a thought he doesn't want to contemplate either, and he sidesteps thinking about it by telling Maria how it went with Peter and Charles. She grows noticeably angrier as she learns they are not cooperating. *Is she upset over being disrupted from tending Matt, or is her hatred for Shashenka's top guards that strong?* Through clenched teeth she says, "Find Jacques and ask him to bring Alastrina here. After she arrives I'll leave Matt in her care, and we will get answers from those two."

An hour later, Maria joins Dmitri and Vladimir in the torture room where Peter is restrained. There is a murderous glare on her face. *I thought as much—this is personal.* "Damnu ort! I think you are too stupid to realize who the real power was behind that despicable troll you called your master. I am here to remind you."

The wizard conjures a red energy ball and hits Peter square in the chest. He gasps and sputters as she intones a spell and then nods at Dmitri. "Ask him whatever you want—his answers will be true. Lies will inflict severe pain upon him."

He's never seen the wizard use a truth-compelling spell against anyone—this magic was beyond her while Shashenka was alive. Dmitri's thoughts flicker over the betrayal that led to Elizabetta's capture. "Tell us everything you know about Teresina De Luca and Milo Kohler."

Peter glares at them and hollers, "Do what you want to me. I'm not telling you anything."

The wizard shakes her head. "I see he needs a dose of cooperation." She casts another spell. "Try again."

Dmitri repeats the demand. The second spell seems to work, as Peter begins talking, but it becomes obvious whenever he tries to skirt the truth or tell a blatant lie—he screams in pain, and his body spasms. The first hour is torturous to watch. There are moments when Peter clenches his teeth or bites his bottom lip to keep from talking—his upper teeth and fangs nearly sever his bottom lip, and blood runs down his chin and soaks the front of his shirt. He spits a spray of blood at the three of them, but they jump back quickly to avoid being hit.

Smirking, Maria blasts him with another red energy ball. It strikes Dmitri that she may be enjoying this just a little too much, but he won't rein her in, not yet. Doubtless Peter deserves a little retribution—Dmitri can just imagine what the Druzhinniki has done to her over the years.

The wizard says, "I won't heal you, but if you bite your tongue off, I will repair it. This will be less painful for you if you tell us what we need to know."

Peter continues his resistance for another half hour and then finally breaks. *Typical thug—no real strength. That son of a bitch wouldn't have lasted more than ten minutes under Shashenka's torture.* A measure of tension leaves Dmitri. The interrogation is grueling, but at the same time it seems to have sated Dmitri's bloodlust for now. *I may get through this yet.*

"Milo's spies said Teresina was seen meeting with the werewolf and Dmitri and Elizabetta. Shashenka summoned her to Venice. When she arrived, she refused to talk, said her dealings with you were none of his business. We locked her in a cell, and Shashenka spent a day teaching her a lesson. She conditionally agreed to tell us the nature of your meetings—she wanted a profitable business deal out of it."

The circumstances of Teresina's betrayal make more sense now, but they don't lessen Dmitri's hard feelings. The fact that she wanted to turn a profit at their expense is telling—she has no loyalty or honor. *Even Justin won't ignore that. She's going to die.*

Peter says, "Shashenka agreed to her terms and doubled the fee the wolf paid her. She was sent back with orders to report all new developments every twenty-four hours."

"Do you know what she reported?" Vladimir's smooth demeanor reflects in his voice, though Dmitri knows his own barely contained rage and Maria's fiery disposition are making Vladimir appear calm, almost aloof.

"Teresina gave us the names of Belyakov's business associates who were helping the stinking mutt, and we put them under surveillance." The doomed vampire clears his throat. "She also said that Elizabetta somehow overcame the witch's spell and became aware of her past, and that the Markovs were planning another revolt. But she said their support was minimal and mostly came from isolated werewolf packs near the estates." He glares at Vladimir and Maria. "We didn't know you were traitors too."

The information paints a picture of Teresina that is an enigma. The rogue never revealed she was in Shashenka's employ or reported anything that would have prepared their side for Shashenka's countermoves. At the same time, it appears that she was selective in the information she provided to Belyakov.

*Not minimal, just selective. That doesn't excuse her betrayal or bring Sofia back or return Elizabetta.*

Dmitri shifts their focus—he needs to find his wife. "What's the connection between Milo, Guillermo, and Shashenka?"

Peter meets Dmitri's hostile stare with one of his own. "Milo is a jackass. Shashenka put up with him because he was proficient in handling business affairs. I don't know how he discovered the shadow realms, but he's been trying for the last two decades to find someone who would turn him. Master had no intention of giving him that gift, and after he learned that you had done so, Milo was marked for death."

*Bullshit! Shashenka said he was pleased and planned to reward Milo.*

Vladimir frowns. "Are you sure about this?"

"Yes. He'd already given orders—Milo is on our hit list."

He's obviously speaking the truth, but it doesn't tell them about Milo's connection to Guillermo or how the sorcerer fits into Shashenka's plans. Dmitri's hands curl into fists as his claws come out—he can feel them puncture his palms. It provides a modicum of relief from his desire to rip their prisoner apart.

Peter is no longer fighting the compulsion. His body

relaxes. "I don't know how Milo found Guillermo, but he arranged a meeting between the sorcerer and Master after the bounty was placed on you and Elizabetta. The timing was perfect too—just days before your damn mutt sent the notices for the business acquisition of Stern-Grenze."

Dmitri's rage swells. His first encounter with that despicable worm resulted in Milo being turned into a vampire—a huge mistake. "Are you telling us that Shashenka orchestrated the trap Milo set for us in Germany?"

"Master figured you were greedy enough to give in to Milo's demands—he didn't expect the additional request. Guillermo was willing to go there and capture all three of you. He almost succeeded too, from what I heard. But those bitches lied; we didn't know any of the Druzhinas were helping you." Peter gives Vladimir another hateful look. "If Shashenka really is dead, then every one of you Druzhinas turned traitor."

Vladimir doesn't take the bait. "Where are they now?"

"Milo was supposed to be killed at your meeting in Machu Picchu." A muscle tenses in Peter's jaw. "If he's not dead ... I don't know where he or the sorcerer went."

"Damn it!" Dmitri rakes a hand through his hair. "Would Guillermo have protected Milo and Teresina and moved them to safety?"

Peter shakes his head. "That sorcerer is a raving lunatic. I don't think he has loyalties to anyone but himself."

Dmitri's eyebrows move higher underneath his long bangs. *Interesting ... explains why he didn't stop us from killing Shashenka.*

"Why wasn't I told that Shashenka was meeting with a

sorcerer?" Maria confirms what Dmitri suspected—she didn't know about this.

"Master feared Guillermo, what he's capable of. He said the sorcerer hated his own kind more than any other shadow realm species. Master knew the power ranks of your people—he didn't want you hurt." Peter sneers. "It's too bad Master didn't know you're as deserving of death as the rest of your comrades."

Vladimir levels his cold gaze at the vampire. "How did Shashenka contact Guillermo?"

"Some kind of weird stone device."

*A redecrystapiezo.* For the next couple of hours they question Peter at length about Shashenka's interactions with Guillermo, but it becomes clear that Peter has little knowledge of their meetings. Guillermo always came to Shashenka, often transporting into a private room so that most in the coven weren't aware of his visits. Frustration builds as Dmitri realizes they've reached a dead end. *How am I supposed to find Elizabetta? We've wasted too much time already.*

Dmitri's blood boils, and his fangs push against his lip as they slide down. Before Vladimir or Maria can stop him, he slides his dagger out of its sheath, flies across the cell, and slices Peter's throat. His free hand tangles in the former guard's hair, lifting the head as he swipes the blade through twice more to decapitate the vampire. Bloodlust turns his vision red—the motion of the dagger blurs in his frenzied slashing and stabbing. He doesn't even know if Peter made a sound. He doesn't care, either ... and he's not finished by any stretch of the definition.

When he turns, Vladimir is blocking the doorway. "Dmitri, calm down ... you can't lose it like this." Their eyes lock in unspoken challenge, only breaking contact when Vladimir attempts to grab Dmitri's arm.

Dmitri lunges at his friend. "My wife is out there somewhere. For all we know, that demented sorcerer has already killed her."

The two men tumble into the hall, and to Dmitri's relief, Maria doesn't stop him. His brief glimpse of her enraged face as she stares at Peter's body tells him she's had enough of these games too. *Good, it's time to finish this.* He breaks free of Vladimir and runs to Charles's cell—Kees and Stephan finished questioning him earlier—but when Vladimir reaches the doorway, Dmitri already has Charles's head detached from his body. Fury blazes in Dmitri's eyes as he turns to face his friend. "Finish them! I'm done here. It's time to find my wife."

*No more excuses ... they're not stopping me from going after Elizabetta again.* But his good fortune of no interference from Maria runs out. The moment he steps into the hall, she casts the immobility spell, then silently watches Dmitri's frozen body with a sad but determined look.

Vladimir calls for a couple of Druzhinas to bring a torch. When Stephan and Victoria arrive, Stephan steps into Peter's cell with the torch and comes out a moment later. He walks past Dmitri, shaking his head, and goes into the cell behind him. The stench of burning hair and flesh confirms the end of Peter and Charles, but even the relief and slight satisfaction Dmitri feels aren't enough to calm his bloodlust. He's been pushed too far for too long.

Vladimir and Victoria carry Dmitri toward the great hall without a word. That suits Dmitri fine—immobility spell or not, he's done talking. *I'm going to find her even if I have to destroy everything standing between us.*

The Druzhinas and Jacques form a perimeter around Dmitri—it's obvious to everyone now that his bloodlust is out of control. He no longer cares. They've become an impediment, a barrier between him and his mate. Remembered images and sounds won't stop flooding his mind with memories: Elizabetta broken, bleeding ... Teresina's smug expression ... Shashenka taking sexual pleasure from his wife. *My wife!* Milo handing him the envelope that put them within reach of Guillermo ... the sorcerer's staff run through Elizabetta. *She's gone, she's gone. I have to get her back!* Rage wires every cell in his body to kill. The echo of that single thought feeds the inferno blazing in his mind.

Dmitri barely notices when the wizard approaches with Alastrina. Then he realizes that the two are supporting Matt between them, and the sight of the mongrel allows another thought to wiggle in. He wants, no, needs that wolf at his side during the hunt for Guillermo.

Matt is deathly pale. His breaths are heavy and labored, but he slowly raises an arm and extends a shaky hand, placing it on Dmitri's shoulder. "Damn, man." Matt shakes his head. "I'm too sick for your shit right now. I shouldn't even be out of bed, but they said you've gone wacko." He takes another shuddering breath. "I want baby vamp back as much as you do. But going off on a murderous rampage will not find Eliza. We need to do this together, or you may be the one to kill her."

The last few words crash into Dmitri, and the bloodlust recoils, wavering between striking back or slinking into the hole in his heart.

The wolf looks at Maria. "Can you thaw him out now?"

"Yes, but everyone needs to be ready to subdue him if he tries to make a run for it." Maria moves between Matt and Dmitri—the protective gesture doesn't go unnoticed, even in Dmitri's state—and releases the immobility spell.

For a moment Dmitri just stands there trembling with rage, fighting to stay in control and survive the riptide of bloodlust trying to drag him back into mindless darkness. *I need him. We can get Elizabetta back.* He's unable to speak, but he keeps his eyes locked on Matt's. *We have to do this together. I have to keep it under control.*

"Okay, buddy, okay." Matt takes a step forward, but his balance isn't there, and he's too weak to stand on his own. Dmitri's reflexes kick in, and in one quick move he repositions himself at the wolf's side and helps Matt over to a chair. Matt manages a weak, lopsided grin. "Now, let's talk about this. I found Eliza before, and I will find her again."

Dmitri sits in the chair next to Matt while the others move to keep them surrounded. *Breathe, relax ... let it go, focus.* Minutes fall around them in silence, and then Matt and the rest of their friends begin to discuss the search for Elizabetta. The longer they talk, the more Dmitri recognizes the truth behind their words—they're done thwarting his efforts to find her.

Relief wraps him in a gentle embrace. When he's able to control his emotions, Dmitri finally joins their conversation. He agrees that the maxians may be their best source for finding Guillermo, but he feels that Milo is the key to uncovering information faster. But Milo's whereabouts remain a mystery too, and they're no closer to discovering his location than before.

About a half hour into their planning, Matt passes out. Dmitri is on his feet and lifts the wolf out of the chair before Maria even reaches them. The wizard tries to take his pulse as Dmitri carries him back to Elizabetta's old bedroom, but once they have him tucked in bed, she makes room for Alastrina to administer another healing spell; as a sorceress, Alastrina's fae blood allows her to conjure more potent and effective healing remedies than other maxians can. Still, the wolf's pallid, clammy skin and raspy breath and the underlying scent of illness are a brutal reminder of Matt's deteriorating condition.

After the spell is cast, Alastrina shoos them away before she leaves to mix another potion, but Dmitri catches up to her in the hall. She cocks her head and points a finger at him. "Vampire venom is the most destructive poison there is, more so to a werewolf. A pureblood fae could possibly heal him faster—fae medicine is far beyond anything in existence." She pats Dmitri arm. "I'm doing my best, but his healing will be slow, if he survives at all. This may take days or weeks."

"We can't afford to lose him, and we don't have days or weeks," Dmitri roars as anger threatens to unleash the bloodlust he's barely keeping contained. *Don't lose control ... don't set it free.*

Alastrina merely nods and asks Dmitri to walk with her to the kitchen to prepare the potion. "I'm nearly as old as

Guillermo," she says. "In our searches I have learned a few things about him. I do not believe he intends to kill Elizabetta ... at least not right away. It's more likely he is preparing to use her in some manner to further the chaos of this world."

The sorceress takes a deep breath. "I don't know how or when. If he repeats past habits, then right now he's still working on bringing his plans together. We have time, and you need to be patient, smart, in your efforts to find him and get Elizabetta back."

*Use her how?* Dmitri hopes that doesn't mean Guillermo would mess with Elizabetta's mind the way Shashenka did. *Who will stop her if no one is there to remind her who she is?* He can't fathom her surviving it again. Echoes of her words filter back: she'd rather be dead than go through that again. *But how would she even know?*

Alastrina continues counseling him as she prepares the potion. Then she shares something that she confides she wasn't willing to say in front of the others. "I know the fae are extinct thanks to Guillermo, but I don't believe the veils between this world and the fae realm are lost to us. There may be medicines there that will heal your friend. And if the stories my father told me are true, we may also find devices that will help us find Milo and Guillermo."

"Veils?" Dmitri gives her a questioning look; he always thought they were a myth.

"For lack of a better word, doorways ... conduits which allow one to move between Earth and Seelinara." She sees his puzzlement and adds, "That is the name of the fae world—Seelinara, or Land of the Fae."

The thought of using fae devices to find Elizabetta faster ignites Dmitri's hope and sets his determination on fire—he wants to leave immediately for Seelinara. "Do you have knowledge of these veils? Can someone find them?"

Alastrina shakes her head. "Sorcerae have looked for them since Guillermo wiped out the fae. I never tried myself; I was busy within the maxian realm, and later too involved attending to the supreme council's business to take interest. But I'm willing to do so now if it means ending that vile sorcerer before he unleashes hell on this world again."

"If there are devices in Seelinara that will help track him, why hasn't anyone gone to get one before now?" Something feels off, and Dmitri isn't sure what is behind the fear wafting off the sorceress. *What is she hiding?*

The sorceress explains the rumors of what may await anyone who succeeds in getting through. Some, she claims, are afraid the fae world itself will attack them as a threat. Others believe it's a haunted world and are unwilling to risk the wrath of fae ghosts. There is also the possibility the veils were destroyed, or that remnants of the Black Plague are still active in the space between Earth and Seelinara, particularly if Seelinara's environmental healing abilities preserved any bodies of the fae who died from the disease. The last thing they need is an active plague on Earth.

She takes a deep breath. Even so, she adds, those brave enough to try have failed so far. "There's also the slight chance that we may be wrong about the fae being extinct, and that comes with its own perils."

Dmitri presses her, but she doesn't know anything

beyond her father's warnings never to go there uninvited; those who were foolish enough to attempt it without fae consent disappeared as if they never existed. His brows draw together. "So why would you risk it now?"

"I don't believe the fae survived. There'd be no reason for the fae world to preserve their bodies, and the plague may not be the threat some think it is. All fae had a natural ability for using the environment in conjunction with their own physiology to call on whatever magic they needed for healing themselves or others—that healing magic, regardless of form, should still be there. That aside, I'm willing to go because I fear that if we don't capture Guillermo soon, our luck will run out. At that point it will be more than your wife or Matt who needs saving."

She pauses to scrutinize him. "There's also the issue of the bloodlust and how it's distracting you from completing what needs to be done to prevent the power vacuum the council warned you about. Some who fought here are already complaining about their cut or share. Once the others know Belyakov's entire dominion fell, it will escalate and spiral out of control if you're not focused. If that happens, you can guarantee that Guillermo will take advantage of it and may become even more of a threat than he is now."

"The other Druzhinas are more than capable of handling the aftermath, whether I'm there by their side or not."

Alastrina's tone becomes brusque. "Everyone is looking to you for leadership and direction in the wake of this war, and you're leaving them like a rudderless ship. In the short time I've been here, I've seen the split single focus you have for your wife and the werewolf. You're inviting the very thing the council warned you about, and it will only lead to chaos."

Dmitri doesn't appreciate the reminder. In any case, he believes the risk of further upheaval is an exaggeration designed to manipulate him for someone else's agenda. Most in their realm aren't stupid enough to provoke the Druzhina. As to the supposed risks of going to the fae world, he's willing to take them if it means getting Elizabetta back and saving Matt's life. Right now those are his two top priorities, and the maxians can go to hell if they think he's going to abandon Elizabetta and Matt to lead the vampire realm into tranquility. *We can save them both—I know it.*

When he recommends they share Alastrina's plan with the Druzhina, she becomes agitated—she insists this be kept between him, Matt, and Maria. "We can't risk too many knowing how to get into or out of Seelinara, if we can even find it ourselves." Seelinara, she explains, holds plants, stones, and natural or fae-made devices which could destroy the Earth realms; it's too great a risk for that kind of knowledge to pass to this world or anyone living in it.

Dmitri questions why it's okay for Maria to go, but Alastrina claims that she won't go against the wizard on this nor make the mistake of leaving her behind. According to the sorceress, Maria has become more than a little possessive of Matt, and Alastrina suspects there's a deeper connection between the two than the wizard may even be admitting to herself.

Dmitri's mind races over the interactions he's seen between the wolf and the wizard—he can't disagree. But regardless, he'd rather have the wizard with them on this journey, as he's come to trust her in ways he trusts few others.

Still, Dmitri doesn't know if it's possible to keep this trip a secret from the Druzhinas, and he isn't sure any of them will let him out of their sight after the way he killed Peter and Charles. The sorceress insists that she has an idea and elicits his promise that he will follow her lead when the time comes. *I don't have a choice if we're to save Matt and gain the advantage over Guillermo.*

While the potion is cooling, Alastrina lays out her plan. They will look for a veil to Seelinara as soon as Matt is well enough to travel. Dmitri begins to protest—that could be weeks away—but she assures him that the wolf's condition only needs to be stable when they leave. She and Maria can work their magic to care for Matt as they search for a veil, and if they succeed they may be able to find the medicine needed to heal Matt faster once they arrive.

"We can use the excuse of taking Matt to convalesce at Garbh Eilean—it's peaceful there. I will go through my father's papers and hopefully find a clue to the location of a veil."

For a moment Dmitri recalls the days and nights he spent with Elizabetta in the sorceress's sea cave home, and he's not sure he can handle returning to a place that holds such precious memories. But the promise of Seelinara, of what it can offer, is too much for him to pass up. He looks at the sorceress. He knows she's eccentric, yet her generosity and compassion for others makes her a rare gem in the supernatural realms. *Is the fae world too good to be true?*

"How soon can we leave?"

# CHAPTER 8: ELIZABETTA

## Secrets

Elizabetta doesn't know how long she was unconscious, but when she comes to she finds herself in Ramira again. *What about my body? What if that hideous spider decides to make a meal of it?* The thought rattles her, and several minutes pass before she realizes that Ramira is in what appears to be a sparring or training room. Various weapons—swords, knives, maces, and flails—line one wall. Mats cushion the rest of the walls and cover the floors. The ceiling is high, though she estimates the room to be only fifty square feet.

Ramira is bent over, hands on her knees, in the middle of the room—she's sniveling at her instructor, an Asian man in martial arts clothing. "This is too hard. I'm never going to get it. Why can't my uncle go with me and use his magic against the Druzhina?"

"Your mind and body are weak—you need to learn how to fight, to defend yourself. Only a fool fights the Druzhina unprepared."

*Oh, he has that one right.* Elizabetta would like to send her without training at all, but she doesn't know if the witch would be the only one harmed. If something bad were to happen to Ramira, would it free Elizabetta from this strange connection or kill her too?

Several minutes fade away while she watches the instructor patiently work with Ramira, who spends most of her time complaining and whining. *I wish she'd shut up. He could teach me a few new moves.* Elizabetta learns that the instructor's name is Michio Urakami. His instruction in the Shaolinquan fighting style is so knowledgeable and skillful that she suspects he's not just an elite martial arts expert— he's likely from the dark ages and possibly one of the first to practice and master this style of fighting.

When Michio concludes the lesson for the day, Ramira moves on to another instructor. This one seems to have some type of military background, with his skill being in stealth and avoiding detection. He never reveals his name, and Ramira only refers to him as "Sir." Again Elizabetta struggles to get anything out of the lesson because of Ramira's constant caterwauling. After the umpteenth time Ramira whines, "I can't do this," Elizabetta screams, *Shut up, you whiny brat.* To her surprise, Ramira ceases her complaints and pays attention for a while.

*Did she hear me? It's just a coincidence, right?* Still, it's unnerving, and Elizabetta is unwilling to explore the pos-sibilities. She needs a break from Ramira, that's all—sheer desire to kick the witch's ass should be compelling Elizabetta's body to find them. It doesn't, and for whatever reason her link to the annoying witch persists for hours.

The only benefit Elizabetta can see is that it has given her a glimpse of the compound where she is being held.

Wherever they are in the world, the elevation is low; she can smell the sea. Tall, thick hedges border the property, blocking her view of what lies beyond it, and in addition to a rather large mansion, there are two outbuildings of sizable proportions. One holds the training room where Michio made every attempt to teach Ramira something. The other building remains a mystery for now. Elizabetta wonders which of the three structures provides an exit from the large underground facility her body is in. She may be able to use this information later, if she can find a way to escape the dungeon without the giant spider stopping her. *Or spiders. Leave it to Guillermo to have mutant spider guards. What a sick bastard.*

After her training is finished for the day, the witch goes to her room, showers, and dresses in a pair of pajamas. For what feels like endless minutes, she sits at her vanity and stares at herself in the mirror. The young witch never talks to herself—it seems unnatural and leaves Elizabetta with no idea what kinds of thoughts are going through her head, other than the sullen and angry side she shows. A part of her wants to feel sympathetic toward Ramira—she remembers the way her own life and memory were stolen from her—but the more she's around the witch, the more she dislikes her.

Ramira climbs onto the bed and flips open a book. Elizabetta doesn't recognize the author or title, and the poor composition of the story makes her desperate to find a way back to her own body. She's never been away from it for so long. *What if I never go back?* Nor is she thrilled about leaving her body unattended, knowing what is lurking in the shadows of the dungeon.

Someone knocks on the door, and when Ramira answers it, Dahliorn is on the other side. He just stands there glaring in silence until she moves aside and allows him to enter. Ramira's eyes follow him as he goes to the chair in the corner and sits down. The witch glances at Dahliorn every now and then, but neither says a word. Elizabetta thinks the hostile looks from him are for the witch, not her, but in any event she would rather study Dahliorn than see the dreck on the pages of the book Ramira is reading. He's a puzzle she needs to solve if she has any hope of getting out of this mess. *I wish she'd talk to him. Say something, damn it.*

"Are you going to sit there and stare at me all night?" Ramira's tone is scathing.

*Not what I had in mind.*

Dahliorn says, "Yes."

*I'd even take him, someone I barely know. over no one protecting me—that spider could be cocooning my body right now. What happens to me if my body dies? Would I live on inside Ramira?* A violent shiver pulses through her, and then a quick shudder courses through Ramira too. *Wait, what?*

"Listen here, you grotesque demon," Ramira says. "I'm warning you ... stay away from me. You don't need to be in my room. You can go sit in the hall."

"I can't do that, and you know why." The cold look Dahliorn gives her sends another shiver through the witch's body. *Coincidence, right?*

"Why can't you and my uncle get it through your thick brains? It didn't work, and he won't risk undoing it because he doesn't know what it did to that stupid vampire underground. I don't care if she dies—she's useless to us now. Until Uncle figures out how to fix this mess, I don't want you anywhere near me ... you're a freak, a disgusting, repulsive mutant. I wish you were dead."

*What is her issue with him? If she wants to see a mutant, she ought to visit the dungeon.*

There's a brief flash in Dahliorn's eyes, and if Ramira hadn't been glaring at him, Elizabetta would have missed it—she swears that his eyes lightened and glowed a brilliant green. *What kind of maxian is he?* That's three times now that she's seen a change in his eyes, twice red and now light green.

Ramira continues her verbal tirade, but when she starts throwing small objects—books, knickknacks—Elizabetta's last ragged nerve ignites in an internal ball of fury. *You ungrateful bitch, he doesn't deserve this. Leave him alone!*

"I'm not ungrateful," Ramira snaps.

*She heard that.* Elizabetta doesn't understand how her thoughts can affect Ramira, but a mix of fear and hope tangle inside her. This may be something she can use to her own advantage—if she can figure it out.

Dahliorn's eyes search Ramira's as the woman stares at him. His lips don't move, but Elizabetta is almost certain she hears his voice in her mind.

«Stay quiet, little dove ... don't direct your thoughts at her. She mustn't know you're there.»

*Where's Matt with his crazy-train clichés when I need*

*him? I must be losing my mind.* Elizabetta's rational side argues she's not, but her brain struggles to wrap around how it's possible for Dahliorn to speak in her head this way. *Hello? Can you hear me?* She sends a torrent of questions to him, but a parade of mute minutes slide past before he sends another mental message.

«Wait until she's asleep. We'll talk then.»

Ramira picks up her book—the only one Elizabetta wishes she'd gotten rid of—and resumes reading, but Elizabetta ignores the words on the page as she mulls over the strange interaction with Dahliorn. She wonders what his story is and how he fits into Guillermo's twisted life. Ramira seems to have a cold, hateful streak, one driven inextricably deeper by Dahliorn's mere presence, but he shows depth and warmth in spite of her outlandish behavior. *She can stop her fuming and go to sleep anytime now—like twenty minutes ago would be perfect.* When Ramira next glances up at him, Elizabetta tries to send a plea through the woman's eyes. *Help me.*

Dahliorn's gaze narrows as he shifts in his chair. He almost looks uncomfortable—but at the same moment expectant. Ramira yawns and places her book on the nightstand. Without another look at the man in the corner, she turns off the light and shuts her eyes.

Silent minutes linger in the shadows until Ramira's breaths slow—she's asleep, leaving Elizabetta trapped in the darkness behind the witch's closed eyelids. The reminder of how little control she has over herself makes each second boom louder than the last. There is no sound of movement from Dahliorn. She begins to think that he has changed his mind and isn't going to talk to her after all, and then a slight noise catches her attention and a moment later he speaks in an almost inaudible whisper.

Lost in her attempt to sort it out—she doesn't recognize the language—Elizabetta startles when she hears him say, «Little dove, can you hear me?»

«Yes, but how is it possible for you to speak with me like this?» Her mind races ahead with questions, but they fall in a tangled heap at his unexpectedly quick response.

«I've placed a spell on you that allows you to communicate with me in this manner.»

*Oh my God, he heard me!* Elizabetta mentally frowns—she's somewhat certain most maxians do not have this ability. Then she realizes he's not reacting to her last thought. «Can you hear everything I think?»

«Only those thoughts you choose to speak to me.»

There's some relief, knowing she'll have a measure of privacy from him. «Who are you? What are you?»

A long pause settles between them—Elizabetta can't see from within the darkness whether her question somehow offended him. *Do the blind have this same issue, or do they use other senses to gauge reactions?* The speculation does little to help her adapt to this new form of communication.

When Dahliorn does send a reply, it carries a hint of sadness. «I'm a sheridauk ... a dark fae.»

«I thought the fae were extinct.» Silence follows her comment, driving her frustration level higher.

She can hear him shift in the chair. «I don't know how many fae Guillermo killed or if the fae were wiped out. I came here to assassinate him.»

*And?* She's about to ask when Dahliorn says, «My mission failed ... I have been bound and held for centuries.»

He pauses again, but Elizabetta doesn't know how to respond. She gently probes for more information; if she is to trust this fae, she needs to know more about his background. To her surprise, Dahliorn is somewhat forthcoming. *It's a start.* But it's obvious he's not kept in a cell, and she wonders how Guillermo forces him to stay.

«I know you have many questions, but our conversations will often need to be brief. This must remain our secret, little dove. It's more important for me to tell you to be patient and to warn you against sending direct thoughts to Ramira.»

«Why?» Before he can answer, another question leaps from the jumbled mass of concerns clouding her mind. «And why do you call me little dove?»

«Until you learn, it's too risky. Ramira could take control of your mind.» He pauses, and she can almost hear him smile as he says, «You're the peace-bringer. I have waited a long time for you.»

*Peace-bringer ... yeah, right. Maybe he's not entirely sane after all.* She's feeling crazy enough on her own, and she doesn't need weird sidetracks—she needs to know how to get out of this nightmare and away from here. But at least he may help take the raw edge off her new constant companion, frustration. «Will you tell me what is happening to me?»

There's a ring of truth to his words. «Guillermo used an ancient unity spell. He meant to bind only your memories and knowledge to Ramira—so she could access what they need. But it would have destroyed your brain and left your body in a vegetative state you'd never recover from. I had to protect you.»

«What?» Panic races through her at full tilt. «Oh God, am I going to be okay? Is there any way out of this?» She's back to imagining her body hyperventilating again. Logic tells her she should be curious why he feels the need to protect her, and from what, but fear pushes logic into the backseat as it grips the steering wheel tighter.

«It is forbidden magic—outlawed by the maxians centuries ago in an agreement with the fae. When Guillermo cast his spell against you, I countered it with my own to protect you.» Although there was no way for Dahliorn to fully prevent the merge, he explains, he bound Elizabetta's consciousness to her memories and knowledge and tethered all three to her body, hoping it might allow reunification someday. «I added a barrier that will shield you for a while too,» he says. «Ramira won't know you're there, at least not right away—or not at all if we're careful. They think the spell failed. We must let them believe that until we are ready.»

*Ready for what?* While Elizabetta is grateful that Dahliorn provided a measure of protection, she doesn't like the idea of remaining connected to Ramira. What little he's telling her allows logic to lock fear in the trunk, but she needs to know more, and she doesn't even know which questions to ask.

«I must teach you how to access Ramira's mind. We will eventually take control of her, but you must learn to use your mind in ways you never have before. Guillermo needs her help to achieve his goals, and he's groomed her for years to that end.»

Ramira stirs and rolls over. Neither of them speaks for a few minutes.

*Can't he break Guillermo's spell so we can help each other escape?* «Why is he using her and me this way?»

She can hear Dahliorn leave the chair and start to pace. «He considers her weak since she had no more than the ordinary powers of a witch—she's beneath him, almost meaningless—and he hoped to combine your abilities with hers. He didn't know she'd lose one power to gain the other, and the protection I cast on you sacrificed all of her magical powers and mostly prevented her from gaining yours.»

Again her mind is reeling. The pacing stops, and she hears the bedframe squeak. «And before you ask, no, it's not possible for me to release either of you from his spell. Either Guillermo must remove it, which he never intends to do, or it will cease when he is killed.»

Thoughts of killing the evil sorcerer are never far from Elizabetta's mind, but she has no idea how it's possible, especially since she's spending more time in Ramira's body. Vengeance swells inside her, demanding her focus. *I may have to kill her before I can get to him.*

Almost as if the witch heard her, Ramira turns onto her back and sits up. Her eyes open wide, and fear drenches her words. "What are you doing? Get away from me, freak!"

*Whew ... I thought she meant me. I've got to get the whole projecting my thoughts thing under control.*

Dahliorn rises from the edge of the bed and rushes across the room to the chair in the corner. There's a green glow to his eyes as he meets Ramira's gaze, but his jaw is clenched tight even as he says, «Rest now, little dove. We'll talk again soon.»

In the next instant Elizabetta is back in her own body. She sits up and looks around the dim room and then checks herself for bite marks. When she realizes what she's doing, she laughs out loud—if a giant spider had bitten her body while her mind was in Ramira, she'd likely be dead. Then she stills. *What will happen to my mind if my body dies while I'm in the witch?* Elizabetta gets off the cot and stretches her stiff limbs, huffing. *At least it would have a reason to be in a state of rigor mortis.*

She suspects that Dahliorn somehow sent her back to her body when he told her to rest, but she has no idea whether it was inadvertent or if he meant to give her time alone to think. Whichever it was, Elizabetta appreciates the chance to process the critical details he shared, though she finds herself more intrigued by the little he revealed about himself. *How does a fae get captured by someone less powerful?*

Maria said once that fae magic rivaled that of a wizard, and Elizabetta can't fathom why Dahliorn's mission failed. As a sorcerer, Guillermo shouldn't have been able to defeat a pure fae. Then she recalls that Dahliorn said he is a sheridauk, a dark fae, and she wonders what that is or what it means in terms of magical powers. Still, it's remarkable that at least one fae survived. *Is that why he's sad? There aren't any fae for him to go home to.* She knows how she'd feel if she were alone in this world, if she never saw Dmitri again.

Elizabetta returns to the cot and lies down, thoughts of Dmitri filling her mind. *I miss him so much.* Between being in Ramira's mind, worrying over the mutant spiders, and figuring out the dark fae, she has not allowed herself the luxury of dwelling on Dmitri or sparing more than a fleeting thought for Matt. Her heart aches with the unknowns of the future ahead of her and the threat Guillermo poses to all of them.

There's no way for her to know if the fighting at Machu Picchu is over or if the Druzhina is still trying to take over the estates. A part of her still can't believe Shashenka is dead. *At least I got to see the end of him. That bastard can rot in hell.* But she feels robbed of the chance to celebrate their victory.

Her thoughts linger over the way she and Dmitri fought side by side, and the pride she felt when he allowed Maria to deliver the final blow. Her voice breaks as she whispers, "*Dmitri ... ti amo e non smetterò mai di amarti.*"

*Are Dmitri, Matt, and the Druzhinas looking for me? How will they find me here? Is there a way to free Dahliorn from Guillermo too?* Her mind is a tangle of questions as she drifts off to sleep.

# CHAPTER 9: DMITRI

## Race Against Time

Now that Belyakov's forces have been eliminated at Novgorod, Dmitri doesn't want to wait one more day to start the clandestine search for a veil to Seelinara—and yet he can't risk revealing their intentions to leave. Besides, Alastrina and Maria claim that allowing the Orde de Maxia to help the Druzhina close out the war will give them the time they need to make certain Matt is stable enough to travel. It takes effort to hide his agitation, but he reluctantly agrees to complete the unfinished business of the unclaimed estates.

To his relief Victoria and Anna make arrangements with a local vampire coven to watch over the castle until a new owner is announced. Jacques promises to personally deliver Dmitri's report to the council, oversee the estate distribution, and send envoys to quell any disputes that arise from the change of ownership. The high warlock's determination to help prevent a power vacuum is obvious, and Dmitri appreciates the extra effort Jacques is giving to their cause. "Remember what you and Elizabetta have fought for all these many long years," Jacques tells him before leaving. "Stay focused on the tasks ahead—it's worth seeing this through."

At the moment Dmitri is feeling anything but diplomatic, but he respects the high warlock and owes him a debt of gratitude at the least. For now the only way he can repay it is to live up to Jacques's expectations. "I will." He gives a faint smile. "Thank you for taking these final instructions to the council, and thank them on the vampire realm's behalf. We wouldn't be here right now if they had not helped us."

Dmitri watches Jacques walk away and hopes he doesn't break his word and lose control. At least the situation with Matt provides a distraction to keep his mind off the vengeful desires boiling beneath the surface. The wolf's condition hasn't improved over the last three days, and Dmitri can smell the growing scent of death on him. He holds his breath for a moment as he enters Elizabetta's old room. Matt's eyes are closed, there's a gray tinge to his face, and his breathing sounds more ragged than even a few hours ago. The maxians sit on either side of the bed, looking defeated.

Glancing up at Dmitri, Maria says, "I'm glad you're here. Alastrina and I were just talking about being wrong."

"Wrong about what?" He folds his arms across his chest, worried they might have changed their minds about finding a way into Seelinara.

"About waiting any longer." Maria places a cold, wet cloth on Matt's forehead. Fear shadows her words. "He's dying, Dmitri ... it doesn't matter what spells or potions Alastrina and I try. The venom is killing him—he's suffering so much—and nothing seems to help."

*Damn it.* Dmitri's jaw tenses and his focus returns to Matt's sallow complexion. He doesn't want to admit it, but somehow over the last few months, the mongrel has managed to become his friend. If Matt dies, it won't just be Elizabetta and Maria who will mourn his loss. "What are you saying? Are we going to risk taking him to find a veil, or is it too late?"

*I can't lose him—he has to help me find Elizabetta.* The bloodlust spikes, trying to compel him into action. Dmitri wants to lash out to save both of them, but then the inferno fizzles, nearly extinguishing, when he considers it may be too late for either. He roughly rakes a hand through his hair twice as he swallows and clears his throat. *Have I already lost them?* He looks at the wizard and sees her pain. Maria sniffles, wiping tears from her eyes.

Alastrina says, "I think we need to try, but I don't know if we'll find a veil soon enough. I need to go through my father's papers so we have a starting point for our search." She pauses. "Even if we do reach Seelinara, Matt may be too far gone for fae medicine to save him now."

*I can't let him die. I won't let him die.* "Maria, get Henri in here right now with an EPM. Alastrina, work your best spell to stabilize Matt. I'll carry him, do whatever it takes to get him there. You do what you can to keep his heart beating until we find the veil."

When Maria and Henri enter the room, Vladimir and Anna are with them. Immediately their noses wrinkle at the smell of death that permeates the air—they almost appear to stop breathing. Vladimir says, "Maria said you're taking him to Alastrina's home?"

"Yes." The lie springs from Dmitri without a second thought. "Her father's ancient writings may describe a spell or potion that will save his life."

Anna offers to go along and help, and both Dmitri and Alastrina scramble for excuses—leading to more lying when they have to explain why they'll lose contact and don't have a reasonable estimate of how long they'll be away. Dmitri hates lying to his friends, but there's little choice if he's going to save Matt and Elizabetta. With that in mind he deflects further unwelcome questions or offers of help by asking Vladimir to stay in touch with the maxian council and do what he can to finish with the aftermath of their war. His friend acquiesces and promises to put some of the Druzhinas on the search for Elizabetta as soon as the outstanding issues are dealt with—even the smallest bit of information may help Dmitri and Matt once they come back. *We will return.*

Lifting Matt from the bed, Dmitri says, "We really need to go now before it's too late for him."

Vladimir and Anna wish them success, and a circle forms around Dmitri and Matt as the maxians link their group for travel. Henri utters the magic command to mutaport them away, a quick bright flash follows, and in the next instant they arrive in the middle of the small drawing room of Alastrina's sea cave home.

Dmitri's brows pull down at what he doesn't hear or see when he looks at the wolf in his arms. *Shit. Matt's not breathing.* He lays Matt on the floor and places his ear over the wolf's chest. No heartbeat. "Damn it, no!"

Dmitri places his hands near the end of Matt's breastbone and begins chest compressions at the same moment Alastrina casts another spell. Maria kneels next to Matt and breathes into the wolf's mouth whenever Dmitri reaches a thirty count and pauses. For several minutes they work to revive him, then Maria sits back and sobs. "We waited too long ... he's dead."

"No!" Dmitri unlocks his fingers and strikes Matt's chest above the heart with the side of his fist. "Damn you, mutt ... don't you die on us now!" He hits the wolf again and again, begging, ordering him to wake. "Don't you dare destroy a part of Elizabetta's heart by leaving her this way."

After several blows he feels Alastrina pull his arm aside. "You have to let him go."

"Keep fighting for him!" He glares at the sorceress. "He's stronger than this ... cast another spell. You will not quit on him ... do whatever it takes. Maria, keep a finger on his carotid artery and let me know the moment there's a pulse." He jerks his arm free and resumes pounding on Matt's chest.

Another few minutes pass before Maria's hand juts forward and she screams, "Stop. He has a pulse—he has a pulse." Tears stream down her face, and her sobs and laughter break the heavy silence.

The pulse is weak, erratic, but it's there; Matt remains unconscious, though for the moment he's still alive. Dmitri realizes he's shaking with relief himself. When it appears the wolf's heart will stay beating, the sorceress tells him to take Matt to the same bedroom Dmitri and Elizabetta used not too long ago. He stops in the doorway, and his heart twists in pain—the memories of his time here with his wife bring a mix of longing, sorrow, and fresh anger. He takes a deep breath, hoping to detect her scent. Instead he nearly gags—the pungent smell of death on Matt is already claiming the room.

Dmitri gently deposits Matt on the mattress, and the second he has the covers adjusted, Maria is there with another cold, damp rag to lay across the wolf's head. She looks up at Dmitri. "Thank you for not giving up on him."

He nods, but has no words. A moment later Alastrina hollers for Dmitri from the kitchen. He finds her dragging two sizable trunks out of a cabinet in what Dmitri thought was the pantry. Looking at it now, he realizes it is mostly a storage area for her magic ingredients and ready-to-use potions.

Together they carry the trunks into the bedroom to do their research at Matt's bedside—Alastrina is afraid they will miss critical signs if the wolf takes another downward turn. Dmitri pushes Matt's bed against the wall, and Alastrina conjures a long, narrow table and three stools. Within minutes they have opened the trunks and are ready to start their search for a veil or at the least a spell or potion that may preserve Matt's life until they find a way into Seelinara.

Dmitri's confidence shatters immediately when he realizes that he doesn't recognize the language on the pages lying open before him. "I can't read this. Is there another way I can help?"

Alastrina looks through the stack of journals and holds one out to Dmitri. "This contains maps of Earth and Seelinara ... it may show the location of the veils."

Dmitri snatches it out of her hand. But there are no legends or scales, and he isn't sure how he'll recognize a veil even if one is marked on a map. He flips through page after page, goes from the back to the front, and then looks at the back again. Frustration mounts—he's all but useless. "What would the mark of a veil look like? There's nothing here to tell me what is on these maps."

The sorceress moves next to Dmitri and studies the map before them. Then she starts flipping the pages too and mumbling to herself. "If you look at each one closely, you'll start to see elements that are repeated on each map. The veils shouldn't be common and may only show up on a few."

A snarl rumbles from Dmitri, and he closes his eyes a moment while he rakes his hand through his hair twice. Then he nods at the sorceress as he refocuses on the first map in the journal. The two maxians consult with each other on spells and potions, deciding what to try next, but he tunes them out, clenching his jaw. *Locate a veil, get to Seelinara, save the mongrel, find Elizabetta.*

The trio spends hours scouring the papers and journals, Alastrina casting a stability spell every time Matt's respireations grow too shallow or slow. The maxians concoct one potion after another but find defeat with each attempt. *How can all their magic be this useless?* His apprehension over Matt's condition keeps Dmitri's bloodlust at a tolerable low boil, but he still can't find anything that seems to indicate a veil's location.

Exhaustion sets in; they've been at this for over twelve hours. Alastrina suggests they rotate, with two continuing the search while one sleeps for three to four hours. Maria is the first to take a respite, only she doesn't go to Alastrina's room as the sorceress offers. Instead she crawls onto the bed next to Matt, clasps his hand in hers, and lays her head on his shoulder. Within minutes she's asleep. Dmitri pauses to study his two friends. *Just how close have they become?*

Another few hours pass before Alastrina wakes Maria and goes to her room to rest. Dmitri, unable to keep the tension from his voice, updates the wizard on their lack of progress. Maria leaves the writings aside and opens a journal containing maps. She scowls as Dmitri tells her that apart from obvious markings—rivers, streams, roads, mountains, terrain features, and elevation—he's not found anything that stands out as a possible veil location. He doesn't tell her he is losing hope that they will ever find Seelinara. At the very least, their progress is too slow. If Matt dies, it will either push Dmitri's murderous impulses beyond control or hinder his ability to find Elizabetta before it's too late for her too.

"Dmitri, did you notice these?" Maria points at a symbol on a map.

He nods. "They're on every map, always near what looks to be cliffs or mountains alongside a body of water. Lakes, rivers, streams, and oceans perhaps, but given the curved lines and wispy branches, I think it represents areas of weeping willows. Leaf-bearing and conifer trees seem to be drawn on these maps too."

Maria rips a page out of one journal, flips through another journal, and tears a page from it as well. She lays one on top of the other and lifts them up to the light. "Is it possible ..." Her voice is a whisper. "Dmitri, look at this."

He leans over and bends his head near hers. "What am I looking at?"

"Your willows. Look, they're in the same place on both maps. These two have identical outlines with different interior features, and one is marked Earth—the other, Seelinara."

Dmitri snatches the pages out of her hands and holds them closer to the lamp. Disappointed, he shakes his head. "It's too common; it's on every map in these journals. Alastrina said it'd be limited, unique to just a few maps."

Breathless, Maria says, "I think you are wrong. These may be the veils." She jabs a finger at the curved and wispy lines, then rushes from the room. A moment later she returns with Alastrina.

"My father always said the veils were few." The sorceress rubs the sleep from her eyes and shakes her head as she reaches for another journal. "Let's find a few more maps with a similar outline—one from each world."

Before long they have several maps torn from the books and compare one set after another. Even with different interior features, each map that has a similar boundary seems to line up with one of Dmitri's willow trees. Maria's theory seems suddenly plausible. *Why didn't I see this? We've lost so much time ... it's been right in front of me.* Dmitri shoves his hands through his hair, gripping his skull.

*If these are veils, we need to go—now.* "Where's the closest one to Garbh Eilean?"

Again they dig through the maps. Alastrina excitedly taps her finger on a page, her eyes growing wider with each repetition. "Right here. There's one right here!"

"Here, here—or on this island?" Maria darts a quick glance at Matt.

"On this island." Alastrina turns the map around to show Dmitri and Maria. "See here, this slight depression behind the tallest point? That's right above this cavern."

Elation and disgust fill Dmitri. To discover a possible veil so close to their location is beyond what he hoped for, but the hours they lost because of his assumption that the symbols were willow trees has put Matt in greater peril. "We can't afford to lose another minute. This one is close enough that we can mutaport up there."

Alastrina looks at the two of them. "On the chance we're wrong, I recommend we take the boat around and hike up. If it doesn't work, we'll need a way to get back to the sea cave."

Maria frowns. "If it's there, how do we open it? I don't want to subject Matt to a long travel distance if we have to come back." Her tone seems to suggest that they're making choices that will kill him. The silent accusation rankles Dmitri, especially after the way both maxians just up and quit resuscitation efforts on the wolf when their group arrived here.

"I don't know." Alastrina glances at the papers and journals again. "Maybe the answer is in this mess."

Dmitri deflates like a popped balloon. *We're running*

*out of time.* He shoves both hands through his hair again and glares at the sorceress. "You're part fae. Why don't you know this?"

She snaps back, "Because I was born in this world and raised in the maxian realm. My father never spoke of such things."

*Useless, I'm useless ... I can't even help them look.* Dmitri picks up a journal and slams it down on the table. Cursing under his breath, he leaves the room. "Let me know if you find anything. I'm going to take a nap."

Dmitri stretches across the divan in the drawing room; it's too short for his long body, but it's better than lying on the stone floor. He closes his eyes and tries to clear his mind. The clock is running out for Matt, and there's no way to know if Elizabetta is alive or nearing her final minutes too. His frustration over the delays is again tempered by a stronger desire to save them both—he mustn't jeopardize them by losing control now.

A hand squeezing his shoulder jolts him awake. Dmitri leaps to his feet, knocking Maria down in the process. "What the hell, Maria?" He blinks to clear the sleepy fog from his mind—he doesn't know when he fell asleep—and extends a hand to help the wizard up. "I'm sorry about that."

Maria dusts off the seat of her jeans. "Next time I'll throw a glass of water on you from a distance. I came to tell you that Alastrina thinks she found something."

He bolts past her to the bedroom. "What do you have?"

"Fae humor?" The sorceress is scowling. "It's a cryptic riddle that reads like gibberish, but 'veil' is mentioned three times. I don't know if it's the spell that opens a veil, or if it's meant to be a clue for opening one, or if my father was just a really horrible poetry writer."

Alastrina turns the page toward him and points to a sketch of an ordinary-looking room with a framed painting above the mantel of a fireplace, and next to it a mysterious passage. She tells him to look closely at the painting—it seems to show an open portal between two different worlds.

Dmitri's jaw flexes. "Read it to me."

"I'll translate as best I can." The sorceress clears her throat. "Veil at cornerstone, shed thee light, while earth and wind hide in plain sight. A spatter of rain the dancing sprite within a ring of fire laughs. Cry a tear upon the veil, where in the shadows pixies sing in mirth. Unseelie and Seelie blood bind untold secrets between thee. One of dark and one of light, only these shall I call to me. Dare ye enter alone without bid or welcome, forever become this side of the veil."

"You're right—that sounds like utter gibberish." Dmitri glances at Matt; there's a stronger scent of death with each shallow breath the wolf exhales. "We need to do something now. There must be other options for going there."

Maria says, "I think we should give Matt another potion, place another stabilizing spell on him, and then go up top. We're a few hours before sunrise, so you'll be safe from the sun. You and I will do what we can to keep Matt comfortable and breathing while Alastrina tries to figure it out. If it doesn't work, we'll have to come back here and ..."

*It will work—it has to.*

Dmitri steps near the bed, ready to scoop the wolf into

his arms, as the wizard fetches another potion. Alastrina mutters an incantation, and the women attempt to pour the potion into Matt's mouth. He chokes and coughs twice before involuntarily swallowing it in his unconscious state. Neither maxian knows if enough of the potion was ingested, but both agree the concoction is too strong—they can't risk giving him more. Dmitri doesn't allow them the opportunity to change their minds. Gathering the blanket around Matt, he lifts him from the bed and heads toward the boat in the cavern. Maria and Alastrina follow him through the drawing room door.

When they reach the boat, Dmitri keeps Matt held firmly in his arms rather than laying him down in the cramped vessel. He whispers in the wolf's ear, "Hang in there, Matt, we're almost there. We're going to get you back on your paws, and then we'll go find your baby vamp." A sardonic huff echoes a single thought—it used to grate on him to no end when the mutt called Elizabetta that, and now here he is using it as a rallying cry to keep Matt alive.

Maria and Alastrina are still debating possible meanings for the riddle, but they're no closer to solving it when they beach the boat on the shore or even after they've stumbled up the steep terrain to reach the plateau on top. The area marked on the map is in a bowl-shaped depression next to a rocky mound, and that combination hides it from the otherwise wide-open view.

Since they don't know the precise location of the veil, or what will happen when they open it, Dmitri stands back a few feet with Matt as Alastrina recites the fae riddle. Nothing happens. Matt seems to react to his disappointment, the wolf's breathing slowing even more. *What if we can't ... don't get it opened in time?* He whispers, "Don't you die on me. Elizabetta will never forgive either of us."

Next the sorceress tries single phrases from the odd riddle. Still nothing. Dmitri can see this is going to take a while, and he backs away a few more feet before laying Matt on the ground, the blanket tucked around the unconscious wolf.

His worry grows as Alastrina continues to fail. She reads each line backward, waits—nothing—and then recites the entire riddle in reverse. Still nothing. Dmitri can see the desperation in the set of her eyes and mouth as she moves to more drastic measures, cutting her hand to drip blood indiscriminately around the depression while she repeats everything she's already tried. Next she places kisses upon the ground, trees, shrubs, and plants. In frustration she hollers, "Open sesame!" That elicits a chuckle from Maria and a deeper scowl from Dmitri.

Minutes surrender to an hour, then two, then three. The predawn colors light the sky. If they don't solve this soon, they'll have to return to the confines of the sea cave home. Then Alastrina takes out a wand and scrawls something on the ground, but he can't read it from this angle. Curious, he stands up and walks over to see what it is—it had no effect, but he's tired of sitting and waiting at this point. In the dirt he sees two words: *"Veascru nonda."*

Dmitri can't resist. "Does that mean anything?"

The sorceress looks up at him and then toward Maria. "I'm not sure. It may be an ancient fae dialect." Alastrina catches the impatient and half-hostile look Dmitri gives her, and quickly she adds, "But it's the first two letters of each sentence of the riddle, and if I'm remotely right, it means 'welcome home.'"

*Ridiculous.* He groans and rolls his eyes as he walks back over to Matt. Alastrina says, " *Veascru nonda!*" A ripping hiss follows a fraction of a second later, and when Dmitri looks back, his jaw drops. There in front of the maxians is a clear, shimmering portal six feet wide.

Dmitri rushes back to the women. "That's the veil?"

The sorceress reaches out and touches the transparent surface—unlike the drawing in the book, the image on the other side seems to be a distorted view of the island's landscape—but her hand disappears, presumably inside the portal or even through to Seelinara. She withdraws her hand and turns to smile at him. "Yes, I believe it is."

## CHAPTER 10: ELIZABETTA

# Settling In

Ramira's shrill voice jars Elizabetta back to wakefulness in time to see the witch shove a chair into the table as she passes it. "I don't want him in my room, Uncle," the witch is screaming. "You have no idea how creepy it is to wake up and find him sitting on the edge of my bed." She reaches her chair and sits in a huff.

"I told you that he will be punished for breaking the proximity rule, but I will not allow you to go unwatched." Impatience and anger coat Guillermo's words, contorting his expression into a mask of disdain. *Just what I want to see first thing when I wake up—sour-puss's usual happy face, otherwise known as "the scowl." It's going to be another long day with these two.*

The witch shudders. "I want to puke just thinking that he might be touching me while I'm asleep."

*Get dramatic much?* Elizabetta knows they are discussing Dahliorn, but she hasn't heard or seen anything to suggest he's the exaggerated threat Ramira is making him out to be. Aside from his strange glowing eyes, he seems well behaved in the presence of the spoiled brat. *If I were him, I would have at least slapped her or knocked her on her butt by now.* Elizabetta suspects that if he wanted to kill the witch, she'd already be dead.

Guillermo says, "We're still seeing slight changes from the spell, and we can't take the risk. Without knowing what went wrong, there is no telling if this is a side effect and if it will get worse."

Ramira actually lifts a pitcher and slams it down, splashing orange juice on the table. "I don't need to be watched! My powers are gone and I look like a filthy vampire, but I can still go into the sun and eat human food—I have no cravings for blood."

*Look like a vampire?* Elizabetta has seen the sniveling witch in the mirror and hasn't noticed any vampiric features. Dahliorn talked of stripping Ramira's maxian powers, but he said nothing about the witch inheriting Elizabetta's natural traits. *What else did the spell give to that witch-hare?* She tries to reach out to Dahliorn, but he doesn't reply. He's not in the room, though—it leaves her wondering if their ability to talk only works over short distances.

Ramira is still sulking. She picks at the food on her plate and glares when the sorcerer reassures her that he will address the problem with Dahliorn, but for now she must stick to her schedule—Michio is expecting her after breakfast. Elizabetta watches through Ramira's eyes as the witch stands and leaves the room, mumbling under her breath, "Uncle needs to kill that freak."

She continues grumbling to herself the entire way to the training facility, where she once more whines, complains, and makes only feeble efforts to take the proper stances or perform correct moves. For two hours Elizabetta watches and listens—sitting on the sidelines is driving her insane. If she had the opportunity to control the other woman, at least the lesson would progress and give Elizabetta a chance to learn. Michio remains consistent in his instruction, outwardly ignoring Ramira's defeated attitude. But more than once Elizabetta finds herself cheering when Michio takes Ramira down to the mat. She wishes he'd do more of it.

When Ramira moves on to her next instructor, Elizabetta's delight increases—Sir is even less patient with her antics, and he meets her resistance to training with force. Elizabetta can see that he is using fear to motivate the woman, but Ramira keeps bellyaching—she's obviously clueless, even when he overpowers her and drives her to the ground. Near the end of the lesson, when he again takes Ramira by surprise, he pins her to the ground with his knee to her sternum. With teeth clenched and muscles bulging, he produces a knife and holds it to her throat. "You're dead."

Ramira screams, "You cut me."

Sir rises and backs away, wiping the blade on his pants before putting it back in the sheath. He looks at her with contempt that radiates off him like a blast furnace. "You're wasting my time."

*Not half as bad as she's wasting mine.* Elizabetta does a mental eye roll as Ramira storms off toward the mansion and races upstairs to her bedroom to inspect the small slice on her throat. In the mirror Elizabetta notices the slight trickle of blood, and the sight ignites her hunger; it's been months since she fed last. She watches in eager anticipation as Ramira uses a finger to catch and lift a droplet of blood. The witch stares at it for what feels like a teasingly long minute to Elizabetta. Then Ramira's hand rises, and she samples the blood but gags—and somewhat to Elizabetta's amusement, the witch runs for the bathroom and heaves into the toilet. *Really? One little drop of blood, and she's sick?*

When Ramira moves to the sink to rinse her mouth, she looks at herself again in the mirror, and for the first time Elizabetta sees two underdeveloped fangs. *Huh, it is true.* Ramira leans closer to the mirror, giving Elizabetta a chance to inspect the fangs. They are short and blunted and could tear flesh, though they seem impractical for feeding. But it's what Elizabetta doesn't see that catches her attention the most. Ramira's fangs appear solid, missing the two ducts that inject venom or draw blood.

*How is that possible?* Her speculation runs rampant, but one thing is clear—Ramira was never bitten by a vampire. Once a human takes vampire blood to neutralize the venom, they are turned; there is no failure rate. It's another topic to add to her growing list of questions for Dahliorn. They need to fast-track her lessons, whatever those may be. The sooner he teaches Elizabetta what she needs to know, the sooner they can end Guillermo and reclaim their lives.

«Dahliorn?» She waits but gets no reply. Throughout the rest of the afternoon and into the evening, Elizabetta's attempts to reach out to him go unanswered. With each passing hour her fear grows that he's injured or is still suffering under Guillermo's hand. *We've got to get out of here. What will happen to me if Guillermo kills him?* The panicked thought seems to drive her back into her own body, but it's outside of what she's come to think of as the normal transfer by Dahliorn, and it only heightens her worry for his safety.

Elizabetta rubs her face before she climbs off the cot. Her body feels even stiffer than before, and she wonders if her prolonged absences are causing permanent damage. The room is too small for the nervous energy buzzing inside her. To release it Elizabetta goes through a series of exercises—jumping jacks, push-ups, sit-ups, and running in place—then practices advanced forms of the moves Michio showed Ramira earlier. The more she sees of the master martial artist, the more certain she is that he trained with the original masters of this fighting form. *I'd love to learn directly from him.* She chuckles. *Bet he'd enjoy working with me over Ramira too.*

When she finishes the routine, Elizabetta paces, giving an occasional glance toward the door; her twitchy nervousness hasn't gone away. For a moment she considers breaking out, but fear of crossing paths with the spiders dashes that thought. Still, since Guillermo cast his unity spell she's seen no one but Dahliorn in this room, and that was only to replace her doorknob.

She calls out to the sheridauk again, «Are you there? Can you hear me?» Her brow furrows when she hears what sounds like a groan coming through the mental link she shares with him. «Dahliorn? Are you all right?» Nothing.

The silence stretches on, and Elizabetta wonders if he's hurt or merely out of range of their communication ability, or if she imagined the noise. But Dahliorn didn't say whether the mind-to-mind communicating spell had limitations—perhaps he can hear her at greater distances than she can hear him. For several minutes she mulls over the connection between them, then draws a deep breath and launches into what she hopes isn't just a one-sided conversation.

Elizabetta tells him about Ramira's training and describes the witch's underdeveloped fangs and the way Ramira's reaction to tasting blood heightened her own hunger—she needs to feed soon. Some of her comments are met with grunts or groans. It bolsters her theory that he can hear her but that the distance is distorting what he's saying in return. *Or am I garbled too?* She doesn't want to contemplate the possibility that he is injured and unable to do more than project painful sounds.

In frustration she returns to the cot and lies down. Asking questions seems pointless since she can't decipher Dahliorn's responses, so instead she bounces ideas at him. Now is not the time for either of them to be alone. «If we can't use her to kill Guillermo, maybe I can make her smuggle my body out—once I know how to control her.» She pauses to sort the flood of ideas. «Oh, better yet, I can turn her in to the Druzhina.»

Elizabetta offers to collect or share intel that may help them with their plans too—there's a slight chance that something she sees or hears through Ramira will be useful—but in truth, Dahliorn can provide more information about Guillermo and this compound than she ever could.

The sheridauk has indicated that Guillermo is away almost as much as he is here. The few snippets of news Elizabetta's heard point to growing problems in all realms, and doubtless the sorcerer is busy meddling in others' affairs, taking full advantage of the many now on the slippery slope into pandemonium and war. The strangeness of her captivity makes it impossible for her to speculate how many days have passed, but her internal senses suggest that more than a couple of weeks have gone by. She doesn't want to think her friends are failing to prevent a power vacuum, but she has no idea what, if anything, Matt, Dmitri, and the Druzhinas are doing to get everything under control. It raises her anger that she's not there to help them, but the thought is tempered by not knowing whether they are looking for her or if such a search will divert their attention and resources.

It seems a cruel twist of fate to be taken from Dmitri once more. So much time has been stolen from them together already, and though Elizabetta tries to envision a day when nothing comes between them again, it doesn't kill the ache in her heart. Nor does it fill the hole next to it where she holds her dearest friends.

The edges of the darkness creep in, and Elizabetta recognizes that she's about to shift back to Ramira's mind. She sighs. *This is a miserable way to live.*

The witch's room is quiet—she's awake but reading.

Page after page of the awful novel turns as Ramira finishes one chapter and starts on another. *Why did I have to return to her for this?* She envisions ripping the book out of the woman's hands and throwing it out the window—she's desperate to see if Dahliorn is there and if he's all right, but Ramira won't look up. *What I need is to learn how to control her.* Granted, Elizabetta is getting better at tuning out the annoying woman when she's inside her head, but doubtless the only way she'll succeed in doing something about her situation is if Dahliorn teaches her what she needs to know.

Ramira growls in disgust when someone knocks on the door, but at least she slams the book down on the night-stand and goes to answer it. When the door opens, Elizabetta's heart lurches—Dahliorn is standing there with his eyes cast downward, and the exposed areas of his body are covered in cuts, welts, and bruises. His left eye is swollen shut, and a muscle in his cheek twitches with each subtle grimace.

"I hope you learned your lesson this time." Ramira steps to the side, allowing him to enter, but her eyes follow him as he limps toward the chair in the corner. When Dahliorn reaches it, he wraps one arm around his ribs as he turns to sit. Even that movement is slow and looks painful. *Great, another evil master who gets his jollies from torturing others, and he has his own cheering section, too. Why am I not surprised?* Extreme and sadistic abuse is something Elizabetta knows very well from life inside the Belyakov coven; her own husband bears hundreds of scars from Shashenka's brutality.

Elizabetta seethes with anger at that thought. *Guillermo will pay for this.* She wants to say something to hearten Dahliorn's weariness but doesn't want to alert Ramira to her presence—Elizabetta is enraged just enough to accidently do so.

The door closes with a shuddering bang. The witch returns to her bed, where she glares at Dahliorn for several long, hateful minutes. He keeps his eyes on the floor in front of him. There's an arrogant ring in Ramira's voice as she says, "Maybe you finally understand your place. But I'm warning you that if I catch you anywhere near my bed again, I will tell Uncle." Then she mumbles, "Perhaps I'll get lucky, and he will kill you next time."

There's no reaction from Dahliorn, not even a blink. *This is either going to break my heart or unleash my bloodlust.* She can only imagine the long, lonely, horrible centuries he's lived here with the Sanchezes. When Ramira finally looks away from him and resumes reading, it is both a disappointment and a relief for Elizabetta—she's grateful the nasty witch's eyes are off her potential comrade and possible friend, but she'd rather keep watch to make sure he's going to be all right.

The silence in the room is oppressive, saturated with boredom. Ramira seems content to read the entire night. Elizabetta fumes; she'd rather be training and learning how to defeat this witch or at least plotting Guillermo's takedown with Dahliorn. The shadows of night have long been the active hours of her life, and sitting around trapped with nothing to do fuels her impatience and feeds the deepseated need for vengeance. There's not been one sound from the corner where Dahliorn sits either, and Elizabetta's heart goes out to him—in some ways he's as stuck in this monotonous cycle as she is.

Ramira finally falls asleep, giving Elizabetta the long-awaited opportunity to speak to him. «Are you okay? How badly are you hurt?»

«I'm mending, but it will be slow. Guillermo restricts my abilities to pull upon fae magic for healing.»

She isn't sure what that means; she knows so little about the fae in general. *Don't tax him with curiosities—stay on point.* «Could you hear me earlier today?»

«When I was conscious, yes.» There's a pause, and sadness echoes in his next words. «I need to heal. Sleep now, little dove.»

Before Elizabetta can protest, the familiar darkness transfers her back to her body, and drowsiness robs her of even a second or two to think.

When she wakes, she's almost surprised to find she is still in her cell. The dim light gives her no idea how much time has passed, but it seems that her returns to Ramira usually come within moments of becoming conscious. Elizabetta lies there waiting for the shift to happen, and when it doesn't she's baffled as to why. Then an odor claims her attention. *Human blood.*

Her fangs involuntarily come down, and she bolts up to look around the room for its source. The burning ache of hunger in her throat increases. No one is here—not even a dead or unconscious body. She draws in a deep breath and sniffs like a hound tracking its quarry. *Where is it? What is it?* There's something about the smell that seems off, as if it is neither in nor out of a human body. *What is that funky odor? Rotting corpses don't even stink like that.* It's certainly not a box from the blood bank like she received from Dmitri in Big Sky.

She's still trying to puzzle it out when something catches her eye—two oblong white objects appear to be stuck to the underside of the cot's frame. Elizabetta kneels, crawling closer for a better look—the blood scent is stronger now—and she is reaching for one of the objects when recognition hits in a tidal wave of revulsion, sending her scrambling back.

*Spider silk.*

Elizabetta stares at the cot, shuddering. *That thing was in here while I slept?* The repulsive thought keeps her pinned against the opposite wall. She stares at the silk orbs, her skin crawling. *Are those egg sacs?* They certainly look like it, but she can't understand why they smell of human blood. *What if they hatch? When will they hatch?*

"Pluck a duck, I've got to kill them ... I wonder how pissed mommy will be?" Elizabetta approaches the cot in slow, deliberate movements—she wants to be prepared in case several hundred spider babies pop out. She's destroyed egg sacs before, but her hand shakes as she again reaches to grab the first one.

*What is this thing?* There's no hardness—it feels like a water balloon. She lifts it to inspect it closer. The scent of blood drives her hunger up another notch. Elizabetta has no idea what is inside, but her instinct to feed takes over, and in spite of the disgust rippling through her, she sinks her fangs into the sac. *This is so revolting—I can't believe I'm doing this.* But aside from the strange taint from the spider silk, the human blood is clean and tastes good. When the sac is empty, she pushes her tongue against the roof of her mouth several times in an attempt to get rid of the spider taste. It doesn't work, and she's still hungry. She grabs the second sac and drains it too. Her brows furrow as the orb deflates. The quantity of blood has sated her as much as a full human feeding would, which seems impossible since the volume appeared to be half of what an average body holds. Curious, she tears open one of the deflated orbs, and to her relief she finds nothing else inside.

*Why would a spider bring me blood? It's not like it can fatten me up to eat me.* The only conclusion she can reach is that it is under orders from Guillermo to keep her alive, but she's not sure how he would know if she's even conscious and able to feed, let alone why he'd allow her to retain her strength. It doesn't make sense regardless how she rearranges the puzzle pieces.

She shudders again and has to laugh. *Can this place get any weirder?* The interminable hours she's spent here in Guillermo's dungeon have been the most bizarre of her long and seemingly cursed life. Unlike the time she lived as Eliza, she doesn't have the luxury of denial, to claim it's not real; she knows the supernatural world exists. *What else happens in the shadow realms that I don't know about?* Now Elizabetta has a better appreciation for Matt's sometimes squeamish attitude. She chuckles. What she just did is one experience she never wants to repeat, even if she is thankful for the meal. *Dahliorn better be ready to go into supersonic teaching mode—I will find a way out of here before I need to feed again.*

At least there is one thing in her favor: a single feeding will sustain a vampire for four to six months, which means they have time to put together a good plan. Given her minimal level of physical activity, Elizabetta may be able to stretch that time to seven or eight months if needed, but the thought of being here that long drives icicles through her bones. *Please find me, Dmitri, Matt ... I want to go home.*

# CHAPTER 11: DMITRI

## Seelinara

Dmitri rushes over and lifts Matt's limp body from the ground. The maxians are waiting for them in front of the veil. There's no sound or movement from the wolf, but Dmitri doesn't slow as he passes between Maria and Alastrina and straight into the shimmering portal. There is a slight resistance, followed by a surge of warmth the moment he breaks through the barrier. He squints against the sudden sunlight. Then his eyes adjust and focus, and the sight on this side of the veil freezes him midstride. *What kind of world is this place?*

He turns in a circle. The portal is closed, the women stand near him, and everywhere he looks the forest goes on for endless miles. Trees the size of redwoods rise hundreds of feet in the air, and their huge trunks, covered with rough green bark, disappear into a thick canopy of foot-long purple leaves. Bright blue sky shows wherever the coverage is thinner, though the spacing of the trees provides enough shade for Dmitri to remain out of direct sunlight. There are sounds that he assumes are birds and other creatures, even if he hasn't seen any yet. His gaze shifts to the forest floor. It's blanketed with unfamiliar grass, plants, shrubs, and bushes, most of which are green, but some have tiny flowers in a variety of colors. The vegetation is dense and will be difficult to negotiate unless they mainly traverse animal trails.

The rumors suggest the fae were annihilated over six hundred years ago, when Dmitri was still human. Doubtless whatever smaller paths they once used are now gone, reclaimed by the forest centuries ago. Looking around, he wonders if there weren't many fae to begin with. He expected something more developed, maybe even advanced beyond Earth standards, but all that remains are the forest sounds around them. Evidently Guillermo's assault spared the wildlife in this world, at least.

"Where to?" Dmitri looks at Alastrina, but the sorceress just stares into the woods. He raises his voice to gain her attention. "Which way do we go?"

She blinks. "Uh, I-I don't know."

"Damn it, we can't stay here." He repositions Matt over his shoulder and looks at the ground in front of him—they are standing in the vegetation near the intersection of two worn trails. *Forward, back, right, left? Forward is as good as any—we need to move.*

He's walking away from the veil when Maria calls out, "Wait. The map showed a symbol that resembled a wheel spoke. It's north of the veil, and I think it may be a town or a city."

Dmitri looks around again. He has no idea which way is

north in this strange place. Using the sun as a guide is not without risk, as it may not rise in the east here. With Matt still over his shoulder, he steps off the path and circles the nearest tree, looking for moss; if it grows here, it may indicate which direction is north. There's nothing on the trunks but the same rough green bark. Next he looks to the shadows, but the sun is directly overhead, and he's unable to guess which side of the vegetation may be north. *Midday, damn it.*

"We need to pick a direction and go. We can't stand here all day." Neither woman says anything in reply, and Dmitri, exasperated, growls.

He gives one more quick glance to the area, looking for landmarks, and instructs Alastrina to mark the tree nearest the veil—they'll need to find their way back here. Then he walks at a rapid pace along the path in front of him. The trail ahead may have been a fae path once, as it shows signs of long-term heavy travel and seems to have influenced the vegetation growth along its edges. Still, he finds it a bit peculiar that such well-worn paths remain. The only explanation is high animal population, though he has no idea what kinds of beasts and creatures may inhabit this area. *Eventually we'll have to find some sign of past civilization.* At this point it doesn't matter to him where they go, as long as they try to go somewhere.

Alastrina disrupts his thoughts. "Before we came here I honestly doubted Seelinara was a planet and thought it was hidden on Earth. But after seeing this forest, I don't think so anymore."

*Planet?* Glancing back over his shoulder, Dmitri says,

"Did you see anything in your father's journals that reveal-ed how time works here?"

"Nothing other than the shift in time we saw when we came through."

Maria, surprisingly, has more information than the sorceress. "I saw subtle references to time, but much of it didn't make sense. One entry seemed to indicate time ran faster here, and another, slower. I think a day may be longer too."

Alastrina gives Maria a questioning look. "Why do you think that?"

"It was in another riddle—something about twenty-seven to go and the sun dancing across the sky while the moon waves good-bye. Your father was anomalous in the way he kept his journals."

The sorceress laughs and is about to reply when Dmitri spins toward an unfamiliar noise and motions for quiet. For several long seconds they stand still and listen, but whatever it was seems to be gone now. The hair on the back of his neck prickles. Still, dismissing it as a trick of the forest sounds, he decides to walk on again. "When we find a building or a town, do you have any idea what we're looking for?" Nothing the sorceress has told them so far gives him a clue—his imagination is running wild.

Alastrina doesn't answer right away, and he begins to think she won't tell them, but then she says, "My under-standing is that apothecaries housed the most potent med-icine. All fae had access to them in the event an emergency required more than their individual skills allowed."

Over the next hour Dmitri grills Alastrina about the fae

world while they follow the winding path through the forest. He can almost feel the sense of loss as the sorceress describes a civilization so unlike anything on Earth that it's difficult for him to fathom. The fae seem to have known a balance unheard of in the Earth realms. Not that they didn't have political problems or wars, but there were fewer instances of such strife in their history even between the light and dark fae—Seelie and Unseelie—or the countless subspecies of light or dark.

The sorceress rambles on while Dmitri scans the forest for any signs of life or threat. "According to my father, it was the separation of the heavens themselves that created the Seelie and Unseelie. Fae were the hybrid children of angels and demons."

"Typical ... so light were good and dark were evil." Dmitri adjusts his grip on Matt and maneuvers the wolf's body back into his arms—he can't see Matt's face or watch for the rise and fall of his chest in the other position.

The sorceress says, "Not true. Same as there are fallen angels, there are risen demons. The potential for good and evil resides in each of us, and life brings out the strongest traits of the two and shapes who we are, who we become."

"Are you telling us that angels and demons are real?" Maria's tone is incredulous, but Dmitri is more open to the possibility of their existence, of the propensity for good and bad in all living beings. Even though he became something many humans consider evil, he has kept a code of honor based on solid morals and scruples. The taking of human life is an unfortunate and horrible part of who he is, but is he any different from a mountain lion that kills a deer? The mountain lion is not necessarily evil but must take a life to survive. If it were possible to drink shallow from a human and prevent the vampire venom from infecting them, he would do it. As it's impossible to turn all humans they feed from—it would tip the balance of survival—he sees killing the victim as a mercy, saving them from a long, painful death. *The same fate Matt is suffering now.*

Alastrina says, "Yes, angels and demons are real. My father claimed that both were present in the fae realm."

"Then why wouldn't they have protected the fae from the plague?" Dmitri's brow furrows; knowing they exist doesn't tell him what kind of beings they are or where he or the women can find something that will save the wolf.

The sorceress chuckles and shakes her head. "I don't know. I'm maxian, not fae, even if I am a halfblood."

A slow, ragged exhale from Matt catches Dmitri's attention, and he hurries to set the wolf on the ground. Alastrina is by their side and in the middle of an incantation when Matt stops breathing.

"Damn you, Matt! We haven't come this far for you to die on us now." Dmitri begins chest compressions, silently cursing himself for thinking of the fatal outcome of vampire venom. Precious seconds sneak away between his effort and Maria's life-sustaining breaths as Alastrina finishes the spell. *It's not working. Don't you leave me ... us.*

In between breathing for Matt, Maria lifts her arm and points. "Alastrina!"

Dmitri's head whips toward whatever she is looking at—he gasps, breaking the rhythm of the compressions. Several green vines inch across the ground. One slithers over his calf until it reaches Matt and wraps around the wolf's wrist. More vines attach themselves to Matt's torso, neck, and legs. "Get them off him!" He wants to stop pumping Matt's chest, but he refuses to allow death a stronger hold than it already has; desperation enters a frenzied dance with fear. "Kill every last plant and tree if you must to save him."

But Alastrina reaches out to stop Maria as the wizard pulls at the vine around the wolf's neck. "Don't—let them go."

"Are you crazy?" Dmitri hollers, thrusting his palms against Matt's chest. "They could kill him."

"Father used to say the forest was alive here, that it had its own abilities and magic. I think the vines might help."

A moment later a surge of energy knocks Dmitri and the two maxians away from Matt. They scramble forward to resume their efforts to revive the wolf, but more vines quickly restrain them. A faint golden glow covers Matt's body as Dmitri struggles to free himself. "Alastrina?" Panic sweeps into his bones as his attempts to pull the vines away fail.

"Don't fight it, Dmitri. It appears the forest needs us out of the way." Alastrina's body relaxes, and the vines loosen their hold on her, straightening her blouse when they let her go. She singsongs her joy. "Oh, what wonders our eyes will see."

Conceding goes against Dmitri's instinct to fight back, and he continues thrashing against the vines holding him. More green tendrils join those already wrapped around his legs and arms. Bloodlust pounds his earlier fears into submission—he can't, no, he won't lose Matt to a damnable

upside-down planet. It's clear they put the wolf's life in even
more peril by bringing him here. *A mistake I'll rectify when
I get free!* Maria repeats something, but her words don't
register—Dmitri is too busy writhing in anger against the
plants that seem to be much stronger than he is. He extends
his claws, and his fangs come out. He can't accept the idea
of being beaten by a plant in battle, not with so much at
stake.

Then Maria's touch startles him, and he finally hears
what she's saying. "Look, Dmitri, look!" She's pointing at
Matt. His gaze darts past the wizard to his friend's body.
The golden light pulses with each rise and fall of Matt's
chest. *How is that possible?* He stops fighting the vines for a
moment, and one by one they loosen, moving away from
him. Even without the restraints, Dmitri remains rooted to
the spot and gives Alastrina a questioning look.

The sorceress shrugs. "It seems to be helping—he's
breathing again. Isn't it wonderful?"

The three of them fall into silence as the strange golden
glow beats a steady rhythm. Minutes dance by. The pulsing
light seems to travel through the vines, but trying to trace
it visually is impossible with the way the forest swallows the
vines in the surrounding vegetation. After what feels like
hours, the daylight begins to fade and the first vine finally
lets go, retreating into the woods. Then another vine slips
away, followed by another, and yet another. When the last
one unwinds from Matt's throat and disappears, Dmitri
races forward to feel the wolf's pulse. It's stronger than it
has been, but not as strong as it should be, and the smell of
death remains.

*Is he getting better or still dying?* "Did the plants cure him or not?" Dmitri's gaze shifts between the maxians. He's almost beside himself with this delay.

Alastrina kneels next to Matt. "I don't think so—his color is still bad. But they may have bought us some time, stabilized him. Pick him up, and let's keep moving. We must go now!"

Dmitri doesn't need to be told twice, and he scoops Matt off the ground to resume their march along the unknown trail.

By now the night shadows have grown, presenting a new problem—the maxians do not see as well in the dark as Dmitri does. He instructs Maria to grab hold of his shirt and for Alastrina to do the same behind the wizard. *We are not stopping until we find an apothecary.* But as true darkness settles over this strange world, a phenomenon they never expected occurs: thousands of soft, winking lights illuminate the edges of the path, hovering in no discernible pattern within six inches of the ground. He notices that the lights are reactive to their presence—they blink on, staying ahead of Dmitri's group by about a dozen feet, and go out moments after the group passes by.

The development lifts his sagging hope that they might find medicine to heal Matt in time. Dmitri estimates they've hiked at least eleven or twelve miles from the veil, and his arms and back are stiff with fatigue, but he's reluctant to stop and cost them fragile seconds the wolf may not have. Once more Matt's breaths have become sporadic, his color worsening, and the smell of his body's decay has increased to nauseating levels.

Time is a blanket over the silence between them, allowing the nighttime sounds of the forest to filter overhead—a further reminder that they're not on Earth. The cadence of what Dmitri presumes are bugs helps him maintain their pace. It's not until he hears Maria cursing under her breath that he looks back at the maxians. The wizard's face is pinched with pain, and her tired eyes meet his gaze. "I'm sorry, but we have to stop. My shoes weren't meant for hiking, and my feet are blistered. I need to do a mending spell." She mumbles, "I should have worn better shoes."

Doubtless both women could use a break, and he grudgingly admits to needing one too. "When you're done with your feet, is there something you can do about the rigidity in my arms and back?"

Alastrina says, "I can take care of that while Maria tends to herself."

Dmitri lays Matt on the ground and stretches as the wizard removes her socks and shoes. Maria's jaw tenses as she inspects the damage to her feet. They are more than blistered—they're swollen, and a few of the sores are bleeding. When the maxians begin casting their spells, Dmitri's eyes close in relief. *Must be a wondrous sensation to wield magic to one's own benefit.* The pain leaves his body, and his muscles loosen, leaving him refreshed.

It takes fewer minutes for Alastrina to attend him than it does for Maria to heal her own wounds. He notes that in comparison with the wizard, the sorceress is doing remarkably well—she doesn't even look tired. Unsure whether she's hiding her condition, he questions her.

"I think my body is reacting to something in the

environment here. It's almost as if I'm gaining strength and stamina." Alastrina exaggerates a shrug. "Perhaps being half fae gives me an advantage over you."

"Where did those come from?" Maria's hand stops in midair above a pair of dark-green moccasins lying partially tucked under the flap of her pack.

Alarms ring in Dmitri's head when the maxians deny that they conjured them. Scanning the forest around them, he finds nothing in the shadows, and the night sounds are the same as they have been since it grew dark. *How could any living creature sneak up on us that way and not be seen?* "I think we should get moving again—I don't like this."

"We may have to wait until the vines let go of Matt." Alastrina kneels next to the werewolf, who's once more wrapped in the plants, their golden pulse beating in rhythm with his heart.

Dmitri says, "This forest doesn't feel right. I'm beginning to question if the fae are extinct at all." *Something is out there, watching and stalking us.*

"Well, at the moment I'm not going to knock it. This place is helping us and keeping Matt alive." Maria slips on the moccasins—they seem a perfect fit, and she marvels aloud at the impossibility that they appeared out of no-where.

Alastrina turns in a slow circle as she scrutinizes the dark woods around them. The underlying fear Dmitri saw in her before they left Novgorod is showing in her eyes again, and he begins to realize she may have held more conviction for fae rumors than she let on.

Dmitri scowls at the delaying vines, wishing them away. Almost as if they heard him, they withdraw in haste, and his eyes widen with surprise. "Let's go."

The women fall in behind him, and their group sets off along the illuminated pathway once more—alert to the shadows now. Still, Dmitri takes a few seconds to observe the sky whenever it comes into view. None of the stars are familiar, and there's not one recognizable constellation anywhere among them. *Are we even in the same galaxy?*

Three hours after resuming their trek, Maria whisper-shouts, "Wait, what is that?"

Dmitri turns to look. Though the predawn sky has lightened, they've yet to see anything slither, creep, crawl, or fly. "What did you—"

"I thought there was a child clinging to the side of that tree over there, but ... it seemed to disappear into the trunk."

They step off the path and approach the tree. The silence of the forest is unnerving, and the sensation of being watched has Dmitri's fangs and claws itching to come out. Alastrina traces the grooves in the bark, but she can't find an opening in the tree. *Is Maria hallucinating, or did she really see something?* Dmitri urges them to start walking— the longer they're here in the forest, the more disconcerting it becomes, even though they still haven't seen so much as another living thing.

As the sun rises slowly above the horizon, Dmitri notices the trees are thinning ahead of them. He asks Alastrina to check it out—he needs to know if it's a clearing or if the terrain is changing into an open plateau or prairie. While he can withstand a few painful moments of sunlight, it's not safe for him to remain in the direct sun. But he doesn't want to spend another night in the bizarre forest.

The sorceress stares at him for a moment—fear reflects in her face—but to his relief, she sprints off and is soon out of sight. *I hope it wasn't a mistake sending her alone.*

Alastrina returns fifteen minutes later. Breathlessly she says, "I think it's the wagon wheel area Maria saw on the map. The trees are fewer—still enough shade to limit your exposure to the sun. But we may have a problem."

Dmitri's brow furrows. "What kind of a problem?"

The sorceress blows out a long breath, the disappointment evident on her face. "This path leads to the center of the hub, and other paths lead away from it ... there is nothing there. Nothing but the pathways and forest."

"What?" Maria shrieks. "No, that can't be—there has to be something there. We've come all this way ..."

Dmitri's heart sinks. He looks down at Matt—the wolf's color is now a greenish gray. His scent rivals that of a decaying corpse. If it weren't for the magic plants of this forest, Dmitri doubts that Matt would still be alive, and yet even the vines seem unable to heal him. *Is he too far gone to save? Would it be kinder to let him die?*

Tears roll down Maria's cheeks. She whispers, "We're going to lose him. We can't save him without the fae medicine." Her shoulders slump as she lifts a shaking hand to the wolf's chest. "I'm so sorry, Mattie."

The gesture is rankling, and Dmitri steps back. He can't accept failure, not on this—if he does, then it may well mean he'll lose Elizabetta too. The bloodlust that's been simmering starts to boil again. "He's not dead yet. We press on ... let the vines sustain him as we keep going."

Shock reverberates in Alastrina's voice. "You're not suggesting we leave him behind?"

"I will never leave him behind. We'll stop more often, let the vines do what they do, but there has to be something out there ... we just have to keep looking."

Dmitri doesn't linger to continue their debate—he pushes forward, whispering every now and then, "Hang in there, Matt, we're almost there." The occasional exposure to the sun blisters his skin and sets his determination on fire. Matt looks even more ghastly in daylight. There are dark-purplish shadows beneath his eyes, his cheekbones are more pronounced, and his skin has a mottled gray-green tint—in Dmitri's long life he has seen very few corpses look worse. *Poisoning by vampire venom is a horrible way to die.* Even fae medicine may not reverse the effects now, but he isn't willing to give up, not yet.

When they reach what appears to be the hub of the pathways, they pause to decide which direction to take. Alastrina was right, there's nothing here—not one abandoned building, nor even ruins to suggest a structure ever was here once.

Maria pulls out the map. At least now they have an idea which way is north, though the only symbols that stand out, besides the veil, are basic terrain features—hills, water, more trees. A rise in the terrain on one side shows the forest spreading up a mountain, and somewhere off to what Dmitri has labeled "East" is the sound of running water. But there appears to be no end to the woods around them.

The air is less fragrant here, and Dmitri notices the air currents seem to move in invisible, meandering streams. *This is unnatural, not right.* Something about this place gnaws at his fight or flight instincts, but he can't find the source of the threat he's reacting to. A sinking feeling uncoils within, claiming every nerve as it pulls Dmitri down— they're going to fail. There's not been one sign of the lost civilization since they entered Seelinara.

Dmitri lays Matt down, and the vines creep across the ground to wrap the wolf the moment he lets go. "Maybe we came through the wrong veil. Did we bring any other maps?" He glances hopefully at the maxians. "Alastrina, was there anything in your father's writings that indicated whether the veils can be used to transport to other areas within Seelinara?" His mind races to consider possibilities they may have overlooked.

The sorceress shakes her head. "No and no. And the veils don't work that way. They are doorways connecting this place to Earth."

*Damn it. We have to find a town, an apothecary, or Matt will die.*

"I don't know where to go," Maria says, and her look of despair hits too close to his own feelings as his thoughts move from Matt to Elizabetta. *I can't give up.* Anger and disappointment war for equal room inside him; malevolence rises from his depths. *I'm going to destroy this world, burn it to ash if we lose Matt.* Pushing both hands through his hair, gripping his skull, he tries to stay rational and calm. "We have to keep moving, that's all there is to it."

He turns back toward Matt, and as he approaches, the

vines release the wolf. Matt's head lolls back when Dmitri lifts him off the ground. *Thwarted by fate again ... east, south, west ... in order, quickly.*

The women scramble to catch up with him, but they're only fifty feet down the new path when a large animal leaps from behind a bush and onto the trail ahead. Dmitri's fangs slide out, and his claws lengthen—this may be what's had him on edge since they arrived in the clearing. His eyes follow every movement the animal makes. Shiny jet-black fur covers its sleek body. The strange beast has what appears to be some type of armor or plating on its throat, chest, and belly, and long, thick claws protrude from the five-toe pads of its feet. Large, stout fangs extend beyond razor-sharp teeth. A ridge along its neck, between its humped shoulders, and down its back contains what seems like a layer of spikes or quills lying within a serrated trough. The physical traits and form are similar to, yet vastly unlike any bear, wolf, or big cat Dmitri has ever seen. It's almost as if nature started to blend the three, only to discard them for something entirely different.

The animal's mouth twists into a vicious snarl as the creature growls, and the spikes on its back stand on end. Its eyes flash red. *Is that a demon or an animal?* Dmitri starts to move backward, but his voice remains cautious and quiet. "Maria, Alastrina. Go back, but whatever you do, don't turn and run."

For each step they take, the beast advances, maintaining the distance between them. Dmitri hears the crackle of magic behind him; he suspects the maxians have readied energy balls and bolts, but he won't risk taking a look to confirm it. He himself can't fight with Matt in his arms, which means that if the beast charges, he may be forced to drop Matt in order to protect them all.

They're almost to the hub when he hears Maria whisper, "Oh no, there's more of them."

This time his head whips around to see multiple beasts blocking each of the paths. Alastrina has a look of sheer terror. There are seven of the creatures now, and whatever they are, they seem to be the same species—the only difference is their coats. They range in shades of black, white, gray, and brown, and the daylight doesn't hide the way their black eyes glow red, amber, or green.

When he and the maxians have pressed back against the tree at the center of the hub, Dmitri lays Matt on the ground and pulls out his dagger. His blood boils in fear and rage as the massive beasts gather in front of them. While being in this unfamiliar land has subdued his violent urges, he's not sure it will last. If given so much as a sliver of a chance, he will try to take down as many of these creatures as he can. Perhaps it will give the women the opportunity to escape.

The beasts inch closer, some snarling and growling. The serrated troughs keep their quills at rigid attention as their tense muscles ooze power and strength. *Do we even stand a chance against these animals?* His claws extend and his fangs slide down. He doesn't know if they can win, but either way he's not going down without a fight.

Alastrina releases the white orb she's holding, but the magic seems to strike an invisible barrier a foot in front of the brown animal she aimed at, and the orb fizzles away.

Dmitri swallows the lump in his throat. Vines slither up his body—before he can even try to move free of them, the plants wrap around him, binding him to the tree. He hears Alastrina scream and Maria curse—the vines have bound them too. *This is the day we're all going to die.*

Then a gray beast moves next to Matt and sniffs along his body, and the growling and snarling stops. The biggest one, the black beast they first encountered, takes another step forward and cocks its head to the side before looking at the other animals. Dmitri recognizes they are intelligent—not mindless, instinct driven. It's almost as if they are communicating in some manner.

There is no escape, and trussed to a tree, they can't even defend themselves. Dmitri steels his resolve to meet his death with honor and waits for the black creature in front of him to lunge forward and tear him to pieces—he's prepared even for that.

*Pop-pop-pop ... woosh-woosh-woosh ... thud-thud-thump!* What he's not ready for is the sting of a dart slamming into his chest instead. *Pop, pop, pop ... woosh, woosh, woosh ... thud, thud, thump!* Confused, Dmitri stares at the tiny needles protruding from just over his heart. *What the—*

# CHAPTER 12: ELIZABETTA

## Mapping Blind

Elizabetta has begun to develop a limited sense of time, but she almost wishes she hadn't. Nights and then weeks pass on repeat, like she's stuck in *Groundhog Day*. Most days when Elizabetta awakes, she's immediately transferred into Ramira. Then she spends hours listening to the worthless witch rant, gripe, and complain to anyone around her, even her uncle. *I wish they'd just kill each other and get it over with.* In fact, arguments between Ramira and Guillermo occur almost daily, which surprises Elizabetta—she knows he's powerful enough to stop Ramira's tantrums, and she well remembers the punishment he dealt out when she, Dmitri, and Matt tried to take him on. He looks angry enough to take action now, but usually he just quarrels back. Dahliorn claims it's because of some twisted revenge plan the sorcerer has molded for well over a few centuries; apparently Guillermo refuses to be robbed of the pleasure of ending his brother's family line when the right time comes.

Though the tension between Ramira and Dahliorn continues, at least the witch's attempts to goad him fail. Elizabetta wants to believe that the silent communication between her and the sheridauk is partly responsible for the fact that he hasn't been punished since the beating inflicted on him two weeks before. For her, at least, strength and hope intertwine and bond their growing friendship. A perk that allows an increased focus—the less he engages the witch, the sooner Ramira goes to sleep, giving Elizabetta more opportunity to train with him.

Dahliorn is teaching her how to identify and access Ramira's mind and body by using what he terms the internal perceptual senses: hearing, touch, mind-sight, and thought construct. At first it's difficult and very confusing. Elizabetta can't physically touch the woman, and she's left in total darkness whenever Ramira is asleep. Night after night, despite Dahliorn's instruction, Elizabetta fails—or rather, she doesn't succeed. *Nothing like lessons in futility.*

«Try again, little dove, but don't try with all your senses. Just use one,» he tells her for the umpteenth time. «Remember, each strand of energy will feel different; there may be a pulse or burst, like static shock, or you might feel heat or cold. When you do find one, you need to establish a way to identify what it does and where it's located in her brain.»

Elizabetta projects a groan, hoping he'll get the message that she's ready to have a complete conniption fit and fall in it. «I'm working blind in here. How am I supposed to know if my interaction even works?» *I need a virtual reality console for this.*

There's a long pause before Dahliorn says, «I've sent her into a deep slumber—she will not wake. I will watch and let you know what reaction she has if you find and access a strand.»

Elizabetta imagines herself moving slowly through a building, staying alert for any sensation that may indicate the presence of one of the elusive energy strands. «You know, if we figure this out, I really need to put it to a map of her body in my mind. Otherwise I won't have any idea how to locate a strand when we need it.»

Dahliorn says through their link, «Work out whatever system you need. Now concentrate.»

*Killjoy bubble-buster.* A tingle to her insubstantial left catches her attention. Elizabetta approaches it with caution—she has already learned that when she rushes these exercises, she finds nothing. The tickle of its presence becomes stronger as she envisions her hands outstretched and ready to grab whatever it is. Of course she feels no-thing—she doesn't actually have hands—and when the tingle suddenly moves from in front of her to behind her, she realizes that she must have walked through it. Elizabetta takes an imaginary step back and tries to visualize the strand again. *Huh, Tron without the colorful environment and computer mainframe. It's too real—lifelike.* This time when she reaches forward, she feels a prickle move up her nonexistent arms. *Got it.* «I found one! What do I do now?»

«Tug or push on it, bend it to your will—give it a command.»

Elizabetta considers his instruction for a moment. Earlier he explained that mental strands may give a glimpse of a thought, dream, or memory—but she's not seeing any images now. *Good.* This must be a physical strand, which is what she needs to force movement of Ramira's body. Elizabetta decides to pull back the one she's holding, but it slips out of her illusory grasp. She reaches for the tingle strand again, this time willing herself to believe it has a ropelike substance that she can tug. It works—the strand remains in her invisible hold.

Excitement fills her with a giddiness she's not felt since she was a child. «I did it! What did it do?»

The movement was too subtle for him to notice. She'll need to draw on it a little longer and give him time to examine the witch's body in order to find it.

Elizabetta grabs the strand and rings it like a church bell—inwardly she's grinning from ear to ear like a fool, but she can't help herself. This victory is one step closer to finding freedom again. Then she hears Dahliorn laughing. «What's so funny?» She's still pulling on it.

It takes him a moment to compose himself. «You're wiggling the big toe on her right foot.»

*You've got to be kidding me. After all this, all I get is a big toe?* She lets go of the strand as her mood deflates.

«Try to find another.» Dahliorn attempts to cover his amusement, but Elizabetta feels it through their link.

"Keep snickering at me, and I'll kick your sheridauk butt when I see you next." There are two more snorts of laughter before Dahliorn falls quiet and she's able to refocus.

For the next several hours Elizabetta explores the darkness for more energy strands. This time she doesn't allow herself to get excited, because she doesn't want to feel the disappointment—and most of what she finds controls the toes, foot, leg, arm, hand, and fingers on the same side of Ramira's body. It is a slow, daunting process. The only differences Elizabetta can discern between the strands is the level of their tingle; larger body parts have a deeper resonance, while the smaller ones move up in intensity. Dahliorn speculates that she has found the left side of Ramira's brain and that Elizabetta won't activate any left body movements until she crosses to the right.

*This is just too weird. Never thought I'd map a human brain.* Elizabetta still doesn't understand how this helps her—she can only control one strand at a time—but she forces herself to stay focused while she color-codes the map she's creating in her mind, choosing shades of blue, green, and purple for physical motion on the right half of Ramira's body. The left side she'll paint in oranges, yellows, and browns. White and gray will define the mental elements of Ramira's brain—when she locates them.

The longer Ramira remains asleep, the more Elizabetta's confidence grows as their experiment continues. She even recovers a sense of humor, laughing with Dahliorn when she sweeps an imaginary hand across the strands like fingers on piano keys and he relays that the right side of Ramira's body jumped, twitched, and wiggled all at once.

Then Elizabetta discovers there are some systems better left alone. She locates a new type of energy strand, one with a cold presence; curious, she pulls on it. Her nonexistent hand lets go when she hears Dahliorn gasp. «What's wrong?»

A few long seconds pass before he says in a serious tone, «We'll have to stop our lesson here for the night.»

«What did I do?»

«You triggered her bladder release. I have to clean this up.»

Elizabetta tries and fails to restrain a giggle. «I'm not sure about our progress unless we want to embarrass her when she goes to fight.»

«I'll need to put you to sleep now, little dove.»

«Wait. Let me finish marking this strand before you send me back to my body.» Elizabetta selects red for the "do not touch—use only in an emergency" category.

Dahliorn puts her to sleep, and she's soon lost in dreams of Dmitri—a phenomenon she has endured ever since she told the sheridauk about her husband. Nearly all of her dreams are about Dmitri now. *Is Dahliorn responsible for that too?* If he is, she doesn't have the heart to tell him that such dreams are difficult for her—when she wakes to find that she's still trapped in Guillermo's dungeon, the ache in her chest deepens. *I miss Dmitri so much. Will he ever find me?*

Over the next few nights Elizabetta and Dahliorn continue mapping the strands. The impulse threads are the most exciting; they're unpredictable and make Ramira's muscles twitch or cause her to cough or sneeze. For something no bigger than a brain is in size, its network is amazingly vast—it takes Elizabetta six nights even to stumble across the mental strands. These energy signatures, she notices, seem divided by warmth or deep buzzing surges instead of the tingling she's become accustomed to with physical motion. Active cognitive thoughts feel hot, while memories are warm, and dreams, tepid. The buzzers, as she comes to think of them, appear connected to Ramira's subconscious and conscious decisions; the latter have a faster rhythm.

Elizabetta's next big challenge will come while Ramira is awake: Dahliorn wants her to practice accessing Ramira's memories and listening in on active thoughts. He assures her that as long as she doesn't project a direct thought to Ramira, the witch will never know she's there. Still, nervous excitement and anticipation course through her at the thought of testing her new skills. There's a lot that can go wrong if she screws up.

Later that morning, after Elizabetta transfers into Ramira, she shuts down her piggyback view of the outside world and pictures the virtual room where she has constructed a three-dimensional map of Ramira's brain. She can't resist being ornery and flicks an impulse strand as she passes it. The room lights up around her as Ramira raises a hand to scratch at her nose. The sudden burst of magenta is overwhelmingly bright for a second, but it gradually dims until blackness reclaims the space. *That's interesting—my color-coding is now part of triggered reactions. Sweet.*

Desire to see propels Elizabetta to stop in front of an active thought strand and tap into it, bathing the area in white light. She's not quite ready to be immersed in the dingy grays of the witch's memories, although she'll need to do it while Ramira is awake. Memories lie too close to the subconscious, often forming sleeping thoughts that serve as a base for dreams, which means that viewing memories while the witch sleeps almost guarantees she'll be caught snooping.

There's a slight static discharge before the heat pours over her, revealing Ramira's mental grumbling—a preview of the complaints she'll verbalize throughout the day. *Great, another fun day ahead in the life of the spoiled bitch. It's time to find out what makes her tick.* Elizabetta releases the thought conduit and moves toward the memory strands. In her experiments with Dahliorn, she's learned that while memories are still warm, they develop the echo of a thrum—the older the memory, the more faint the sound. She looks at several memories before choosing one with a weak signature, wrapping an illusory hand around it.

Elizabetta startles when light bursts around her. She finds herself sitting at a table in a cottage, and when she looks down, she sees two small arms with tiny hands folded in her lap. *Ramira as a child?* A bowl of stew is placed before her, and a woman's gentle voice—Ramira's mother, evidently—encourages her to eat. A moment later a chunk of warm bread is set next to the bowl. She looks up through her child eyes across the table at a man and woman seated with her. *Her parents.* Emotions surface in a cascade of love, trust, adoration, and comfort. The adults don't talk, and Ramira says nothing as she picks up her spoon to eat.

Halfway through the meal, a door behind Ramira's father flies off its hinges and crashes to the floor. Her father's chair topples over as he jumps to his feet, conjuring some type of energy in his hands. He tosses it toward the doorway as a man steps through, but it merely bounces off the intruder. Elizabetta's blood boils as her own memories echo in the background of her mind.

*Guillermo.*

Ramira's little body sits frozen at the table, her fear spiking as the sorcerer laughs and thrusts both hands at her mother. The woman sails across the room, hits the rock hearth, and doesn't move again—blood trickles from the side of her head. Ramira screams for her mother but remains in her seat at the table, trembles running through her small body. She seems so young, afraid, yet somehow understands the danger of being herself hit by such strong magic.

Guillermo makes a backhand motion that sends her father crashing onto the table. The edge of the tabletop catches Ramira in the chest and knocks her chair backward. Wood cracks from the impact of her father's body and splinters as the table collapses to the floor; a large, jagged piece impales Ramira's shoulder, and she cries out in pain. A moment later her father's screams ring out, and then all falls silent.

It takes a moment before Elizabetta lets go of the strand. She feels sick. Guillermo just burst into that home and killed two people without saying a word—Ramira's parents, his own brother and sister-in-law. *Why would she be with him, then?* There's too much she doesn't know.

Elizabetta grabs another faint memory strand adjacent to the one she just released and watches it play out, but it doesn't make sense. She's seeing it double vision, almost as if two similar memories are layered over top of each other. Ramira, panicked and confused, lies on a bed with Guillermo hovering over her, tending to her shoulder wound; it seems to be the same one inflicted by the broken piece of table in the scene Elizabetta just accessed. Then the memory comes into sharper focus until only one layer is discernable, and with it anger and hatred swell inside Ramira as Guillermo reassures her that they'll get revenge against the vampires who killed her parents. Matching emotions rage inside Elizabetta, but for different reasons. *What the hell? How could she not know?* The true memory is still there, but somehow Guillermo has blocked Ramira from reaching it.

For hours Elizabetta accesses different memories, trying to follow them in chronological order so she can understand what that monster has done to his niece. It becomes clear that he has altered Ramira's memory and that the conflicting double-vision memory strands she discovers are the overlapped buried and planted memories. She learns that Guillermo raised Ramira after her parents' murder and to some degree spoiled her as a child, but as the memories continue Elizabetta realizes that he was grooming the witch from day one to do his bidding—whatever goodness Ramira may have possessed as a child erodes over the years as she matures and carries out Guillermo's sinister plans. Though he taught her magic suitable to her level as a witch, every spell Ramira casts harms something or someone. Together they murder humans in dark magic rituals, set forests or buildings on fire, and slaughter vampires, werewolves, and maxians who cross their path.

Each revelation intensifies Elizabetta's dislike for the witch, a feeling that quickly grows into hatred. The Sanchezes remind her too much of Shashenka and the Belyakov coven, and of how once again she is trapped in a life she doesn't want any part of. Guillermo and Ramira are every bit as evil as Shashenka, maybe more so—at least where the sorcerer is concerned.

Elizabetta keeps digging through memories, almost desperate to find something good remaining within the witch, but as she watches Ramira growing older, the woman seems only more despicable. The witch is obsessed with finding a lover and seems frustrated that Guillermo won't allow her to get involved with a man until they achieve their goals. He claims it's because they won't know who is worthy of her until then, and he doesn't want her distracted with romances or affairs. He dangles it like a carrot in front of a horse—and she chases that dream, that promise, as if it's tangible. *Doesn't she know it's nothing but a mirage?* Elizabetta suspects the witch may not care, she's so determined to do what it takes to see that reward. It's sad that Ramira has never known love of any kind, but as far as Elizabetta is concerned, it doesn't excuse the heinous acts she's committed against others—people burned alive, spells cast to ruin lives or destroy the most loving relationships, and injuries inflicted which leave victims less than whole in body or mind. Elizabetta finally turns away from the virtual room. She's seen more than enough for one day.

The outside world comes into focus, and Elizabetta realizes that Ramira is sitting at the dining table with Guillermo, eating supper. *Just what I want to see—not.* The two of them are discussing her training and make vague references to upcoming assignments meant to test the witch's skills. *These two must be stopped.* Elizabetta seethes. The best way to accomplish that is for her and

Dahliorn to escape, find the Druzhinas, and deliver the justice that is way past long overdue.

Guillermo moves away from the table and asks Ramira to show him her defensive skills. Elizabetta can feel her eyes roll—the witch couldn't defend herself against a human in a fair fight, let alone hope for a chance against any supernatural being. Sure enough, when the evil sorcerer grabs her from behind, she's unable to break out of his hold.

"Uncle, you're hurting me!"

He spins her around, a sudden hard look in his eyes. "You said there's been no interaction between you and Dahliorn. When has he touched you?"

"What?" Ramira blinks, lowering her gaze to his chest. "No. I told you he just sits in his chair all night. He doesn't even speak unless he has to."

The vein in the center of Guillermo's forehead bulges as if it's about to burst. "You reek of him. Your body is saturated in his magic." Malevolence wraps each word in a stranglehold of evil intent.

*Oh God. How does he know that? He's going to kill him!* Elizabetta tries to warn Dahliorn, but she doesn't know if he can hear her.

Ramira gulps and tries to pull out of his grip. "Uncle, what's wrong? You're scaring me."

He shoves her back, and she reactively reaches for the sorcerer's arm, but he jerks it away from her and storms toward the door. "Dahliorn! Dahliorn!"

Shouts erupt from the hallway. Ramira runs over and looks out the dining room door, and fear surges through Elizabetta; Guillermo has the sheridauk in an invisible grip and pinned against the wall. Fury radiates off the sorcerer's body—Elizabetta almost expects him to combust—as he says, "You are forbidden from touching her. Why is Ramira layered with your residual magic?"

Dahliorn's words choke out as he struggles to speak against the hold on his neck. "She ... nightmares, eased ... sleep."

The sorcerer's arm swings outward, sending Dahliorn hurtling into the opposite wall. He lands on the floor with a heavy thud. Elizabetta's mind flinches at the sight. Then she notices that the almost upside-down position of his body has allowed his shirt to slide up, exposing a silver band with symbols on it around his waist. This isn't the first time she's seen something like it—the spider had a similar band. *Is that Guillermo's idea of a shock collar, how he controls others?* She watches in horror and growing anger as the psychotic sorcerer slams Dahliorn's body into the floor again and again. *I have to stop this, but how?* A narrow silver cord of light springs from Guillermo's hand and coils around Dahliorn's ankles, jerking the sheridauk toward him. A split-second decision to risk exposure has her shouting, hoping that the witch will react as she has before when Elizabetta projected a strong desire through thought.

*Stop this! Stop it now.*

Ramira walks toward the men while Elizabetta holds her imaginary breath, unsure what to expect. "Uncle, stop. He's telling the truth. I have been having nightmares again."

*I don't think my projection worked.*

"Then he should have informed me. It's not his place to touch you in any way."

Guillermo uses his magic to lift Dahliorn from the floor and propel him down the hall. The memory of being moved the same way in the apartment at Mettlach flashes through Elizabetta's mind, but within seconds they are out of sight. Ramira returns to the table and requests dessert. *Compassionate to unaffected in nothing flat.* Elizabetta knows Guillermo is going to punish Dahliorn, and there is nothing she can do about it. Clearly Ramira is as heartless as her uncle. *A Jekyll-Hyde personality—the only explanation for her intervention.*

Thoughts and questions ricochet off one another until Dahliorn's soft tone snatches her full attention. «Rest now, little dove. I will see you soon.»

«No, don't—» *This is bullshit! One of these days I'm going to wrest this control from him.* «Put me back in Ramira.»

«Too dangerous.» The sound of a cry comes through before Dahliorn blocks their connection.

«Damn it, don't shut me out!» Elizabetta jumps off the cot and punches the wall in frustration, ignoring the damage to her knuckles; she wants to argue with him, but even if she got past his block, it could make whatever he's enduring worse.

*There has to be a quicker way out of this nightmare.* A few deep breaths help somewhat, but she's too agitated to calm down completely. Her progress with Ramira is too slow. There's no indication that anyone is searching for her. She's beyond fed up with others controlling her life. Elizabetta feels a twinge of bloodlust—a dangerous sign that she may lose control if she doesn't find a way out soon.

She considers making another escape attempt, only this time it's not the spiders holding her back, but worry over what will happen to Dahliorn if she leaves him behind. Somehow Elizabetta must use Ramira against Guillermo, but the witch hasn't called on magic once since Elizabetta's been around her. If Ramira is magically impotent, it's a potential advantage and detriment, but the latter seems a bigger setback—Ramira doesn't seem to possess the speed or strength of a vampire either. *How does Dahliorn expect me to do this?* It seems impossible to use the powerless witch to bring down her uncle.

«Are you there?» No reply. Elizabetta knows she needs to do more on her own, but she's at a loss as to what her next step should be. Shaking her head, she lies down on the cot—fatigue has caught up with her—and moments later she falls asleep. This time, instead of dreams about Dmitri, nightmares from Ramira's memories plague her mind.

## CHAPTER 13: DMITRI

# Only One of Three

Low voices murmur in conversation, but Dmitri doesn't recognize the language. For several minutes he struggles to open his eyes. When his eyelids flutter open, a strange room comes into view: the ceiling seems to be a canopy of trees and the walls a mix of green plants, stones, and compacted dirt. Moving shapes are outlined against the wall, though between the shadows and his blurry sight he's not certain whether they're humanoid or animal.

Dmitri turns his head to the right, blinking a few times as one of the shapes comes into sharper view—a man. The stranger's head cocks to the left and then to the right before he begins speaking in the same unknown language. Two other men step forward and lift Dmitri between them. An image of a dart in his chest flashes through his mind, and he realizes that he was drugged; whatever it was robs him of his ability to resist as the men carry him from the room.

Dmitri finds his feet as they haul him down a long hall

and through a large set of doors to what looks like a huge amphitheater constructed of natural materials. The walls remind him of abalone, but aside from occasional seams of what looks like granite, the pearlesque slabs are unfamiliar—he's unsure if they're of natural or synthetic origin. Stone benches make up the rows of seating, filled with several dozen beings who stare at him with curiosity, disdain, and concern.

Steep, wide steps lead from four sets of doors, including the one he just entered, down to a recessed stage. Maria and Alastrina stand on the edge of a white circular platform below, and lying in the center is Matt. *Where are we?* The maxians seem as confused as Dmitri over this turn of events. Maria's eyes dart about the room and meet his gaze with uncertainty, but Alastrina is obviously struggling to keep her composure; fear radiates off her in waves. *Who are these people?* Dmitri's pulse quickens. *Fae are supposed to be extinct.*

The two men escorting Dmitri deliver him near the maxians and step a few feet away as a tall man with a strong build and angular features approaches from the opposite side of the platform, studying them a moment before raising his eyebrow and addressing the three of them. A quick glance between Maria and Alastrina tells Dmitri that they don't understand his language either. Then the man looks up at those seated in the large room and speaks with someone in the crowd.

A woman walks down to the platform and stops in front of Alastrina, hesitating slightly before settling her hand over the sorceress's heart. Drawing a deep breath, the woman closes her eyes as the sorceress's body trembles beneath her touch. When the stranger's eyes open, she looks at Alastrina for a moment before she moves over to Maria, repeating the same action with the wizard. After she places a hand over Dmitri's heart too—he feels nothing but the heat of her hand—she nods, takes a step back, and turns to the tall man. "Children of Enethura," she says in English. "Though they speak many languages, this is most commonly understood among them."

The man approaches them again, scowling at Dmitri and the maxians. "Is this true?"

Alastrina sounds unusually timid. "We speak English, but I don't know what Enethura is."

"It is what we call your world. I believe you call it Earth."

Dmitri's brows furrow—they don't have time for this nonsense. He needs to know whether these beings can help Matt or not. "Are you fae?"

The tall man's movement is so swift that Dmitri flinches when he appears mere inches from his face. "You do not speak out of turn here."

Instinct to rise to the challenge has Dmitri leaning forward, but he restrains himself from striking the first blow. One on one he might stand a chance against the man, but there are far too many others in this room—it'd be suicide to start a fight.

The man steps back and looks between the three of them again. "Which one of you leads?"

Dmitri exchanges looks with the maxians, unsure how to answer. While he's reluctantly leading the Druzhina at this time, he has no say over the sorceress or the wizard. He doesn't want to speak for them or on their behalf.

Alastrina's voice quavers. "We are equals. We all lead."

The man's head cocks to the side, and his eyes flash red. "I sense fae in you."

Alastrina gulps. "I am a maxian, a sorceress ... my father was fae." The man glares at her, and she adds, "Efurrid, my father was efurrid."

The man's nose wrinkles as he looks her over from head to toe. "Seelie ... rock sprite," he mutters.

Dmitri's muscles twitch with the need to fight or flee—it takes every ounce of discipline to remain where he is. He doesn't know what a rock sprite is, but it's clear this man holds contempt for them. *Is Alastrina's presence a threat to them?* Except for the one woman, these people seem hostile, and he's not sure what they intend to do with the four of them.

The man says to Maria, "And you?"

"I'm maxian, a wizard."

He gives a curt nod and fixes Dmitri with a cold stare. "You are a night child." Dmitri assumes he means vampire, and he nods but doesn't say anything.

"Why do you bring a dying and half-rotted moon child to our world?" The man stands rigid, power and yet indecision showing in every muscle that twitches.

*Half-rotted ... how far gone is Matt?* Dmitri clears his throat and tries to keep his voice even. "To save him."

"Are you not his enemy?"

"He's my friend."

The man resumes speaking in his own language for several minutes, discussing something with the small group standing near the platform. Dmitri's gaze slides over Matt—long seconds steal another piece of the wolf's life with each short, sharp breath he takes. His color is horrid. *We're going to lose him. We don't have time for this.* "If you're fae, save him."

The other people go quiet, and the man's eyes narrow. "He is not our problem."

The woman who approached them earlier steps forward. "There is no evil in their hearts, my king. He speaks the truth—they seek help."

*King? What the hell is going on here?* For a long, tense minute no one moves or says a word. The woman clasps her hands together, her voice calm but with a hint of pleading. "They do not know—they did not expect to find us. Their fear is for their friend and others they left behind."

The king gives her a cold look, and Dmitri swallows hard. *This is not going well.* But when she asks if she may speak with the newcomers, the king deliberates with those around him for only a moment more before he nods his assent.

The woman moves to stand in front of Dmitri. "You say you want to save this moon child, but is it not your venom that kills him?"

Dmitri shakes his head. "Another of my kind did this. This werewolf is my friend. He's important to us."

"So you claim, and yet you do nothing."

The woman's accusation wraps his mind in confusion. "We have no medicine to help him." They've exhausted every possibility available to them, from hope to spells to potions—at this point they don't have time for lengthy discussions. He nods toward Alastrina and Maria. "Their magic can't save him. We brought him here to find an apothecary, to seek fae medicine that can save his life."

The woman scowls at him. "There is no fae magic or medicine that can save one from a night child's venom. There has only ever been one antidote."

"We've tried everything—"

She steps closer to Dmitri, and her eyes blaze gold. "Lie! You withhold the only cure."

*How can she say that after all we've been through to bring Matt here?* Anger pulses through his veins, forcing his fangs to lengthen while his muscles coil, ready to strike. "I didn't do this to him! We have tried everything we know."

She cups a hand to his cheek, and her tone carries disappointment as she whispers, "One of three negates. Think, night child—the truth is there."

*Three what? Only cure ... truth?* Furiously his mind races, trying to make sense of what she's saying. A single thought repeats amid his speculation: *Venom, saliva, blood. Are those the three?* Venom is as deadly to a werewolf as it is to all other living things. Matt is dying proof of that. Saliva neutralizes vampire venom when it's mixed before applied, like when he placed Elizabetta's mark on the wolf, but it is less effective and slower acting if applied afterward. Vampire blood must be ingested to set the DNA change at a human's transformation—

An idea sparks. *Could it be that simple?* Werewolves often come in contact with vampire blood during a fight, with no ill effects. Fangs fully extended, Dmitri runs to

Matt's side, dropping to his knees and puncturing his own wrist as his other hand cups the back of Matt's neck. Dmitri is shaking. He doesn't know if he's doing the right thing or ensuring Matt's death, but neither the strangers nor the maxians are moving to stop him. *I hope this doesn't kill him.*

He places his wrist over the wolf's lips, allowing blood to trickle into his mouth, then lifts Matt's neck and head so his lips part wider. Blood fills the wolf's mouth and spills out the sides. "Drink ... damn it, Matt, drink." Matt half chokes and gulps, but Dmitri keeps his arm in place. A long minute later the wolf swallows again. The punctures on Dmitri's wrist begin to close, and he lifts his arm to his mouth to reopen the vein before aligning it with Matt's lips again. A second time the wolf's mouth fills with blood before he swallows. Dmitri's eyes widen as some of the mottled coloring lessens. Until Matt's tongue presses against his arm, Dmitri isn't aware he's been holding his breath. He exhales sharply, his breath quickening. *How is this possible? The hell we went through to bring him here, keep him alive ... and the cure was always at hand?*

Moments later Matt's canines lengthen, though the other wolf attributes remain dormant. Dmitri winces when Matt's fangs pinch his arm—but as long as the wolf keeps drinking, he has no intention of withdrawing his blood offering.

When the punctures begin to close once more, Dmitri wriggles his arm loose and moves to pierce the vein a third time, but the woman stops him with a smile. "That should be enough."

Dmitri looks up at her in astonishment. "I didn't know." He shakes his head. *If I had given Matt my blood days ago, he never would have suffered like this.* He places a hand over Matt's heart and feels it thrum stronger with each pulse.

The woman addresses the king in their native language, and their discussion continues, seemingly oblivious to the minutes slipping away. But the wolf's respirations are getting stronger, more even. Dmitri is beside himself. *How did we not know this? We almost lost him. I could have saved him so much agony.* He can't escape the guilt weaving its way through him—Matt suffered needlessly and could have died over something as simple as blood. His mind flashes back to when Shashenka left Elizabetta near final death. Then, at least, Dmitri risked the consequences of offering his blood to save her. He can't understand his failure to even consider it for Matt.

*Blood ties ... we share a bond that only blood can bring.* This changes the relationship between him, Elizabetta, and Matt; they are kindred now. The wolf is among their ranks the same as those among the Druzhina are their brothers and sisters—a dubious honor, to say the least.

When the strangers' conversation ends, the woman looks at Dmitri. "Collect your friends—follow me."

Without hesitation, he scoops Matt into his arms and nods at Maria and Alastrina, who move to his side, following the woman up the stairs, out of the amphitheater, and through another door. To Dmitri's surprise, they are back out in the forest on one of the trails near the hub. He looks around—no buildings anywhere, not even the huge amphitheater they just exited. *Are they letting us go?* His mind struggles to process what just happened, but he's unwilling to say anything that may jeopardize their chances of getting off this insane world.

After a five-minute walk, the woman stops in front of what seems to be a thicket. She looks at them for a moment, and her eyes sparkle with golden flecks as she reaches for a gnarled piece of wood. A door opens, revealing the interior of a home. Dmitri's jaw drops. The woman just laughs as she steps inside. "You only see forest because that is what we wish you to see. Would you like to see the truth that your eyes hide?"

Unable to form a response, he simply nods. Stunned silence engulfs them as they look around. They are standing in the middle of what appears to be a very large castle complex. *Maria was right, the wagon wheel on the map marked civilization.* Towering walls several stories high shimmer in iridescent colors that remind Dmitri of polished abalone, much like the walls inside the amphitheater. Small rows of stone and wood buildings line the street, which moments before was no more than a path through the forest. The structures appear to be shops offering goods and services. The strange meandering of the wind makes sense now; it was moving around the objects they couldn't see.

There are people, or more accurately, beings—Dmitri assumes they are fae—everywhere. The sounds are similar to those of any town he's been in on Earth, and he marvels at how the beings must have blocked the smells and sounds from reaching their group. *How is that even possible?* Many of the beings are humanoid in appearance, but it's clear that they are otherworldly. Some have unusual shapes to their eyes or ears. Others have skin colors in shades of green, white, black, red, or blue. A few beings are winged and small, though others are bulky and huge—everything from the grotesque and inexplicable to the beautiful and breathtaking. More startling is that some among them look like what most people would term angels or demons, or at the very least angelic or demonic in origin.

A shiver runs up his spine. *Were they around us this whole time? Did they follow us from the veil?* His thoughts drift back over the strange noises, the child Maria said she saw, and the moccasins that appeared out of nowhere. *What were those beasts who pinned us to the tree?*

The woman clears her throat—she's still waiting by the open door. Her appearance, too, is altered, revealing her true form. *What the hell?* She is ghost white with unnaturally blue eyes, silver-blond hair, and pointed ears. Razor-sharp teeth show in her smile.

Dmitri glances around the castle grounds once more before he follows her inside. She shuts the door behind Maria and Alastrina and leads them to a room with what looks to be a bed. "Your friend may rest here for now. Permanent quarters will be found for all of you later."

Dmitri lays Matt on the bed as the maxians stand nearby. "We won't need permanent quarters. As soon as Matt is able to travel, we'll be leaving."

The maxians nod in agreement, but a peculiar expression crosses the woman's face. "You came here uninvited, and King Altheron did not welcome you. You'll be taken to the Enethuran village in the forest of lost souls; your home is there now."

Alastrina steps toward her. "We came uninvited because we believed you were all dead, extinct. But if we're not welcome to be here, then why would you force us to stay?"

"It is the law. As part efurrid, you must surely know this from the records your kind keep."

The color drains from the sorceress's face. "The last line of the riddle."

Maria clasps a hand to her throat, muttering under her breath, "'Dare ye enter alone without bid or welcome, forever become this side of the veil.'"

"What the hell does that mean?" The thought of never leaving this place, of losing his freedom once again, of never finding Elizabetta, unleashes the violence Dmitri's been holding back. He lunges for the woman. She turns into a vapor, disappears, and then reappears in front of the outside door. Dmitri races forward and catches her, spinning her around to face him. His hand clamps around her throat.

Maria mutters the immobility spell, and then she and Alastrina pry his fingers off the startled woman's neck. The wizard says, "I'm sorry—he's barely been in control of his darker emotions since his wife was taken."

"That is unfortunate, but it does not change the law."

"You don't understand. If you try to keep him here, his bloodlust will destroy him, and he will harm or kill anyone who stands in his way."

Maria's words do little to dampen the rage tearing through Dmitri's frozen body. He strains futilely against the magic's hold as every thought and desire funnel toward a single course of action: destroy. *Destroy everyone and everything.*

Several seconds build an uncomfortable pause between them. The woman says, "I will bring this to the king's council. You may free him of your spell once I leave, as you will remain in this home." Without another word, she exits the dwelling.

The sorceress walks over to the door and finds it locked. With no apparent way out, the maxians agree to release Dmitri, though they back as far away from him as possible before Maria frees him.

*I've got to get out of here. I have to find Elizabetta.* Dmitri flies across the room, and for several frenzied minutes he claws, kicks, and rips at the door, walls, and windowless portals surrounding it. Even the latter can't be breached—the barrier looks like an open window but is more impenetrable than bulletproof glass. There is no way out through this room.

Dmitri sprints deeper into the house—into what appears to be a kitchen—but his efforts prove just as fruitless. He finds the same result in the bedrooms and bathroom.

When he reaches the room Matt is in, the sight of his friends stops him—Maria and Alastrina stand on the bed over Matt's prone body, holding energy in their hands. His gaze shifts to Matt. The wolf is still unconscious, but he looks better; the mottled gray-greenness is almost gone, and there is more natural color in his face. Even Matt's breathing is steadier, a little less short and shallow.

Dmitri looks up at the maxians, takes a deep breath, and swallows hard, pulling against the rage. *These are my friends—I'm supposed to protect them. I must regain control.* "I won't hurt you, but somehow we are going to get out of here as soon as Matt is on his feet."

Maria absorbs the magic back into her palms and steps off the bed. "Agreed. We'll do everything we can to convince them to let us go home."

"He's looking better."

Alastrina says, "Yes, he appears to be healing now. I still can't believe that the cure was as simple as giving him vampire blood. I wonder when that knowledge was lost in our history."

"I can see why it needs to be safeguarded, but it is something the maxian realm should be aware of in the future." Maria sits on the edge of the bed and takes Matt's hand. "I really thought we'd lost him."

A voice from the doorway startles them. Dmitri whirls around to see the same woman who brought them here.

"From the beginning of time there has only ever been one cure," she says. "The night children know this. I'm surprised this one didn't."

The accusation spikes Dmitri's anger again, and he takes a step toward her.

Alastrina puts out a restraining hand. "If it was known once, then it is something that has become long lost to those of us who live on Earth now."

Her words don't cool the blood boiling in Dmitri's veins. "I left my mate in peril to keep this werewolf alive! If I had known, he would have been healed a week ago, and we'd be searching for my wife right now."

"It sounds as if you have an interesting tale. Come, tell

it." The woman turns and walks away.

*Foolish, turning your back on me!* Before Dmitri can lunge at her, Maria and Alastrina grab his arms, holding him back. After a few tense seconds and a couple of threats from the maxians, Dmitri reluctantly follows the mystery woman to another room. He's too busy fighting murderous impulses to appreciate the strange beauty of the home, though he's aware natural materials comprise the structure and furnishings. Alastrina and Maria sit on something that resembles a sofa; its block shape changes to a seat, conforming to their bodies. The woman sits on a smaller lump that becomes a molded chair, and she stares at Dmitri as if waiting for him to start talking.

Dmitri remains standing and folds his arms across his chest. He is reluctant to share any information with these people until they answer a few questions of his own. "Are you fae, and are you going to let us go?"

Alastrina says cheerfully, "I think introductions are in order. I'm Alastrina, and this is Maria, and Dmitri."

"Oh yes, pardon me. It has been a very long time, and I forgot that Enethurans prefer their social customs. I am Milnea." She looks over at Dmitri. "The elders will decide whether to hear your petition. It will take some time. Sit, tell me your tale."

# CHAPTER 14: ELIZABETTA

## Tests

An unknown number of days pass before Elizabetta is transferred into Ramira again. She keeps a keen eye out for Dahliorn, but he is nowhere to be seen, and no one mentions him. «Dahliorn? Please, are you there?» Nothing.

By the end of the day, Elizabetta's fear is growing that something horrible has happened to the sheridauk. Guillermo is capable of inflicting grievous injuries and relishes in the pain and demise of his victims. But she won't allow herself to think the worse. *He's healed himself by now and is just busy. I know that must be it.*

After Ramira retires to her room for the night, a knock at the bedroom door sends a burst of relief through Elizabetta—all her worrying was nothing more than wasted energy. But then a tidal wave of disappointment floods her with uncertainty. She expected Dahliorn would be standing in the hall, and instead there is a man she's seen around the estate. *Another stooge, great.* He seems to be Ramira's new guard, and his presence forces Elizabetta to consider all possibilities.

«Dahliorn! I have to know if you're all right.» Again nothing. Dread, fear, and hopelessness set in as Elizabetta contemplates the loss of the only ally she has here. Unwilling to give in to worry, she tries to pay attention to the conversation the witch is having with her new guard. Something big is about to go down, but she's missed most of what they've said. Key words echo in her mind: test, new phase, assassination. Each one screams the truth of her situation. *This is something bigger than just Dahliorn.* Now they have Elizabetta's attention, and they stop talking. *Figures.* A hundred different thoughts race through her mind as Ramira falls asleep, leaving her no opportunity to learn more tonight.

The absence of Dahliorn is noticeable over the next week, and the weight of his disappearance threatens to drown Elizabetta in despair. She continues trying to reach out to the sheridauk, but all her efforts are met with silence. Everyone else has gone on as if he never existed. With reluctance Elizabetta acknowledges that even her shifts in and out of Ramira feel different, as if they are no longer under his control. *What if he's dead?*

Any chance of learning the sheridauk's fate is further thwarted by Guillermo. Almost daily now, the sorcerer is away "on business," as he says, and he seems particularly interested to hear about Ramira's training and her progress—or lack thereof—each time he returns. The cheerful way he gloats over the deteriorating state of the human and shadow realms' affairs increases Elizabetta's trepidation. The odds favor that whatever the Sanchezes are planning won't bode well for anyone.

If what the sorcerer is saying is true, then the shadow realms are in serious trouble, and the power vacuum the maxians warned about is well underway. *All our hopes and efforts ... destroyed, gone. What have we brought the world to?*

It's too much—captivity, separation, and now loss ... loss of control, of lives, of Dmitri, Matt, Dahliorn, and the future the Druzhina was supposed to be building. She's at a breaking point but can see no way out ... no way to escape, let alone kill the evil son of a bitch who has done this to her. Although she's not in her body, she can feel the tears that must be running over her cheeks. *I'm done ... I can do no more.* She sends a final thought to Dahliorn, wherever his soul may be. «I'm sorry I couldn't protect you. I hope you've found peace ... I'll miss you.»

To her utter shock and great relief, he finally responds. «Little dove, are you going somewhere?»

«What? Where are you? Tell me you are okay. I thought he killed you. What is going on—why aren't you here with Ramira?»

«Guillermo has forbidden me to be near Ramira except to protect her when she's on assignments from now on. My injuries are still healing, but I will be fine.»

Alarms scream in her head when he explains the meaning of assignments—it ties in with the few scattered mentions of Ramira's upcoming challenge. Guillermo is going to test his niece's skills as an assassin. The sorcerer's intent, according to Dahliorn, is to take out the top leadership of each shadow realm while he continues plunging the human world into anarchy. *Dmitri, Matt, Jacques?* If Elizabetta needed any proof that the feared power vacuum is happening, this clinches it, and she knows Guillermo will boost its devastation a hundredfold if given the opportunity. The icy chill of despair is shattered by a new surge of determination as she realizes two things: not only is Dahliorn alive, but they still have a chance to stop the sorcerer. A euphoric optimism swells inside her over the renewed possibilities. *We can do this! But what if we can't?* Uncertainty allows doubt to take root, but that will only lead to a resurgence of helplessness, which she can't allow.

Their only hope in stopping Guillermo is in overcoming their situation, and that leaves one option: Elizabetta must resume training so she can turn Ramira against her uncle. «Can we even still train?»

There's a long pause before Dahliorn answers. «Yes, but it will be more difficult, as I will not be able to see what you are doing.»

They spend the next few hours practicing what Elizabetta has learned, but Dahliorn seems off, distracted, and he's not giving her any clues as to why. *Is it because of his injuries?* She tries to focus on the lesson, though his mood nags at her even as she forces herself to pay attention. While she has a large portion of Ramira's mind mapped out, she's yet to learn how to influence the witch's conscious decisions and actions, something Dahliorn maintains carries the highest risk of exposure. Elizabetta will need to learn how to blunt Ramira's awareness and quickly eliminate, by tampering or direct manipulation, any memory strands that may reveal her presence or the actions she's taken.

As they move through the exercises, Elizabetta asks Dahliorn about what she's discovered in Ramira's past. He confirms what she suspects—Guillermo has been altering Ramira's memory since the day he killed her parents, but he has never fully wiped and reset it. The sheridauk seems surprised to learn that Ramira's true memories are still there. For a moment it gives Elizabetta hope that maybe the wretched woman can become good again once her uncle is gone, but then Dahliorn tells Elizabetta how he's watched Ramira change into something as corrupt as her uncle. Although his magic ability is limited, the sheridauk tried to protect the child, casting minor spells to help her resist the evil and hatred Guillermo poured into her. But in the end it only hindered her progression into what she's become, earning him harsh punishment.

Dahliorn reminds her that he's still limited in what he can do, regardless of the restraint on his magic—wielding it will leave a trace on Ramira. That's how the sorcerer discovered what Dahliorn was doing to protect the witch when she was little, and he was tortured for it. He was caught in the same manner before his latest beating.

Magic, when used on another, always leaves a trace on the person it's used against, and from what Dahliorn describes, it is like a calling card. Anyone with the ability to sense and read a magic signature can identify the maxian or fae who cast it if their paths cross. If it weren't for the monster Ramira is now, Elizabetta would almost feel sorry for the pathetic witch. Instead her sympathies align her closer with the sheridauk and begin to cement her feelings of friendship.

The awkward silence returns, and Elizabetta refuses to push her nagging concerns aside again. «Dahliorn, what is going on? I know something is up—what aren't you telling me?»

She can almost envision him drawing a deep breath in the lingering pause before he says, «Guillermo is sending Ramira to Paris for her first test. She is to assassinate one of the maxian supreme council members.»

The news settles like a brick in Elizabetta's stomach. While she doesn't know all the council members, she owes them a debt of gratitude for helping to end Shashenka—her team couldn't have done it without them. *I'm so glad she can't access my memories and use me for this.* «We have to stop her.»

He promptly reminds her that they're not ready; she's not far enough along with her training to use what she's learned. «Damn it.» Elizabetta's mind whirls. *We need to start cramming—faster, harder. I'm a quick learner—we can do this!*

Dahliorn breaks the silence that grows louder between them. «I'll be with her, to keep you safe.»

«You mean, to protect her?»

«I mean, to protect you. The merge between you and Ramira binds you—there are risks you're unaware of. Risks resulting from the spell Guillermo cast on you.»

«You're flipping kidding me?» The shock reverberates into a new kind of fear. She knows the proverbial other shoe is about to drop, and she's not sure she wants to hear what Dahliorn's keeping back.

He says, «Your consciousness, your essence of being, is

bound with her. While you may not bear physical pain from any injury inflicted on Ramira, there is a chance that if she dies, it may claim your life too.»

«What? No. Back up right there.» She knows Ramira's skills are lacking; if the witch has to face anyone in a fight, the odds are high that she will be injured or killed, which means Elizabetta may suffer the same fate. At the same time, the witch needs to be defeated, and as a Druzhina Elizabetta must protect the intended target. It's absurd that she survived everything Shashenka threw at her, and now she's faced with allowing others to die or losing everything because she's trapped inside this useless witch. Denial settles into her bones—she can't let this happen. She won't let this happen.

She'd give anything to swallow the lump that must be growing in her throat, about to choke her. «Well, first let me tell you that dying is not an acceptable outcome. Second, looks like we'd better do all we can to make sure she lives.»

The echo of minutes becomes louder before Elizabetta realizes that Dahliorn is quiet—her earlier suspicions are screaming in her head now. «Okay, out with it. You're still holding something back.»

A few more seconds taunt her as they pass her by. *Tick, tick, tick ... cue the* Jeopardy *theme music. God, he's infuriating!* Dahliorn says, «Just know that Ramira will be well protected.»

«What is that supposed to mean?»

«A spider will be lurking in the shadows. Please don't be afraid. I will never allow you to be harmed.»

*Un-flipping-believable! Shit. Let's just keep throwing shoes onto the pile.* Even though she isn't in her own body, the thought makes her flesh crawl—and it's Ramira who shudders, but Elizabetta barely notices. *Accidental, or is my training coming through?* She doesn't pursue that thought—Dahliorn's words are on repeat in her head. The idea of being anywhere near that hideous monster is more than a little unnerving, and she doesn't share Dahliorn's confidence that the creature can be trusted. *Well, of course, what could possibly go wrong with one of Guillermo's mutant pets?* Logic steps in and waits for her to stop ranting, and when she does, it points out an obvious benefit: the spider's protection, if it does its job, may be the very thing to save her life.

She's still mulling over that disturbing thought when Dahliorn puts her to sleep. Unlike other times, tonight there are no dreams for her—just the empty unknowing darkness of unconsciousness.

It seems as if it's mere moments later when Elizabetta wakes and once more shifts into Ramira, who is preparing for her mission. Hot tears run down the witch's face as she changes into her fighting gear—even Elizabetta feels the echo of their heat, and she reaches out and accesses the active thought strand. Panic, fear, loathing, and uncertainty snarl Ramira's mind. The test will be a combination of stealth and hand-to-hand combat. But the witch knows that she is no match for the maxian, especially without her powers—a point she argued with her uncle. Guillermo's cold response was twofold: get over the loss of her powers and don't fail, or they'd part ways. If he intended to boost her confidence or assuage her fears, he missed the mark, and his final words only shattered what remained of both.

Even now they run through Ramira's mind: "You'd better fight as if your life depends on it. I want that maxian dead. Fail in this mission, and I may just kill you myself."

The witch washes her face before she goes downstairs to receive final instructions—she doesn't want Guillermo to know that she's been crying. So many times over the years she has disappointed her uncle, and it wrenches her heart that she never seems to please him. She's been punished before for failure, and while it thrills her when it's Dahliorn at her uncle's mercy, it's never an experience she wants to repeat.

Ramira's emotions may be in turmoil beneath the surface, but Elizabetta's own emotions slide the skilled killer in her closer to the surface. Though she is trapped, her blood oath as a Druzhina remains—she must protect her friends and allies. Determination splits her focus between listening in and figuring out how to foil the witch. Ramira doesn't stand a chance—even if she somehow survives, her demented uncle may carry out his threat. *I may be dead regardless.* This leaves Elizabetta with one choice if Ramira somehow gains the upper hand in the fight: she may have to sacrifice herself if it means giving the advantage to the maxian. She'll just need to find a way to stop Dahliorn and the spider from engaging in the fight.

Elizabetta accepts the path she's chosen, and when Ramira descends the stairs to the ground floor, she sees

Dahliorn waiting with Guillermo near the mutaport. Guillermo hands a slender object wrapped in a cloth to Ramira.
"You're to bring the head back. I want you to leave this
near the body."

The witch takes the object and unfolds the fabric, and
Elizabetta is certain that her own heart skips a beat—it's
her horse-head dagger, the match to the one Dmitri carries.
She scrambles to figure out what possible message the
sorcerer intends to send by leaving her weapon behind. *Are
they trying to make me look like the killer, like I've gone
rogue?*

Ramira tosses the cloth on the table and slips the dagger
into her waistband. "I will not fail you, Uncle."

"Don't defy my orders, Dahliorn, or I may permanently
sever a limb this time." Guillermo glares at the sheridauk,
who joins Ramira on the mutaport.

Elizabetta's mind races. «Don't you dare save her. Her
target may be a very dear friend, and I will stop at nothing
to ensure she fails.»

Dahliorn's eyes widen. «I can't let you do that. I must
keep you alive.»

«No! I will kill us both before I allow her to harm someone I care about.»

Ignoring his pleas, she mentally puts herself near the
divide between the motor skills halves of Ramira's brain.
For decades Elizabetta used her vampiric influence to sway
others, and she wonders if that is the reason Ramira
sometimes seems to respond to her thoughts. If so, she may
be able to send the command for Ramira to turn Elizabetta's dagger on herself. *Maxians are mortal, even if they*

*do live a long time. I have to strike her heart.* Regardless of what Dahliorn says, she will do whatever it takes to disrupt the woman's intended actions. She raises her imaginary hands—she'll know which energy strands to pull when she sees their destination—and holds tightly to the command she'll send when the time comes. *I will not allow her to kill anyone.*

Still standing on the mutaport, Ramira glances up at Dahliorn. Elizabetta sees the resolve in his eyes—he'll do everything possible to protect her. She's equally determined to thwart his plans. *Speaking of ... where's our big, hairy eight-legged protector? Is the spider waiting for us or being sent after we arrive?* She wants to shudder; at least she doesn't have to look at that ugly mutant right now.

The white light of the mutaport flashes. Elizabetta is ready to face whatever may come.

A fraction of a second later they are standing in what appears to be someone's private study. Ramira looks around the room and then makes her way to the door and down a hallway, looking into the rooms they pass. Elizabetta doesn't recognize the place, but no one seems to be around, and she hopes whoever does live here isn't coming home anytime soon.

After a thorough search of the house, Ramira moves out to the garden. It's daylight, leaving the witch second-guessing the wisdom of a midday attack. She instructs Dahliorn to hide in the shadows of a hedgerow alcove as she takes up position nearby. Elizabetta is baffled as to why the

witch picked this spot—given what they've seen of the
property, the best place for an assassin to wait is inside the
house in the master bedroom. *Foolish woman, she's helping
me out here in ways I never hoped for, and she's too
inexperienced even to know it!*

Hours pass, and night falls. Dahliorn has retreated into
the shadows, and although Elizabetta knows he is there, she
can't see him when Ramira looks his way. There's been no
communication between him and the witch, and no sound
from the house either. *Maybe the target's not coming home.
Their mission may fail yet, and mine will succeed.*

The sound of the back door opening mangles
Elizabetta's optimism. Then a man comes into view, and her
heart plunges to the ground as rage pulses through her.
Ramira's breathing quickens, matching the frantic desperation consuming Elizabetta. *No, no, not him.* The nightmare is all too real, and she just wants to wake up.

Jacques Boucher, the Orde de Maxia's council leader,
walks over to a bench near a lighted fountain and sits down.
Ramira begins to creep up behind him while Elizabetta
prepares to counter the witch's attack. *He can't die this
way. I won't allow it.* Elizabetta grabs for an energy
strand—she must act now before it's too late. She finally
wraps her imaginary arms around the one that controls
Ramira's foot and uses her mental weight to pull it back.
She barely processes the thought that some of her training
has paid off.

The witch trips and stumbles—and the *umph* that
escapes her as she hits the ground alerts Jacques to her
presence. He has a magic orb ready in his hands the

moment she scrambles to her feet. For a few tense seconds they stare at each other, then Ramira charges at him. The warlock releases the orb, knocking Ramira on her backside. Elizabetta silently cheers when he begins to mutter an immobility spell.

Then out of the darkness, Guillermo's spider rushes past the witch and leaps on Jacques. Ramira doesn't waste a second to regain her footing and run at the warlock again. The spider's swift and fluid movements stun Elizabetta— Jacques's face is a mask of sheer terror as he tries to defend himself.

The creature's huge mandibles position its fangs to swipe and tear at the warlock's face, gouging out his eyes. Then the spider uses its legs to pin Jacques's limbs to the ground, and as its fangs pierce his shoulders, the blinded man twists and writhes—but he is unable to throw the creature off.

A knife is in Ramira's hands the moment she drops to her knees next to Jacques. Her hand tangles in his hair as she lifts his head. "My uncle sends his regards."

The warlock's screams reverberate pain and horror across the garden as Ramira slashes the blade across his neck. Too late, Elizabetta realizes she should have made another attempt to distract the witch—her own fear and terror over the spider kept her attention riveted on the hideous creature. Nausea rolls through her as Jacques's life seeps out in a growing pool of blood. Grief rocks her to the core. It was Jacques's leadership that helped gain her and Dmitri the maxian council's unanimous support of their overthrow of Shashenka. If not for the words he said to her later in Xi'an, she would have given up before they'd even started, and Shashenka would still be alive. Jacques fought alongside them at Machu Picchu. Now he is gone. *He's gone ... no, no, no.* Elizabetta had the ability to interfere and give Jacques a chance in return, and she failed.

The spider is still standing on Jacques's lifeless body. Dahliorn says something, but Elizabetta is too lost in the aftermath of this horrible moment to pay attention to either of them. Words Jacques spoke to her filter back, but with a different meaning to her now: "The shock ... has left you too close to see objectively—to see the gift ... given to those ... fighting on your side." But what good could come of this? "Make the shadow realms proud, Mrs. Markov. Go lead them and win this war." *He was a good man—he didn't deserve to die this way. I will exact blood justice for his life.*

As the spider moves away into the shadows, she hears Dahliorn speak again. «It's over—you're safe now, little dove.»

Rage burns through her—guilt, remorse, and heartache spar for room in her battered soul. «Where were you? Why didn't you ...» There has to be something more than just his desire to protect her; good beings don't allow evil ones to murder others. Ever. *He's hiding something, he's not who—*

Her silent words freeze when Ramira reacts to the silhouette of a tall man appearing in the doorway at the back of the house. *Oh God, not again. This can't be happening.* Emotions threaten to overwhelm Elizabetta. *I can't ... I just can't—*

The vampire steps out into the garden; his sharp eyes take in the bloody scene but seem to miss Ramira deep in the shadows. *Vladimir. What is he doing here?* It doesn't matter; Elizabetta will honor her oath as a Druzhina and do all she can to help him. *What if I can't save him?* Her thoughts flicker to Anna. She'd be devastated by her mate's loss and would never forgive Elizabetta. *I have to ... I can't fail him too.*

The Druzhina approaches slowly, scanning the garden as he comes nearer the spot where Jacques died. Ramira darts a quick look around, and Elizabetta realizes the spider is nowhere in sight—neither is Dahliorn. *I'll need to be fast ... I can't let either stop me this time.*

Vladimir circles the fountain, obviously unaware of the danger. Elizabetta's mind is screaming for him to see the threat. The witch repositions the horse-head dagger as he turns his back to her—and when he crouches to examine Jacques's remains, she starts to leap forward.

*No, don't touch him!* Elizabetta attempts to take control of the witch's arm, to force Ramira to stab herself in the heart, but it's not working; it requires too many different strands, and she is only causing the witch's limb to jerk and twitch. Enraged, Elizabetta wrenches another strand, and Ramira's knee buckles, sending her to the ground.

The action gives Vladimir the opportunity to attack, and he launches forward before the witch can scramble to her feet. Elizabetta pulls the strands to release the witch's grip on the dagger. The weapon drops from her hand as Vladimir grabs Ramira by the throat. "Who are you?"

*Don't struggle—don't fight him.* Elizabetta looks into Vladimir's alert and steady gaze. *Make it fast ... kill her now!* She concentrates harder on sending a command to the witch. *Surrender! Stop! Don't move ... he'll kill you ... you don't want to fight ... you're tired ... stop, relax!*

Ramira's body relaxes and her arms drop to her sides, but she doesn't say a word. Confusion radiates off her—giving Elizabetta hope that the witch's mission will fail.

Vladimir's voice booms, "What are—"

Without warning Guillermo's pet slams into them, knocking both over—his legs push Ramira clear as they tumble to the ground. *Where the hell did he come from?* Elizabetta doesn't see the sheridauk anywhere—he must still be lurking in the alcove, perhaps following his orders this time not to get involved. She hopes so; it's hard enough dealing with this nightmare. She doesn't need his interference too.

The spider advances on Vladimir as the vampire rolls and tries to gain enough distance to stand and fight back against this new foe. *Damn it!* Vladimir doesn't move far enough away—the spider pounces on him, driving its fangs into the vampire's shoulders. Elizabetta's bloodlust surges as Vladimir howls in pain, his claws swiping at the creature over him. She knows he'll never stop fighting. And neither will she. *Get up and kill that spider. Do it now!* Ramira rises to her feet, picks up the dagger, and leaps at the creature. The dagger slashes forward and stabs the mutant spider's body behind its head. The unexpected blow staggers the monster sideways.

Dahliorn shouts, «Elizabetta, don't do this.»

*No friggin' way!* Vladimir scrambles to his feet, blood soaking his shirt—disbelief and revulsion in his eyes as he takes a defensive posture. *I said, kill the spider!* «I told you that I will not allow her to kill him. I will kill her first ... die if I must.»

A *click-click* chatter comes from the spider, and its eyes seem to track both Ramira and Vladimir at once as its front legs rise in an apparent fighting stance. Vladimir looks between the woman and the creature—uncertainty reflects in his hesitation to move. The spider too turns slightly, ready for either the vampire or witch to advance on it. When Vladimir lunges at the mutant creature, it moves so fast that Ramira—and Elizabetta—lose sight of it for a moment. Before anyone can react, the spider has the witch in its grasp and is darting away from the garden.

Ramira struggles against its hold, but her efforts are like a gnat attacking an elephant's ass. Elizabetta is too lost in her own bloodlust and attempt to break free to realize the witch is still acting out her commands. The spider reaches the hedgerow, climbs up, and looks back, giving her a glimpse of the fallen vampire. There's no movement or sound from Vladimir, but she knows he can survive if she can somehow overpower the spider and keep it away.

«Elizabetta, stop sending her commands.»

Dahliorn's plea enrages her further. «No. Where are you? Help us kill this monster.» There's a long pause—if anything, it makes Elizabetta even angrier. *Damn it, I need his help for once!* The creature ignores Ramira's thrashing and twisting as it drops to the ground and runs off, still carrying her.

Then Dahliorn shatters her control. «I can't allow that ... sleep now, little dove.»

## CHAPTER 15: DMITRI

# *A King's Command*

Tremors of bloodlust pulse through Dmitri as Milnea states for the fifth time that she is forbidden to reveal certain facts. He refuses to tell their story until she answers his questions first. Maria and Alastrina talk quietly between themselves, having given up trying to resolve the impasse an hour ago.

He rakes a hand through his hair. He doesn't understand why Milnea can't even admit that they are fae. *If they're not fae, what are they?* "Look, I realize you are trying to protect yourselves, but I'm telling you that we are no threat to you if you allow us to go back," he says yet again. "But keep me here against my will, and I will find a way to destroy you."

Milnea sighs. "That is precisely why your kind is not trusted—and we are a distrustful species to begin with. I can assure you that the uninvited and unwelcomed never cross a veil."

*I swear, if we ever get out of here, I will not miss this place or its people.* He's lost count of the number of ways

she's already said that—all the while refusing to explain
why. It only pushes him closer to the breaking point. He's
had enough. "You will not stop me from going back to save
my wife. I demand to—"

A steady, rumbling growl comes from the doorway
behind him. "Does anyone want to tell me where the hell we
are? I mean, unless I'm delusional and fell into some hobbit
hole, then I'd lay odds we're not in Kansas anymore."

Dmitri spins around and sees Matt leaning against the
wall, upright but weak. He rushes to the wolf's side. "I'm
not sure you should be out of bed yet. You almost died and
still look like you belong in a grave."

Matt gives him a crooked grin. "Just help me to a seat.
You two have been at this for hours, and I want in on this
conversation."

Alastrina moves to a chair, and Dmitri settles Matt next
to Maria.

"Mattie!" The wizard throws her arms around the wolf's
neck. "I thought I lost you, Mattie."

Milnea looks Matt over. "It's good to see you're doing
better, moon child."

"Yeah, about that, anyone want to bring me up to speed
here? I told you I was too sick for your shit." Matt frowns at
Dmitri. "Last thing I remember, we were talking about
ways to flush out Milo and Guillermo."

"Guillermo?" Surprise rings out in Milnea's voice. "Are
you talking about the Enethuran sorcerer?"

Dmitri glares at the infuriating woman. He'll be damned
if they're going to cooperate after the way she's dodged and
refused him. "Don't! Not until she starts answering our

questions."

Matt shakes his head and blows out a breath. "It's time someone starts answering questions around here, or we're never going to get out of here to find baby vamp." His gaze shifts from Dmitri to Milnea. "Yes, we are talking about that evil pile of crap."

Her eyes widen, and she says under her breath, "I have to go." Then she darts from the house before they can say another word.

*What is with these ... they must be fae. What else could they be?* Dmitri's at the point that he no longer cares. *We need out of here.* He rushes to the door, but she's locked them in again. His fist slams into it as he curses under his breath. Another low growl pulls his attention toward Matt—the look on the wolf's face serves as a reminder to calm down.

Dmitri paces the room as Matt asks again what's happened since he blacked out in Novgorod. Maria and Alastrina fill him in on what he missed, but what Dmitri notices during their exchange is the way Maria keeps in constant contact with Matt—her fingers sweep through his hair, she holds his hand, and there are moments when she rests her head against the wolf's shoulder. In response, Matt puts an arm around her and kisses the top of her head. For the first time Dmitri sees the depth of emotion between the two, and he is certain that this ordeal has tipped them deeper into a relationship. *Is it a passing affair, or do they share a bond?*

When Maria tells the wolf that Dmitri saved his life— first at Alastrina's home and then twice after they arrived here—Matt stands somewhat shakily and grabs Dmitri into a hug. An awkward few seconds sneak away before Dmitri lifts his arms and pats the wolf on the back. Before pulling away, Matt says in a tone too low for the women to hear, "I'm beginning to see what Eliza may have seen in you. You're a damn good vamp—thank you for saving my furry ass."

*I can't believe the way this mutt wormed his way into our lives and hearts.* Dmitri won't admit that aloud; instead he replies in an equally quiet voice, "Let's just say that I realize what Elizabetta sees in you too. Seems we're stuck with each other now."

"Now that's what I'm talking about." Matt grins as he retreats to the sofa.

Dmitri finally sits down and joins the maxians in telling Matt about their journey through Seelinara, including the less-than-friendly reception they received from the king. Matt is particularly concerned over their captors' reaction to Alastrina's fae heritage. She tries to assure him that efurrids are mischievous at best, but they are peaceful, and there is little reason for the king to harbor hostility toward them. But to Dmitri it makes about as much sense as the nervous and scared reactions they saw from those in the amphitheater—before he gave them reason to fear them. *Hell, we didn't even expect to find anyone alive on this planet.*

Which, for Dmitri and Matt, brings up the biggest mystery: why those on Earth concluded the fae were wiped out during the Black Plague. Alastrina lived during that period, and the only excuse she can offer is that they knew the plague was hitting Seelinara harder than on Earth. Then when the veils stopped working, it was believed that whatever fae magic operated the veils must have died with them. *All this on speculation?* None of it explains why the fae cut themselves off from Earth. Dmitri intends to ask Milnea, regardless if she's willing to answer—at some point she's going to have to give them some information. *I'll see to that.*

He's about to move their conversation toward escape, when Milnea opens the door—followed by several of the beasts who aided in their capture. *Seelinaran version of guard dogs?* Dmitri assumes the large creatures have been sent as a deterrent to keep him in line. But to his surprise, Milnea says, "King Altheron has requested your audience. Come with me."

Dmitri exchanges a glance with his three friends, then moves to help Matt. He isn't sure where they're meeting this king, but if it's back in the amphitheater, it may be too far for Matt to manage without assistance—the wolf is still weak and recovering. *I wonder how his strength and skill stack up against these animals?* Matt is of equal size when he's in his wolf form, but he is in no condition to fight anyone at the moment. Dmitri notices Matt's eyes rake over the beasts following them—he suspects Matt is inclined to try talking their way out, though if all else fails, they will need to fight to leave Seelinara.

This time Milnea leads them to a side entrance of the castle. The guards at the door nod at their entourage as they pass. Dmitri expects to be taken to some type of great room again, but he's baffled when they climb several flights of stairs and proceed down a long hallway on the top floor. Numerous guards line the corridor ahead; two large wooden doors with ornate gold plating and knobs are on the other end of the hall.

A single guard bows his head as they approach. "The king is waiting for you in his private chambers, my lady."

*My lady? Is Milnea royalty here?* Dmitri follows her through the door, supporting Matt at his side. The rooms here are lavishly decorated, filled with natural furnishings adorned with colorful throws and pillows—almost the equivalent of a living room or parlor. But what Dmitri notices most is that there are no guards on this side of the hall door.

If the beasts leave them alone, it may be possible to make a move against this king and demand their release. From what he saw of the king earlier, Dmitri estimates that he has a good chance of taking the man in a one-on-one fight, or at least of holding the king hostage until they reach a veil. He is determined to watch for the first opportunity to take action—one way or another they are leaving this place forever.

Milnea instructs them to remain standing until the king invites them to sit, and a moment later King Altheron enters the room. Unlike many of the others they've seen, the king has features resembling those of a man and not some otherworldly being. He looks each of them over but addresses Matt first. "Your companions brought you here without your knowledge or consent. When you are well enough to travel, you will return to Enethura."

Matt grimaces. "If it's all the same to you, I'd rather not

leave my friends behind. They only did what they had to do to save my sorry ass, and I'd be in your debt if you'd allow them to go home with me."

The king's eyes narrow. "They have broken the law and have not been pardoned."

Dmitri clenches his teeth to stop the outburst balanced on his tongue. He feels Matt sag against him—the mutt has no strength to keep standing. *Maybe we won't be escaping today. With the condition he's in, he couldn't run five feet, let alone miles with these beings chasing us.*

The king seems to notice and waves a hand. "You may sit—we have matters to discuss, and this may take some time if you remain as obstinate as you were with Milnea."

Maria moves to Matt's side and sits next to him, but she keeps a respectful distance and doesn't touch the wolf. The beasts that followed them into this room back off too and recline on their haunches along the walls, leaving King Altheron and Dmitri the only two still standing.

Dmitri studies the man, and his certitude grows that these beings are indeed fae, though he's clueless about discerning the species. They still don't know whether the king is Seelie or Unseelie, and from what Alastrina has said about Seelinara, this information is needed to properly interact with any fae. *I will get that answer.* He selects the chair nearest the unknown man—a twofold advantage. It's an added barrier between the man and Dmitri's friends, and it provides Dmitri with the opportunity to take the man hostage if the beasts attack.

The king gives him a penetrating look. "You claim to lead equally, yet your actions suggest otherwise, night child."

When Dmitri doesn't respond, King Altheron says, "Deny it if you wish, but I know a king when I see one."

That provokes Dmitri out of his silence. "I am not a king, nor am I a leader of any realm. I'm just a vampire who took a stand to help free my kind from a despotic ruler." *A feat we've yet even to celebrate.*

"Believe what you wish, night child—you cannot change what you are." King Altheron waves his hand in a dismisssive gesture. "I must hear what news you have of the sorcerer Guillermo. Before you resist, know this: I can compel the truth."

Matt says, "Just tell him what he needs to know, Dmitri. We're burning too much daylight here, and it's not getting us any closer to getting baby vamp back."

King Altheron shifts his gaze to Matt. "Who is this baby vamp you speak of?"

"She is his wife and my best friend, and she is in danger. That demon sorcerer you're so interested in kidnapped her, and we intend to get her back. If that stupid vamp in Novgorod hadn't hit me with a dose of venom, we might have found her by now."

"Your wife was taken by Guillermo?"

Dmitri's nostrils flare, but he gives a curt nod. "Yes."

"You will tell me about the sorcerer."

The king levels an invasive gaze on Dmitri, leaving him feeling exposed and bared as a strange weight settles inside him; the desire to tell this man everything he wants to know grows stronger with each second that leaps off the clock. Dmitri intends to say no more than is necessary, but from the moment his mouth opens he is unable to stop talking. Despite his efforts not to, he reveals everything to the king—their struggle in winning freedom from Shashenka, the many years of torture and sacrifice, and the two encounters they've had with Guillermo. When he falls silent, Alastrina provides a history of the evil sorcerer, and she doesn't stop either until all of her knowledge of Guillermo is added to Dmitri's divulgence.

King Altheron looks toward the beasts lining the wall and dismisses them. Dmitri's back straightens. *Wait ... wait.* He begins to shift forward. *Now!* He's about to rise out of his chair when King Altheron's eyes flash green, and the desire to attack ceases as if Dmitri's need to do so never existed. It's unsettling, to say the least—not even vampiric influence is that swift or thorough. *What kind of power and control does he have over us?*

The king temples his fingers in front of his lips, and the silence balloons to such an uncomfortable level that it's almost a relief when he finally speaks. "If Guillermo is still alive, then it means my warrior failed in his mission, and that the maxians still haven't taken care of their problem." His fists clench, and Dmitri notices a slight trickle of blood ooze from the closed right hand. "When Guillermo unleashed the evil that slew many throughout the Enethuran and Seelinaran realms, I sent my best warrior to end his life. The decision was made to close the veils and cease interaction with Enethura when he disappeared and never returned. As long as the maxians allow that sorcerer to live, we have no desire to give him access to harm us again."

Alastrina says, "The maxian realm had no knowledge

that you sent anyone. When contact ceased between our worlds, we believed the plague had ended all life on Seelinara."

The king levels a hard look at the sorceress. "Then how did you unlock and activate the veil you used to get here?"

"It was a riddle in my father's papers. *Veascru nonda* was hidden in its message." Alastrina darts a glance between the intimidating man and Dmitri—uncertainty is etched plainly across her face.

"Your father violated a treaty we hold with the Seelie court by preserving that information. While your kind has wide latitude in recording history and details, even going so far as to imprint those records into stone, none of you have the right to disregard an order given by royal decree. Does he yet live?"

Alastrina hangs her head. "He died during the plague."

"So you admit that you are Seelie, you are a fae?" Dmitri stares at the man, hoping he'll finally reveal their nature.

The king stands, his facial features transforming in an abrupt shift—the black face of the beast they first encountered in the forest. His eyes glow red. "Do not confuse me with the light fae. I am the Unseelie king!"

A growl erupts from Matt. Dmitri's eyes narrow. *Bingo, gotcha now. What the hell kind of dark fae are you?* King Altheron's words unleash a torrent of questions in his mind, but he settles on one: "What do you want from us?"

Manlike attributes return to the king's face as he sits back down. "I will give you the chance to earn a pardon. Three of you will return to Enethura, find Guillermo, and learn what happened to my son. If you do that, you will be considered welcomed here and thus free to leave of your own volition."

"Your son?" Dmitri cocks an eyebrow. *Really? He sent his own son?*

"If that sorcerer killed him, then I charge you with avenging his death—you will provide proof of that deed. If my son is being held captive, then you will rescue him when you free your wife."

"What is his name?" Dmitri feels as if he's been pushed into a deal with the devil, but it's the best one he's had in his quest to find Elizabetta.

"We don't offer our names unless asked, and you have not asked him. He will have to decide whether to tell you when you find him."

Dmitri fights the urge to shake his head in frustration. He's not willing to leave anyone behind, and if the king is desperate, it may give him some leverage to get his entire team out safely. "It would be best if we all go. Guillermo is incredibly powerful—it will take the combined effort of our skills to hunt him down and kill him."

Again a flash of red pulses in the king's eyes. "You will leave the half-breed efurrid as a guarantee of your compliance, and return as I've commanded you. If you fail in your mission or refuse to return, then she will remain here for the rest of her life."

Alastrina's gulp catches Dmitri's attention. Fear is written across her face, and there's a slight tremor in her voice as she acquiesces. Dmitri senses there is something she hasn't told them, but he draws a deep breath to put as much confidence into his voice as possible. "Before I agree to anything, if we are to do your bidding, I have to know ... what exactly are you?"

"Father, let me go with them." Milnea's unexpected words cause a whiplash reaction—all turn to look at her, but none appear more surprised than Dmitri.

*Father? She doesn't look anything like the Unseelie king.* King Altheron's face contorts with a look of disdain. Then it occurs to Dmitri that this may be another deflection, a way to avoid answering his earlier question. He starts to open his mouth, but before he gets one word out, the king says, "We are fae."

"Yeah, but what kind?" Matt rubs the back of his neck. "I mean, you two don't even look alike." *Leave it to the mongrel to say what's on his mind—and mirror what I was thinking.*

The king's jaw tenses. He seems to realize that they will not let this go and finally says, "I am a sheridauk, a dark fae. Milnea is an elemental, a light fae. She is a peace offering from the Seelie queen, and my son's betrothed."

Dmitri's eyes widen in surprised sympathy—he knows what it's like to wait centuries to reunite with a mate—but he keeps the thought to himself.

The king says, "It's settled, then—Milnea will go with you. If you fail in your mission but survive, then she is to bring you back here, where you will live out the remainder of your lives. If you succeed in ending Guillermo's life, she will invite you back to retrieve your half-breed friend."

He levels a cold gaze at each of them, lingering on Dmitri. "Know this, night child ... you will protect the prince with your life. If he is dead, you will discover the details of his demise, but if he is alive, you will return the rightful heir of my throne unharmed. Should he be found alive but perish after you confront Guillermo, then your life is forfeit." The king grants them permission to start their quest as soon as they are ready to go—but he reiterates that the sorceress will remain at the castle until they achieve their goals.

Alastrina tells Maria the incantation necessary to activate the mutaport in her home, instructing her to go to the maxian council chambers and get the support they will need. "Oh, and one more thing ... we left in such a hurry that I didn't look to see if Edward was put out. Make sure he's not inside when you leave my home."

"Are you sure about this, Alastrina?" Maria's tone conveys uncertainty, but Dmitri knows they have little choice.

He stands and approaches the sorceress. "We will do our best to set you free." The look she gives him is pitiable, almost as if she knows their fates are already sealed.

King Altheron nods. "Milnea, I charge you with aiding these Enethurans in their quest. If you fail, your punishment will be to remain in their realm—you will be barred from crossing a veil again. But I warn you, Milnea, you will send them back regardless of their success or failure, or I will consider it a violation of the treaty and declare against the Seelie."

"Okay, no pressure, then," Matt mutters, rising to his feet. Maria moves to support him as the king dismisses them from the room.

Dmitri looks over his shoulder at Alastrina. She meets

his gaze with a dignity appropriate for the gallows. "This may be our best option to right whatever hostility Guillermo caused between our worlds," she says. "I have faith that you can do this, Dmitri." The sorceress manages a half smile, but it does little to boost Dmitri's confidence.

He hasn't fully reconciled his emotions over leaving Alastrina behind when they renter the house they were in earlier. Matt is still too weak to travel any distance—they will need to wait at least a day or two before his strength is sufficient to make the trek back to the veil. Dmitri offers to carry him again, but the wolf wants to walk out of this realm under his own power. *No man, regardless of species, wants to be seen as weak.* It's yet another delay in their search for Elizabetta, understandable as it may be, but Dmitri reluctantly agrees to give Matt the time he needs.

"We will get her back," Matt declares.

Dmitri places a hand on Matt's shoulder. He has no doubt that the wolf will do his best to make that statement true.

# Stop at Nothing

Elizabetta wakes in her cell, fury radiating through every nerve of her body. She had no idea that Dahliorn could send her back across such a distance. *How long have I been asleep?* Trepidation pushes against her rage—she doesn't know whether Ramira and the spider went back to kill Vladimir. «Dahliorn, how could you do this?» *Oh God. Let Vladimir be safe.*

There is no response from the sheridauk, and Elizabetta's thoughts tangle around her throat like a noose with ever-tightening knots of disgust, grief, and hatred. Is Dahliorn so terrified of Guillermo that he won't act against him, or is the sheridauk playing her for a fool? She will never allow Ramira to take another decent life—she doesn't care if it does expose her or gets her killed.

Time slips away. Elizabetta is no closer to answers than when she first awoke. She repeatedly tries to contact Dahliorn, but he's either ignoring her or is too far out of range. Lucky for him if he is still in Paris—she's furious enough to use the witch's hands to rip his head off his shoulders. Vladimir was outmatched with the spider there, and if Dahliorn helped Ramira, then her friend is probably dead. She doesn't know how she could ever look at Anna again, knowing that she had the chance to save Vladimir and blew it. *Damn it. Once I had Ramira under my influence, I should have told that bitch to kill herself instead of attacking the spider.* Elizabetta won't make that mistake again. *This will end one way or another.*

Then the sensation of darkness tugs on her, and a moment later she is back in Ramira. Guillermo is screaming at the witch—his face twists into its standard ugly mask of hate. "Those damn Druzhinas have their hands full now that Shashenka is dead, and you can't even take out one of them when he's alone! And on top of that, you went and attacked the one guard trying to protect you."

*Vladimir's alive.* Joy blooms inside her—she'd sink to her knees in relief if she could. A huge weight has been lifted from her soul. Then the other words the sorcerer said rebound to the front of her mind, but Elizabetta isn't sure if he was talking about the spider or Dahliorn.

The evil witch shouts back, "I told you, I don't know what happened, Uncle. I understood my mission, but my underlying hatred for that freak confused me, and everything spun out of control. It didn't matter that he was there to protect me—I wanted him dead, and I couldn't stop."

*What? Wait ... I know she attacked the spider, but did she attack Dahliorn after he sent me back?*

"Bloodlust?" Guillermo mutters under his breath, and he stares with curiosity at his niece. "Are you sure that you're not having other urges? Cravings, a desire to sleep during the day?"

Ramira shakes her head. "I have fangs—that's it. There's nothing else."

As soon as Guillermo leaves the room, Elizabetta taps into Ramira's recent memories to find the answers she needs. She's already decided to increase her training with or without Dahliorn's supervision, and now is the perfect opportunity to practice what she's learned. The first memory she taps into has a loud thrum. *Too new.* She releases it and grabs another—closer, but not back far enough. The next one shows Ramira supporting Dahliorn as they mutaport back to Guillermo's home. Blood soaks the right side of the sheridauk's shirt and jeans; his breathing is labored, almost as if a lung has collapsed. *What the hell did she do? Is it possible Vladimir caused the injury after the spider ran away with Ramira?* But Guillermo said she attacked him, and Ramira, at least, believes she did too.

Guilt bubbles inside her that she might be responsible for Ramira's actions against him. There's no denying that Elizabetta messed up, acted like an amateur instead of the professional she is. She has no desire to harm Dahliorn unless he proves he's working with the Sanchezes, though a part of her wants to blame the sheridauk; if he hadn't stopped her connection to the witch in his attempt to save the mutant spider, then she might have been able to prevent what happened next.

Elizabetta lets go of the memory and chooses another, this one just a little further back in time—it's within seconds of when the creature ran away with Ramira. But right after the moment Dahliorn put Elizabetta to sleep, the memory reaches an abrupt end. *Did he put her to sleep too? Why would he do that?* It's possible that Ramira attacked the sheridauk in a blackout or some kind of blind rage, which could be why the witch seems to have no memory of hurting him. Elizabetta goes forward and back, searching for something that will show her what happened, but there are no memories until Ramira wakes in Dahliorn's arms— and he's already injured then. Confused, Elizabetta watches the witch help him up and guide him to the mutaport in Jacques's home. The sheridauk is bleeding heavily and struggles to remain upright, even with the witch's support.

*Shit. Shinola. Where is the missing piece?* Elizabetta calls out for Dahliorn again—no answer. She's tempted to give Ramira the command to go check on him, but fear shuts down that thought faster than it formed; the unpredictable witch could black out and attack him again.

It's not until the following morning that Dahliorn steps into view as the witch descends the staircase. Relief floods Elizabetta; he's on his feet, and that means his injuries weren't as bad as she feared. He makes eye contact with Ramira and starts to walk away.

"Dahliorn, are you okay?" The way he freezes midstep suggests he's as surprised as Elizabetta is that the witch said anything remotely empathetic. *Humph, she must be more worried about herself than she's let on.*

He turns back—his eyes flash bright green as he glares up at Ramira. The witch pauses on the stairs, and a long, tense moment settles between them. Ramira is the first to look away. "Listen, freak, I already told you that I didn't mean to hurt you. I couldn't control myself."

Dahliorn turns to leave. *Well, she's unusually contrite, and he's really pissed—great combination. So conducive to what we need to do.*

«Please tell me what happened.» Elizabetta waits, hoping he'll answer her, but he just glances over his shoulder and without a word or another look back continues on his way. Several times throughout the day Elizabetta unsuccessfully tries to get a response from him. She knows he can hear her—it's clear that he's upset and ignoring her too.

After Ramira finishes her training sessions, she spends the evening with Guillermo. The sorcerer says he hasn't determined the cause of her blackout, but the news he relays rattles Elizabetta more: the leadership void in the vampire realm is ratcheting up tension, and there are reports of conflicts between and within the other realms, mostly fights over territory. Their ripple effect seems more than the Druzhina is able to contain. *Jacques was right. We are losing control.* It's just one more way she's failed the maxian council leader, and the ache in her heart intensifies, making her feel physically ill—she wants to throw up.

Guillermo tells his niece that he'll be away for a couple of weeks, but he wants her to remain there and continue honing her skills. The sorcerer grins. "I've waited so long for this opportunity. It's time to bring the humans into the game and let them play."

Ramira laughs. "Humans are so gullible and stupid."

"Yes, and their ignorance will be their downfall." Guillermo pauses. "No one from the shadow realms will be able to stop it, not with their attention diverted as it is."

*What is he up to?* Elizabetta tries to scrutinize him for a clue, but Ramira looks down and picks at a hangnail. "Are you going to unleash another plague?" the witch asks, sounding eager.

"That will depend on how well this unfolds." He nods at her. "We'll keep your focus on the vampire realm first. We need their elite fighters out of the way—send them the same message you delivered to the maxian realm. We can and will eliminate them. Once leadership falls, we'll have more opportunities against the other realms, and that is why your training is so critical. As long as the Druzhina and the coven leaders remain, we will not succeed."

*He's an absolute delusional psychopath. There's no way he can wipe out entire realms.* Then Elizabetta remembers he did exactly that to the fae, and she knows he has the patience to wait centuries for his plans to come to fruition. Determination to stop him strengthens her resolve to use Ramira against him. Once more she's unwavering—she will take action with or without Dahliorn's help.

Ramira whines, "I will do my best, uncle, but it would be better if we could figure out a way to get my powers back. This is going to get me killed."

Despite Guillermo's anger, the witch seems so resistant that Elizabetta again considers whether it's possible to communicate with Ramira—if she could somehow talk with the misguided woman, then perhaps she could tell her that Guillermo intends for her to die. She may need her assistance in taking him out.

She also needs the sheridauk to stop being a stubborn ass. It would be far less risky and messy if he'd simply reengage and do his part. «Will you please talk to me?» A few minutes pass. «Look, I know you're upset with me. I don't know why you protected that abominable creature, but you need to understand—I'll stop at nothing to protect those I love.»

The sheridauk can't or won't respond, and frustrated by his continued silence, Elizabetta collects her thoughts; she must mollify his aching-butt attitude if she wants to move forward. «I never meant to push Ramira over the edge or for you to be hurt. Guillermo's pets are the problem, and we need to eliminate them before they hurt someone else. As long as those creatures live, they will be a threat to us.»

She barely has the words out when Dahliorn's internal voice shouts back, «I will never allow you to be harmed. Did it ever occur to you that you're not Guillermo's only victim?»

*Are you freaking kidding me? Now he speaks up?* «Those things are controlled by Guillermo—they helped Ramira kill a good man. You said yourself that they're an abomination of nature. We have to take them out if we're going to win here.»

Silence is his only answer, and Elizabetta wants to strike out, rip something to shreds. «Fine, don't friggin' talk to me. I thought we were in this together, but I can see that you have your own screwed-up priorities.» She's more determined than ever to control and better manage Ramira—on her own if necessary—and to take out those mutant spiders one at a time if she has to. «I won't allow them to kill everyone I care about. You can either accept that, or you're on your own.»

There's a tinge of sadness as Dahliorn says, «I won't allow you to put yourself at risk that way. You are the peace-bringer, little dove. I will sacrifice myself for you, but I will not do so even one moment before I know that this world is free of that evil sorcerer. You may hate me and we may even become enemies because of it, but this is the way it must be.»

His comments make little sense to Elizabetta—beating her head on the wall seems more logical than the excuses he keeps coming up with. «Fine, whatever ... you do what you need to do, and I'll do what I have to. But I promise you that I will stop Guillermo and Ramira, and before this is over, those spiders will be dead.»

Elizabetta tunes back in to Ramira, who has gone from whining about how fighting without magic will kill her to shouting at her uncle that his plans stink. The sorcerer is on the verge of reaching his limit too, and when he conjures a red ball of energy, Ramira shrinks back in her seat.

"You have tested my patience enough. We will not debate this point again." Every syllable is saturated in rage. Guillermo unleashes the energy, and as it slams into a wall, he gives her one more cold look and leaves the room.

*Great. This is going so well—not.*

# Into the Storm

Two days pass before Matt is well enough to travel. Several sheridauks in beast form escort them to the veil, accompanied by Milnea and two pixies she asked the king to allow to accompany them—she insisted that one or both could be sent back to deliver messages should they need fae support. Dmitri steals a glance at the little creatures now. They appear to be male and female, with the taller of the two no more than four inches in height, and the other a good half inch shorter. If not for their tiny stature and wings, they would look human, though their exaggerated flying and gestures are anything but small—something made abundantly clear when the highly incensed pixies realized the Earthlings, as Matt quipped, couldn't hear a word they spoke. Listening devices pressed into a fold of the ear now allow Dmitri, Matt, and Maria to clearly hear the pixies' tiny voices. Since then the creatures have toned down their wild movements, but not by much; they are very animated, and Dmitri doesn't quite know how to take them.

Matt seems to have developed a rapport with the pixies right away and spends most of his time bantering with them on the hike to the veil. Dmitri isn't sure how well the little ones fit into their plans, given his group's assignment—the pixies' mischievous and playful nature doesn't quite mesh with the seriousness of what lies ahead.

When they arrive at the location of the veil, one of the sheridauks transforms into his humanoid shape to speak with Milnea before the portal is activated. He demands a drop of her blood, which she gives without hesitation. Dmitri watches with a mix of fascination and curiosity as the man says something in their language and then wipes the blood on the rock wall in front of them. A moment later he speaks the words to open the veil, and Dmitri's group steps through into the darkness on Garbh Eilean.

Milnea glances back as the veil closes, saying with a sad smile, "They added my blood to the forbidden." She seems to sense their confusion and adds, "I cannot cross back into Seelinara—the veils will not allow me to pass. Only the king can remove me from the forbidden now and grant my return."

Dmitri scowls. The fae are a complicated species that make little sense to him, but after being held in Seelinara against his will, he does understand her desire to return home. "When we find Guillermo, we will learn what has happened to your betrothed."

The male pixie, Tavorell, flies past Dmitri's ear, circles around, and lands on his other shoulder. "King Altheron wouldn't have sent you otherwise. The prince is too important, and it's best for all of us, especially you"—he drags a finger across his throat—"to find him alive."

Before Dmitri can reply, the other pixie, Liathera, hovers excitedly in front of him and gushes, "If he's the prophesied one, that will further drive the women wild. A pixie would give up her wings to be large enough to spend a night with him."

Milnea turns back and scowls at Liathera. Tavorell's wings flutter as he dashes upward and snags Liathera, seating her on Matt's shoulder with the command to stay put and be quiet. He zips through the air toward Milnea. "Ignore her, my lady. She comes without a filter and has a death wish."

As their group begins the descent to the boat, the little pixie-man explains the prophecy, and Dmitri is thankful to gain some information—though he is still displeased with the way the Seelinarans avoid most questions. "The ancient ones told of an age of great silence between Seelinara and Enethura," Tavorell says, "with an evil one born of both worlds as the cause. During this time a great prince would rise and be lost."

Liathera launches off Matt's shoulder and flies between Maria and Tavorell, batting her eyelashes as she flutters a hand over her heart. "A great, fine-looking, and swoon-worthy prince."

"Shh! I'll dust you if you can't behave, woman." Tavorell swats at her and clears his throat; his tiny voice lowers as a mask of seriousness settles on his face. "It is said that the prince's redemption lies with the peace-bringer, an Ene-thuran female who will come to suffer for a long era under the power of two realms before fate delivers her to the lost prince." Tavorell flies backward as he holds eye contact with the wizard. His tone turns ominous. "Together they will face great peril, but the bond forged between them will seal the prince's fate. If he survives, the peace-bringer will return him to Seelinara, where she will gain the king's favor. This will give rise to a new alliance, a true peace between our world and yours—one that will last for all time."

Before Dmitri can ask a question, Milnea says, "We have reason to believe that Guillermo is the one born between worlds. The prince has been missing for what is likely centuries on Enethura. If he is the one prophesied, we will find him alive, and the peace-bringer will be with him— ready to deliver him back to us."

Matt whistles. "What if he's dead?"

The elemental drops her gaze to the ground. "It will mean the time is not now."

They reach the boat, and Dmitri steers them toward the cavern's entrance. If Guillermo is this evil one and the fae prophecy is true, is it possible that Elizabetta is the peace-bringer? His wife certainly suffered under magic and at Shashenka's hands for centuries. *How will we know for sure?* The idea isn't a welcome one—all Dmitri wants is a quiet life with Elizabetta. He'd even give up being a Druzhina if it meant they could live the rest of their unnaturally long lives in peace.

Maria opens the access to the cave, and they dock the boat at the stone pier, debating where to go next. Maria and Matt lean toward Paris and the maxian council; they reason it's best to keep the council informed in case their help is needed to find Elizabetta, end Guillermo, and free Alastrina. Dmitri wants to use the redecrystapiezo to contact Vladimir instead. His instinct is to gather information about what has happened in their absence and finally start the search for his wife. The Druzhina should have those details, but the maxians may not. On the other hand, he doesn't relish revealing their lie, and there's no other way to explain the sorceress's disappearance and the presence of the three Seelinarans.

Then there's the added problem that they may have to answer for either an all too brief or an extended absence; none of them know how much time has passed here on Earth. In Seelinara, Milnea explained, time is controlled by the Seelie and Unseelie royal timekeepers, who can speed it up or slow it down depending on the needs and whims of Seelinara's kings and queens. Hours, weeks, or months may have passed on Earth since they walked through the veil, and the possibility that Elizabetta has been in Guillermo's clutches for months leaves Dmitri with a sick ache inside.

Milnea and the two pixies offer no opinion, leaving it up to Dmitri to decide which way they will go. With great reluctance he concedes to the logic his friends have laid out—they will go to Paris.

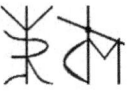

The catacombs are empty when they arrive. Maria follows the instructions Alastrina gave her and steps onto the raised platform in front of the dais. She gives her friends one more look and draws a deep breath, and Dmitri recalls the way she addressed this same council and helped him and

Elizabetta gain the support they needed to end Shashenka's tyrannical reign. "Supreme council, hear me now in my time of need. Answer my call and hear my plea."

A few moments pass and nothing happens, but then they see a few robed council members enter from the hidden doorway behind the dais. Dmitri scans for Jacques, but the warlock isn't among them. A white-haired woman in long, flowing robes steps forward. "Why do you summon us in this time of grief, wizard?"

*Time of grief?* Dmitri searches the somber faces of the council members. A sense of foreboding blankets him in suffocating layers of denial.

Maria clears her throat. "We have just returned from Seelinara and bring news of your fellow council member, Alastrina Anirtsala. She is being held by Altheron, the Unseelie king. We came to seek your assistance in finding a lost fae, the king's son. We must either return word of his fate or return this prince alive to secure the release of Alastrina."

The council members lose their decorum, with several voices raised at once, and the white-haired woman raps her wand on the sphere. "For the record, I am acting High Witch Josephina O'Mordha. You may not be aware, but High Warlock Jacques Boucher was murdered a fortnight ago."

Dmitri feels a chill claim his body, his mouth going dry. The consequences of losing Jacques are dire: they may fail at keeping order, which in turn could unleash Dmitri's bloodlust. His mind races through his final words to the warlock, and his promise to try to maintain control. Time just became a bigger enemy than it was before. *If he died two weeks ago ... how much time has passed?* Dmitri's eyes narrow as he steps forward. "What happened? What's today's date?"

"October seventeenth."

Dmitri staggers back as if she punched him—four months have passed. *Have they even helped search for Elizabetta?*

Sadness radiates from High Witch O'Mordha's gaze. "Something we suspect is an unearthly creature attacked and killed the high warlock in the garden of his home. His body bore the puncture marks of something not natural to this world, and his head was missing when he was found."

A lump catches in Dmitri's throat. "What kind of punctures?"

"Large, very large. That is all we know. One of your Druzhinas happened upon the carnage while the murderer was still there. He was similarly assaulted, but his report claims that he was attacked by a spider."

"A spider?"

"Yes, according to Vladimir Jagr, he was attacked by an arachnid of size and proportion not seen before or known to be possible."

*Did someone cast a spell that resulted in hallucinations?* He looks back at Milnea. "What is the prince? Is he a sheridauk like his father?"

Milnea nods, then shakes her head. "Yes, but we have no fae with arachnid traits."

High Witch O'Mordha clears her throat. "You should also know, Mr. Markov, that the power vacuum we warned you about is happening. In your poorly timed absence, disputes have risen—not only between realms but within the maxian, werewolf, and vampire realms themselves. We have heard rumors that human governments are shifting their allegiances, and there is talk of war. Rogue maxians are killing our own without mercy, and many of us are withdrawing to our inner sanctums to protect ourselves."

*We were only gone four months. How have things become this bad this quickly?* Dmitri's hand swipes twice through his hair as he considers the high witch's words. "Is Guillermo responsible?"

"This we do not know." Josephina draws a breath. "The council withheld a vote to select a new leader pending Alastrina's return. We will need to confer on how best to proceed in light of Alastrina's capture, Miss D'Arcy's request, and the current circumstances surrounding the shadow realms."

The witch begins to turn away, and Dmitri blurts out, "I must find my wife—she may be the key in resolving all this. The fae believe their missing prince may be with a foretold peace-bringer, and my wife—"

Josephina's scowl as she looks back pins Dmitri to the spot. "Legends and prophecies from Seelinara are the least of our concerns! I recommend that you return to your people and regain control. Stop this upheaval before it dooms us all."

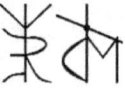

A few days later Dmitri's group gathers with the Druzhinas at the villa in Venice, where Vladimir set up their base of operations while awaiting Dmitri's return. The other Druzhinas seem unhappy with his deception but somewhat understanding of the circumstances, though it may take him a while to fully regain their trust. Their reception of Matt is far more favorable—the mongrel has endeared himself to them and earned their respect. The Seelinarans they greet with an assortment of skepticism and curiosity.

All are given the means to hear the pixies, and as the others are occupied talking to them, Vladimir pulls Dmitri off to the side. "I wanted to make sure you got this." For a moment his gaze holds Dmitri's, then he pulls a horse-head dagger out from behind his back. "The woman who attacked me at Jacques's home dropped it during the scuffle. The spider ran off with her before she could pick it up."

A lump forms in Dmitri's throat as he stares at the weapon. *How did she get Elizabetta's dagger?* He clutches it as if Elizabetta will lose her life if he doesn't hold it tightly. "Who is the woman, and where is she now?"

Vladimir shakes his head and shrugs. "She is unknown to us and appears to be nothing more than human."

*A human?* "But she was with this supposed spider?"

"If I hadn't encountered it myself, I would be skeptical too. We think Guillermo likely created it, even if the maxian council refuses to consider that possibility."

Dmitri suppresses a shudder. While giant spiders roaming their world may be unnerving, the idea of Elizabetta disarmed is more worrisome still. He can't allow the thought that she might already be dead.

The men join their comrades, who are already seated around a long table in a cubiculum off the primary piano nobile. The first order of business is a full briefing—and it quickly becomes clear that the Druzhinas' reports will not be good.

Vladimir says, "Many were unhappy with the drawing that assigned new owners to the remainder of the Belyakov estates. The conflicts started soon afterward. Smaller vampire covens and werewolf packs have been attacking the compounds in an attempt to seize them for themselves."

"Are those disputes still occurring?" Dmitri looks across at Matt—they don't have time for this. The resolve in the wolf's eyes tells him they're in silent agreement.

Stephan suggests they hold their questions until the end of the briefing. "As Vlad said, it started there, but it has only escalated since. Factions are forming—some are composed solely of vampires or werewolves, but there are a few that contain both species." He takes a breath, then describes the major territorial disputes around the world, which are so out of control that they risk human realm exposure. Most disturbing to Dmitri is the news that a few coven masters have attempted to gain control of smaller covens, seeking leadership of the vampire realm. *Over my dead, rotting corpse—we will never allow another Shashenka.*

The Druzhina, with the help of a few loyal Druzhinnikis, has spent most of the past few months going from one hot spot to the next to quell the unrest, engaging in fights where necessary to end a dispute. Stephan chuckles. "To suggest that we are not popular at this time is an understatement."

While at first the maxians tried to assist, Alexander tells them, they withdrew their help as the situation deteriorated—leaving the Druzhina no way to cover up the conflict within the shadow realms. Given the global nature of vampire interests, the tension among human nations has risen too, and there's been a flurry of meetings at the UN and NATO as rumors of global anarchy spread. "Lines are being drawn, dear brothers and sisters." A sneer curls Alexander's lips. "Alliances between countries are weakening. Monetary systems are threatening collapse, and all-out war is inevitable. The Americans blame the Eastern bloc countries, while those countries blame the West. South America, the Middle East, and China fault both sides and see it as their opportunity to rise as the dominant ruling powers." His somber tone casts its own gravity to his words.

*They haven't had time to give Elizabetta a single thought.* Dmitri looks around the table at each of his friends before his gaze locks on Matt—they have no choice but to do something to calm the global crises, or they may lose all chances of ever finding Elizabetta.

A growl rumbles from Matt's chest. "You need to stop putting out fires and set a back burn. While I appreciate the mess we're in, Eliza is my priority. I'm not willing to lose any more time in starting the search for her. I'll help you vamps when I can, but you need to find a leader for your realm and regain control."

Dmitri narrows his eyes at the mongrel, suspecting but not liking where this is going. *I doubt vampiric leadership is going to solve all our problems. We need to find Guillermo.* The mongrel obviously didn't fully interpret Dmitri's look—they are getting better at reading each other, but Matt fell short this time.

"Why don't you vamps do what we do when it comes to leadership?" Matt shrugs. "Come on, you aren't that dense. Arrange a fight for leadership."

*He went there.* Dmitri wants to throw his hands up in the air.

"A fight?" Victoria scowls. "That's part of the problem now—everyone is fighting."

"No, everyone is trying to kill each other because they won't respect anyone else's claims. Put out a call for all wannabe leaders and make them sign a treaty that says they'll respect and honor the outcome." Matt raises an eyebrow at Dmitri. "There is a dominant alpha among you bloodsuckers, even if you don't realize it or want to admit it."

Kees nods. "The wolf is right. Once a leader emerges and is able to command the control needed to get our realm in order, they can reach out to the werewolves and regain maxian support to bring stability across the other realms."

"I'll check with my contacts and get the search started. If you vamps can pull this off before we leave, then it will make our search easier." Matt takes out his phone to make the first call, but first he flashes Dmitri a lopsided grin. "I told you before, there's a right way to do this—we can't go off half-cocked here. I found her last time, and we will find her again."

*How many more hurdles will fate erect before we are reunited and can go on with our lives?* Matt's steady reassurances help, but Dmitri knows he's reached his limit for patience with the delays. He abruptly pushes away from the table, saying as he walks out, "Do what you need to. I just want to find my wife."

# CHAPTER 18: ELIZABETTA

# Setbacks

The two weeks that Guillermo is away pass slowly for Elizabetta. There's been little communication from Dahliorn—it pains her to accept that the rift between her and the only friend she has in this place may be permanent. She tries to focus on Ramira, hoping to teach herself how to take control of the witch. Or to bring her to their side— every now and then Elizabetta glimpses an act or thought that indicates the witch might turn against her uncle if there were some way to tell her what he's done to her. She won't go so far as to say it's a redeeming quality, but it's a shred of hope worth exploiting.

After discovering that three strands in close proximity to one another seem to have access to all other strands on both sides of Ramira's body and mind, Elizabetta mentally re-designs the virtual room in the witch's head, creating a console that puts the three strands at her imaginary finger-tips. She quickly learns that the configuration allows her to tunnel through them to manipulate all the energy strands in Ramira's brain. *No more running around to hunt down one strand at a time—I like it.*

Armed with her new knowledge, Elizabetta practices at different times throughout the day and night, noting patterns and responses. She creates muscle spasms, changes Ramira's posture, and even assists her in making correct Shaolinquan-style moves during her training sessions with Michio—it builds Elizabetta's confidence when the witch doesn't seem to notice that none of it is originating with her own body or mind.

One indulgence that Elizabetta allows is planting the suggestion for Ramira to go out and watch the sun rise each morning. The centuries she's spent in nights of shadow ended her enjoyment of the sun because of its harmful effects. Now, watching the sun break over the horizon and feeling its warm rays through Ramira is an indescribable joy.

The night Guillermo returns, he calls both Ramira and Dahliorn into his study to gloat over his success; his moles are in place and already pulling strings to manipulate the outcome in his favor. "The maxians are retreating," Guillermo says, laughing, "with my rogues picking them off one by one. The vampires and werewolves are at each other's throats and destroying their own kind as well as their enemies. The time is near for you to get revenge against the Druzhina for murdering your parents, Ramira."

*You lying jackwagon. Look at him, Ramira—he killed them himself.* There's no reaction from the clueless witch, and Elizabetta can almost feel the anger radiating through her insubstantial body. She needs to learn how to communicate with the witch directly. She could really use Dahliorn's help, but the sheridauk keeps his eyes averted from Ramira and ignores Elizabetta's attempts to draw him into conversation.

"What's our next step, Uncle?" the witch says.

Guillermo strokes his chin. "There's word that the Druzhinas are on the trail of the rogue vampire who betrayed them. We are going to use that to lure them to you. When they separate to box her in, you will attack and kill one of them."

*Not going to happen.* Elizabetta notices Dahliorn raise a hard gaze to Ramira; obviously he knows what Elizabetta's thinking. If she could glare back at him through the witch's eyes, she would.

Ramira says, "How soon will you send us?"

"Within the week if possible." Guillermo gives Dahliorn a stern look. "You are only to protect her if her life is in the balance. She may need to be hurt to learn how to fight against these vampires. I can heal whatever damage they inflict."

Ramira swallows hard, and even Elizabetta feels the chill that races through her. *Advantage me.* The witch doesn't fight anywhere near well enough to survive against a Druzhina, and Dahliorn may not be able to interfere soon enough to save her scrawny butt this time. As long as Guillermo's pet is left behind, Elizabetta may succeed at stopping the witch—the mutant is the only thing working in Ramira's favor.

The next few nights pass, and despite Guillermo's scheme to lure the Druzhinas into his trap, which should force Dahliorn to acknowledge Elizabetta, the sheridauk steadfastly avoids talking with her. She wants to give him updates, but since he keeps ignoring her, she doesn't tell him about her progress. She's made near daily advances in what she can do regardless of whether the woman is asleep or awake. Elizabetta has even learned how to open Ramira's eyes when she's sleeping—without triggering a conscious state—and one night she decides to test how far she can go with it.

Once Ramira has entered a deep sleep, Elizabetta orients her illusory body to the virtual console and activates a series of commands. First the witch's eyes open, and then she sits up and looks toward the bedroom door. *Let's take a little stroll.* The guard in the corner rises from his chair when Ramira stands and walks to the door, but the witch's sleeping ears don't hear him ask where she's going. Elizabetta guides her past him and into the hallway. Ramira's movements are jerky and lurching, but Elizabetta is elated; she's actually making the witch do what she wants.

When they reach the staircase, Elizabetta orders a hand to grab the banister rail and forces Ramira to take the first step—the witch wobbles, so she waits a moment for Ramira to steady, then compels the woman to step down again. This time Ramira loses her balance completely. *Shit! Son of a bitch!* Elizabetta sends desperate commands to the witch, trying to arrest her fall, but only makes the situation worse. Ramira's body pitches sideways and bounces off the wall, slamming her onto the stairs and down to the foyer below. *Ooh, ow, ugh ... damn it. Uh-oh, that's going to leave a mark.*

When Ramira's body comes to a stop at the bottom of the staircase, the guard is already shouting for Guillermo. Ramira moans and tries to open her eyes, but they slam shut as she fights to stay conscious. Elizabetta curses herself—stairs were obviously a poor choice for a first attempt. *That was totally brainless ... way to go, Elizabetta!*

Footsteps approach, and agitation and concern ring out in Guillermo's voice. "What happened?"

"I don't know," the guard says. "She got up, walked out of her room, and fell. I tried to catch her but wasn't fast enough." The guard adds, "I think she was sleepwalking."

The sorcerer orders the man to carry her back to her room as he questions him further about the strange way Ramira was moving and whether she responded when he spoke to her. When Guillermo asks if she's been having more nightmares, the guard affirms she has. "She'll need a mending spell after I assess the extent of her injuries," the sorcerer says, but before he dismisses the guard he orders him to send Dahliorn up. "He should be in his room."

A few minutes later Elizabetta hears the sheridauk's soft, familiar gait as he enters the room. Guillermo's voice carries a hint of urgency now. "Take a listening stone and go down to that vampire's cell. I want her watched for any signs of consciousness or movement."

Dahliorn sounds hesitant as he says, "What is going on?"

"I don't know, but Ramira took a bad fall down the staircase." Elizabetta can't ignore the suspicion lurking in the sorcerer's words—she doesn't know if this screw-up is going to reach back and bite her hard this time. "Her guard said she seemed to be sleepwalking, but I need to make sure it's not another complication of the unity spell. I'm wondering if whatever went wrong simply stalled its completion."

«Rest, little dove—I will see you in a few minutes.»

When Elizabetta opens her eyes and stands up to stretch, the pain throughout her body tells her that she did indeed suffer the same injuries as the witch. *Great, just what I need—bumps of knowledge.* She'd rather remain in Ramira to keep an eye on the sorcerer, but she hasn't discovered how to stop Dahliorn's ability to transfer her between the witch and her own body. It's just one more thing she'll need to figure out, and when she does, he'll have to accept that he's not controlling her anymore. *This situation is really getting—*

She startles when the sheridauk disrupts her thoughts. «Do not move or speak aloud when I enter the room. Listening stones are very sensitive and will pick up every sound. You need to lie down and keep your eyes closed to stay relaxed. I don't want to put you to sleep—we must talk.» Dahliorn's command is firm—she knows he won't hesitate to render her unconscious. But they are beyond overdue for a discussion, and she'll play nice to avoid being silenced.

The door opens. Elizabetta hears him step inside the room, moving near the wall opposite her cot; the rustle of his clothing suggests he's sitting on the floor. Unwilling to provoke him by saying something that will upset him, she waits for him to speak first.

«Elizabetta, what did you do?» It's the first time Dahliorn has addressed her by name, but the way he says it drips disappointment.

«I've been learning and practicing on my own since you refuse to help me.» It's true, even if she sounds petulant like Ramira; if he hadn't stopped coaching her, she might not have made the mistake she did. «I just wanted to take her for a little stroll around the house to test my ability to control her.»

Rage filters through his words. «It could have killed you both. Is that what you want? Do you want to die? Do you think your death will stop Guillermo?»

«I'm doing what I can to protect my friends and defeat that son of a bitch!»

Silence settles between them, and Elizabetta inwardly sighs, reminding herself not to fight with him. They can't resolve their issues with Dahliorn glaring at her—she can feel the scorching heat of his eyes on her. «What does Guillermo think he'll learn with you watching me?»

«If you are unconscious and without movement, then he will assume that you're still isolated by the unity spell. Awareness on your part could lead him to discover our deception and make another attempt at the spell. A second cast would bind you permanently—I could not protect you, and you'd never be separated from Ramira again.»

*This just keeps getting better and better.* Elizabetta ponders that for a moment. «You said earlier that if they learned I was in her, she'd take control of me. Am I strong enough to prevent it now, with everything I've learned?»

A sigh comes through their link as she hears Dahliorn move—doubtless the cement floor is uncomfortable to sit on. «No. She was meant to be the host, and once they're past the barrier, the connection will ensure the host has priority and maintains primary control. Guillermo will help her strip your knowledge and memories and make them her own. You won't be able to stop her or get them back.»

«Damn it, Dahliorn. I wish you would have told me this before. I—»

«You wouldn't listen! I've been warning you, but you are willful and headstrong. Your foolish experiment could have destroyed you and our only chance at freedom.»

The impact of the risk she took buries her under ten tons of guilt and shame. If the sheridauk does have her best interests in mind—if he is trying to help her bring down Guillermo—then she has no choice but to set it right between them again, or she may be their undoing. «I'm sorry. I screwed up, but you have to understand this is very unnatural for me, being trapped like this. I just want to put an end to it and get back to my life, my husband. I'll do whatever I have to do to escape.»

Anger again surges in Dahliorn's words. «There is no escape from this. The unity spell will not be broken until Guillermo is dead.»

Dahliorn goes quiet, and the minutes further erode Elizabetta's resolve to do this without him—she lacks true understanding of the magic used against her and the danger it presents. *I need his help.* «Please forgive me. I was wrong to take risks and discount your advice. You must continue to explain the things I don't know or understand so we can make it out of here.»

«Sometimes, little dove, it is best not to know everything.»

*You mean like why it's important for you to keep those hideous spiders alive?* Elizabetta has to restrain herself from groaning in frustration—she wants to jerk Dahliorn to his feet and demand he tell her what he is hiding. «So where does that leave us? How are we supposed to work together to accomplish our goals if either of us withholds information the other needs?»

It's Dahliorn's turn to show frustration. «I need you to trust that I will do the right thing. I will keep you alive, and we will succeed. We can work together, but first you must stop worrying about spiders and start listening to what I'm telling you.»

«God, this is driving me insane.» Elizabetta takes a surreptitious deep breath to calm herself. «Fine, you win on this: I won't bring up the spiders again. But mark my words, when this is over I will make sure that Guillermo's abominations of nature are destroyed.»

«I think you should sleep now, little dove.»

«No! Don't.» When Dahliorn doesn't utter the command, Elizabetta says, «The world is never going to be safe, or us free, unless we take Guillermo out. I can't wait around forever.»

«It's that type of hubris that will get you killed, and it is the same mistake I made.»

*What makes him think I'll make the same mistake?*

To her surprise, Dahliorn admits his own capture was due to his arrogance and foolish pride. He was already the Unseelie king's best soldier when fae infected with the plague began returning to Seelinara with stories of a sor-

cerer trying to wipe out the inhabitants of Earth. As more
and more fae became ill and died, Dahliorn begged for the
chance to prove himself—to end the one who created the
plague. But in his haste to vanquish the nefarious sorcerer,
he didn't take time to think or plan ahead. Dahliorn was so
certain that face to face, his fae magic would far surpass
Guillermo's, he never considered the sorcerer wouldn't fight
him straight on. A rueful chuckle comes through their link.
«I thought that I had succeeded in pushing him into a
corner where he'd have to fight me. It was a trap, and I
walked right into it.»

Elizabetta's eyebrows draw down—she remembers how
well the sorcerer laid the trap that resulted in Dmitri's
capture and return to Shashenka. He narrowly avoided
being executed before they ended their master's life at
Machu Picchu. As for Elizabetta, Guillermo has already
wounded her twice—the beating in Mettlach and the staff
run through her when he abducted her from the battlefield
in Peru. «How did it happen?»

«There are two substances that are tightly guarded on
Seelinara—salt and iron, or rather the rust from iron. The
first burns on contact, and the second acts as poison and can
debilitate a fae by turning their own magic against them—
the latter can be lethal.» Dahliorn explains that it is their
close connection to angels and demons that is responsible—
the benevolent and malevolent spirits form the very essence
of light and dark fae. «Our species long ago began mating
with those from otherworldly realms. Angels and demons
reside among us, or rather they did before the plague.»

Elizabetta detects sorrow, pride, and even a measure of

homesickness in the cadence of his words. Doubtless these memories are more poignant for him since there's likely no one left alive to return to. *If he ever gets the chance to go home.*

«Salt was the Creator's gift to the lesser species—a way for them to ward off those whose spirits might cause them harm. Salt, however, does not make a distinction between good and evil. It burns all alike. We fae also burn upon contact with salt because of the angelic or demonic DNA infused into our cells.»

A few moments pass in silence. Shame coats Dahliorn's words as he finally reveals his failures. «I did not push Guillermo anywhere he didn't want to be. When I followed him inside a cottage, salt rained down upon me, burning me. An open path in the salt led to a door, and I went through it. Too late I realized the room was lined with rusted iron walls and floor. I fell within seconds, and Guillermo placed a silver belt, charmed with fae and maxian spells, around my waist before he removed me from the room.»

The sheridauk claims the silver belt, with its wards restricting and blocking his magic and strength, ensured he'd remain too weak to ever fight back. He's been under the device's control for a little more than six centuries, so long that he's forgotten what it feels like not to wear it.

Learning this detail triggers her excitement when she realizes it's a common tactic, and forgetting her earlier pledge, Elizabetta blurts out, «He uses a similar belt on the spiders. It must be his preferred method of control.» Then she realizes that she violated her promise not to mention the creatures. *Way to go. Keep screwing up, and you'll never get out of here.*

«The belt gives Guillermo much more than mere control.» She hears Dahliorn stand and walk toward the door. «He summons me. Sleep now, little dove.»

## CHAPTER 19: DMITRI

# Issues to Settle

The early returns from Matt's contacts produce no leads, and Dmitri growls as he fights another flood of the darkness pulsing through him. Most everyone is focused on the leadership contest. Dmitri has no patience for it regardless of its necessity, but until they have a starting point for finding Elizabetta, there is little else to occupy his thoughts. Admittedly, keeping his mind busy helps subdue the bloodlust that has become a constant dark companion, but one way or another he will start his own search for his wife—he must. *We have to find her before it's too late.*

"Matt, have your people start looking for Milo too. We have to locate that worm, or we're never going to find her."

The wolf cocks an eyebrow. "They'll do what they can, but—"

"I don't want to hear it until there's something to report."

"Fine, be an ass." When Dmitri only glares, Matt says, "You need to know this isn't that dissimilar to when you vamps took Eliza from Montana. It took a couple of months before I collected enough information to start snooping around the Belyakov estates."

"Damn it, Matt, we've already lost four months and can't afford to wait. That sorcerer may kill Elizabetta, if she's not dead already."

Those last four words seem to throw a switch, and Matt goes from his no-bullshit attitude to brother-friend mode. He approaches and places a hand over Dmitri's heart, his other hand covering his own chest. "She's not dead—we'd feel it here, and I think you know that. We need to stay busy, make the most of our time until we can go after her."

The mongrel has a point; mate and loyalty bonds create a connection that is physically felt by those who hold them. Dmitri rakes his hand through his hair, fighting the anger boiling under the surface. "You're right. Just ... push your people a little harder. Milo is out there somewhere."

Vladimir offers to do what he can. "I'll call Janek and get his people on this too. We will find Elizabetta, but I need you to stay in control."

"I'll keep him from going off the deep end, and witchy-poo will do what she does to make sure of that." Matt winks at the wizard.

Dmitri ignores their laughter. His muscles twitch with the need to retreat to his quarters, be alone to calm down, but they adamantly refuse to leave him unattended. He sighs. They know what he's battling, and no one will give him the opportunity to go on the rampage. Even Matt sleeps in the suite to keep an eye on him during the day. Dmitri has no humor for the situation and glares at the wolf now. "The maxian council needs to make a decision and start helping us. Maria, will you contact them and find out what the holdup is?"

The wizard steps away a few feet to make the call as Tavorell, Liathera, and Milnea enter the room with Sally. Dmitri's focus on finding Elizabetta and the aftermath of Machu Picchu hasn't allowed him time to engage his old friend in conversation, but Sally has been busy too. The master chambers of La Perfezione, where they are gathered now, have been redecorated—a project she took charge of while they were in Seelinara. Apparently she arrived from Xi'an within days of Shashenka's demise and made herself at home.

Now Sally smiles as she strides toward him and wraps him in a hug. "It's good to see you. I've heard you're having a rough time."

His teeth clench and he trembles, unable to force words to his tongue—he feels talked out for the night—but he know Sally is not to blame and allows her to lead him to the divan. She smiles up at him with the same warmth and friendship she has always shown him. "First, I want to thank you for freeing me. Second, I have chosen my room here, and you're stuck with me for-ev-er." She flashes a mischievous grin.

*The neighborhood menace, her threat.* Dmitri tries to smile and fails. "I'm glad you're settled in, but we didn't decide whether to have a coven yet."

"No, but you will ... and I'm already here. You're going to have to deal with it."

"Sally, I'm sorry, but I'm not fit company right now."

Dmitri gives her the best apologetic look he can under the circumstances. *She's just trying to lift my spirits.*

She snorts with laughter. "Oh, hey, like that is something new." She places a hand on his cheek. "I heard about what happened at Machu Picchu, the way you and Elizabetta fought together."

The reminder isn't helping—he feels another surge in the bloodlust coiled under the surface. Sally pats his hand, which is squeezing hers to the point of obvious pain. "Calm down, we're going to get her back," she says. "And when you and the mongrel go to continue your search, I'd like to go with you. You freed me—I want to do what I can to help."

Dmitri closes his eyes as he pushes against the rage inside. *Not her fault, any of it.* "You're no match for what we may encounter. I think it's best that you stay here."

"That's bullpucky, Dmitri. I may not be as skilled as a Druzhina, but I didn't survive the inner lair as long as I did by being stupid or weak."

*I can't trust myself right now, and I don't want to hurt you.*

Mistaking his silence for assent, she says, "Then that settles it—I'm going." Sally grins at Matt and Maria. "When do we leave?"

Dmitri tries to dissuade the blond vampire, but she doesn't relent, and soon Matt is chuckling—and when Dmitri glares at him, the wolf's lopsided grin grows larger. "Looks to me as if she does a great job of keeping you distracted. What do you think, Maria? I say we should bring her along."

Dmitri rises to his feet. "Don't encourage—"

"Matt has a point. I think it's a great idea." Maria flashes a devilish smile, and Sally jumps up, bouncing on her feet, and giggles.

"Yep, it's settled, and I'm going." She stands on her tiptoes and pecks a kiss on Dmitri's cheek.

He growls and grumbles under his breath but finally agrees. *At this rate I'll never be able to give them the slip and go look for Elizabetta myself.* He has to earn their trust, show he's under control, and pretend to follow their agenda. Then an idea sparks, and he redirects the conversation back to the leadership contest.

Most agree that the volatility of the current situation won't allow the Druzhina the luxury of taking full control of the vampire realm themselves—but neither do they want another to rise like Shashenka did and bring them right back to a despotic ruler leading their realm. At the same time it'd be foolish for the Druzhina to relinquish all control or set up a human-style government that won't work for vampires given their nature. They could put themselves at risk if others band against them and call for their removal or demise.

Dmitri understands the necessity for the Druzhina to remain the steady force within their realm, but the debate rages on far longer than he has patience for. He cringes at what they come up with—a hybrid system of government that is a blend of Native American confederacy, American democracy, and British monarchy. The contest will bestow the titles of King and Queen, allowing for mates to rule together. It's not the latter idea—he agrees mates can be effective as a team—it's the use of a royal title that he feels is pretentious and unwarranted at best. At worst, he fears the new ruler will attempt to gain more power or even throw off this new vampiric government they are creating. *President, Chancellor, Prime Minister ... even Supreme Leader is a far better choice for us.*

A notice detailing the tournament rules and the new government system is soon drafted, setting a date two weeks away. The contest will use a bracket system to give each fighter a chance to advance or be defeated; elimination will produce the one vampire with the strength to command respect and lead their realm. There's a clause that establishes the opportunity for their leader to be challenged once a decade should he or she fail to rule in a just and honorable manner. Another clause ties the Druzhina to the ruler as governing council and advisors and states that their unanimous objection can overrule and nullify a decree made by the king or queen.

Even with those concessions, the Druzhinas seem hell-bent on having one of their own in the contest. Anna, for whatever reason, is spearheading the ridiculous idea. "Our reputation and history most already respect," she says. "And it will give us an opportunity to have someone in the fight who can eliminate less desirable prospects." It's not the first time Anna has made this point; in fact, they've been over this a few times now.

Dmitri tries to argue against it yet again. *They're doing this deliberately to keep me from searching for Elizabetta. It's one excuse after another. None of them would be this patient if it were their mate.* What bothers him is that

Vladimir wants a consensus, a vote, rather than allowing one of their rank to do it voluntarily. Dmitri wants no part of the contest, whether spectator, officiant, or participant—it will only serve to unleash his bloodlust against undeserving victims. Plus he has no desire to lead, and given his current state, it's unlikely he'd lose. He just wants to be left in peace and have a chance to live a quiet life if and when they ever allow him to rescue Elizabetta. But once again the argument is going nowhere—Dmitri is the sole holdout on the point—and he capitulates just to end the discussion.

The Druzhinas agree to an immediate blind ballot and prepare to cast their votes. After taking a deep breath, Dmitri jots down Vladimir's name and folds the page before he tosses it to the center of the table with the other nominations. He's confident that Vladimir is the logical choice, based on the years he led the Druzhina during Dmitri's absence, and he is the one best suited to rule should it become necessary for a Druzhina to win the competition. If the others are being honest with themselves, Dmitri believes, they will choose Vladimir too.

When all the votes are cast, Matt scoops them toward himself and calls out the first name: "Vladimir." Dmitri smiles as Sally writes it down. It bodes well that others seemingly feel the same about Vladimir, and for the first time since the whole contest nonsense began, Dmitri relaxes. His smile fades as Matt continues to read the names. Vladimir garners just one vote—Dmitri's. The other eight are for him.

Seething doesn't come near describing what's boiling in

his veins. *They deliberately set me up ... damn every single one of them!* He glares at those seated around the table. Fury and incredulity strangle every syllable as he says, "I don't want this ... I don't want to rule anything."

The determined and unrelenting looks on their faces tells him they're not going to back down. They are ignoring his instability, the danger he poses to others. His much-needed search for Elizabetta aside, the truth is that he's not only unfit to lead, but he might kill someone. *This is bullshit.* Dmitri tries to argue, and one after another his friends push back, a united front against him. He thrusts his hands through his hair, fighting the urge to crush his skull.

Anger rises. *I'm losing my grip, and I mustn't allow that to happen.*

The Druzhinas return three days ahead of the leadership contest, giving them just enough time to test the fight barriers. But before they begin, they meet to report on their missions. Most of them went as a group to locations near the former Belyakov estates, areas in the direst need of intervention to stop the bloodshed between vampires, were-wolves, or both. Their efforts met with marginal success—vampire covens are too eager to grab power to be easily quelled at this time—but Kees remains confident this issue will resolve itself once a new leader is chosen. Dmitri trusts Kees's assessment but doesn't share his optimism that a new leader is the magic cure-all for the problems in their realm.

Justin and Alexander were searching for Teresina and

Milo, but their update also indicates minimal progress. Justin claims that the rogue is constantly on the move, never staying in one location longer than twenty-four hours. He and Alexander try to convince Dmitri that they're closing in on Teresina and have noticed a pattern to her movements; they anticipate that after a king or queen is chosen, the Druzhina can command more resources to bring an end to Teresina's running. *Which brings us full circle— the contest again.* He doesn't doubt Justin's desire to find her—if they are destined to be mates, then Justin is driven by the same compulsion he feels to find Elizabetta—but he does question the progress. Milo is another matter, and neither the Druzhinas nor Matt's people have a single lead. Wherever he's hiding, he is staying put and out of sight— another issue they believe will resolve after the tournament.

*That event is going to put me over the edge. The sooner they get this done, the sooner they run out of excuses to keep me from searching for Elizabetta.* Dmitri sweeps his hand through his hair twice, pausing at the crown of his head before allowing the bangs to fall once more into his eyes. "During your absence thirteen vampires signed up to compete. We need to test and adjust the fight barriers."

Those who stayed behind at La Perfezione have already cleared the ballroom and piano nobiles of their furnishings, and Maria has conjured bleachers along the walls for the spectators. The plan is to allow Milnea to create the fighting cages with her elemental magic; she will manipulate air and water into clear, impenetrable structures. But she needs to find the right mixture of air and water to maintain each shield's integrity, and now that there are enough vampires present, all the barriers may be tested at once after an initial test of one barrier so that there's no risk of any fight spilling into the watching crowd.

Matt, unsurprisingly, volunteers to go first. He starts bouncing on the balls of his feet while throwing punches at an opponent that doesn't exist. Then the wolf says in an exaggerated tone that sprays saliva with each *pah* sound, "Put 'em up ... come on, put 'em up. I'll whup ya with two paws and my tail tied behind my back."

The mongrel's exuberant mood doesn't lessen Dmitri's annoyance with the situation. "I don't think we need to add to the ridiculousness of this spectacle." He folds his arms across his chest. *I'd like to lock all of you in a cage and get the hell out of here.*

Matt shakes his head and laughs. "I told your wife once that you were like a wet towel. You're living up to that, you know?"

Dmitri clenches his jaw shut and marches back across the room as a sudden tremor ripples through him. "Fine! Let's get this done."

He climbs the bleachers to sit and watch. Milnea asks Matt to stand in the center of where one ring will be located. The wolf crooks an eyebrow but complies as her soft, musical voice casts the spell in her native language. A circular shape shimmers and solidifies into a clear barrier around him.

The crazy mongrel spends the next few minutes beating against and punching the barrier and throwing his body into it. Then he says, "Turn around, ladies, or you'll see me in all my glory."

Several of the women are quick to look elsewhere, but Maria hesitates as her cheeks flush in embarrassment. She turns away, while Milnea remains facing forward. Matt strips out of his clothes and shifts into his wolf form. Liathera lets out an appreciative whistle and claps her hands, and Tavorell mutters, "Nymph blood must be in her family somewhere."

Matt gives the pixies a one-sided wolfish grin before he begins leaping, ramming, clawing, and biting at the barrier again. After circling it a few times, he moves to the center and sits on his haunches, yips, and then howls. His wolf snout pulls into another grin, his tongue hanging out the side.

The pixies laugh at him, and Milnea releases the barrier. Maria says, "It's still not a padded dog house, but it has potential."

When their laughter dies down, Dmitri, further agitated, joins the others who are pairing for the full-on test of all the barriers. The Druzhinas who are paired will spar during the test, but those caged alone will have to do their best to attack the barrier itself. Dmitri is in the center cage of the ballroom alone. He doubts it's a coincidence—Maria is behind it, he knows it. She's been watching him closely and doubtless is aware how unstable he is. The wizard may not be wrong—given his precarious hold on rationality, being alone here may work to his favor and prevent him from exposing just how close to the edge he is—but still, he doesn't appreciate her manipulation. He glares at the wizard as his fangs and claws extend.

When she gives the go-ahead for the test to start, Dmitri

unleashes a flurry of punches. In the sudden rush of striking out, the outside world falls away as he takes out his frustration and rage against the impenetrable barrier. Memories pummel him. Elizabetta impaled; him killing the man who tried to assault her centuries ago; Shashenka torturing her; Guillermo twisting her body like a wrung dishrag. Bloodlust explodes to the surface and drives him into a frenzy. *I have to save her!* He kicks, knees, and elbows the barrier, launching his body into the invisible wall surrounding him. His vision turns red—desperation to get free, go after his Elizabetta is the most logical thought to him. He slams his body into the unseen cage one more time, but at the same moment he freezes midmotion, remaining upright. *Maria! That damn wizard.*

*Vent it, get control ... don't let them see.* Once the barrier drops, he'll need to convince everyone standing in front of him that he's all right. They aren't taking any chances, which gives him more time to force the raging darkness to retreat deeper beneath the surface. *Do they know that?* He'd wager Maria does.

Vladimir and Matt are shouting at him to calm down and regain control. Tavorell says, "I can dust him into submission."

Matt's eyebrows arch. "Dust him?"

"It will make him happy and feel good." Liathera giggles and shrugs.

"He'll be more than that, and you know it." Milnea shakes a finger at the pixie. "I don't think you want to lose a wing to undo the spell."

Tavorell grumbles, "That vampire needs a good dose of

dust. He's cranky and irritable."

*I'm going to be more than that if they don't let me go.*

Matt chuckles and looks from the pixie-man to the elemental. "What happens when someone is hit with pixie dust?"

Milnea's gaze is stern. "They become euphoric and can laugh, dance, and sing themselves into a comatose state or even die. If one gives consent, then a pixie can quickly neutralize the effects, but when dust is used against someone's will or awareness, then ingesting a ground pixie wing mixed in nectar is the only antidote. I doubt Dmitri will consent."

The wolf teases that it could be entertaining to watch, but when Milnea suggests that he can satisfy his curiosity and arrange a dusting for himself, the idea seems to lose its appeal.

"Thanks, I'll pass."

Tavorell smirks. "Talk your friend into it later, and we'll have some fun."

"I think we've had enough fun at Dmitri's expense." Sally turns to Maria. "We all know he's having a hard enough time—we don't need to add to it."

Stephan and Kees step forward and grab his arms as Maria releases the immobility spell. He tells the Druzhinas that their hold on him is unnecessary, but a long minute gobbles seconds before they seem convinced enough to let him go. Pain registers for the first time, and Dmitri looks down at his hands and body—his knuckles, knees, and elbows are bloody from his vicious but useless assault against the barrier.

Sally gently takes his hand. "Let's go get you cleaned up."

Dmitri nods. He'll have to fight hard, but he can't lose it that way during the tournament. *Elizabetta needs me to find her.*

## CHAPTER 20: DMITRI

# Royal Selection

With just hours before the leadership contest begins, the participants and their supporters arrive. Dmitri wants to avoid greeting them, but his renewed leadership of the Druzhina and his status as their chosen champion in the fight leave him little choice. Despite his efforts to prove he's managing the bloodlust, he's known all along it's barely under control—and that is going to present a major problem in the next few hours. *I don't know if I can hold it together and keep from killing someone.*

He frowns at the leather outfit lying on the bed. Maria advised him that its thick material would give him the best protection during the fights ahead, but he picks up the shirt and then tosses it aside. With the mood he's in, he'd rather use the psychological tactic of allowing his opponents to see his multitude of scars. He slips into the leather pants and steps out of the room barefoot.

Matt and Sally, waiting in the hall for him, look him over from head to toe. Matt smirks and nods, while Sally's eyes widen. *I take it my fighting attire will serve its purpose.*

Together they go up to the ballroom, where everyone else has assembled to hear the final instructions and sign the treaty, a requirement for each fighter. A few try to argue against it, but it's too late for them to change their minds and back out—the Druzhina is determined to get them under defeat or under treaty. The treaty forbids them to return to their homes and continue fighting to take more than what they already own. It also demands they pledge their coven's fealty to the new king or queen at the end of the event.

Vladimir says, "I want you to understand that if you break your oaths and fail to protect our king or queen, then you forfeit your coven and property. Should our ruler die and have no mate to carry on alone, then the second-place winner of the tournament will take over, and you will pledge them that same loyalty. This is a new era for our realm, and it will be one of unity and peace."

The tournament is designed to send a message to the other realms as well; two representatives from each are present to witness the event. Josephina and Maria will report back to the maxians, while Matt and Raffaele Mancini, the werewolf who became alpha of Vincente Falco's pack after Vincente was murdered, represent their realm. Delegates from Seelinara are also in attendance, but most of the participants and observers must remain ignorant of this until the Seelie or Unseelie royal courts decide to reveal the truth. Milnea uses glamour to appear as a maxian, while Tavorell and Liathera buzz around looking like dragonflies. Dmitri hopes the contestants and their entourages don't give too much thought to the cool fall weather—and the fact that Venice's dragonflies have already migrated to warmer climates.

Vladimir takes a moment to look at each competitor before announcing the rules for the event. "There will be no weapons other than claw or fang. You will fight until one of you concedes or is too injured to continue. You will not fight to the death or strike any blows which may remove head or heart from your opponent. This is a single elimination event—one loss, and you are out of contention.

"There will be an odd pairing number for round two, and one of you will be drawn at random for a bye into round three. The winner of the fourth and final round will be granted full leadership rights and receive the title of king or queen. If the winner is mated, then equal title fitting the gender shall be given to the mate, and either may continue to rule if their mate dies."

The fighters stand in a single line in front of the three ballroom arenas; the remaining four arenas are on the primary and secondary piano nobiles. Most of the competing vampires are from European countries, but there is one each from America, Brazil, and China. Four females are among the fighters, causing grumbling from some of the men, but the complainers are reminded that the competetion is open to all vampires who want the opportunity to lead their realm.

Each contestant is presented with a number that corresponds to the order in which they signed up to take part— Dmitri is number one, a reminder of his reluctant participation. The numbers are placed in a bin and shaken to mix them together. Matt draws the stubs, while Sally calls them out; Maria and the Druzhinas stand ready to direct each pair of fighters to a ring. There will be at least one Druzhina at each arena to monitor the fights.

Excitement shines in Matt's eyes. Sally, bouncing on her feet, waits until she has both numbers in hand to announce the first pair of fighters. "One and seven."

Vladimir motions for Dmitri and his male opponent to enter a ring. Sally continues calling out the pairs that Matt draws: "Twelve and fourteen. Nine and five. Two and thirteen. Four and six. Eleven and eight. Ten and three."

Two men are placed into the ring on Dmitri's right, while a male and female fighter are shown to the ring on his left. It does not surprise Dmitri that Maria remains on this floor, near him. *I wonder if she'll have to lock me down after each fight?* He can't allow that—it will show weakness, no control.

When everyone is in place, Milnea uses English to wield her magic and hide the fact that she's fae. "Water, air, come forth, unite. Bind a wall top to bottom, enclose around at thrice and half my height. Hold within each night child as they fight. Go with the wind at a winner declared and reclaim your nature as water and air."

Matt allows his wolf form to surface just enough to send out a howl, signaling the start of the first round. Before the sound cuts off, Dmitri closes the distance between him and his opponent and strikes the first blow. The man recoils and ducks the next jab—his eyes narrow as he wipes blood from his nostrils. He lunges at Dmitri, but a kick to the vampire's chest sends him flying back into the barrier surrounding them.

"You filthy son of a bitch!" the man hisses.

The rage in the vampire's eyes unleashes the raw fury swirling inside Dmitri and begging for release. As the man rises off the floor, Dmitri catches him by the shoulders and flips him over his head, using the momentum to roll on top and grip the man around the neck. The vampire rakes at his arms, but Dmitri digs his claws into the man's flesh. *Enemy ... Elizabetta ... he must die. Kill!* He's pulling upward with the intention of ripping the man's throat out, when Vladimir shouts, "No death blows."

Dmitri hears the order, but all he sees is his claws ripping flesh—severing arteries, tearing away the windpipe, shredding muscles. He closes his eyes, trying to hold on to Vladimir's words and rid himself of the images of ending his enemy's life. *Not an enemy—an opponent.* His eyes fly open. Through clenched teeth, his body trembling with the need to kill, Dmitri says, "Yield!"

Fear flashes in the man's eyes, and he croaks out, "I yield."

The barrier surrounding Dmitri and his opponent shimmers away, and Vladimir and Matt rush forward. The wolf pulls Dmitri off his defeated foe as Vladimir drags the man away. Tremors rack Dmitri's body as he stumbles back into Matt's arms. "I'm okay. Let me go." His tone is harsher than he intends.

"Are you sure, bud?"

"Yeah, I'm good." Dmitri takes a few deep breaths to steady himself further and feels Matt's arms drop away— but the wolf's hands hover, ready to grab him if he makes a rash move.

The other two matches are still in progress, though the female in the arena nearest Dmitri's is struggling—he can see that she doesn't stand a chance against her opponent. The two male vampires fighting on the other side are more evenly matched, but Dmitri suspects the taller man is going to lose to his Chinese opponent. The shorter man's movements are concise, fast, and well aimed, and exert raw force with each blow.

The woman next to Dmitri rasps out, "I yield." The man shoves her away, and Matt's hand clamps down on Dmitri's shoulder as the barrier around the two fighters drops.

The woman averts her gaze, cradling an injured arm, but Dmitri feels a measure of respect for her tenacity and lack of fear. She went against a formidable and well-trained fighter—one that would be a challenge even for him—and she made a valiant effort. He says, "You fought well. Don't be ashamed of your loss."

"Screw you!" She glares at him with disgust and hatred, then turns and pushes her way through the crowd.

Dmitri blinks as he watches her disappear from view, but he shakes his head and allows his attention to fall on the two men still fighting. The shorter man makes a series of moves that combine blocks, punches, and sweeps, and the instant his opponent falls he jumps on top of him. One hand is raised, ready to strike the man's throat, and the other hand clasps his foe's forehead—if he delivers the blow, it will stun his opponent. The man concedes without demand, and the victor rises to his feet, bows, and turns toward Milnea.

Twenty more minutes pass before the matches on the

first and second piano nobiles are decided. One more of the female vampires is eliminated, but the other two—the Brazilian and American—have earned the right to go on to the next level. Maria tosses the victors' numbers into the bin. The second round will take place in the ballroom; only three rings are needed, since the seventh fighter will receive a bye into the third round.

The first number drawn is the lucky winner of the bye; it goes to the American female fighter, who flashes a smug grin. Dmitri's opponent for this round is a burly man whose accent indicates he's Russian. While Dmitri is slightly taller, the man outweighs him, and it's clear his opponent will use his weight as a weapon.

When Matt's wolf howl signals the start, the Russian proves Dmitri right. The man is quick to move in with brute force, unleashing a series of punches and kicks designed to stun and knock down an opponent. Dmitri dodges the initial onslaught and strikes back with a low round-house kick. His bloodlust remains mostly in check, trickling to the surface as he waits for the man to make his move. *I need to take this man from behind, get him off balance.* Predictably, the vampire throws another round of direct, front-on hits. Dmitri tucks into a crouch a split second before he jumps to the side and past the man. Then he straightens to his full height, one arm extending to wrap around his opponent's neck as his body rotates behind the burly man. Once he's pinned the other vampire against his chest, Dmitri jerks the man's upper body as he steps back; the man loses his footing, and Dmitri repositions his arm to cup his foe's chin as his free hand grabs the vampire's forehead. In one quick, hard twist Dmitri wrenches the man's neck, and the vampire's body sags as he loses consciousness. Dmitri drops him to the ground as the barrier disappears, and he feels a sliver of pride for managing the bloodlust so well this time.

The other two matches are still in progress. He watches as the Brazilian female fighter takes down the male vampire. Her movements are swift and sure, and a sneer curls her lips as she steps out of the ring. The Chinese man wins his match seconds later.

The thought of fighting either woman doesn't sit well with Dmitri. With the darkness swelling below the surface, he fears that he may hurt or even kill one of them far more easily and with less intent than he would a man, whether he means to or not. It's almost a relief when the third round matches are announced—he'll go against the Chinese vampire. Dmitri knows that he'll need to be mindful, though, of the man's stature and speed.

Vladimir leads them to an outside ring, and the American and Brazilian females take their places in the center ring as Milnea erects the shields. Another wolf howl sends the fighters into motion. Dmitri and his opponent bow and then circle one other, each waiting for the perfect moment to deliver the first blow. When the man reveals a crane stance, Dmitri suspects that his foe plans to use his speed and proximity for a series of short, rapid strikes. In response Dmitri crouches into a praying mantis posture, an effective form of defense against that fighting style.

The man launches his attack, and Dmitri delivers a combination of blocks and hits, which fall short—he's actually at risk of losing the bout. *Druzhinas fight to win, fight to live—always!* Rage seeps to the surface. The man's fighting posture is no match for Dmitri's long limbs and speed, and even when the other vampire transitions to a dragon stance, it's not enough to prevent Dmitri from getting the upper hand. Dmitri allows the man to flip him facedown on the floor and straddle him. But then, with his palms against the floor, Dmitri kicks up, his back arching, and his feet strike his opponent in the back of the head and shoulders.

The man stumbles forward as expected, and Dmitri leaps to his feet, pressing his advantage, pummeling him with a series of blows. The other vampire's timing is thrown off; he's still defending low when Dmitri's hands jut forward and grab the man by the head. In a twisting motion Dmitri lifts the vampire and slams him to the floor. He follows with a few hard blows to the man's neck with his leg before pinning him down. The pressure Dmitri exerts against his throat is more than the vampire can resist, and he chokes out his concession. Dmitri leaps to his feet, presses his palms together, and bows to a worthy opponent.

He breathes deeply through his nose, attempting to clear his mind as his body continues to pulse with the malice he struggles to reign in. *I've been using the bloodlust to win, and I don't know if I can hold it back now.* In his next bout he will face a woman, and she will be at greater risk of harm if he loses control during the match. His mind races for a way to bow out. Desperate, he gives Vladimir an imploring look, but his friend closes his eyes and shakes his head.

The American, a female vampire from New York, wins

the bout. As her defeated opponent limps away, the victor says, "Told you I'd win, you stupid bitch."

Dmitri notices the woman is similar to Elizabetta in size and build, but her chiseled features seem harsh and pinched—her body language screams contempt. *She's unpleasant, but I don't want this ... I don't want to take her life.* He isn't certain that he can maintain control, and that scares him more than anything—but it's not chivalry behind his fear of killing her. It's the fact that if he loses it, they'll never allow him to go after Elizabetta, never take the risk or give him a chance to prove himself again. *I can do this. I have to do this. Pin her, hold her, force her to yield.*

Vladimir shows the American and Dmitri into the center ring, cautioning them to have a clean fight. When the match begins, the vampire goes on the attack immediately while Dmitri counters her with defensive moves. It becomes clear that she is using a combination of fighting techniques—mixed martial arts, boxing, and something that looks like a deranged wraith. Without striking back, he blocks her blows as she hits, kicks, and claws at him.

"Fight me, you prick!" Her shriek is guttural and filled with frustration. Dmitri can hear his friends shouting at him to take her down, to end this fight. The outside world begins to dim—bloodlust feeds the fury trying to claw its way free. She's igniting the fuse he's desperate to keep extinguished, but he can't bring himself to fight back. He's too far on the edge now—all it will take is one blow, and he'll doom himself.

*No!* He jumps back and slams into the barrier as, in a flurry of dips and swipes, the American's arm finds a way past his block. Her claws leave deep slices across his abdomen. *I can take it. Don't strike back—let it go.* The woman leaps forward and wraps her arms and legs around him, her fangs tearing into his shoulder. He tries to push her away, but her mouth finds his ear—and when Dmitri feels his earlobe tear and the blood flow down his neck, he explodes and breaks her hold, throwing her back several feet. Her body slams into the barrier, and she slumps to the floor.

*Enemy ... no. Elizabetta ... enemy. Kill her. No! Druzhinas don't lose. End the threat, now!* The bloodlust begins to surge to a deadly level—his body is positioned with claws ready to strike the blow that will end his opponent's life. *I can't kill her.* His mind screams for Elizabetta—she needs him. He can't help her if they lock him up. Dmitri can still hear the others shouting at him. His claws are fully extended. *I can't ... I can't.* He forces the hand to open, retracting his claws, and angles his palm toward the American. Through gritted teeth he says, "I concede!"

Shouts and whistles ripple through the crowd, but the silence coming from Dmitri's friends drowns out those cheering in celebration. A mix of disappointment and disbelief is visible on every ally's face. Dmitri chokes down the lump in his throat. *They'll never understand.*

The barrier drops, and the American sneers. "You're a worthless pile of shit. You don't deserve to be king."

*Nothing like gratitude ... I just spared her life and handed her the vampire realm. I hope this wasn't a mistake.* There's no fight left in him; he feels hollow, gutted.

Maria mutters a healing spell and applies a poultice to

stem the bleeding from his torn ear. The American gives them a dirty look and marches up to Vladimir. He dips his head in a show of respect for their new leader. "Congratulations on your victory, Constance. Allow me to bring this event to a close, and then we'll discuss your new power and status."

"Let's get it over with quickly. I want to go back to New York."

Vladimir nods and casts a disbelieving look at Dmitri before he says, "Contestants, guests, this is a new beginning for our realm. Constance Bledsoe has won the right to lead our people. She is our queen, and you will treat her with the dignity and respect befitting her position.

"To those who participated, thank you for your valiance and self-control. As you return to your covens, you are cautioned to remember the treaty you signed. Cease hostilities against others in the vampire and werewolf realms. The Druzhina will hold you accountable."

Vladimir steals another glance at Dmitri, then points toward the werewolf and maxian representatives. "They will spread word throughout their realms and request the same of their kind. Our new era of peace and stability begins tonight."

## CHAPTER 21: ELIZABETTA

# Decoys, Spies, and Bait

The loud bang of a door slamming against a wall jars Ramira awake and sends Elizabetta scrambling to release the witch's legs from the scissor kicks she was experimenting with. Guillermo barks at his niece to follow him to the study. *What is this all about?* Tense, Elizabetta watches through Ramira's eyes as the witch slips on a bathrobe and hurries after him into the study. The sorcerer appears agitated again. *Did he notice I had control, or is he up to something?*

Frustration slithers through Guillermo's voice. "We have a problem. Those damn vampires are trying to bring peace across the shadow realms. My spies report that the Druzhina held a contest and appointed a queen to lead them— some American vampire. Now truces between the werewolves and vampires are sprouting up all over. We can't have that—not when the humans' financial and social collapse has just begun. Not when we're nearly ready to lure a Druzhina into the first trap. We're at the pinnacle of achieving everything we've worked for over these last few centuries."

*A queen? Great, the world is on the brink of disaster, and the Druzhina creates an archaic form of leadership.* Elizabetta's mind races with this new information. Elevating any vampire to royal status is like holding a cup filled with water or gas and throwing it on a house fire—neither does a bit of good. *How much power did they grant the new vampire queen? Is she a mouthpiece, a figurehead?*

"What can we do to stop it, Uncle?"

"We have the humans where we want them. We will need to assassinate the vampire's new queen too, and take out a werewolf who seems to influence wolf packs around the world." Guillermo's face contorts with disgust. "Another damn American. The problem is that he's all over the globe. He jets between his businesses in the United States and back to wherever the Druzhinas are. Apparently he helped the Druzhina bring down Shashenka and is often still in their presence. He'll be much harder to isolate and take out."

*Matt? Oh, hell no. Not going to happen.* The queen likely is well protected, but Matt—if he were always with the Druzhinas, it might lessen her fear for his safety, but his trips alone to the States will put him at greater risk. *I wish I could get a message to him.*

"What about the Druzhina? Are you still going to lure one for me to fight?" Ramira shifts in her chair, and the active thought strand indicates that she's unhappy with the prospect. Elizabetta smirks at her discomfort. *Suck it up, cupcake, and take the ass-kicking—you deserve it.*

"It appears they may be returning to their normal routines, and as soon as I have word that one of them is going after that rogue again, I will set the trap." A sinister smile spreads across Guillermo's face. This is the real reason behind his briefing, he tells his niece—he's almost ready to send her on another assignment. But this time it won't just be her and her guards; she'll have walking bait for company. A knock on the door disrupts their dispute, and one of Guillermo's servants announces the arrival of Milo Kohler.

Rage surges through Elizabetta at the sight of the despicable vampire—she swears her pulse pounds faster. *I'm going to kill you someday, you crusty old maggot.*

Milo merely nods at Ramira and takes a seat opposite Guillermo. "You summoned me?"

"I have a job for you."

The vampire shifts in his chair, and Elizabetta notices the way he bristles—there's a possibility Ramira might just get herself and this worm killed. The thought makes her smile.

"Will it pay the debt I owe you?"

Anger flashes in the sorcerer's eyes. "I own you! You will do my bidding whenever I have need of you, or I will kill you."

Milo fidgets and swallows hard, but he nods.

"I want you to lead the Druzhinas to that rogue who double-crossed them. She's going to be the bait." The look on Guillermo's face is evil and cold as he pulls a map from his desk, his long, thin finger tapping the location of Venice. "The Druzhinas are currently here." His hand moves as he adds, "The rogue is in Budapest at the moment, but she's on the run and will be gone from there within the next few hours. The one I have tailing her says she's predictable."

He looks at Milo. "She loops back. For each two new locations, she revisits the one before them and then changes direction. Her habit seems to be to go north two towns or cities, return, and go east two more. She repeats this until she's gone south and west as well, and then she flies to a new location, and that one becomes the hub of her movements." *Vampire goes loop de loop and dies on a Saturday night. Good!* This is actionable intelligence the Druzhina can use, but once more Elizabetta is unable to help them on any level.

Milo says, "If you know this, why not just get word to the Druzhina and set them up that way?"

Guillermo roars, "Because they are too stupid to see what is in front of their eyes!" He takes a breath and continues glaring at Milo as he explains that a courier will deliver a message to the rogue to set up a meeting. When she accepts and a location is set, he will send an anonymous note informing the Druzhina of the details—or just enough information to lay the trap. "Your whereabouts will be known to them, but hers will not. They're anxious enough to capture her that they will wait for you to lead them to her."

"You do realize that they want me dead? They'll all come after us."

*Oh, you got that right, slimeball. You were a dead vampire the moment Dmitri turned you.*

Guillermo shakes his head. "I've already planned to control how many they send. My niece"—the sorcerer nods at Ramira—"and at least one of her protectors will be there with you. She has a job to do."

A scowl puckers Milo's forehead, but he remains quiet as Guillermo outlines the rest of the plan—or part of it. Elizabetta quickly realizes that the sorcerer is telling Milo just enough to satisfy the vampire's curiosity and allay his fears. There are so many holes in the scheme that she's unsure whether Guillermo intends for Teresina and Milo to escape unharmed, or if he's willing to sacrifice them so Ramira can kill a Druzhina.

Sure enough, after Guillermo dismisses Milo—informing the vampire that he will remain in the guesthouse on the sorcerer's estate until they are ready to activate the plan— he provides more information to Ramira. The trap will be sprung as soon as Guillermo confirms the Druzhinas are closing in on Teresina; Milo and Ramira's team will be sent to the general area via mutaport beforehand and arrive at the prearranged location once the Druzhinas are where they need to be. From the sound of it, Elizabetta fears he may indeed succeed in controlling how many Druzhinas respond, since word will only be sent to the ones already trailing the rogue, leaving no time for them to rally the others. Milo's presence is meant to be the splitting maul that divides the Druzhinas if they are working as a pair.

Teresina is merely a decoy—Guillermo doesn't care what happens to her. She means little to him at this stage in his overall plan. Her only role is to lure a Druzhina inside, where Ramira can then prove herself capable of killing one of the vampire realm's most elite fighters. The sorcerer has no inclination to protect Milo either—he sees it as a way to end the despicable creature. Elizabetta's desire for revenge against those two vampires leaves her actually supporting one of the sorcerer's plans, and she finds that vexing. *Disturbing ... but good.*

Given the new developments, Elizabetta's training in memory manipulation needs to go into high gear—this time she refuses to be a victim along for the ride. Guillermo is activating key parts of his plan, and their time is running out to stop him. After the sorcerer dismisses Ramira, Elizabetta convinces Dahliorn to help her make her first attempt at messing with the witch's head.

Unlike monitoring active thoughts or even long-term memory, altering working memory and short-term memory requires precise interaction because it must occur while Ramira is awake. Anytime the witch registers Elizabetta's presence, the active thought must be blocked or erased quickly from Ramira's working or short-term memory. Elizabetta can't allow a single memory to transfer to long-term storage. She will need to perfect the technique or risk exposing herself to the witch.

She's not even sure it's possible to maneuver fast enough to disrupt the pathway. «I feel like a juggler trying to toss knives while tap dancing and watching a monitor for alarms.»

Dahliorn chuckles. «It will take practice for you to master it. Now concentrate, and let's try this again. Remember, keep it simple.»

*Simple, he says ... tap into active, block working, erase*

*short-term, give commands, monitor action, don't get caught. Nothing like asking the impossible.* Still, she focuses, tapping into Ramira's active thoughts. The witch is done with her training for the day and standing in the shower. With illusory hands in place, Elizabetta creates an electrical surge, gives the command, and erases the short-term memory as Ramira rinses the soap out of her hair. The witch starts to reach for the conditioner, but her active thoughts show confusion—she knows that water was just running through her hair, but she's suddenly unsure whether she shampooed.

When Ramira reaches for the shampoo again, Elizabetta nearly bursts with excitement. «I did it! Dahliorn, it worked.»

She wants to try again, but he cautions her in a stern tone, «She can't have too many of these moments close together, or she may report new or unusual experiences to Guillermo.» Ever since Ramira's "sleepwalking," the sheridauk tells her, the sorcerer has worried that her unexplained behavior is a residual side effect of the failed unity spell, and he's been tenacious about finding a way to fix whatever went wrong. According to Dahliorn, Guillermo is determined to gain access to Elizabetta's memories, knowledge, and skills—and the strategic boost that a proper uniting will provide his quest to upset the world and remake it to his liking.

An idea comes to Elizabetta, but she isn't sure if it's good, bad, or even possible. «Since we're tampering with her memories, is there a way for me to remove the blocks and alterations Guillermo's made over the years?»

Dahliorn says, «The blocks may disappear when Guillermo dies—that is, if Ramira outlives him. Alterations cannot be undone.»

«Why not?»

Seconds tick by while Dahliorn seems to think about her question. «I believe they are often based in truth, and they overwrite portions of memory or take the empty spaces where others were stored.»

«Is there any harm if I poke around and experiment?»

«Only to the degree that you may reveal something Ramira will adversely react to. For example, if you somehow unveil her true memories of her parents' deaths, she may break down mentally or go into a rage and try to kill Guillermo.»

Elizabetta would laugh out loud if she could. «The last part sounds like a bonus.»

«It would be if we knew she were capable of doing the deed. But the risk of failure is too high.»

He doesn't have to explain—Elizabetta understands now. «Her loving uncle already considers her disposable. We can't risk him killing her as long as I'm tied to her.»

She can hear the pride in his words. «You're learning, little dove.»

Their conversation ends when Guillermo summons Dahliorn to assist him in searching fae records for an incantation that may work as a patch and allow Ramira to pull Elizabetta into her the way the failed spell was meant to. Dahliorn says it was common for fae to protect their personal records and magic books with misdirection glamour and with spells—often dark magic—that hide the true intent of the words. Because he's a full-blooded fae, the sheridauk has the ability to decode and see past the glamour.

According to Dahliorn, dark magic serves a purpose, but even among full-blooded fae its use was tightly monitored and controlled to prevent inexperienced or malevolent fae from causing a catastrophe. Guillermo himself is unaware that Dahliorn is well experienced in dark magic—it's how the sheridauk was able to meddle with the attempted unity spell.

Before he sends her back to her body, Dahliorn says, «I left you a present on the frame of your cot. It's a tiny crystal that will fit above your ear canal—place it there, and you can listen.»

Back in her cell, Elizabetta hangs over the edge of the cot and discovers the crystal hidden in the connecting corner near her head—it's the diameter of a pencil lead and as thin as a wafer. She picks it up and presses it into her ear. As voices trickle through, she startles at the sound of Guillermo's voice. He's snarling in his typical unpleasant manner. "This had better work, Dahliorn."

"I've already told you that I can give no such guarantee. This is ancient and forbidden magic that I never practice."

Elizabetta chuckles at his not-quite-a-lie. She's learned that fae are truthful beings, but they are selective in what and how they say things. Dahliorn claims to be quite skilled at dark magic, but when he says he never practices it, he merely means that he's refused to do so on Guillermo's behalf. Of course, his ability to cast any magic is largely hampered by the silver band around his waist—even when he tries, he often fails.

She notes Ramira's voice next and almost doesn't recognize it; hearing it from within Ramira's mind sounds different from hearing it with her own ears. "I'm not happy about this, Uncle. What happens if it boomerangs like your last spell and finishes transforming me into a vampire?"

Guillermo says, "According to the text Dahliorn revealed, it will only pull your weakest trait into one of strength. I assure you, it's the vampirism that has stolen your magic but trapped you midchange. There is no way for you to fully transform without a vampire's second bite and blood."

*What a lying sack of shit. Doesn't Ramira know anything about other supernaturals? One bite, that's all it takes—one bite, and you're either dead or turned.*

The sorcerer ignores Ramira's low-throated groan and mutters a spell in a language Elizabetta suspects is a fae dialect.

«Dahliorn, what's he trying to do?»

«Find a way to salvage the botched unity spell.»

She isn't sure what that means—or even worse, if it's possible. She doesn't want to be a husk, a stooge, a non-being without awareness. Long, bloated minutes reveal nothing, and then finally she hears Guillermo speak. "Do you feel anything?"

Ramira says, "No. I feel the same."

"Squeeze this." Guillermo is silent for a moment. "Are you even trying?"

"Yes, I'm trying, Uncle. I'm squeezing as hard as I can."

The sorcerer makes one of his dissatisfied grunting sounds. "Tell me if you can hear this—it should be discernible to vampire ears.""

A sound pings and grates through the tiny device in Elizabetta's ear, and she shudders. *Jeez, that's worse than fingernails on a chalkboard.*

Guillermo's tone is hopeful. "Did you hear it?""

"Hear what?""

"Let's go outside—we need to see if it gave you speed instead." Moments after the sorcerer gives Ramira the command to run, he bellows, "Why didn't this work?""

*Obviously she didn't gain speed either.* Elizabetta cheers another failure—there's no telling how vampiric ability would aid these two.

"You told me this would work, Dahliorn.""

"Perhaps the strengths connected to her vampiric physical traits cannot be elevated due to the mutated state of their nature.""

Elizabetta cringes at the sorcerer's threatening tone, but curiosity gnaws at her. «Did you meddle again?»

«No. The spell really does boost one's weakest trait, but I took a gamble that Ramira's greatest weakness is a lack of compassion.»

Elizabetta roars with laughter. «Does that mean that we're going to see a kinder, gentler killer?»

«Guillermo is pushing for solutions to the unity spell.» There's no humor in Dahliorn's tone. «I had to give him something to keep him from trying a different spell that might force you out of the shadows.»

The comical situation doesn't seem so funny all of a sudden. The sorcerer has grown impatient—too many aspects of his plan are falling into place, and he'll demand to see progress soon. *We are running out of time.*

## CHAPTER 22: DMITRI

# The Search Begins

When the Druzhinas, Matt, Maria, and the Seelinarans meet privately with the new vampire queen, it becomes clear rather quickly that Constance has her own ideas of how to rule her new kingdom—and they're not what the Druzhina intended. She's power hungry and despotic. Bitchy and rude seem to be her best traits. Her first order grates against everyone else in the room—she doesn't want maxians or a werewolf in on their discussions and demands they leave.

*What have I foisted upon our realm? More proof that I'm not fit to rule, either—this was a mistake.* When Vladimir refuses to send them out, Constance questions what authority and power her title conveys. Vladimir tries to be diplomatic; he suggests that both will grow over time, but that for now she needs guidance from the Druzhina to come into her potential as a just leader. Then he reminds her that the Druzhina is not only there to do her bidding—within reason and established vampiric law—but also to keep her in line.

Constance's reply is to attempt to disband and dismiss the Druzhina on the spot. *She will not shut us down and prevent me from finding Elizabetta!* Bloodlust spikes, and Dmitri rises out of his chair and leaps to attack her. Stephan and Justin stop him before he can touch her. Maria gags and binds Dmitri to his seat as Constance flashes him a contemptuous glare. She wears disrespectful and haughtiness as if they were designer labels.

"Mark my words"—Constance glares around the table—"in time I will have the trust and respect of our kind, and when I do, you are all finished."

Vladimir levels a hard look at the woman. "We will never allow you that level of power."

A long minute passes as they stare at each other. Then Constance demands to leave, and they cram what should be an in-depth briefing into a twenty-minute summary. Once they finish, she stands and glares once more around the room. "My home is in New York, and from now on you'll make arrangements to see me there. Except for that coward." She points at Dmitri. "I don't want him in my presence again." The queen turns on her heel and storms out of the room, the door shuddering as it slams shut behind her.

Before a bloated silence can settle among them, Matt gives Dmitri a pointed look. "Boy howdy, when you vamps screw up, it's on a grand scale."

Anger writhes through Vladimir's words. "We'll correct it when the time is right—she just signed her death warrant." He gestures toward Dmitri. "Let him loose, Maria."

Dmitri closes his eyes as the wizard releases the spell. They're waiting for an explanation—he knows it. He can't admit to them that his bloodlust was borderline out of control, that he would have killed her if he hadn't thrown the match. But he needs an excuse, and finally Dmitri settles on one based on his earlier reluctance. "I'm sorry. I didn't want to rule, and I thought we could guide her ... it was a mistake not to defeat her." He nearly chokes on the partial lie at the end—he's still convinced he did the right thing by not killing her. *Now they won't have a reason to stop me from finding Elizabetta.*

Vladimir nods. "What's done is done. We'll leave Constance in her new role until peace returns to the shadow realms. She evidently didn't read the fine print in the treaty. We are a governing body—she can't disband us, but we can declare her unfit to rule if she tries to rise as a dictator."

Dmitri grimaces at Vladimir's words; if she does, it will be his fault. *Let this all be worth it.* Katherine recommends they assign two Druzhinas to keep an eye on Constance in New York and to attempt to educate her about her new role as queen. No one wants the assignment. They put everyone but Dmitri's name into a bowl. Alexander and Victoria are chosen, but when Stephan grumbles about being separated from his mate and partner, Alexander offers for Stephan to go in his stead. Dmitri approves the arrangement—he understands the need for mates to remain together during a long assignment. Victoria and Stephan will do what they can to get their new queen in line.

Vladimir and Anna offer to concentrate their efforts on

quieting the conflict in the vampire and werewolf realms now that they have a queen. Katherine and Kees will assist them as needed, but their primary focus will be retracing Milo's movements prior to the battle at Machu Picchu—this may be their sole lead to wherever Milo is hiding. *That son of a bitch will tell us where Guillermo is, or he'll die slowly.*

In the meantime, Alexander and Justin will resume the search for Teresina. If the pattern they noticed before the leadership contest has continued, then they should be back on the rogue's trail within days. Dmitri is hopeful they'll have positive news to report soon—he can't take much more of this waiting, but even he has to admit that they still lack a starting point to search for Elizabetta.

Several Druzhinas stand to leave, and Dmitri glances around the room, his eyes settling on Vladimir. "I notice that you suggested missions for everyone save me."

Vladimir nods. "There's a reason you were chosen unanimously to represent us, Dmitri. I know you look to me to lead the Druzhina, and I filled that position after what Shashenka did to you and Elizabetta. But the two of you were our leaders before, and we need you to be in a position to field our reports, manage our movements, and give us our assignments as you see fit."

The thought is disconcerting, and Dmitri chuckles ruefully. "I'm in no condition to lead anything, Vlad, and I just proved that point. We're all going to pay for the bad decision I made by allowing Constance to win something she never should have had within her grasp."

A hand settles on his shoulder, and he is surprised to see Milnea smiling down at him. "I know that I am not from this world, but whether you know or accept it, you are a leader, Dmitri. Your kind needs you, and you will rise to meet this challenge."

He's heard similar words before from Jacques, who urged him to do just that, but he wants no part of leading anything—even more so without Elizabetta at his side. Speaking just loud enough to be heard, he says, "I'm too damaged, too flawed to be an effective leader again."

*I'm too close to the point of no return, and you don't want to see me go over that line.*

At sundown, the departing Druzhinas leave to begin or resume their missions. The villa feels even emptier after they leave; Antonio was the sole local to survive the battle when La Perfezione was taken, and now he and Dmitri's small entourage are the only residents. Milnea has suggested they spend their time searching historical records for clues to Guillermo's whereabouts—repeated events, plagues and illnesses that kill the young and healthy, and patterns of human conflict that aren't easily explained by normal disagreements. "The one we seek will have left his footprints along the trail of time," she says with a certainty that suggests the Seelinarans know more about the sorcerer than they've shared. She's confident they will discover something about Guillermo.

Sadness settles over Dmitri as thoughts of his wife take his attention away from the book in front of him. *Will I ever see her again?* So far their efforts have failed to produce viable leads, and the more time they waste, the more likely they won't rescue Elizabetta in time. Dmitri doesn't know if Guillermo is torturing or abusing her, and any speculation leaves him feeling sick inside. He drags a hand through his hair as if it will sweep away the darkness struggling to come out.

It doesn't escape Dmitri's attention that Matt has moved behind Maria and begun massaging her shoulders. Within minutes the mutt has her sitting on his lap as he continues to work the muscles in her neck and back, every now and then nuzzling the wizard's neck. They murmur softly between them as Maria flips pages in the book they are skimming for clues. *I wonder what Elizabetta will think of their blossoming feelings?* Dmitri only hopes that Matt and Maria find a balance—now is not the time for either of them to be distracted. His gaze returns to the book before him, and a sigh escapes as he refocuses his own attention.

In his periphery he notices Milnea looking around the table. "I think this may be something," she says. "It says here that the flu pandemic of 1918 was unusual in that it was deadly to healthy, strong adults. There's also a reference to the second wave being more deadly than the first. The one between worlds—Guillermo, as you call him—used plague as a weapon against Seelinara. This seems to fit what he would do."

No one says a word as her comments sink in. *Is it possible that Guillermo has attacked in such a way more than once?* Even so, Dmitri isn't clear how Elizabetta fits into these plans if this is the sorcerer's preferred method of killing others.

There's a golden spark in Milnea's crystal-blue eyes. "Do

you have a map that shows Enethura?"

Antonio retrieves another book from the shelf and opens it to a map, laying it in front of Milnea.

She looks up at him. "Now show me Étaples-sur-Mer, France, and the location where the Black Death started."

"I'm sorry, miss, I do not know this information." Antonio appears embarrassed as he retreats to his seat.

Maria walks over and places her finger on the map. "The Black Plague started in this area"—she points to central Asia—"and the flu pandemic started here." Her finger trails across the map to France.

A confused look crosses Milnea's face. "Does anyone know Guillermo's whereabouts in relation to these events?"

The wizard shakes her head but takes out a redecrystapiezo to call the historian at the Orde de Maxia library in Dublin. A smile spreads across her face as the call ends. "I think we may be on to something here. Guillermo was known to be in the central plains of Asia when the Black Plague broke out. He was also near Paris ahead of the flu pandemic."

Milnea looks around the table again. "Are there other major plagues that killed large numbers of Enethurans?"

It only takes them a few minutes to list the top ten most deadly plagues, which Maria cross-references with the historian in Dublin. Guillermo was in proximity to at least seven.

Dmitri says, "I don't see how this helps us locate him now."

A pixie buzzes past Dmitri and lands on the table in front of him. Tavorell's little chest puffs out. "It leaves a trail, and most creatures form habits and patterns. We can narrow down the most likely area your sorcerer returns to in between."

There's a hint of excitement in Maria's voice. "I think he's right. The seven plagues we can connect Guillermo to most recently are England, Italy, and France, with the other locations further back in time from when he was known to be in Asia or Eastern Europe."

"So what does that mean, witchy-poo?" Matt looks over her shoulder at the European map in front of her.

The wizard explains that the seat of maxian power spans England, Scotland, and Ireland. Guillermo's philandering father was in part of Celtic heritage, and together with the sorcerer's fae mother was said to have caused many problems in Northern Ireland, including land and money disputes and illegal uses of magic that brought censure from the maxian council.

Milnea leans her elbows on the table. "Before you continue, tell me who Guillermo's mother was."

The wizard places another call to the Dublin historian. When the call disconnects, she looks curious, and her tone conveys the same to Milnea. "The name of Guillermo's mother was Birneal."

Milnea pales and stares without blinking for a moment. "It's confirmation of what we feared, which is very bad news. But it may also be conclusive proof of the prophecy."

Liathera mutters something and begins to sob. "Hearts will break all across Seelinara if our prince is lost." She floats down and slumps on the table. "All is lost," she wails.

When Liathera's sobbing becomes hysterical, Tavorell

wraps her in his arms, trying to soothe her. Milnea draws a deep breath and explains that Birneal was the daughter of the previous Unseelie king, Lefian. "She was impetuous and pernicious. Against King Lefian's orders, she ran away with a maxian wizard in this realm and was stripped of her crown and title. For years she petitioned for the return of her rights but was denied. It is rumored that she and her husband ran afoul of the maxian realm too and were executed. Is that true?"

"Yes." Maria's voice is barely more than a whisper. "Guillermo's parents meddled in the crusades and nearly brought defeat upon the Europeans. It triggered the Church's war against the maxians and led to centuries of witch-hunts. The elder Sanchezes were put to death because of it."

Several minutes gobble the silence between the wizard and the Seelinarans as they stare at each other with horrified faces. Dmitri is lost in his own thoughts. They have grossly underestimated their foe; Guillermo has been setting the stage for revenge for centuries. *At least as long as I have lived.* The sorcerer likely has a vast network of minions and has acquired resources that dwarf what Dmitri, the Druzhinas, and Matt have at their disposal. The revelation tells him that they may never know how the sorcerer plans to use Elizabetta to achieve his demented goals.

It's Tavorell who breaks the oppressive quiet and answers questions Dmitri hasn't even thought of yet. The pixie walks up and down the length of the table as he tells them of Guillermo's ambition. With little power and position among the maxians, the sorcerer apparently felt he was due his mother's right of inheritance to the Unseelie throne. But before the Black Death was unleashed, King Altheron overthrew King Lefian, and in Seelinara rights of royal inheritance belong only to the ruling bloodline. Guillermo had no grounds to continue his petitions and was cast out of Seelinara, his blood added to the forbidden when he didn't cease his protests. The sorcerer has not been able to cross a veil since.

The puzzle pieces start falling into place. Guillermo is an orphan child denied prestige and title in both worlds. Dmitri, mesmerized by Tavorell's pacing, says to no one in particular, "This is retribution, isn't it?"

Milnea nods. "I think so. He can't rule either world, so he is willing to destroy both or hurt as many as possible as he gains control. Guillermo likely believes that he succeeded in wiping out those on Seelinara, and it's left him no way to return to the fae realm. But nature, population, and circumstances keep thwarting his attempts here. I fear that he means to keep trying until the situation is ripe for him to take over Enethura himself."

*To what possible end?* Dmitri shakes his head; he can no longer remain quiet with his concerns. "My wife is but one vampire among many. How could she possibly help further Guillermo's goals?"

Silence again engulfs them until Tavorell says, "In the history of Seelinara, a race targeted for annihilation requires one of that race."

At Dmitri's puzzled expression, Liathera flies over to him. "Dark magic allows such a captive to be used against their own kind. It's why pixies are prone to dust first and ask later."

A razor-sharp stone settles in Dmitri's stomach. "In what ways can this dark magic be used?"

Milnea sighs. "It can take many forms, depending on the ability of the one wielding it. Spread a poison that kills the targeted species. Use knowledge from a stolen mind. Send one to assassinate their own kind ..."

"If Guillermo has taken your wife for any of these reasons, she is likely lost to us already." Tavorell hangs his head.

A torrent of maleficence washes through Dmitri. Warring images flicker in his mind: Elizabetta in his arms ... being forced to decapitate her ... rending Guillermo flesh from bone ... cities demolished in his hunt to find her ... finding her too late ... her burnt head and charred remains. "No. No, Elizabetta ..." The words begin as a horrified whisper, rising in pitch with each one. He bellows, "We have to get her back. Now."

Matt is out of his chair within seconds and at Dmitri's side, clamping a firm hand to Dmitri's neck. He shoots a dirty look at the pixie. "Keep riling him, and I'll feed you to him, little pixie-man. Remember"—he turns to Dmitri—"you can feel her—I can feel her. She is alive, and we are going to get her back."

## CHAPTER 23: ELIZABETTA

# Small Victories

As if her situation wasn't bad enough with Guillermo trying to push his agenda forward, Elizabetta is now dealing with Ramira version 2.0, and she has no idea how to take it. The change in Ramira—from catshit nasty to whatever this is— is so subtle at first that even Guillermo doesn't notice. She is more polite to the staff and her instructors, and she's courteous, grateful. *Weird.* But it's when Ramira seeks out Dahliorn for a private conversation that Elizabetta gains her first measure of respect for the witch. He looks as stunned as Elizabetta feels when Ramira apologizes for the way she has treated him—the witch expresses a level of remorse and embarrassment that Elizabetta didn't think she was capable of feeling. When Ramira admits that her uncle is solely to blame for the sheridauk's condition, Dahliorn all but slumps in apparent astonishment.

*Condition? Does she mean the belt?* Elizabetta waits for Dahliorn to acknowledge the comment or for one of them to reveal what the witch means, but neither says a word. When curiosity gets the best of her, she asks him outright, «What's this about a condition?»

Dahliorn's reply comes through in a curt manner. «It's not important.»

*Fae and their bullshit secretiveness.* «It is important. Are you sick? What has the sorcerer done to you?» Her questions go unanswered, probably in part due to the way he's transfixed, gawking at Ramira—though Elizabetta isn't sure if the look is meant for her or for the witch.

After being trapped for the last few months inside Ramira, Elizabetta is accustomed to her surly and rude attitude; the witch's old aloofness and lack of empathy made it easier to consider killing the coldhearted witch when the time came. Now this change leaves Elizabetta less certain whether Ramira deserves death or if she can be salvaged as a person in some way. *Can this stop her from putting her new skills to use? She's helped him kill so many already.* Still, while the witch may display more compassion, even some of the world's more prolific serial killers were well liked and considered charming. And it's clear that she will continue to do Guillermo's bidding—she shows the same eagerness to please him and carry out his plans.

In a way, the improvements make Ramira more of a threat. The witch now does two sessions a day with her instructors, and her new attitude shows in the progress she's making in her fighting technique. Michio, unlike Guillermo, does notice the change in Ramira—though he believes it is because of her training that she is coming into balance with her mind, body, and spirit.

It's after one of Michio's sessions that Guillermo storms

into the training room—something he's never done before—and he's more than a little pissed at Ramira, who
ignored the minion he sent to fetch her earlier. He shouts,
"Come now, hurry, we have little time."

*What is going on here?* Ramira follows her uncle to the
mansion and keeps running until she reaches her room. The
witch wastes no time shedding her training clothes and
donning her fighting gear, which she buckles as she races
down the hallway and into the atrium. Elizabetta looks
around with the witch—Guillermo, Milo, and Dahliorn already stand near the mutaport. There's no need for an
explanation from the sheridauk. *They're going after a Druzhina.*

Fear ticks up as she wonders which of her friends is
tailing Teresina. The sorcerer is correct in his assumption
that if there are two of them, they will divide to catch both
Milo and the rogue. She suspects that Milo will run; he's too
much of a coward to stand and fight. Dahliorn usually
manages to stay out of Ramira's fights unless Elizabetta
intercedes, which means that if the witch is left to her own
defenses, the Druzhinas will be the victors. The witch's
skills are still no match against the elite fighters; any of the
Druzhinas should be able to stop her. Elizabetta must force
herself to be a spectator this time.

Once Guillermo sends them through the mutaport, they
arrive in a dark alley between two multistory buildings.
They don't linger, and when the street comes into view,
Elizabetta doesn't recognize anything beyond the Roman-
ian language displayed on the shops and buildings. Inside
the nearby hotel they enter, a pamphlet rack indicates

tourist attractions for Targu Mures. *The heart of the Transylvanian plains. Interesting place to be hiding.* The clerk signals a bellhop to show them to their room and gives them a suspicious look when Ramira claims their luggage was lost by the airline. After a few tense seconds, they're shown to a room on the seventh floor.

Dahliorn sits in a chair near the window, but Ramira and Milo pace while they wait for word from Guillermo. There is little talk among them as the minutes slip by, other than a final review of their plan. Guillermo's courier is waiting for Teresina to provide the address where Milo is to meet her; Ramira and Dahliorn will follow Milo there, though at a discreet distance, to make sure the Druzhina meeting Teresina is behind the vampire. When Ramira arrives where Teresina is waiting, the witch and Dahliorn will move in and catch the Druzhina by surprise. If there is more than one Druzhina, then Milo is to run for an exit—to draw one away while Ramira engages the other. Guillermo expects that Teresina will flee the moment they initiate the assault.

The way Dahliorn keeps shifting nervous glances at Ramira suggests he is worried Elizabetta will interfere. «I'm staying out of this one. She lacks the skill to take any of them in a straight-on fight—she will get her ass kicked this time.»

A nearly imperceptible nod is his only response. Elizabetta wonders if Guillermo's pet will be there and almost asks, but then refrains—that subject never goes well.

The bellhop knocks on the door, holding an envelope, which Ramira takes as she thanks the young man. She closes the door and reads the short note: "It's an industrial park off 151D Road." The rogue has included instructions for Milo to meet her in the southeast section of a building under construction.

"Is there a time?" Milo clasps his trembling hands together. Fear punctuates each word.

*You should be afraid, you son of a bitch. Your betrayal was your death sentence.*

A dry laugh comes from Ramira. "The top of the witching hour."

"That's less than thirty minutes from now, and we're over sixteen kilometers away." Milo glances at his watch. "She chose a location on the other side of town from this hotel she told me to stay in, and we're on foot."

Dahliorn stands and starts toward the door. "Give me five minutes to borrow a car from a guest."

When the sheridauk returns, a set of keys dangles from his hand. He looks at Milo. "There's a red Skoda Fabio in the middle of the lot. I've already unlocked it."

The plan is for him and Ramira to get into the backseat before Milo comes down, but Ramira says, "First I need to let Uncle know to alert the Druzhina to Milo's departure from the hotel." There's tension in her voice when the call ends. "He's already done it; his contact says there are two Druzhinas in the lobby waiting."

*Is Dmitri one of them?* A wave of nervous excitement washes over Elizabetta—she will have that answer soon. Dahliorn tells Milo to wait for two minutes to give him and Ramira time to get past the Druzhinas and hide in the car. The vampire nods when Dahliorn reminds him to act natural and not panic—Elizabetta wants to laugh. The worm is acting like he's already shit his pants and is about to toss his cookies too.

In the elevator, Ramira's active thoughts worry over confronting a Druzhina—and whether her skills are enough to survive. Elizabetta finds it amusing, considering that Milo is more likely to be snatched before he even reaches the car. If that happens, they won't need the Druzhinas to follow him to the rogue—he'll be forced to take them to her. Elizabetta prefers they take him upon sight, as it will prevent Ramira from attacking either of her friends.

They successfully avoid the Druzhinas, to Elizabetta's dismay, and reach the red car. Dahliorn sits on the floorboard, while Ramira lies down on the backseat. A few tense minutes pass as they wait, but then the driver's side door opens and Milo gets into the vehicle. Under his breath he says, "They followed me, but they're breaking into a car a couple of rows back."

"Give them a moment before you pull out." Ramira adds, "We need to make sure you don't lose them."

*You're going to be the one to lose.* Elizabetta hears Milo take a couple of deep breaths before he turns the key and starts the engine. She can feel the change in Ramira's mood; the witch is apprehensive too and can't seem to lie still when Milo confirms the Druzhinas are following them.

At Ramira's insistence, Milo parks as close to the meeting place as is practical—it will help her and Dahliorn avoid detection after the Druzhinas follow him inside. Once he leaves the vehicle, Ramira counts twenty seconds before peeking out the window. No one is in sight. She sprints from the car to the back door of the building but glances at

Dahliorn before she opens it. His serious expression screams "ready for anything."

As they walk quietly through the warehouse, Elizabetta notices that Dahliorn is directing their movements. *He must hear better than I can.* They slow their approach when Milo and Teresina's voices grow louder. The rogue is arguing that she's not interested in the job Milo claims Guillermo wants to hire her for. Elizabetta wonders where the Druzhinas are, but she suspects they're giving Teresina and Milo a couple of minutes in order to gain information on the purpose of the meeting.

Then Dahliorn stops Ramira and pulls her into the shadows next to a cabinet along the wall. Through the witch's eyes, Elizabetta follows where he's pointing—the Druzhinas are just coming through the doorway into the large open area beyond.

"You sold me out!" Teresina's shrill accusation puts Ramira and Dahliorn into motion, as the Druzhinas move out of the tenebrous cover of the dimly lit warehouse: Alexander and Justin, who split up just as Guillermo predicted. Alexander runs after Milo as Justin—to Elizabetta's surprise—charges toward Teresina. The look on the rogue's face is conflicted, but then her gaze darts past him. "Watch out behind you!"

Justin turns around just in time to avoid Ramira, who meant to leap on his back. The witch stumbles forward a few steps when she misses, and Elizabetta watches with pride as Justin's fangs drop down and he takes a defensive posture. *You're toast, Ramira.*

Ramira lunges at Justin and attempts to fight with her

minimal martial arts skills, but his movements are swift and accurate—they're meant to repel his opponent, not seriously injure or kill her. Doubtless he can tell she is little more than human. Ramira foolishly thinks she stands a chance against the Druzhina, and her naïveté plays into Justin controlling the fight and readying her for a takedown.

He proves it three seconds later when he throws a block that captures her arm as he spins into position behind her. Through gritted teeth he says, "Who are you?"

Ramira snarls and groans as she tries to work free of his hold. Her eyes dart around the room, and Elizabetta knows she's looking for Dahliorn, but he's nowhere in sight. Much to her relief, the damn spider doesn't appear to be here either. *Don't screw up my sacrifice for you—kill her already.*

"Do you have any idea who she is?" Justin's question is for someone behind them, and when he pulls Ramira around, Elizabetta sees Teresina standing a few feet away. She won't meet Justin's gaze, but she hasn't run. *Yet.* "I've never seen her before."

Alexander's booming laugh breaks the building tension. "It's a three-for-one night. I think we crashed a party, dear brother."

Panic surges through Ramira—her body trembles—but Elizabetta can't help mentally smiling at the sight before her. Alexander has Milo in a secure grip and is pushing him toward the others. *I could almost kiss him for capturing that worm.*

Justin starts to reply, when Dahliorn steps into view. The sheridauk's eyes glow a brilliant red—Elizabetta suspects it has something to do with his fae powers—and he says, "While I am willing to let you leave with the two you came for, I cannot permit you to take her."

*Hmm ... so this arrangement didn't allow for Guillermo to send his mutant. Can't say that hurts my feelings.*

"Who and what the hell are you?" Justin growls.

Dahliorn mutters something, and before anyone can react, he rushes forward two strides, rips Ramira out of Justin's hold, and flees the building. Elizabetta hears shouts from her friends but not the sound of running feet. She understands—Milo and Teresina were the targets, and the Druzhinas will not risk losing them. Only after their captives are secure will they turn their attention to this new threat.

The sheridauk runs at incredible speed, and Elizabetta doubts a vampire or werewolf could catch him as it is. His strength is impressive; he seems to have no need to readjust his hold on Ramira as he weaves through the industrial complex, not slowing until they are a couple of miles away. Given his slender yet well-toned physique, his endurance is expected—but still remarkable. He doesn't even sound winded from the run.

When he sets Ramira on her feet, her eyes move over him once before she shifts her gaze past his shoulder—she's not making eye contact long enough for Elizabetta to assess him. "Thank you for getting me out of there. I failed again." The sadness in her tone reflects the humiliation Elizabetta knows the witch is trying to work past.

Dahliorn stares at her as if he's unsure what to say. Instead he speaks to Elizabetta. «I didn't do it for her. I did it to protect you.»

«Would it have been so awful if she was captured? It could have provided them the information they need to find me.»

«Guillermo may kill you if she's captured by the Druzhina. It's too much of a risk.»

Frustration bubbles to the surface. *Maybe I'm not that valuable if he'd dispose of me so fast. Advantage or disadvantage?* She ponders that thought, and then an idea comes to her. «Does he ever check on me?»

Dahliorn takes a deep breath when the witch finally meets his gaze. "We should contact your uncle and have him arrange to transport us back to the island."

Ramira's face scrunches into a half grimace. "He's going to be very angry again."

"Yes, but we must go back."

While the witch is on the phone with Guillermo, relaying the bad news of another failed mission, Dahliorn says, «Aside from the day he cast the unity spell, I do not know if he's returned to your chamber.»

The compound is large enough, and the underground facility seems huge—there has to be somewhere the sheridauk can hide her body. «You know he'll send her again. If you can hide me someplace that will be very hard to find, it will buy us time.»

Ramira looks back at Dahliorn in time for Elizabetta to see him scowl.

«Time for what?» he says.

She lays out her impromptu plan with as much haste as possible, but before she can talk him into it, Ramira calls over her shoulder, "Uncle Guillermo is sending someone to pick us up." She's already begun walking to the nearest street corner. "He'll take us to a house with a mutaport, and we'll meet with him upon our return."

Dahliorn says, "How upset is he?"

Another grimace crosses Ramira's face. "He'll decide on punishments after he hears how I screwed up this time."

When they arrive at Guillermo's estate, the sorcerer is waiting for them in the dining room, glaring—and it's Dahliorn he addresses first. "What happened?"

The sheridauk doesn't hesitate to provide a recap, though one which emphasizes that Ramira was outnumbered and that the rogue never ran off as expected. Dahliorn claims he had no choice but to pull Ramira out of there; he even postulates that Teresina might have helped the Druzhinas had he joined the fight. When the sorcerer questions what happened to the bait, Dahliorn confirms that the Druzhinas have them in custody now. The sorcerer slams a fist on the table and storms out of the room, muttering something about wards and protections.

Dahliorn rises to leave too, but Ramira grabs him by the arm. "Wait! I—" She glances toward the hall, pausing as if to make sure her uncle is out of hearing range. A moment later she raises the exact question Elizabetta has about the story the sheridauk told Guillermo. "I thought fae can't lie. I did fail. You said I was outnumbered, but it was just me and you against the two vampires until the other Druzhina came back with Milo."

A gentle smile breaks across his face as he looks at her. "I didn't lie."

Ramira's active thoughts show she doesn't understand, but Elizabetta does—the sheridauk counted her in. *Sneaky, but good—damn fae. Still, a win. Small victories.* Inwardly she smiles. With Milo captured, it's only a matter of time until Dmitri finds her now.

## CHAPTER 24: DMITRI

# *Answers*

The unexpected developments of the last few hours have Dmitri pacing faster as bloodlust boosts his anticipation for the answers which soon may come. For months there's been nothing to go on—no leads, no clues—and now, out of nowhere, a major break. *Not just one, but both.* He shakes his head, trying to process what seems unbelievable: Justin and Alexander will arrive any moment with Teresina De Luca and Milo Kohler. *We will finally be on the move to rescue Elizabetta—I will get her back.*

With those thoughts filling his mind, he doesn't hear what Maria says until she repeats it. The others are deciding how best to handle the interrogations; the wizard wants to assign specific teams to question each prisoner, but Dmitri plans to be there for both regardless of who else takes part in the questioning. There may be details which will benefit him in their search for Elizabetta, and he doesn't want any small piece of information overlooked or considered trivial.

A buzz of excitement ripples through the group waiting near the main doors of the ballroom as the Druzhinas bring in the prisoners. *The traitors.* Rationality flees when Dmitri sees their faces, and he lunges forward with every intention of ending them where they stand. Matt moves to physically restrain him. The mongrel's body is tense, though, and Dmitri can feel the tremors pulsing through him—a clear sign that Matt, too, is fighting to keep himself in check.

Antonio and Sally help Alexander take Teresina to the wine cellar, where she'll be shackled until they're ready to question her. Justin rotates to keep his back to Teresina—it appears deliberate—while he forces Milo to sit on a chair in the middle of the ballroom. The vampire's hands are bound behind his back, but Milnea erects a barrier around him as Maria places the spells necessary to gain his full cooperation. He has no choice but to truthfully answer their questions, and Dmitri is grateful they won't lose more time playing games.

Liathera blurts out, "Where is my prince?" Everyone ignores her.

Dmitri snarls, "Where's my wife?"

"I don't even know who your wife is." Milo's answer is unexpected, but it occurs to Dmitri that there was no visible sign of pain that a lie would produce.

"She's been snatched by Guillermo Sanchez." He glares at the reprehensible vampire. "Where is he?"

"Where is my prince? Tell me, or I'll dust you to death." Liathera bangs her tiny fists on the barrier as puffs of pixie dust roll off her harmlessly.

Milo doesn't answer her, of course, because he can't hear

her little voice. Instead he squirms and looks away, and it's clear that he is fighting the compulsion to answer Dmitri's question. A groan escapes him. "He's at ... I can't, he'll kill me for telling you."

Matt's canines are showing as he stalks the perimeter of the barrier. "You should have thought of that before you betrayed us—you're dead either way now. It's your choice how painful your last few hours will be."

The mongrel presses his palms against the barrier, deep growls rumbling from his chest. More than once his wolf features surface while he stares down the vampire. In a different situation, it would almost be amusing; not too long ago Matt voiced his unease at executing Milo, and now he looks as if he'd relish the opportunity to do the deed himself. It's a bit disconcerting that the closer Dmitri and Matt become, the more alike they seem to be—well, aside from the wolf's odd sense of humor.

"Where is Guillermo?" Dmitri says again, his tone terse.

Again Milo tries to resist, but the intense pain from his noncompliance proves the effort futile. He finally gasps and sputters, "Rat-Rath-Rathlin Island. He's at his estate on Rathlin Island."

"Northern Ireland," Maria says.

Tavorell flies in front of Dmitri, his little chest puffed out with pride. "See? Creature of habit, returning to what he knows. Rathlin Island is one of the known areas where Guillermo's parents lived."

Dmitri swats at the pixie. He doesn't want the little winged creature in his face as he glares at Milo—this is personal, and the doomed vampire's manipulation and betrayal made it so. "Tell us about his estate."

Milo's resistance diminishes as more and more answers pour out of him. *He clearly has no tolerance for pain.* They learn that he fled from Machu Picchu when the fighting started, and—not surprisingly—he didn't slow down until he reached Cusco. After returning to Germany, he went into hiding as rumors began circulating of Shashenka's fall. He knew he would pay dearly if the Druzhina found him.

Milo tries to claim that he had no choice—that Shashenka and Guillermo plotted together, leaving him at Shashenka's mercy given their long association. That alone, he insists, is the reason he requested to be turned—he wanted to make it harder for anyone to hurt him or end his life. Milo considered it an insurance policy on his future, a move he never thought would backfire. Now it has, and he knows final death awaits.

"I didn't know that sorcerer could find me." Milo gives a sardonic laugh. "I had already resigned myself to staying in the shadows of this world for a millennium if necessary, to ensure my survival. He claimed I owed him a debt for his failure to capture you three in Mettlach, but then he set me up to be captured by you."

"We would have found you eventually." Dmitri pushes against his desire to end the vampire right now—he knows better than to destroy a source before their leads are investigated.

Milo gulps but continues providing details about Guillermo's estate and the little he knows of the sorcerer's plans. Guillermo clearly used him and Teresina to attempt to trap and kill a Druzhina—it is discomfiting that the

sorcerer was able to manipulate and lure them so effect-
tively.

Justin barks out a laugh. "That sorcerer is nuts if he
believes he can take on any of us."

Maria reminds him that besides Dmitri's capture before
they ended Shashenka, Guillermo has since made three
such attempts—Elizabetta, Vladimir, and now Justin and
Alexander. "Who are the woman and man Guillermo has
sent for these missions?" she asks.

Milo shrugs and claims that he doesn't know anything
about the man, but Guillermo referred to the woman,
Ramira, as his niece. *Niece? Is the man related too?* But
then Milo's description of the man sends an excited murmur
through the small crowd around Dmitri. Liathera lets out a
shriek of joy and crashes to the floor. Tavorell swoops down
to check her and assures everyone that she's okay; she
passed out from the excitement.

*I think this just went sideways with their prince.*

The barrier around Milo shimmers and turns black.
Dmitri looks at Milnea, who says, "We must discuss this
development privately. He's describing the king's son, I'm
sure of it." Her ghost-white skin pales even lighter than its
normal milky state; even her attributes lose definition,
almost as if she's fading away. "I don't know why he would
be helping Guillermo. I fear the possibilities."

They're discussing the issue—Guillermo may now have
access to fae dark magic—when Liathera comes to and
buzzes around, growing more agitated when they try to
dismiss her arguments in the prince's defense. Tavorell
mutters again about nymph blood in her family as she

protests, "We must give the prince a chance to explain."

Matt looks between the Seelinarans and Dmitri but directs his question to Maria. "You told us once that fae magic rivals that of a wizard. How could a sorcerer overcome a fae?"

Maria shakes her head and purses her lips. "I don't know. It shouldn't be possible—maybe he joined Guillermo willingly ..."

The more Dmitri learns about this prince, the more he's leaning toward this possibility. *Why else wouldn't he join forces with Elizabetta and help them both escape?*

"The sorcerer could have exploited fae weaknesses." Tavorell tries to say more, but Milnea cuts him off abruptly. A silent exchange lingers between them long enough to put Dmitri on edge—they're withholding something important, maybe even critical.

Then the Seelinarans begin to argue in their native language. When it turns heated and the pixies make threatening gestures—Dmitri assumes they're trying to dust Milnea—the elemental retaliates by calling up the wind to blow them across the room. Then she wraps both in a bubble and pulls them back toward the group. "You will not threaten me!"

Tavorell glares back at her as he kicks the surface of the bubble he's trapped in. "You can't keep me in here forever, elemental. I'll gladly give up both wings if it means teaching you a lesson."

"And I'll part with my wings if it means helping my mate teach you a lesson." Liathera's tiny arms fold across her chest as she sits in a huff.

Matt and Maria look at each other and say, "Mates?"

"That's enough, all of you!" Dmitri's tone brooks no argument, and the Seelinarans become quiet. "We need to understand what we are up against here if we are to succeed in ending that sorcerer and getting my wife back."

Milnea says, "Tavorell is correct. The sorcerer, being half fae, may have known how to overpower the prince. We have vulnerabilities, which I will not reveal. But I will say this much: if the sorcerer used that to his advantage, then he may have full control of the prince and will use him as a tool, a weapon against others."

Dmitri frowns. The reaction from the tight-lipped fae is expected, but secretiveness isn't going to help them complete their search for the missing prince and return him to Seelinara, let alone rescue Elizabetta.

The barrier around Milo returns to a transparent state, but the vampire has little new to add. Ramira, he insists, was supposed to kill a Druzhina, and the fae was there to protect her if anything went wrong. Milo doesn't know anything about Elizabetta—he claims he never even heard mention of her when he was at Guillermo's compound. *Is she at the estate, or is the sorcerer hiding her somewhere else? Is she already dead? No ... Matt's right, I would feel that permanent loss.*

After a brief discussion with the others, Dmitri determines that Milo knows nothing more that will help them, and he turns to the vampire. Cold hatred carries in his impassioned but official pronouncement—he maintains control. "Milo Kohler, I claim the right of blood justice against you for your perfidy in betraying your own kind.

But as much as I want to end you right now, you will be kept alive until we are certain there is no other knowledge you may possess that will aid us in finding Guillermo Sanchez. You will be placed in shackles and kept here until such time as you are no longer needed, and then I will put you to final death."

While waiting for the bastard to be taken to the cellar and for Teresina to be brought up, Dmitri reflects on the information gained through Milo. He's hopeful that once the rogue is compelled to cooperate and tell the truth, they will garner enough intelligence to go after Guillermo. *I've waited long enough to find and free my wife.* With that thought in mind, he turns to face Teresina as they bring her into the room.

The rogue's eyes take in those in front of her, but even Dmitri sees the sadness that flickers across her face each time her gaze sweeps over Justin. The Druzhina turns away, refusing to look at her.

"Justin, you may leave if it is more comfortable for you to do so." Dmitri's tone is kind—one look at Justin's face, and he understands the sting her betrayal inflicts on his friend. Dmitri has no words to describe the depth of what his friend must be feeling, but the heartache is obvious to everyone in this room.

The Druzhina shakes his head. "I must hear this—I have to know why she turned against me."

"I didn't turn against you!" Teresina's voice is strong and pleading. "I did what I had to—I had no choice."

Dmitri strikes the invisible cage. "You profited from your choice. You willingly provided information that almost doomed us to failure!"

She looks down, and a tremulous sigh parts her lips. "I know you don't believe me, but—"

"Maria, compel her. We're losing time here, and I'm not going to dance in circles with this bitch." Dmitri waits for the wizard to invoke the spells, then says, "I'll say it again: you profited at our expense."

Teresina winces. "I walked into a trap, and your master tortured me for information. If that was all he'd done, I might have been able to resist." Tears roll down her face, and her gaze locks on Justin for a moment before she looks down at the floor. Her voice is barely audible. "I did resist until ... until Shashenka and one of his henchmen began raping me. If it had only been their bodies, I might have withstood even that, but ... I couldn't bear the pain of the devices and weapons they used to violate me."

An uncomfortable silence settles over the room. Dmitri recalls what Peter said during his interrogation—and the way he avoided going into specifics. Now he understands why. He shudders, remembering the reprehensible order Shashenka gave for Elizabetta to be raped at Big Sky—and how it would have ended had he not pretended to carry out his master's demands. While he may be volatile right now, Dmitri is not a heartless monster. But something doesn't add up. *Why did she turn it into a profitable venture?*

He studies Justin for a long moment—doubtless the same question and many more are racing through his mind. The Druzhina's hands are clenched, his nostrils flaring; rage and pain are etched on his face. Dmitri would like to give his friend privacy and time to find his own answers, but he can't let go of the way Teresina played them all. Until she explains the money, he won't give her another chance to dupe Justin, if that is what she's doing. Their history as Druzhinas binds them as brothers—the closest to family any of them have in this long life. He will give them time to talk when this is over.

Dmitri turns back toward Teresina. "So tell us why you decided to twist this into a money-making scheme."

Teresina hangs her head again but explains that her reputation was too well known. She was already under threat, and possibly being tracked; by bringing money into the equation, she gave what little information she did share with Shashenka more credibility. It also, to a small degree, was recompense for what Shashenka did to her. "I regretted fleeing the moment I left." Her eyes again dart toward Justin. "I was ashamed of the role I played, the way your master revealed me as a traitor to all of you"—a tear rolls down her cheek—"and to Justin. I was afraid of what you might do to me if you won the battle."

"Why didn't you tell us ... or at the least tell me about your capture and the deal you entered into with Shashenka?" Justin's question is unexpected, and Dmitri studies his friend's face—the vampire appears heartbroken, and devastation pierces his tone. If there were any doubts about Justin's feelings before, Dmitri has none now.

Teresina draws in a deep breath. "Shashenka claimed that I wasn't the only mole, that he had two others in your ranks. For all I knew, you were one of them, Justin. I was afraid that if I revealed too much, your master would find out."

Dmitri, Matt, and Maria immediately look toward Alexander, but he shakes his head and puts his hands in the air. "I swore my blood oath to you, and I have not broken it."

There's a ring of truth to his statement, but Dmitri can't shake the nagging doubt. Tavorell flies a couple of circles around Alexander, saying, "Perhaps you should question your friend here. If he betrayed you, you will know soon enough."

"There's no need to spell me—I'm telling the truth."

Maria utters the truth spell nonetheless, and Alexander continues to insist he is not a mole and knows of no others. Then he gives Dmitri an imploring look. "Brother, I know that I have wronged you in the past, and I truly am trying to make up for my transgressions against you. I do not believe these moles existed, but that they were a hollow threat to keep the rogue in line."

The Druzhina has a point, one that Dmitri must consider, but he needs to know for certain. He asks Maria to put each of them, including himself, under a truth spell. The wizard moves from one Druzhina to the next, then on to Matt, Sally, and Antonio, and to Dmitri's absolute relief, everyone checks out. If there were moles, they might not have survived the battle at the estates or Machu Picchu, and the only one of consequence Dmitri's side lost was Sofia— for the way she fought and died, he knows she wasn't in league with Shashenka. The only ones not tested are Maria and Elizabetta, but Dmitri understands the truth of the wizard's enslavement to Shashenka. She never would have helped their master in any manner, and Elizabetta waited centuries to kill him.

That leaves the question of Teresina. Dmitri collects the others and leaves Justin and the rogue alone in the ball-room. "When we return, let us know your decision on what-ever justice or punishment you feel is due for her betrayal."

They retreat to the library and go over the details they've learned about Guillermo. Within minutes their plan takes rough shape. They will leave Antonio to look after the villa while the rest of them travel to Rathlin Island to scope out Guillermo's property and try to discover whether Eliza-betta is even being held there. If she is ... *Our long wait is almost over. I'll finally get her back.* But they can't begin the search for her until other matters are taken care of, and Dmitri hopes his friend has had sufficient time with the rogue. Every minute now is at Elizabetta's expense.

When they return to the ballroom, Dmitri's eyebrows arch in surprise at the sight before him: both Justin and Teresina are on their knees facing each other, their palms and foreheads pressed together against the barrier between them. Dmitri can see that both have shed tears, and his heart wrenches. A part of him still wants to destroy Tere-sina for her betrayal—but how much of that desire is driven by the ever-present bloodlust coursing through him? *Justin loves her ... even now he loves her.*

In the seconds it takes to stride across the room, Dmitri makes a difficult decision, one that goes against his need for blood justice—he'll accept whatever Justin proposes. "Have you decided, brother?"

Justin nods and stands to face the others. "I won't make the decision you seek. We're unbound, and I have forgiven her, but I understand that none of you may be able to."

*Unbound.* Dmitri's eyes narrow. He doesn't need any explanation—an incomplete or yet–to-be-sealed mate bond doesn't make the pull between them any less.

The look Justin gives Dmitri is crushing—his friend knows that Teresina isn't blameless for Elizabetta's capture. "My desire is to let her go, give her a chance to prove herself loyal ... I know that is not what you have sought. Grant one kindness, though: if you execute her, end my life too. I choose to follow her and have no wish to remain once she is gone."

The Druzhina's words prove Dmitri's assumption correct, and without hesitation he clasps Justin's shoulder, conveying assurance. "We will not execute your intended mate. She will be granted a reprieve, a chance to earn her place among us. I charge you to stay with her, watch over her, and keep her from interfering as we continue our search for Elizabetta."

Dmitri releases his grip but holds Justin's gaze. "Make yourselves at home here until we return or call you to us. Alexander, stay with them and keep an eye on both." *We need to make sure that she's not fooling Justin and seeking a way to escape.*

Alexander nods as Milnea releases the barrier. Teresina runs into Justin's arms, but she turns her face toward Dmitri. "I will never forget the debt I owe you for sparing my life. Please allow me to make it up to you by providing my services as needed."

Dmitri sputters in disgust. "Is profit always your biggest motivator?"

She manages a faint smile. "I meant to convey that my

services are at your command. No charge."

A hand clasps around Dmitri's, and he looks down to see Sally standing next to him. "I think I might like her—I see she can muddle her words as well as me."

Although Dmitri still has reservations about this new arrangement with Teresina, he can't help laughing at Sally's perky acceptance of the rogue.

She squeezes his hand again and bounces on her feet. "Now, are you ready to go find Elizabetta and finally bring her home?"

Dmitri starts to reply, but Matt beats him to it. "I was born ready myself, and I don't think there'll be any stopping Dmitri. Something tells me he may be worse than a bloodhound now that we have a trail."

# CHAPTER 25: ELIZABETTA

*New York*

The activity at Guillermo's compound returns to the boring normalcy of Ramira's daily routine, Elizabetta's stealth training, and dribs and drabs of how Guillermo's plans are progressing in the human and shadow realms.

Televisions throughout the mansion are left on at all times as news trickles in of the growing unease. Allies are turning against each other and forging new alliances with old enemies. Governments have toppled in the smaller, less stable countries, and the escalating unrest is threatening to bring down the superpowers as well; several developed nations have already begun moving military assets as peace talks break down at the UN and NATO.

But while these developments bring Guillermo great pleasure, he is noticeably displeased by the decrease of fighting in the shadow realms, which have calmed considerably after the vampire realm chose a leader. Guillermo rants, stomps, and throws anything he can get his hands on—he even blasts a television with a bolt of magic.

Elizabetta almost expects him to cry out, "Curses, foiled again." The sorcerer is a demented real-life version of the cartoon character Snidely Whiplash, but he is more than the stereotypical villain—he is the reason that stereotype exists.

As if to prove her point, a report on the Druzhina arrives, and he smacks the table with his palm so hard that his wine glass jumps and topples over, spilling its contents across the table. Elizabetta swears he is on the verge of losing his mind. "They aren't in control! The vampires will fall, and I will bend them to the point of breaking until you destroy them." *Oh, really? Good luck with that.* Guillermo stares across the long dining table between him and Ramira; he looks like he's going to have a stroke, and Elizabetta wishes he would. "It's time to send the Druzhina a message," he says.

Ramira waits patiently for him to continue, but the active thought strand Elizabetta taps into tells her that the witch already knows what's coming next.

Guillermo doesn't disappoint. "I'm sending you to New York in the morning. I will allow a one-time release of Dahliorn's ability to glamour you both so that you may infiltrate the vampire queen's court and assassinate her."

*A one-time glamour? Are we talking disguise or weapon?* «Dahliorn, what can you tell me about glamour? Guillermo's going to compel you to use it on yourself and Ramira so that she may assassinate the new vampire queen.»

There's a slight pause before he replies. «It's a fae ability to induce others to see something that is not true.»

She detects an underlying hint of fear in Dahliorn's response, though she's unable to discern whether it's the glamouring spell or its consequences that frightens him most. «What is putting you on edge?»

A couple of long minutes pass without a reply. Guillermo and Ramira are discussing her upcoming mission. The vampire queen lives in a penthouse in New York City and has a rather large entourage, but her actual coven is small—only six, including her. Guillermo is confident that if Dahliorn's glamour can get them past her followers, Ramira should be able to kill the queen.

*Disguises, then.* «Dahliorn?»

Finally the sheridauk says, «The sorcerer must risk unleashing my fae power to enable that level of magic, which means that he will ensure that he has full control over me first. Only one other time has he done this ... he restrained me in rusted iron bonds and poured salt over me until I relented.»

Elizabetta recalls the damage both cause, and she imagines it's no less painful than Shashenka's perverted naval cat. Memories of being tortured combine with images of Dmitri's scars—she can't abide Dahliorn suffering that way, and she pleads with him not to resist. *I don't want to see him burned to dried-out, crispy bits.*

A bitter chuckle rumbles through their mental link. «He will expect my resistance, and I dare not disappoint him in that regard.»

Ramira is almost finished packing when she is summoned to a room in the dungeon. Dahliorn is strapped to a gurney, writhing and groaning in pain—the sorcerer has him stripped naked, and a thin layer of salt sizzles across the sheridauk's body, searing his flesh. Red welts and blisters cover almost every inch of exposed skin. Elizabetta is shocked to see that the silver belt is lying to the side and no longer fastened around his waist. Doubtless Guillermo removed it after he covered the sheridauk in the first grains of the caustic substance.

Dahliorn's body trembles with the futile effort to resist, and Elizabetta's heart clenches—she watches in horror as Guillermo rips a handful of salt from the bag and dribbles it over the sheridauk's body. His screams ratchet up in pitch as the addition burns his skin. His body arches and pulls at the restraints. The sight sickens her; she can't just stand by and let this go on. «Please do what he demands—end this torture. We can find a way to defeat them, but stop this.»

Dahliorn's gaze flickers to Ramira, and his eyes close as his mouth opens. Half-choking, he speaks in what Elizabetta has come to recognize as his native tongue, and she watches in almost macabre fascination as Dahliorn's appearance shifts. The gaunt shadowing of vampiric eyes appears in darkened circles beneath his lower eyelids. Fangs and claws become visible, and both look as if they could be deadly. *He really does look like a vampire, and a handsome one at that. Color me impressed.* She wonders what Ramira looks like now, but she'll have to wait until the woman checks her own appearance in a mirror.

The sorcerer places the silver belt around Dahliorn's waist and mutters an incantation that causes the symbols on it to glow momentarily before returning to their normal dull state. Then with a wave of his hand, he swipes away the salt from Dahliorn's body. "I have reactivated your shackle, but know this, sheridauk; if you allow the glamour to slip before I give you the command to remove it, then you will be burned by the packets of salt embedded between your waist and the belt." A smug smile crosses Guillermo's face. "I will not be there to counter it, and you know as well as I that the salt will eventually burn clean through your body."

Dahliorn's eyes drift toward the silver belt, and he nods but doesn't look up. "I understand. I will not fail in this task."

Grimacing, Dahliorn gingerly places one foot and then the other on the floor and shuffles toward his quarters. Elizabetta cringes at each painful step he takes, and she's struck by the similarities of his and Dmitri's tortured existences—both men have endured what no one should ever experience. She's not naïve, and she understands that being good isn't a free pass to avoid all the bad in life, but the shadow realms seem to take it to extremes. *Both deserve far better than what this life has given them.*

In many ways Dahliorn reminds her of Dmitri and Matt—good men with compassionate hearts, and each possessing the intelligence that makes for a great leader. She watched Matt rise from a lone wolf on the outer fringes of a mixed pack in rural Montana to an alpha wolf respected around the world. Dmitri was a leader in his own right before he suffered under and then helped eliminate one of the most tyrannical vampires that ever existed. She can't help but wonder what—if fate had been different, and the fae species had not been destroyed by Guillermo—Dahliorn might have become to his people.

Elizabetta allows her thoughts to wander further, trying to envision him free. She knows little about his culture, but she can see the strong, resilient sheridauk being a great leader. It saddens her to think of the dreams and future he'll never have, and of the loneliness he'll face for millennia—he's expressed no desire for a mate from Earth. She can almost see him choosing to return to the fae realm and living the rest of his existence alone.

The empty ache in her heart returns as her thoughts move back to Dmitri and Matt. *Where are they? Are they looking for me?* She can't help wondering whether they are close to finding her. Doubtless the Druzhina has gleaned all they can from Milo and Teresina, and she hopes Milo sang like a meadowlark and gave them her location. *I need you to find me, amore.* But she doesn't know what would happen if they did rescue her while she's stuck inside Ramira in New York.

Elizabetta turns her attention back to the witch—they're entering her bedroom—and taps into her active thoughts. *This should be good.* Ramira immediately goes to the mirror at her dressing table. Her blunted fangs look more mature, natural, and Elizabetta detects the hint of a shadowed circle below her eyes, but Ramira doesn't seem to see these changes—she mutters aloud as she wonders what she looks like to others. Still, there is little doubt in Ramira's mind that the glamour worked. Guillermo wouldn't have released Dahliorn otherwise, and the threat of the salt is likely enough to prevent Dahliorn from removing the glamour before they complete their mission.

After Dahliorn sends Elizabetta back to her own body that night, she tries to engage him in conversation, but he declines, citing the burns he must heal before their departure. She exercises most of the night, feeling disappointed that the sheridauk is in no condition to move and hide her body—the upcoming trip would be the perfect opportunity to try that escape method. Her body will unfortunately remain where it's been for months now, and the extended period she'll be away may lock her body in a rigor mortis–like state, something she's not looking forward to when they return.

Elizabetta wakes disoriented to find she's already been transferred back to Ramira—something that has never happened before. The witch is standing near the mutaport. Dahliorn and Guillermo are there too, and the latter is recapping his expectations; Dahliorn receives his usual admonition to watch and protect Ramira but not to interfere with the witch's responsibility of ending the vampire queen's life.

Curiosity burns within Elizabetta—a mix of eagerness and dread-filled anticipation at the opportunity to meet the woman the Druzhina has installed as queen. *Is she a good, moral leader? She must be, right?* Elizabetta has no idea why the Druzhina chose this route for their realm, or how her friends came to select the female who now leads the vampires. She's also unsure to what degree she should attempt to protect this queen, and if there's a possibility the queen may be a threat in and of herself. Dahliorn has claimed his knowledge of the mission is almost as vague as her own; the only aspect Elizabetta is certain of is that he will not be happy if she does anything to stop Ramira.

The mutaport activates, and seconds later they find themselves in a dark alley—it's the middle of the night in New York, but the noise of people and traffic is louder than Elizabetta expected. Once they have their bearings, they move in the direction of the apartment Guillermo arranged, chosen for its proximity to the vampire queen's lair. It will provide Ramira and Dahliorn a base as they work to penetrate the queen's court.

The dingy one-bedroom apartment is furnished, but the worn-out furniture makes it obvious that their stay here will be anything but comfortable. Missing knobs, inoperable light switches, and stains on the furniture and floors seem to confirm that building maintenance and upkeep haven't occurred in the last decade or two. In a selfless moment, Ramira suggests they share the queen bed, but the appalled look that crosses Dahliorn's face is a clear signal that he'd vastly prefer the discomfort the sagging couch offers him.

In the remaining few hours before daylight, they venture out into the neighborhood, taking an elevator to the floor below the penthouse suite where the queen resides. It's an unremarkable floor with standard tenants, but it far surpasses their rat- and cockroach-infested building. Dahliorn tells Ramira what he detects about the queen's closest neighbors as they pass each door; over half are human, while the remaining are vampires. It amazes Elizabetta that there seems to be no security at all. *Why would they leave the queen unprotected? Isn't she in danger from other vampires or those from other realms?* Of course she is—

Ramira is here for precisely that reason.

The following evening Elizabetta wakes, confused, as her senses return. Music is blaring, blood scents the air, and the crowd is a mix of vampires and humans—Elizabetta feels the nausea wash over Ramira at the sight of vampires openly feeding on the humans or engaged in sexual activity. *Hell of a way to wake up—now I'm hungry.* The black walls with red ceiling borders add to the debauched environment in the dimly lit nightclub. The witch stands with Dahliorn near the dance floor, where several humans and vampires are grinding and swaying together.

Three vampires mingle nearby, sipping blood from crystal goblets. One keeps looking over his shoulder at them; after a few moments he approaches, and Elizabetta can feel a burst of nervous excitement ripple through Ramira as his eyes rake over her from head to toe and back up to her breasts. Elizabetta shakes her insubstantial head. *Hello, face is up here.* The man's gaze doesn't shift upward.

"Hi. You're new here, aren't you?"

Ramira says, "Yes, we just arrived yesterday. Quite a club you have here."

"It's not mine, but it has perks for those like us." His broad smile gives a glimpse of his fangs. "I'm Jax, and you are?"

There's a bloated pause as Ramira scrambles for an answer. Elizabetta nearly laughs at the quandary—the unprepared witch knows she needs to protect her true identity but never gave thought to the fact that someone might ask her name. "I'm Debbie, and this is John."

Dahliorn shoots her a scornful look. No doubt he didn't

consider false names either, but he doesn't seem pleased with the one she chose for him.

Jax reaches out and shakes Dahliorn's hand. "Good to meet you. Nice-looking gal you have here."

"She's not mine." Dahliorn's tense posture carries through to his voice.

Jax shrugs. "No biggie either way. Did you two come to meet Queen Constance? We seem to get a lot of gawkers now that she's been crowned, so to speak."

*So that's her name.* Elizabetta tries to size up the vampire, but Ramira's lack of attention keeps the witch's eyes darting around the crowd.

"Oh, is she here?" Ramira feigns an innocence that sounds like the lie it is. "I mean, yes, we came to see this new queen of ours. What's she like?"

Jax spends a moment looking over each of them. "She may show up here later—she does like to party." He doesn't go into any detail that is helpful to Elizabetta, but it confirms the easy access the witch may have to get near the queen.

The other two vampires who were with Jax wander over, and he introduces them—they take in Ramira and Dahliorn, clearly assessing the two. It seems that none of them are on close personal terms with this new queen. Elizabetta speculates that while they are aware of who the queen is, they are not part of the large entourage that is rumored to surround her.

About an hour later, their new friends become animated when a woman enters with several others following her. Jax points at the group—all are well dressed, and several appear to dote on the woman. "There's our mighty new queen now." Ramira rises from her seat, but he puts out a hand to stop her. "Best watch from a distance. She doesn't take to any of us getting up in her face."

Ramira's eyes narrow, but she sits back down. For the next hour she watches Queen Constance interact with the club's patrons—she's dismissive with some and raucous with others, all the while keeping herself the center of attention. Though she takes turns dancing provocatively with a few of the men who came with her, she seems unattached to any of them. She even acts uninterested in the humans, preferring blood in a champagne flute. *Pretentious much?*

Then another pair of vampires moves into view, and Elizabetta's reaction causes Ramira's breath to catch in her throat. *What are Stephan and Victoria doing here?* Seeing a pair of familiar faces is unexpected, and it leaves her feeling torn. She may have the opportunity to learn how close they are to finding her—but Ramira's risk levels just spiked through the ceiling.

«Dahliorn, see those two by the pillar behind the queen? They're Druzhinas, and I think they are here to protect her.»

Dahliorn seems to ignore her comment and asks Ramira to join him on the dance floor for a slow dance. But as they sway to the music, he whispers, "There's at least two vampires nearby protecting the queen."

"How do you know?" Ramira doesn't keep her voice quiet, and he scowls at her. "Shh. Their actions are clear. They are not here for fun, and the way they're watching the crowd tells me that they are looking for threats."

*What is he up to?* At least he didn't out Stephan and Victoria as Druzhinas, but her mind races: setup, personal agenda, desire to thwart her, secret orders, none of the above, or all of the above. *It'd be great if he'd toss me a clue.*

When Constance moves onto the dance floor, Ramira guides Dahliorn to close the distance between them; the not-so-inadvertent bump against the queen gives the witch the opening she was hoping for. "Pardon us, we didn't mean to crash into you, your majesty."

The use of royal recognition seems to win Ramira consideration from Constance. "Try not to let it happen again." Then the queen's eyes drift over Dahliorn. Constance licks her lips and cocks an eyebrow, and then she pushes her dance partner at Ramira and pulls the sheridauk to her. Her body presses into Dahliorn as her hands cup his ass. She purrs, "Dance with me."

Ramira's active thoughts take in every nuance of the queen's interaction with Dahliorn—she is mildly amused that he isn't spurning her affections. Elizabetta mentally grimaces as the witch realizes they just found their ticket in. *That bitch. She's going to use Dahliorn's sex appeal to infiltrate the queen's lair.*

# CHAPTER 26: DMITRI

# *Barriers*

Dmitri's disparate group arrives on Rathlin Island and takes in the low-lying countryside from a cliffside hill. The mostly wide-open terrain is sparsely populated, and he believes they'll locate Guillermo's compound with little effort. But when they stop to check the map after an hour of hiking, it becomes clear that somehow they altered their course and are nowhere near the sorcerer's estate. They should have found it within a half hour of their starting point.

After the third time they end up astray, a surprised look widens Maria's eyes. "Misdirection. Guillermo's property may be warded and spelled—it's confusing our sense of direction and causing us to move away whenever we come close to it."

Tavorell instructs them to wait while he attempts to locate the property—he believes his skills and magic will allow him to get past whatever is hiding the compound. To no one's surprise, Liathera announces she'll go with him.

Twenty minutes later they return and appear coated in sweat, though Tavorell beams with satisfaction. "It's a strong misdirection spell, but my powder armor deflected the magic and allowed me to stay on course. The property is there, as Milo described it. I can lead you to it, but you must not follow your instinct to go in other directions."

As the pixies hover in front of Dmitri, he realizes it's little glistening clouds of dust falling off them, not sweat. They're confident their powder armor will work well enough to get the entire group to the estate.

"Lead the way, little pixie-man." Matt laughs, and a smirk tugs at the corners of his mouth. When he sees the questioning looks on his friends' faces, he says, "Oh, come on, surely you see the humor in this. We're about to blindly follow two pixies to find an evil sorcerer."

Sally scrunches her nose. "I don't see how that's funny at all."

"Ignore him ... he has a warped sense of humor." Maria looks at Tavorell, but not before Dmitri catches the wink she gives Matt. "Show us the way, Tavorell."

The pixie's chin lifts with pride as he flies off ahead of them. Within minutes Dmitri is struggling against his natural instinct to choose a direction—like the others, he can't shake the overwhelming desire to turn, reverse course, or veer off. There's slight comfort that everyone reacts the same way; otherwise they might be scattered all over this small island. *It's beyond me how we keep getting lost on a strip of land that is no more than four by two–plus miles in size.*

Liathera buzzes around them, encouraging them to focus

on Tavorell. Dmitri knows they're faltering again, but he swats at her when she hovers in front of him.

She dodges his swipe and repositions herself in front of Matt. "Watch me and follow along."

The wolf grins when Liathera begins to sing and dance in the air, stepping, twirling, and shaking her hips. *Of course, no inhibitions—Matt plays right along.* Dmitri's brows furrow in worry. He's not sure how sane the pixie is and whether they should follow the tiny Seelinaran at all. To his bemusement, though, the strange dance routine seems to entice his companions to follow along. Even Tavorell's backward glances go from scowls to grins. Dmitri, embarrassingly, is as affected as everyone else by the compulsion to do as Liathera instructs.

"Did she pixie us?" He looks at Milnea.

She laughs. "No, but their kind is known for silly antics that can be addictive to watch. I believe in your folklore there is a story about a pied piper—the truth behind that story is a pixie who was hired to lead the rats away."

"So Liathera is mesmerizing us?" Maria tries to stifle a giggle.

Milnea's head dips in confirmation as Matt says, "Wait, is that the cha-cha?" Then he starts to mimic the moves. In counts of three the wolf steps forward and back, slides sideways, and resets with a rocking step as if he's going to step back, but instead he goes forward. Dmitri's jaw is slack as he watches Matt embellish the movements by throwing his arms out or up, swaying his hips—a bit suggestively whenever Maria looks at him—and tops it off with a few twirls.

Dmitri chuckles in spite of himself and then laughs harder when he realizes that all of them, with the exception of Milnea, are cha-cha-ing their way through the countryside. *Elizabetta would never let us live this down.* Almost as if the wolf read his mind, Matt quips, "I'm gonna love telling this story after we get baby vamp back."

It seems as if they have been dancing for mere seconds, when the pixies stop and hover; Tavorell folds his arms across his chest and impatiently taps his tiny foot. A long minute passes before Dmitri realizes the pixie's yelling at them to stop dancing—they are at the boundary of Guillermo's estate. Liathera is literally rolling in the air with laughter. Dmitri shakes his head to clear it and starts to walk forward, but Tavorell punches him in the nose, bringing him to a stop. The hit feels like a bee sting.

"Don't touch the barrier—you may trigger an alarm."

Dmitri notices the confusion on everyone's faces, likely matching his own. He doesn't see anything but undeveloped property—no different from the majority of the island, save a thick grove of trees surrounding the clearing. "This is it? There's nothing here."

"It's not glamour—the pixies and I would see through it." A look of concentration washes over Milnea's face as she mutters something, but it's not clear to Dmitri what she's trying to do. She says, "Maria, can you see the magic pulsing around this empty area?"

Maria squints and tilts her head one way and then another. "Yes ... there are many layers to it. I suspect there is a ward to give the illusion of an undeveloped property. Give me a few minutes to study it and see if there's a way to remove it without setting off any alarms."

Tavorell's small size allows him to be the guinea pig to test the barrier—since it's likely Guillermo's wards and spells are meant to thwart larger beings, something the size of a big bug shouldn't trigger an alarm. Maria tries several incantations to penetrate the invisible barrier, but each time Tavorell touches the invisible wall, he is repelled. For hours the Seelinarans and Maria work together, but their every attempt fails.

Dmitri doesn't want them to give up, but the sun will rise soon, and there won't be enough shade to shelter him and Sally. When he mentions the need to return to Venice, Milnea orders the plants and trees to provide them cover. Astonishment drops his mouth open as two trees with a tangled mass of limbs and thick canopies of leaves move toward one another—not walking, but somehow using their roots to pull and creep across the ground, stopping when only a few feet separate them. Then an assortment of shrublike plants begin to climb up the trunks, weaving a natural screen that blocks the sunlight. As the sun inches across the sky, the vegetation screen moves too, continuing to shade the vampires. Given his team's failure to take down the sorcerer's shields so far, the plants are the only thing keeping the vampires alive.

Still, it's exhausting for everyone as the hours drag on, and Dmitri can't begrudge them a break when a haggard-looking Maria turns and says, "I need to rest for a bit."

Matt, leaning against a tree, says, "Come here, witchy-poo. You can use me as a recliner." He pats his lap and the wizard settles with her back against his chest, her head resting against his shoulder. Matt wraps his arms around her as she drifts off to sleep. Dmitri can't ignore the pang of jealousy—not of the wolf holding the wizard, but because of his longing for Elizabetta. *I would give anything for her to be in my arms again.* Dwelling on those thoughts will only drive his bloodlust to the surface, and he forces himself to observe his friends instead. He still doesn't know whether their deepening friendship is interfering with their commitment to find Elizabetta.

Dmitri's tone is quiet, so as not to disturb the wizard. "You've grown quite fond of her, haven't you?"

A smile stretches across Matt's face, and he kisses the top of her head. "Yeah, she's special." The wolf seems lost in thought for several long seconds before he grimaces and says, "I'm just a mongrel destined to protect special damsels in distress." There's no humor in his tone, though, and Dmitri senses something off about the comment.

Maria doesn't stir, but Liathera lands on Matt's shoulder. "I think that brooding vampire is rubbing off on you. Let me dust you—it will stop the foolish gloom pouring from your mouth."

The melancholy that began to settle across Matt's face melts into a grin. "Hey, it takes great talent to say stupid shit at precisely the right moment. I think I'll pass on being pixie-alized."

The pixie shakes her head. "You Enethurans have no idea what you're missing. I'm telling you ... best time ever."

Matt leans his head back against the tree and closes his eyes as Sally cups a hand to Dmitri's ear and whispers, "It's quite a coven you're gaining here—vampires, maxian, werewolf, even fae and pixies. What a crazy blended family ... I like it."

*Family? Is that what this is?.* Sally inserted herself into his coven whether he wanted to lead one or not. Matt, by default of his friendship with and loyalty to Elizabetta, and now by Dmitri's blood, is an extended member already. But until now he had not considered that Maria's presence was out of anything other than a sense of duty, to keep him in line. Always fewer answers than there are questions, and in that regard the Seelinarans don't fit either; success will return them home, or Milnea will be left behind when he, Maria, and Matt are sent back to face punishment if they fail to find or return the prince alive. He doesn't want to think about that because it will mark an even bigger failure—losing Elizabetta forever.

When Maria wakes from her nap an hour later, she resumes her attempts to tamper with the wards protecting Guillermo's property. The day has been tough for Dmitri— the possibility that Elizabetta is mere yards away, waiting for them to rescue her, eats at him like a cancer. The sun is setting when Tavorell finally passes through and disappears on the other side of the barrier. *Progress?* Dmitri jumps up just as Tavorell's little arm pokes back through and Liathera swoops forward to take his hand. Without warning, Tavorell pulls her through the magical shield.

Dmitri holds his breath as everyone waits to see if the pixies will set off an alarm. When the grounds of the estate remain quiet and nothing comes back through the barrier but Tavorell and Liathera ten minutes later, there's an audible ripple of relief that seems even to include the ambient noises of the surrounding area. Dmitri wants to go after Elizabetta right now, but he forces himself to stay put and listen to the pixies' report. They claim that the compound matches the details that Milo provided. *As expected, given the spells he was under.* The pixies also located an underground entrance, something Milo didn't tell them about, and Tavorell feels it may be worth exploring if they can find a way for all of them to cross the ward.

Maria steps up her efforts, her confidence boosted by the possibility that she's on the right track. Liathera and Tavorell continue flying back and forth through the barrier, and soon Milnea offers to join them and test her ability to cross too, but she turns to half mist as a precaution. When the elemental manages to put a slender arm through the barrier, they again wait to see if an alarm triggers—there's nothing but the same quiet as before.

"Wish me luck." Milnea smiles as she steps through.

Twenty minutes later she returns, and the excitement pouring off her is contagious. "It's an elaborate estate—a three-story mansion that could house a good number of beings, and two large outbuildings that, from the windows, seem to be training and housing facilities. The underground door isn't locked, and I did peer inside. Whatever is down there is kept in the pitch dark."

Dmitri takes a deep breath—it's the most logical place for Elizabetta to be. "Are we ready to do this?"

"Hell, yeah. We've waited long enough to find this asshole and get baby vamp back." Matt quickly strides toward the barrier, but Maria's arm shoots out, her palm splaying across his chest, stopping him.

"I know we're anxious to get in there, but we still don't know what we're dealing with here. We can't saunter in like we own the place."

For several minutes they debate the best approach, keeping in mind the wizard's admonition against haste. Most agree that Guillermo has either isolated Elizabetta in the underground structure or hidden her nearby in the mansion. Milnea is inclined to believe Guillermo wouldn't allow Elizabetta out of his sight, but Dmitri tries to persuade them against searching the mansion first. To back up his argument, he points out that Milnea saw signs of at least one or more beings inhabiting the house—someone could be home.

Tavorell volunteers to go alone. He believes that he can find a way in and explore without detection, and though it doesn't sit well with Liathera—she pouts over being left behind—any more than it does for Dmitri to remain on the outside of the barrier, he can't argue with the logic of the tiny pixie doing an initial probe without alerting whomever is inside to their presence. The pixie gives them a mock salute as he flies backward through the barrier.

A full night and day pass before he returns. The frown on his tiny face is an unwelcome sight. "I searched every nook and cranny of the mansion," Tavorell says, his scowl deepening. "Aside from a few servants and the sorcerer, there is no one inside that house or the outbuildings. I started to look underground, but the place is huge and could take days to search."

Dmitri's blood boils—he can't accept the idea that

Elizabetta is not here, just because the pixie didn't find her. They haven't come all this way to quit. "Aside from not completing a search underground, did you overhear anything that may indicate my wife's whereabouts?"

"No, and I even followed the sorcerer around in hopes that he might reveal something of use to us. His attention seems riveted on events in the human world—the escalating conflict between governments of Enethura has his rapt attention."

*Has that situation become worse?*

Matt's expression turns grave. "What world events?"

"The humans are about to unleash something they call World War III, and the sorcerer seems to be directing some of the pandemonium. Guillermo made a few calls while I was watching him. He's directing the use of military forces and nuclear armaments on every continent. There's a lot of chatter about who will drop the first bomb, or if traditional warfare will be bypassed in favor of launching nuclear weapons."

Maria blanches, and the panicked look on her face matches the sick, writhing feeling in Dmitri's gut. "Why would he do that?" She frowns. "It will annihilate everything and everyone on this planet."

Dmitri says, "Some will survive, but they'll be too weak to stand against him. We have to stop Guillermo and then dispatch the Druzhinas to influence the human leaders to turn away from this path."

Apprehension resonates in the wizard's tone. "I don't know if I'm ready to fight Guillermo's power. The maxians have sent other wizards before me, and all of them died trying to defeat or capture him. He's far more powerful than he should be."

Matt stiffens, a low growl rumbling from his chest.

Dmitri blurts out, "There's two of you. Can't you defeat him together?" He understands why he, Elizabetta, Matt, Sofia, and Katherine failed in their fight against the sorcerer after Milo set them up, but he expects more from two magical beings—a wizard and a fae—who are supposed to be powerful even on their own.

The maxian and elemental both try to answer at the same time, and Milnea stops so that Maria can explain her position. "I still don't know what I'm fully capable of as a wizard. For centuries I was denied the time or knowledge to work with my natural abilities. Only since the battle at Machu Picchu have I discovered that I can cast stun, truth, and compelling spells. I don't know what else may come to me when we need it, but I may not be powerful enough to confront him yet."

To Dmitri's surprise, Tavorell provides more unsettling news. "The sorcerer is steeped in the dark magic arts of not only Enethura but Seelinara as well. The residue is so strong, he reeks of it."

"What does that mean?" Sally's gaze darts between the Seelinarans and the wizard, fear saturating her tone.

Milnea is visibly upset. "That Guillermo is tapping into evil magic infused with the power of the most awful demons known to any realm." She draws a deep breath. "And if the sorcerer is doing more than merely relying on the dark arts of evil demons—if he is summoning or controlling them— then no, we can't defeat him. Only two species can counter that type of darkness. The first is an angel, and not just any angel, but one that is equally powerful in the arts of divine magic. The other is a demon of equal or greater sortilege mastery."

*Angels, understandable, but summoning more demons to fight demons?* It sounds too close to selling one's soul, and if that is the only way to kill Guillermo, it may be a price too steep to pay. Trepidation claims every cell in Dmitri's body. For the first time he considers that there may be no stopping the sorcerer.

"I'll return to Seelinara and request that King Altheron send an angel or demon." Tavorell flies off without waiting for an answer.

Maria touches Dmitri's forearm. "Perhaps we should go back to Venice and wait for help from Seelinara."

Dmitri glares at her. "We can't wait that long!" *We have to do something to put a stop to this now.*

Matt lets out another growl, and Dmitri notices how the wolf's canines lengthen. "Baby vamp is in there somewhere, and from what I know, neither angels nor demons exist in this world, or they stay well hidden."

But the wizard won't give up; she reasons it's for the best if they are ever to stand a realistic chance of stopping Guillermo. Anger swells inside Dmitri, the heat of bloodlust trickling to the surface. His body shakes with the need to unleash it, to punish anyone and everything standing in his way—with spikes of the raw impulse to kill. *I will end that son of a bitch. I will get my wife back.* Even as he takes the first step toward the barrier, there's a modicum of satisfaction—he has waited long enough.

Before he can penetrate the invisible wall surrounding Guillermo's compound, Maria slaps the immobility spell on him. "I'm sorry, Dmitri, we can't let you go in there alone. It's certain death if you do, and that won't help free Elizabetta or stop the sorcerer."

Milnea places fae restraints on Dmitri's wrists, and Maria releases her spell. He starts yelling at them, demanding to be let go, then rakes his shackled hands through his hair. The vitriol of his own accusations soothingly strokes his bloodlust. "We need to get her back. We can't keep allowing the effort to find her to get sidetracked."

Stepping between Dmitri and Maria, Matt says, "We won't be of any use to her dead, and I think you know that the others are right. If we expect Maria to face down that mad magician, then we need the right kind of firepower on our side."

Matt's defense of the wizard settles like razor blades in Dmitri's stomach—doubtless Maria's reluctance to go without additional fae help has swayed the mongrel's opinion. *Why?* Their gazes lock, and Dmitri sneers. "Just how special is Maria to you? You used to be focused ... not anymore. She's become a major distraction to you, hasn't she?"

Matt grimaces, and equal amounts of hurt and anger punctuate each word. "I don't want to lose either Eliza or Maria, but I will make damn sure that we do this right and get them both out of this mess alive."

"You stopped giving a shit about Elizabetta!"

"Stop it!" Sally moves between the two men—her palms repeatedly strike Dmitri's chest. "Just stop it, Dmitri. Do you think we're doing all of this just so both of you can end up dead? For someone who wants to rescue Eliza so badly, you're sure doing everything you can to get her and everyone else killed. Is that what you really want? Or are you still suicidal and using this as an excuse to take her out with you?"

Her outburst knocks the air from his lungs. All he manages to do is stare as if he's never seen her before. Matt grabs his arm, mumbling that she has a point and that Dmitri's elevator isn't going to the top floor anymore. The wolf uses that as an excuse to issue orders, but Dmitri is still frozen by Sally's dressing-down. The blond vampire gives a curt nod to Matt and moves to take Dmitri's other arm, and together they drag him away from the property.

# CHAPTER 27: ELIZABETTA
## Drastic Measures

Over the next week, Constance demands more time with Dahliorn, which allows Ramira the opportunity to scope out the queen's court. Of course, she discovers that it's not really a court at all, but a luxury suite with expensive furnishings. There's a stark absence of governmental structure. Guillermo's assumptions are proven true—she has only a handful of coven members, and protection and security are nonexistent inside the suite, with the exception of Stephan and Victoria. The queen apparently prefers her guards stay in the hall or in the ground floor lobby.

Elizabetta longs to talk with her friends but has no way to do so, not even through Ramira or Dahliorn; they're busy taking advantage of the large number of outside vampires coming and going, and Ramira, at least, is trying to ingratiate herself with the new queen. But Elizabetta can observe the Druzhinas, and their interactions with the queen confirm what she already suspects about their new leader: Constance is an overbearing and arrogant woman who's nearly drunk with her perceived power. She's made more than one threat against the Druzhinas in Dahliorn and Ramira's presence but seems easily placated and side-tracked with flattery. The way Ramira lights up and cheers the queen on is well received and lifts Ramira in status surprisingly quickly.

Soon Constance is demanding private talks with Ramira and moments behind closed doors with Dahliorn. So far the sheridauk has avoided sexual intimacy with the queen, thanks to his limited powers of deflection, but he worries that the trickery will eventually fail if her desires become strong enough to push past it. Her demands for sex are repugnant to him, and he insists he will refuse her, which puts their mission at risk. It's enough to propel Dahliorn into a decision-making role, and he urges Ramira to do what she came to do.

Elizabetta, oddly, finds herself in agreement with Dahliorn. The conversations between the queen and Ramira reveal Constance's long-range plan to dismantle and banish the Druzhina—she holds a hatred for them that Elizabetta doesn't understand, but what she's seen of the new ruler tells her enough. The Druzhina made a serious mistake in elevating this vampire to power.

Ramira, on the other hand, has come to view the queen as a potential ally. She even calls Guillermo to plead her position—she believes Constance may be an asset in their quest to destroy the Druzhina. The sorcerer rebuffs her, clearly upset by the suggestion. Using a combination of veiled and blatant threats, he reminds her that the vampire queen will herself grow too powerful once the Druzhina is gone. She must be stopped if their plans to destroy the vampire realm are to come to fruition.

"Your uncle has a point," Dahliorn says after Ramira throws her redecrystapiezo across the room.

She glares at the sheridauk. "I don't care! I still think it's a mistake not using that vamp bitch to do what Uncle wants done. If I didn't know better, I'd swear my uncle was trying to find a way to kill me. I'm no match for any of those Druzhinas, and we all know it."

*She hit that nail on the head.* Elizabetta adds, «We may have to push the issue if Ramira is ever going to finish this mission.»

A questioning scowl narrows Dahliorn's deep-green eyes. «Why do you want one of your own dead? What happened to you protecting them from Ramira?» He tells the witch that he needs to think, and she flops on the bed to pout.

«Constance needs to be removed from power, or my kind will suffer.»

Dahliorn lies on the couch and drapes an arm across his eyes. «What are you suggesting?»

«If Ramira won't act of her own accord, then maybe it's time I bend her to my will and force her to carry out her orders.»

Dahliorn jumps up from the couch. Incredulity, anger, disbelief, and shock fight for real estate on his face. «It's been a while since we practiced manipulating memory—the risk is too great. I can't guarantee that you'll succeed in keeping yourself hidden from her. Don't do this. We must convince her to make this decision.»

Ramira's active thoughts tell Elizabetta that the odds are slight—the stubborn witch is actually contemplating defying her uncle. «How much longer do you think you can dodge the queen's bed? What do you think Guillermo will do if Ramira refuses to kill the queen? If you can't convince her in the next twenty-four hours, then we may have no choice but to force her to it.»

Dahliorn doesn't answer but resumes arguing with Ramira over the need to bring this assignment to an end. Elizabetta half listens to their discussion; she has a plan of her own. *I'll be doing our kind a favor in getting rid of that queen.* During a lull in the witch's arguing, Elizabetta feeds points to Dahliorn, which he relays to Ramira.

"You've already gained Constance's trust, and you spend at least a half hour alone with her every night. You need to take advantage of that."

"I still say it's a mistake." Ramira leaps from the bed and plants herself in front of the sheridauk. "Uncle is going about this all wrong."

Dahliorn keeps opening his mouth as if to say something contrary, but his frustration results in a series of groans and growls before he says, "What if you're the one who's wrong? What if you use her to wipe out the Druzhina and then find that you've lost the access to finish her afterward? You do understand that she will become more than a figurehead to her kind—it may be all but impossible to get close enough to kill her."

If Elizabetta could nod or add her approval, she'd do so. Still, his words seem to have an effect, and Ramira finally agrees to follow through on Guillermo's plan. Dahliorn's lips press into a tight line—it's obvious he is considering the veracity of her promise—but he sighs and tells the witch he'll try to lead the two Druzhinas away when she meets with the queen next. "This may be your best chance to succeed. I can guarantee that if you fail, we won't get close to the queen again, and your uncle will punish us both."

When nightfall arrives, Ramira and Dahliorn make their way to the queen's penthouse in silence. Unease has the sheridauk hounding Elizabetta. «You must let her do this—don't interfere.» He doesn't waste a moment before seeking out Stephan and Victoria, engaging them in small talk while they wait for Constance to make her appearance. Elizabetta's glad for the chance to learn a bit more about the situation the vampire realm is in. Neither Druzhina hides the fact that they are in disagreement with Constance; they find her abrasive, brash, and impulsive. But when they reveal the lengths they went to in installing this ruler, it becomes clear that they hold some resentment toward Dmitri—they blame him for throwing his fight.

It doesn't make sense that Dmitri would deliberately lose to anyone, let alone Constance. Elizabetta sends silent words to Dahliorn: «What fight? Try to find out what they're talking about here.»

His head inclines. "Do you mean to say that one of your own purposely lost?"

Stephan nods. "Yes. He was in the fight to weed out the worst of the contestants, but when he ended up in the final round, he conceded the match." To Elizabetta's frustration, he seems content to leave it there without elaborating further.

*That isn't like Dmitri ... what was he up to? Why would he do that?*

"It doesn't sound as if you approve of our new queen."

Dahliorn's attempt to elicit more from the Druzhinas seems to work, to Elizabetta's surprise—she isn't sure if they're baiting the sheridauk or making sure it's well known throughout the vampire realm that the Druzhinas aren't the queen's puppets. Neither one bodes well for Constance.

"As long as she refuses our counsel and continues her efforts to disband us, then no, we do not approve of her," Victoria says. "If she comes to her senses and works with us instead of against us, then it will be another matter—she may yet benefit our realm."

*Good luck with that.* What Elizabetta has seen of Constance tells her that their new queen has her own idea of power and how to rule her kingdom, and nothing the Druzhina says will ever change that.

Constance approaches, interrupting them, and demands Ramira join her. Elizabetta expects that Dahliorn will draw out his conversation with Stephan and Victoria once Ramira follows the queen away, and that leaves it up to Elizabetta to push Ramira into taking action. Dahliorn warns her a final time not to interfere—the witch must be the one to act—and Elizabetta acknowledges the risks on all sides. She'll remain patient for now.

The door closes behind Ramira, and immediately Elizabetta can feel the nausea roll through the witch—Constance has two goblets of blood waiting for them. All the blood around here has Elizabetta feeling like a human on a diet who has chocolate cake waved under their nose at every meal. But Ramira swallows hard. "I appreciate your generosity, your majesty, but I just fed and couldn't squeeze another drop down my throat right now."

*Good one. I'm sure it'd be a dead giveaway if she started vomiting.*

"I have a proposition for you, and if you agree, I'll order another round to toast our partnership." Constance takes a sip and flashes a bloody grin at Ramira—Elizabetta is inwardly laughing. *Note to witch, if you can't stand the sight of blood, don't pretend to be a vampire.* "After our last conversation, I began wondering how far you might be willing to go to help me get rid of the Druzhina."

The words send a chill through Elizabetta, but Ramira reacts with eagerness. "I'm willing to do anything I can." Whatever progress the witch made at growing a conscience seems to be eroding the longer she is around the vampire queen, hatred and revenge reclaiming her focus. Ramira proves it when the queen asks her why she despises the Druzhina so much, and the witch, leaning forward, says in a conspiratorial whisper, "Vengeance."

"Vengeance?" Constance crooks an eyebrow.

"Yes. Everything that has gone wrong in my life is because of them." A noticeable spike in Ramira's blood pressure catches Elizabetta's attention, but Constance is unaware due to the glamour. "When I was younger, they killed my parents, and now they want my uncle dead. I was turned by one of their women, and in two recent attacks by their men I've barely made it out alive."

*Sheesh, what a liar—a real piece of work.* A tinge of

sympathy spars with Elizabetta's outrage. Ramira doubtless believes almost every word she uttered, but unknown lies permeate her beliefs—with the exception of the Druzhina wanting Guillermo dead.

Constance studies Ramira for a moment. "Do you know why they took those actions against your family?"

"I don't know why they killed my parents, but I know that I've waited a long time for a chance to get justice for their cowardly acts."

The queen smiles. "I think we can come to an arrangement. I'll invent an excuse to send one of the Druzhinas with you to collect a payment from a rival. If you can kill that Druzhina, we'll blame it on the rival, and I'll help you kill the second one when we meet to discuss what happened."

Ramira nods, her pulse beating faster, and Elizabetta taps into her active thoughts. Everything the queen says pulls the witch further away from any consideration of ending Constance's life. *The stupid bitch is going to back out and botch this mission. Not going to happen.* Elizabetta's mind is made up; the queen is obviously corrupt enough that the Druzhina will not be upset by her loss once they find out that she made the decision to end the problem. *If they ever find out.*

Elizabetta looks over the virtual controls inside Ramira's mind. She's learned enough by now to hijack Ramira's body with more control and smoother moves, but if the queen has any fighting skills—and the tournament she won suggests she does—then it may be difficult to take her out if it comes to a straight-on fight. This leaves Elizabetta with only one real choice, and she can already hear Dahliorn's arguments against such action. But she must do something, and this may be her best or only chance.

As the two women continue to talk, Elizabetta waits for the perfect moment to strike. She knows that Constance has been training Ramira in how to style hair—the queen wants the witch as her lady-in-waiting, and they practice for it nightly. It will give Elizabetta the best opportunity to strike, regardless of whether Dahliorn agrees or approves. *I'll tell him afterward.* She doesn't need a distracting argument now.

The steady tick, tick, tick of minutes stretches into an hour before Constance moves over to a dressing table and hands Ramira a brush. As the bristles rake through her long strands, she resumes plotting with the witch; she's determined to set up Victoria and Stephan's murders for the following night. *Dream on—that is never going to happen.*

Elizabetta gives Ramira all the control the witch needs to continue the conversation, but she begins to take over Ramira's movements and subconscious thoughts, using a combination of thought projection, vampiric influence, and manipulation of physical action strands. The witch's hands keep working the brush through the queen's hair, gathering the strands in one hand. She leans forward and places the brush on the table. The queen prattles on, her excitement growing over how they will use her rivals to bring the other Druzhinas into a trap and kill them all at once.

*You're already in my trap, you bitch, and you are going to die.* Ramira's hands pause. Elizabetta refocuses, prodding the witch to put down the brush. Snippets of their conversation filter through as Elizabetta concentrates.

"... careful to lure one or two ..."

*Section the hair and begin the braid ...*

"... will protect you ..."

*Now weave the plaits together ...*

"... is one needs a slow death ..."

Then the queen names Dmitri, and Elizabetta pushes against her rage and steadies herself. She's about to learn whether she can take this level of control and conceal it, or if she'll lose her chance of ever being free of Ramira.

In a swift motion Elizabetta's imaginary fingers work the energy strands as she propels her own mind to saturate Ramira's brain with vampiric suggestions and commands—allowing her to overcome the witch's conscious abilities. She directs the witch to wrap the long braid around her own hand and sends Ramira's other hand reaching for the dagger hidden beneath her shirt. *Time to do this.* Elizabetta pushes strength into a dual command, which has Ramira pulling the queen's head back and bringing the blade to the vampire's throat. The witch, emotionless, shows no hesitation, reluctance, or reaction as the blade slices deeply and in one smooth pull severs the jugular vein. Constance's hands rise as if to defend against the attack, but Elizabetta forces the witch to step backward. Unable to utter a sound, the queen tries to stand, but the chair topples over and Constance lands with a thud. Elizabetta swings Ramira's leg over the queen's body and forces her to kneel on the woman's chest and pin the vampire to the floor. Wide, terrified eyes stare back in muted horror, but

Elizabetta's in assassin mode and barely notices. *Sever the head, now!*

The sensation of being pushed against catches Elizabetta by surprise. The witch has become aware something is happening beyond her control, and the macabre sight before her seems to have spiked an intense desire to stop herself from this madness. It's too late for regrets—the deed is done. Elizabetta tries to get the witch on her feet so she can find something to ignite and burn the queen's head, but the power struggle for Ramira's mind and body has begun, and Elizabetta is in uncharted territory now.

Ramira whispers, "What have I done?" Panic and remorse saturate her tone. "I-I didn't mean for this to happen."

*Shut up! Burn the head.*

"No. I'm not going to do that."

Elizabetta is in too much trouble to consider the level of awareness the witch is exhibiting by refusing the command. *If you don't finish her, she will kill you.*

The witch shakes her head and backs further away. Nothing Elizabetta tries reverses her course. *Damn it, Ramira, if you don't finish her and the others see this, you'll be dead regardless of whether they can save their queen.*

"I don't want to do this."

*You have to, or you're dead.*

Ramira clutches her throat and shakes her head as if trying to clear it. "What is happening to me?" A heavy pause settles into the silence of the room as the queen's body bleeds out. The witch rushes toward the dressing table and stares at herself in the mirror. Her pulse ticks up, eyes widening, and her mouth falls agape.

An image of Elizabetta's face flashes into view over the top of Ramira's face, and their combined shock is met with a jolting flinch. The witch gasps. "It's you!"

Elizabetta's image fades, but not before her murderous glare locks with Ramira's frightened eyes. *Shit, I'm losing control.* She taps into the memory strands and attempts to wipe the memory of recognition from the witch's mind, but this time she can feel the resistance from Ramira as the witch begins her own race to take control of them both. The sensation is like an arm-wrestling match—Elizabetta gains ground, only to waver and start to lose it. For what seems like hours she strains to slam the witch into full submission, but the effort is exhausting, and she can feel her mental strength weakening under Ramira's will. She's out of options, and she knows it.

«Dahliorn, we're in trouble! I forced her to kill the queen, and she's aware of me now. She's trying to overtake me—»

«Rest, little dove.»

The moment Elizabetta becomes aware of her own body again, she tries to reach out to Dahliorn; she needs to know what's happening. But the distance must prevent communication, or maybe he's too busy fixing her mess to respond. After several tries, she resigns herself to the long wait that is no doubt ahead. If there is one positive aspect to what she's done, it's that Ramira doesn't know how to reattach the queen's head. By the time Constance's coven members discover the body, it will be too late to salvage the queen; if they care anything at all for the vampire, they will burn her head, putting her out of her misery.

The situation with Ramira is another issue. When the witch realizes that Elizabetta's presence is gone, she likely will flee the queen's apartment and New York. But unless Elizabetta's absence convinces the witch that she hallucinated after the queen's murder, then the next time Elizabetta enters Ramira's mind, she may set off another battle for control. It's impossible to wipe the memory of what Ramira saw without Elizabetta first returning to the witch's mind. Somehow she must preempt the confrontation, and she isn't certain how to do that.

*Dmitri ... Matt ... now would be a really good time for you two to come save my butt.*

## CHAPTER 28: DMITRI

# Vampire King

Dmitri nearly succeeds in slamming his bedroom door behind him, but Matt's strong hand clutches the knob and pushes against it.

"Damn it, Matt. I just need a few minutes alone." He's nowhere near as out of control as he was at the sorcerer's estate. He doesn't want to admit it, but Sally's tirade had an impact on him. It's the first time he's ever seen her so angry, and after the accusations he flung at Matt and Maria, he realizes now that he may have crossed a line he'll never come back from—something he ashamedly understood after he calmed down. He sought out each one afterward and attempted to make amends, though he's uncertain if they understood how heartfelt and sincere his words were. *I hope they accepted my apology.*

Still, he can't allow their efforts to find Elizabetta to become sidetracked any longer; they're running out of time. His determination to see this through and not give in to his bloodlust has only been making the angry impulses stronger, and his efforts to resist have failed. Dmitri has to admit that willpower and rationality are no defense against a deeply rooted physiological response. *I need to get Elizabetta back, or I will make the biggest mistake of my long life.*

The wolf squeezes into the room. "I'd rather not have to babysit your ass, but you know that we're keeping an eye on you for good reason."

Dmitri rakes a hand through his hair and stalks off toward the sitting area. Matt doesn't need to remind him of the peril they all face, but Dmitri can't overlook that they each have their own priority: Elizabetta and Maria. He's just not sure to what degree the mongrel holds the wizard's interests above Elizabetta's safe return, or whether Matt's fascination with Maria strengthens or weakens their support for rescuing his wife. "I've already apologized, and I ask with all sincerity, how special is Maria to you? Are my concerns unfounded about your focus on her being a distraction?"

Matt's eyes narrow as he takes a deep breath. "I don't want to lose either Eliza or Maria, and I will make damn sure that we do this right and get them both out of this mess alive."

The ambiguous response leaves Dmitri pondering what is really going on that has both the wolf and wizard sidestepping the issue. He decides to probe for a reaction. "You're aware, aren't you, that Maria cares for you—maybe even a little more than she should? When we thought you were going to die, when you almost did die, she didn't take it well."

"Yeah ... can we talk about something else?" Matt's tone is gruff and dismissive as he sits down in a chair and looks around the room.

Dmitri isn't sure what to make of the mongrel's response. He opens his mouth several times to say something, but everything that comes to mind leads right back to the topic of Elizabetta or Maria. Even though both agreed to move on from Dmitri's earlier outburst, it's left an uneasiness between them, one that grows more uncomfortable the longer they're alone. Dmitri breathes a sigh of relief when Sally enters with a phone in her hand.

Stephan is on the line. "We have a problem, although it's not an entirely bad situation." He clears his throat. "The queen is dead. A couple of unfamiliar vampires found their way inside her lair, and one of them killed her. It was a botched job, and the two got away."

Dmitri listens without comment as Stephan explains what they know. The last one seen with the queen was a recent arrival to her lair, and this mystery woman's male companion had Stephan and Victoria's attention when the attack occurred. Several hours later one of Constance's servants entered her room and discovered the queen's decapitated body. She had bled out, and there was no hope of reattaching the head; they had to finish destroying her.

According to Stephan, the investigation in New York is complete, and he and Victoria are on their way to Venice to go over the crime with Dmitri. The other Druzhinas will also return so they can settle a few matters before they resume their duties. *What is he holding back?* The vagueness of some of Stephan's comments confirms he's hiding something, but Dmitri doesn't want any surprises when they meet. However, Stephan refuses to say anything further until they return.

Two days later the Druzhinas gather in the library to discuss the queen's assassination. As Victoria describe the assassins, Dmitri notices a shift in Vladimir, Justin, and Alexander's demeanors. When questioned, the men are adamant that the suspects are the same man and woman who were present when Teresina and Milo were captured, and that the female was the one who attacked Vladimir. An argument ensues, with Stephan and Victoria insisting the two are vampires, while the other three refute that claim based on their encounters with the mystery pair.

"I don't think they're vampires either." Their heads whip toward Milnea; no one expected the fae to be present, and they watch her warily as she and Liathera approach the table. "The man's description fits King Altheron's son, and he'd have the ability to glamour them to look like vampires."

Dmitri's brows furrow. "What if your prince is in league with Guillermo and assisting him with the dark magic? Will it be considered a failure if we have to kill him?"

"King Altheron didn't give exceptions if the prince is alive when we find him. It won't matter how just or deserved—death will be seen as defying the king's orders to protect and return his son." The elemental's tone sounds detached, but Dmitri suspects she's unsettled by the thought of the prince going rogue.

Matt glares at Milnea. "Risk or not, if your golden boy tries to harm one of us, then we'll take our chances."

"What are you talking about?" Kees leans forward—he's ready to absorb the details and analyze the facts, the way he always does.

A deep sigh blows over Dmitri's lips. "We ran into a problem with Guillermo's estate. Aside from it being heavily warded, there's a high probability that the sorcerer is practicing a very old, evil kind of dark magic, aided by one or more demons. We may not be able to take him out, let alone storm his compound to find and free Elizabetta."

As Dmitri and the others take turns explaining the situation, the Druzhinas go from incredulous to disbelieving—not only that angels and demons do exist but that such an entity may be helping Guillermo thwart them. It only boosts Dmitri's dark mood. Summoning demons to fight demons is one path he refuses to go down, and he doesn't want to debate the point. Regardless of his attempt to steer the conversation elsewhere, they're in the middle of that very discussion when Tavorell flies into the room. *He's alone, no reinforcements?*

Tavorell hovers in front of Milnea while looking at Dmitri. "King Altheron sent two guardian warriors—an angel and a demon. They're waiting in the garden, as neither can enter your home without being invited."

Dmitri freezes in surprise as Alexander shouts, "You brought a demon here? To this realm, this world, you brought an evil creature back with you?"

The pixie stops inches from the Druzhina's face, his little voice buzzing with indignation. "He's not evil. The king sent the angel Nafurael and the demon Zerbadiah. Both are pure. Nafurael has never fallen, and Zerbadiah has risen."

"Precisely my point, little man!" Alexander slams his hand on the table, but Liathera dives down and pokes a tiny finger into Alexander's chest.

Dmitri has never seen her so angry. "No, you don't get it, you big, ugly brute! There is balance to everything in the multiverse, and as surely as angels can fall and be cast out, a demon can rise and be given entrance to the celestial realm."

This information is new to the vampires and Matt, and they fire off questions as Milnea tries to allay their fears. Dmitri is still unsure about involving a demon, but at this point he almost no longer cares, as long as it means ending the argument and making progress in getting Elizabetta back. He stands, leaving them to their debate while he heads for the garden. Of course he doesn't get far into the hall before he hears footsteps behind him. *Matt.* He doesn't look back. *Heaven forbid I should be alone for more than one second.*

Two tall men—average, normal-looking men—wait in the garden. Dmitri's not sure what he expected, but it wasn't this. *Who are they, and where are the angel and demon?* "Excuse me—this is private property. What are you doing in my garden?"

The man with golden-red hair meets his gaze with a fierceness so unexpected that Dmitri's steps falter. Raw power oozes from the stranger. *Not a vampire, but what is he?* The man says, "It is our understanding that we are here at your request. But if we are not welcome, then we shall return whence we came."

Dmitri starts to reply and is cut off by one very agitated

pixie. "I don't think he expected to see you in your glamoured forms." Tavorell jabs a tiny thumb at Dmitri. "Please show yourself so this thick-headed vampire understands who you are."

The strangers look at each other and shrug. Then the one who spoke sprouts gold-and-white wings tinged with red that fan out and flex behind him, while the other, darker-complected man changes shape in the same moment—but unlike the winged creature at his side, his body mass triples and his skin turns a red-ochre color. A crown of horns rings his head, completing his transformation.

Dmitri recoils at the sight and immediately realizes his mistake. *I can't believe what I'm seeing here.* "My apologies ... gentlemen." This is incredibly awkward for him. He looks toward the winged one. "Nafurael?" When the man nods, he says to the other, "And you're Zerbadiah?" He's met with another nod as both otherworldly creatures resume their glamoured disguises. Dmitri sweeps a hand through his hair, searching for a polite response. "Yes, we asked for your help. Thank you for coming. Please come inside so we can discuss the situation."

As Dmitri walks past Matt on the stairs, the mongrel mutters, "This just keeps getting twenty shades more bizarre by the day. I may have to reconsider whether unicorns and leprechauns exist."

Milnea, in all seriousness, confirms they do, and Matt says in an exasperated tone, "Too much information on too much shit I don't want to know about or see." For once Dmitri is starting to agree with the mutt on that point.

Milnea and the pixies no longer glamour themselves with

a human or bug appearance unless outsiders are present, and they invite Nafurael and Zerbadiah to drop theirs as well. She explains to the others that maintaining a glamour takes energy, which consumes and depletes their magic, and she equates it to resting and rebuilding strength—something they'll need to defeat Guillermo. Still, several minutes fall off the clock before the vampires and Matt stop gawking at the new arrivals. *I need to quit staring at them. They're real, and they're here.* The only three who don't look shocked are the Seelinarans.

Once everyone is seated, Dmitri decides a quick briefing is in order, and then the conversation returns to the mystery woman and man who assassinated Queen Constance. Alexander quips that they should give the assassins a medal for doing them a service, but the humor in it dies away when Dmitri reminds everyone that this mystery woman may be the very same one who has made multiple attempts against them. "We can't overlook her as a suspect in Jacques Boucher's murder, either."

When the potential link to Guillermo is mentioned, Nafurael offers his opinion—he believes that whatever threat this woman poses will go away once the sorcerer is dealt with. "It will provide us the opportunity to sever whatever power your sorcerer holds over the woman. If the man with her is indeed King Altheron's son, then we need to separate him from the sorcerer's control too. Only then will we know if the prince's soul is tainted with darkness or if he is redeemable."

Matt rolls his eyes. "You make him sound like a coupon. Is there a checkout line for this?" Liathera dives down and gives Matt a high five.

If it weren't for the stern look Nafurael gives the mutt, Dmitri would be inclined to smile. Instead he keeps his face neutral and tries to reason out the argument in his mind. The angel makes a valid point—if the woman and the prince are both under Guillermo's control, then eliminating Guillermo will resolve that problem. It also means that after all the delays so far, he'll finally be able to put Elizabetta at the top of their priority list, and that's something that has eluded them since she was snatched at Machu Picchu.

"Do you have something of your wife's?" Nafurael keeps his gaze on Dmitri.

His mind races. There's nothing of hers here ... but there is. Without a word, Dmitri runs from the room to retrieve Elizabetta's horse-head dagger from his chambers. He almost forgot Vladimir found it in Jacques's garden—it's been in Dmitri's nightstand ever since. When he returns, he hands it to the angel.

Nafurael closes his massive hand around it as his head cocks to the side. A faint light pulses to his wing tips. "Your wife is alive, but there is something wrong—it's as if she is outside of herself."

The demon blanches and looks almost sick. "Dark magic. The sorcerer is using the forbidden casts. Perhaps he has united her with the mystery woman?"

"That doesn't seem right either. There's a duality to it that I've never felt before. As if part of her remains tethered and yet ... severed." Nafurael hands the dagger to his demon counterpart, who deeply inhales.

"I sense sheridauk powers upon her." Zerbadiah looks at

Milnea—his scrutinizing gaze is unnerving even to watch.
"Do you know what level of magic your betrothed can
wield?"

The elemental shifts in her seat. "I've yet to meet him.
But his father, as you know, is very powerful."

A gruesome smile breaks across the demon's face—ugly,
gnarled teeth with razor-sharp points drip saliva. Several of
the vampires press back into their chairs, including Dmitri.
*It's going to be difficult remembering this hideous being is
on our side.* "I think all may not be as hopeless as we feared
for the lost prince," Zerbadiah says. "We will not know for
certain until we contain the situation, but I suspect he is
protecting the vampire queen, and that may be the odd
magic Nafurael senses surrounding her."

*Vampire queen?* Dmitri shakes his head. "What is our
best course of action, then?"

To no one's surprise—save the Seelinarans and the
otherworldly creatures—Kees is the first to outline a
strategy. "If Nafurael and Zerbadiah's assessments are
correct, then it's logical to use the element of surprise and
storm Guillermo's compound. But I'm not sure if slightly
more than a dozen of us will be enough to breach it, let
alone confront whatever the sorcerer has in store for us if
their numbers are greater than our own. We have no idea
what traps may await or what exactly is in the underground
complex—it could be a whole legion of hellish creatures we
haven't even considered. This may also explain the spider
that was with the woman when she tried to attack Vladimir."

"A spider?" Nafurael raises an eyebrow.

Vladimir details what happened the night of his attack, and the angel confirms there are no such fae creatures— though he speculates it is quite possible that Guillermo has an army of mutated natural creatures ready to do his bidding. Dmitri still can't fathom a spider of that size, let alone a potential army of them. Their lives are immersed deeper in dark magic than he ever wanted even to be near.

"Again, how do we proceed?" In Dmitri's mind there's only one answer. They must do further surveillance—they have to learn what is on that estate before they make their move.

Vladimir leans forward, looking at each Druzhina before settling his gaze on Dmitri. "First we must address the announcement of our new king."

*How is that important?*

Anna is quick to agree. "Yes, we do, and I agree with Vlad—we must announce it before there are ripples of unrest throughout our realm again."

Dmitri is looking at them as if they've lost their minds. A broad, lopsided grin is plastered on Matt's face. Dmitri growls at him, "What's so funny, mongrel?"

Matt bursts into laughter. In between chuckles he says, "He really doesn't get it, does he?"

The wizard and the other Druzhinas are now laughing with Matt, and it only turns Dmitri's mood more sour. Maria bites her lip to stop giggling. "Anna is correct—we do have a king." When Dmitri continues to glare at her, another round of laughter breaks out, and even the Seelinarans join in.

Katherine finally connects the dots for him. "The lead-

ership contest spelled this out, Dmitri. If anything happened to our new leader before she could be replaced in a
challenge, which I'll remind you can only be made once
every ten years, then the second-place winner of the event is
to assume the role. The replacement leader will rule as if he
won the contest outright and has the right to defend his
position when each challenge year comes along."

Realization hits like a jackhammer. *They really are
going to force me into this.* "No. I don't want this. I am no
king! Give it to the third-place winner." Dmitri adamantly
shakes his head—he can't allow this and won't accept it.
Even Jacques wouldn't have expected or supported this
ridiculous position. *Would he?*

Liathera's reply carries a note of finality that feels like a
death knell to Dmitri: "Royalty recognizes royalty. Get used
to it, King Markov."

*That's what Altheron said too. And Milnea, and Jacques,
and Vladimir ... the list goes on. What is everyone else
seeing that I'm not?*

The elemental starts to rise from her chair, but Nafurael
waves her back down. The golden ring around his stunning
blue eyes flares and seems to pin Dmitri to his seat. "You
are very young in comparison with me, and you know
nothing beyond this world. But I assure you of this truth—
the fates exist, and they do the Creator's bidding. You
cannot ignore the paths they offer you any more than you
can avoid your destiny. The fates made you a leader in your
own right, and now it is time for you to lead your realm."

*He doesn't know one thing about me.* "But—"

This time Zerbadiah interrupts him. "Take it from a

demon who knows what it is to resist and walk the wrong path. There are numerous levels in each of the nine realms of hell, and I have spent seven millennia there suffering horrors you could never imagine. I knew my place, yet I resisted and became my own torturer and jailer. Only when I sought absolution and accepted deliverance did I rise to my potential and was freed. It is what the fates decided for me."

*What can I possibly say to a speech like that?* "I lack the strength ... I'm too broken."

"It is not only your wife I read from that dagger." Zerbadiah sits up even straighter than before. "You have fallen far enough. Now it is your time to rise."

# CHAPTER 29: ELIZABETTA

# Doubling Down

Elizabetta paces her tiny cell, anxiety gnawing at her while the discussion among the Sanchezes and Dahliorn continues. She's grateful for the listening device; the sheridauk, fearful that Ramira will take permanent control of Elizabetta's mind, is blocking her from returning to the witch's body. He claims he still doesn't know how Elizabetta's actions affected the shield he had in place for her protecttion. She doesn't think the situation is that dire, but she's unable to argue the point unless she wants to reveal the way she's been practicing control and tampering with Ramira's memories when no one is around. *I've really fallen—no, I dived—into a bucket of shit, and I'm beginning to doubt I'll come out smelling like a rose.*

"Are you sure there's nothing in these scrolls?" Guilermo says to Dahliorn yet again.

The sheridauk's tone conveys certitude. "There are no recorded incidents here that speak to such a problem in a unity spell. Perhaps you misspoke and caused it to go awry."

"My words were precise!" A few tense seconds linger in silence—Elizabetta holds her breath, fearing Dahliorn will be punished for insolence. But the sorcerer says, "Ramira, you say you haven't seen or felt anything unusual since immediately after you saw the vampire's face in the mirror?"

"No, but—" The witch makes another attempt to state her opinion, and like the last three times she's tried, Guillermo stops her.

"Leave us, Ramira—go on to your training lessons." Frustration rings out in Guillermo's voice.

Elizabetta hears a door open and close, and she assumes Ramira left. She wishes the sorcerer hadn't sent her away; she really needs to find out what the witch is thinking, or more importantly, remembering, about attacking Constance.

The sorcerer tosses questions at Dahliorn one after another, and hours pass as he grills the sheridauk about hallucinations, mental impairment, deterioration of the brain, and the possibility that the whole situation was a reaction to the shock of what Ramira did. The latter seems the least appealing to Guillermo, even as Dahliorn tries to reinforce it as the best explanation. He reminds the sorcerer that Ramira lost control and attacked him without provocation after she killed the warlock and tried to kill the vampire.

Their conversation is punctuated by moments of silence and what sounds like pages turning or paper rustling. *He's not going to stop digging for answers.* When Guillermo begins to speculate that he may need to repeat the unity spell, the sheridauk pushes against the idea—but the thought ratchets up Elizabetta's anxiety. The twisted sorcerer is about out of patience, and if he discovers or even guesses at the truth, she will be trapped forever in Ramira.

"Unless you can figure out a way to solve whatever went wrong, I may have no choice." Guillermo's tone is harsh. "Time may be running out to use Ramira against the Druzhina, with the unpredictable state this has left her in."

*And that's Dahliorn's fault? What an arrogant jackwagon.*

A second later Guillermo says, "Get Ramira and meet me in the vampire's cell."

The sound of a chair sliding against the hardwood floor spikes her fear, then panic. «Dahliorn, you've got to stop him. Don't let him do this to me!»

«I don't know if I can.»

For a split second Elizabetta considers trying to make a run for it, and her hand closes around the doorknob—but she doubts she'll make it past the spiders if they're lurking out in the halls, ready to stop her. «If I attack Guillermo from the front, can you help take him from behind?»

Dahliorn sounds defeated. «I can't harm him. It will harm me within seconds.»

«What? Why didn't you tell me this before?» Elizabetta's mind whirls. «How did you ever expect us to use Ramira against him if you can't help me?»

He doesn't answer, and moments later she hears him interrupt Sir, the stealth trainer. A lump grows in her throat as she listens to the sheridauk confirm that Guillermo wants to recast the unity spell. Minutes tattoo the doom she feels into her bones. Then Dahliorn's voice startles her. «Make sure you're lying on the cot, and don't make a sound or movement when Guillermo enters the cell.»

Aggravation temporarily trumps her apprehension and fear; she already lay down when she decided not to run. At this point, with everything that has happened over the past several months, Elizabetta doesn't need reminders. *One stubborn sheridauk will doubtless disagree with me.*

Elizabetta takes a deep breath to steady her nerves. There's the sound of a key unlocking the door, and when Guillermo stands over her, she can feel his presence—she almost flinches when his palm touches her forehead. The sorcerer lifts her shirt, likely checking for signs of the wound that has long since healed. Next his hands push Elizabetta onto her side—he's inspecting her body—and then he rolls her the other way. She recalls what Dahliorn said when he came to her cell with the listening stone, and she wants to swallow the bile rising in her throat—but even that action could give away her awareness. *Don't throw up ... maintain control.*

The sound of Dahliorn and Ramira entering the cell catches her ear, along with a noise that Elizabetta suspects is a cot being placed next to hers. *Oh God, no. Dmitri ...* «Dahliorn, do something! I'd rather die than be trapped forever in her.»

No response from him—it does little to calm Elizabetta, and she considers again whether she should run. She knows she'd never make it; Guillermo would hit her with a blast of magic before she ever crossed paths with one of his mutant spiders. *I have no way out.* Tears threaten to well in her eyes as the realization that she'll never be with her husband again shreds her soul.

Guillermo instructs Ramira to lie down. He must be distracted—it amazes Elizabetta that neither of the Sanchezes has noticed the way her pulse is pounding or her breath has quickened. She tries to slow both, but panic has a viselike grip on her, and she fails to push against the rising pressure urging her to flee.

"Are you ready, Ramira?" The sorcerer uses the soft tone that he often takes when he's manipulating his unsuspecting niece, but fright and uncertainty echo in the witch's reply.

"Yes, Uncle. Are you sure this will work?"

Guillermo says, "I think it's the only way to save your mind from whatever went wrong the last time."

"I'm not losing my mind. I know what I saw, and that vampire is already inside me."

Elizabetta wants to laugh at the absurdity of the situation. Her efforts to hide inside Ramira were so successful that she may now be permanently tied to the crazy witch, with no way back to her own body or the life she always wanted. What makes it worse is that she's done this to herself through her impatience and the rash decision to go against Dahliorn's advice. She thought it was the right move at the time, the best way forward, but now she understands it was one of the biggest mistakes of her life.

The sorcerer draws a heavy breath, and Elizabetta knows he's about to repeat the spell that will doom her forever. Adrenaline surges. The instinct to survive and fight back is about to propel her into action when she hears Dahliorn say, "Wait! There's a spell that may solve the problem with less risk."

Impatience resonates in Guillermo's tone. "And why does it only come to you now? Your timing is rather convenient, isn't it?"

"It's of demonic origin."

*What? Is he that pissed at me that he'd recommend evil?*

Guillermo's voice carries a hint of suspicion. "I thought you never practice dark magic."

"Not all demonic magic is dark." Dahliorn pauses, and Elizabetta's mind trips over the thought that he might be about to untether her from her body. "We know a second attempt may kill them or render them into an unsalvageable state. The mirror bonding spell will also tie them together, but by thought, mimic action, and deed."

When the sorcerer interjects that the unity spell was supposed to accomplish this, Dahliorn says, "No, unity was meant to give one of them inherent control and blend the subordinate's mind, knowledge, and skills into the dominate host. A mirror bonding unites them with equal claim, access, and awareness."

"You're suggesting that we allow that vampire equal control over my niece?" Guillermo shouts in astonishment.

It doesn't escape Elizabetta's attention that the sheridauk is deliberate in his response—her confusion and fear is growing at just how adept the fae is at distorting the truth yet avoiding a lie. "They will have the ability to communicate, and that carries no risk—the unity spell already gives Ramira priority over the vampire."

«Are you freaking nuts? How is this supposed to work?» Elizabetta's panic surges again—she can't risk being taken over permanently by the witch. *What the hell will happen to my body?*

Dahliorn urges her to be patient even as he continues debating the usefulness of the spell with the sorcerer. He sees it as the better of the two options; a mirror bonding spell can be broken, ensuring Elizabetta's chance of separation from Ramira someday, and it won't interfere with the block he placed on the unity spell earlier—if the block is still intact. While the bonding will give Ramira the chance to assume control, it will provide Elizabetta equal access. Given Elizabetta's vampiric ability to influence minds, she may more easily thwart the witch's attempts to take control of her.

Guillermo finally relents, but his obvious displeasure comes through in his reluctant acceptance that it's his best, possibly only option left if he still wants to use his niece as a weapon.

When the sorcerer demands to know the incantation, Dahliorn says, "A pure fae must cast it."

The sheridauk's words send terror spiraling through her—there are too many unknowns. «What does that mean?»

«That unless I am the one who casts it, I will not be able to lift it when the time comes.»

Elizabetta stifles the impulse to sigh with relief when Guillermo consents to Dahliorn casting the magic, but it's not until the others leave the room to prepare for the dark incantation that she exhales audibly. *Will the nightmares in my life ever end?*

Through the tiny ear bud, Elizabetta listens as Guillermo all but interrogates Dahliorn about the bonding spell and the sheridauk's motives for wanting to do a demonic cast, given his aversion for dark magic, and Guillermo refuses to believe this spell isn't dark. The sorcerer is distrustful, and rightfully so; he will need to allow the sheridauk access to all of his fae magic in order to perform the spell. It's a risk Guillermo needs to mitigate if he's to keep Dahliorn under his control.

Dahliorn clears his throat. Elizabetta assumes he'll capitulate to whatever safeguards the sorcerer desires, but when he declares the primary reason is his feelings for Ramira, it gives Elizabetta as much pause as it seems to give Guillermo. "Explain yourself," the sorcerer booms—his voice carries her own shock, dread, and concern.

"When you brought her here as a small child, I cared for her, looked after her. For centuries I have protected and guided her at your command. I don't want to lose something precious to me."

Elizabetta feels sick over the absolute sincerity wrapped around his statement. *This can't be happening. No, God, no.*

"She can't stand you." Guillermo's tone turns icy. "You already know she's doomed, and it's only a matter of time before the unity spell—whatever it did to her—kills her. What difference does it make if she dies tomorrow, next year, or a hundred years from now?"

"Mourning would consume me."

Elizabetta removes the ear bud, trying to sort the not-quite-lies from whatever truth is in his words. She doesn't want to hear any more—everything he said only gives her reason to doubt his true intentions, and the more she tries to rearrange the puzzle pieces, the less clear the situation becomes. *Does he love Ramira? Is he using me to free them?* Elizabetta's confidence wanes with the thought. She's truly alone in this ordeal and has been since the day Guillermo captured her; the chance to escape and return to her life never existed.

Hours, possibly days pass in silence and without any contact with Dahliorn. Elizabetta replays every conversation they've had, running Dahliorn's words through the lens of whose interests were served. She begins to doubt it was ever hers. *I need a chance to dig through all of her memories ... he knows how to do this. Is he tampering with her memories too?* She has no idea when they'll return to cast the mirror bonding spell, but worse is not knowing what any of this means for her or her chances at freedom. *Shit. Shinola. How do I get out of this? Think, think.* The only answer Elizabetta comes up with is that she'll have to continue playing whatever game the sheridauk is orchestrating.

Lost in the never-ending tangle of her thoughts, she startles when Dahliorn finally contacts her—his mental tone is rushed. «Lie down—we're almost to your cell. Remember to act unconscious no matter what happens.»

*Um, okay.* «Care to give me any hints as to what is going on?»

«There's no time ... trust me and do as I say.»

The command drives her distrust higher—it is difficult to close her eyes and go along with this.

Seconds later her cell door opens, and she hears Guillermo and Dahliorn enter the room. She stifles a reaction when she's unexpectedly lifted from the cot. Neither man speaks as she's carried through what she guesses are the same underground corridors where she first encountered the spider. She attempts to make mental notes of their route, counting Dahliorn's footsteps to each turn, and marking whether he goes left or right—it may be the only map she'll ever get for escaping this place.

Finally they ascend a flight of stairs, and she nearly draws in a deep breath when, for the first time in months, the fresh outdoor air caresses her cheeks. *Well, at least I know how to get out of the dungeon now.* After a few dozen more steps Dahliorn lays her on the ground, and it takes every ounce of willpower to keep her eyes closed and not give in to the temptation to sneak a peek.

"You'll follow Dahliorn's commands without question while he prepares and casts this spell. Do you understand?" Guillermo's tone is terse—Elizabetta isn't sure if he means her or Ramira until the witch responds.

"Yes, Uncle. We've gone over this more than once, and I'm fully prepared for what I need to do to gain dominancy over the vampire." Her usual peevishness wraps around every word, confirming Elizabetta's worst fears.

*Excuse me?* «Dahliorn, what the hell is going on?»

«Trust me.»

«Seriously? Just trust you? Just like that.» Anger swells inside her. «You haven't spoken with me in days, and now I'm supposed to give you blind faith? So help me, Dahliorn, if you're selling me out, know this: if I don't kill you, Dmitri surely will someday.»

«There's no time. Trust me, little dove.»

Before she can form a response, she hears Guillermo instruct Ramira to lie next to her and hold her hand. Her pulse races, though she's frozen in fear—there's no escape, and no one is coming to save her this time. It takes an extreme effort not to swallow the lump in her throat as Ramira's hand closes around hers.

"Remember, Dahliorn, although I'm about to give you access to most of your powers, any attempt to escape will fail. I've set iron and salt traps that will stop you even if you incapacitate me. The only thing you'll accomplish is a slow, horrible death."

"I understand, and I will not run." Dahliorn pauses. "May I speak with Ramira privately before we start?"

The sorcerer gives his consent after a long moment, and Elizabetta's mind reels. *What the hell is he up to now? I'm so flippin' screwed, it isn't funny.* She almost gags when she hears Dahliorn lower his voice and say, "Know that I pledge my love and loyalty to you. I have only ever wanted to protect you since the day I first laid eyes upon you. What I'm about to do represents the lengths I will go to keep you safe, always."

*He set me up. That son of a bitch betrayed me!* Elizabetta can feel the panic hammering through her veins as she struggles to keep her breaths even and shallow. She weighs the risks of fighting back. *I can't let him do this to me.*

Elizabetta is about to leap to her feet, when Dahliorn says, "Ramira, may I?"

"Yes."

A second later Elizabetta hears what sounds like a kiss being placed somewhere on the witch's face. She expects the sorcerer to flip out and intervene, but nothing happens. *You have got to be freaking kidding me. Dark fae aren't evil, my ever-aching butt.* «You're a dead man if I ever get my hands on you!»

«Calm down. Trust me.»

*He's insane. I'm inside an asylum, and the lunatics are in control. Damn it, Dmitri ... where the hell are you?*

Her heart almost stops beating when Guillermo gives Dahliorn the command to cast the spell, along with another warning not to try anything foolish. Then the sheridauk's melodic voice begins to speak in his fae dialect, and in between each line he pauses to give Elizabetta instructions. «When I finish, you'll wake—act surprised, confused, scared.» «Cower and keep your mouth shut.» «Allow her to believe she's dominating you.» «Keep your interactions with her brief—don't argue with her.» «Build her confidence that she's in control.» «I'll answer many of your questions later.»

The sheridauk falls silent, and Elizabetta feels herself drawn back into Ramira's mind, but it shocks her when she realizes the witch is entering her mind too. The sensation of Ramira's presence is as if a cold steel ball is rolling around inside her brain. It's unnatural. There is no doubt that this is different from the last time—the witch is physically there to greet her, as in looming over top of Elizabetta when she opens her eyes. Elizabetta sits up and scrambles away from Ramira, who sneers as she rises to her feet. "You're mine now—I own you."

Elizabetta, still sitting on the ground, looks up at Ramira. Her mind is trying to reject the conflicting sensations of seeing and hearing the witch while simultaneously feeling Ramira and herself in both of their minds. "W-what's going on? What have y-you d-done to me?" She isn't faking it; she's scared witless. Ramira is moving around in her head, and it's worse than having a bug fly into her ear—Elizabetta wants her out. Now. But at this moment Elizabetta's only capable of sitting frozen in body and in both of their minds.

It's clear the witch was better prepared for this, and it rockets Elizabetta's suspicions to new heights. Fear and rage battle while she tries to decide if she should ever talk to either the witch or Dahliorn again.

Out of the corner of her eye she sees Guillermo strap the silver belt around Dahliorn's waist. The sheridauk glances at her before looking away. «Ramira will not hear your thoughts or our conversations, but keep your direct communication with her to a minimum until I can instruct you further.»

She doesn't acknowledge him but resists the desire to back away as the witch stalks toward her. It's at Dahliorn's urging that she doesn't strike out when Ramira grabs her by the arm and leads her back into the dungeon. But then Elizabetta's flight instinct kicks in, and she struggles to break free of Ramira. Guillermo is ready and locks her in an immobility spell, which also freezes his niece. The witch, or at least the part of her in her own mind, starts mentally screaming and threatening to get even with Elizabetta— though as long as they're both frozen by magic, it's a hollow threat. *Good luck with that, you bitch. I'll deal with you when the time comes.*

It's not until Elizabetta's deposited on her cot and the door to her tiny room closes that the spell is lifted. *Friggin' maxians.* She bolts for the door, but this time there is more than a simple household doorknob locking her in. Guillermo added a barrier—she can't even touch the door—and it's eerily similar to the maxian wards that kept her prisoner in Xi'an. *Great! This is flipping fantastic. There's no way out.* Rage finally vanquishes fear, and Elizabetta almost welcomes the pulse of bloodlust shooting through her veins.

«Dahliorn, what have you done to me?»

# CHAPTER 30: DMITRI

## Reconnaître

Shortly before midnight Dmitri's eclectic team arrives on Rathlin Island, and, thanks to Zerbadiah's knowledge of dark magic, this time they aren't misdirected by Guillermo's spell. Putting his own magic to work, Nafurael discovers multiple alarms woven into the invisible wall, with varying triggers—it was sloppy luck they didn't trigger an alarm last time, and that was only because Guillermo didn't set the barrier to detect elemental fae, and the pixies were too tiny to trip an alarm at all. "I can only see four options," Nafurael says to Dmitri.

"They are?" Something in the angel's demeanor tells Dmitri that he's not going to like any of them.

According to the angel, the first two options are to go in—alarms be damned—and risk facing whatever awaits them, or to send the pixies back in with Zerbadiah to finish their surveillance. The other two options are to unravel the magical barrier, which could take days, or to place a spell that will alert them should Guillermo leave the property.

Dmitri shoves his hands through his hair and grips the top of his skull. *Can't one thing in my life ever go smooth or easy? Elizabetta ...* "We're going in, and we will deal with whatever crosses our path."

There are several gasps, but it's Maria who blurts out, "It's too dangerous."

*I am surrounded by cowards.* "My wife may be in there! She's been missing for over seven months now. She's waited long enough."

"I think that's Maria's point." Matt places a hand on Dmitri's shoulder. "If we go in balls to the wall and magic blazing, and Eliza is in there, they may kill her before any of us can reach her. Think about that, think about how you'll feel if she dies because we stormed in."

A long, guttural snarl rumbles out of Dmitri as he turns and walks several paces away from the group. He closes his eyes. *Is fate determined to keep me separated from my wife? What gives the fates the right to choose for me?* He's mulling over the wisdom of his friends' counsel when he feels a hand touch his forearm—Sally is standing next to him. Without a word she grabs him into a hug.

"Sally ..." He shakes his head. "I can't keep doing this ... it's driving me insane." He never intended to admit that, and shame fills him over expressing such weakness.

She leads him away from their comrades and lowers her voice. "I know you're tired of debates over how best to proceed, but I think we really need to find a consensus with the rest of them"—she waves at the mix of supernaturals talking among themselves—"before you make a decision."

Uncomfortable, he looks toward the hidden compound.

A long minute passes before she speaks again. "If you don't make the right decision, it will destroy you. I know you well enough by now to know that you won't survive if Eliza dies, especially if it's by your hand or actions."

"But the need for vengeance—I can't keep stuffing it down."

"Bullpucky. You've made it this long without allowing it to take over, and you can push back a little longer. You're stronger than that, and I know it."

Dmitri hates to admit it, but she's right, as are the others. Sally slips her hand in his, leading him back to their comrades. But even with his concession, they're no closer to reaching a decision than before.

The Druzhinas are thinking classically in terms of strategies, suggesting those they've used when carrying out a coup d'état; they believe the same tactics will work now. The Seelinarans encourage further surveillance before any decision is made, and Maria is willing to support whatever is chosen, so long as they make an attempt to take down the protective wards in the meantime. Their voices begin to rise. As a precaution Milnea erects a bubble to shield them while they discuss the matter—it will prevent anyone from hearing or seeing them. They're too close to making a rescue attempt to blow it now by revealing their presence.

Matt finally pulls Dmitri aside, and they discuss the arguments alone while everyone else continues the debate. Once more Dmitri is impressed by Elizabetta's choice for a friend and ally—she was right, the mongrel is very intelligent. *Simple country charm ... that's what she called it once.* It leads others, himself included, to underestimate the wolf, and once again he's proven to be good counsel. Dmitri and Matt reach a decision—now they need to get the others to agree.

They're still arguing. "Enough!" Dmitri pins each one with a fierce glare to quiet them; he's about to flex the power they've thrust on him as king. "We've lost nearly four hours with this debate. This is what we're going to do—there'll be no further discussion. Maria and Nafurael will start working to take down the barrier while Tavorell, Liathera, and Zerbadiah sneak in and complete the reconnaissance of the compound. Milnea will place the snare that will alert us if the sorcerer leaves the property, and the rest of us will wait until the Seelinarans report on their surveillance and Guillermo's wards are taken down."

When no one argues against it, Matt says to Zerbadiah, "Given your size, are you one hundred percent certain that you won't trigger an alarm?"

The demon shrugs and nods, which doesn't instill much confidence in Dmitri, but Matt gives his usual irrepressible grin. "Then let's get this started, or I'll back Dmitri's next suicidal suggestion."

Liathera and Tavorell immediately zip through the barrier. Bowing his head, Zerbadiah takes several steps back and drops his glamour. He flashes a wicked smile as his body dissipates into a barely detectable red-ochre mist that swirls as he too disappears to the other side of the barrier. Dmitri swipes a hand over his open mouth. *Impressive and frightening. It's no wonder people claim demons can enter Earth's realms so easily—what else can he do?* But then he realizes that if Guillermo is using demons too, their challenge to get Elizabetta back safely just ballooned expo-nentially. *Are an angel and a demon enough to help us save her if the sorcerer commands an army of demons himself?*

No one knows how long it will take for the Seelinarans to return or the barrier to come down, or if Guillermo will try to leave the compound before they get that far. Only one thing is for certain—their efforts to break in could take hours to days. As if to prove his point, the sun starts to rise, and Milnea adds an opaque layer to her shield—there are more vampires this time to protect from the harmful rays of daylight. Safely tucked into the bulwark, Sally, Matt, and the Druzhinas keep their conversation focused on vampire realm business, and how best to stabilize the increasing world discord. Dmitri's attention is split among the entire team, as his need for doing something to achieve their goals is a countermeasure to unleashing his darkest desires.

Four nights later Dmitri is struggling to control the violence surging within him and demanding release. He can't keep the memories at bay; each inflicts another cut that bleeds his patience, increasing the risk that he will unleash the worst he can bring to bear if they don't see a positive development soon. Even Matt and Sally's attempts to keep his mood out of dark territory fall short, and both Maria and Milnea are starting to pay extra attention to him—they're ready to subdue him with magic if necessary.

There still has been no sign of the Seelinarans who entered Guillermo's compound; their task may take the longest given the potential size of the underground facility and the unknown number of minions the sorcerer may have at his command. The barrier is also proving a tedious process, and the three working on it—Maria, Nafurael, and Milnea—take frequent rests.

*Something isn't right.* His head snaps up as Tavorell, Liathera, and Zerbadiah come through the barrier, but the expressions on their faces douse Dmitri's joy for their return. *It's bad news.* He swallows hard in a poor effort to steel his resolve for their report, and it doesn't escape his notice that Nafurael moves closer and spreads his wings. *I wonder how the angel will subdue me if this goes as badly as I suspect it's going to?*

"We completed our search." Zerbadiah shakes his head in silent answer to Dmitri's unspoken question.

"What *did* you find?" Dmitri says through clenched teeth.

Liathera's little face crumples into sadness as she stops near his head and puts a tiny hand out to pat his cheek.

Tavorell says, "Nothing."

Dmitri's mind whirls—red floods his vision. He's barely aware that his claws and fangs are now on full display. Nafurael takes another step closer as the demon bends over to capture Dmitri's line of sight. "Your mate was there ... she's not now."

*What does that mean?* Any fear he felt for the demon earlier evaporates. Dmitri steps forward—there's less than a foot of space between him and Zerbadiah now, and he tips his head back to maintain eye contact. "Show me!"

"Whoa, we can't just go rushing in there. We need to hear their full report first," Katherine says.

Kees steps forward in support of his mate's position. "We must know what they learned, Dmitri."

"So speak!"

Tavorell and Liathera take up positions on Dmitri's shoulders as Zerbadiah delivers their news. "We entered and went straight to the underground facility—that's where we found evidence that your wife was there. It took three days to search that facility, and we found nothing living. There are no other prisoners, no hidden army or giant spiders. There is evidence of at least one or more spiders, and we found animal and human remains—some were dried husks and others were wrapped in spider silk, undergoing liquefaction. Aside from what appeared to be its lair, only one cell was in recent use. I was able to confirm your mate's presence with my senses, and—"

Dmitri stiffens.

Liathera leaps into the air. "Wait, it gets worse."

Matt groans, "You've gotta be kidding me."

Vladimir seems to recognize how close Dmitri is to losing it and urges the demon to finish quickly. Stunned silence engulfs them when Zerbadiah postulates that they may have misjudged the sorcerer's level of protection—he suspects that their passage through the underground complex may have disrupted an internal ward and set off an alarm. When they went above ground, they discovered that the mansion and outbuildings were deserted. Whoever had been there had fled.

"That's not possible." Milnea shakes her head in disbelief. "Nothing caught or went through my snare."

Maria mumbles, "Mutaport ..." She turns to the elemental. "A maxian transportation device."

The perplexed look on Milnea's face tells Dmitri that she never considered it. He doesn't wait for her response. Before anyone can stop him, he pushes through the barrier himself.

The estate is bigger than he realized, and his eyes dart over it in a wild attempt to find the entryway to the underground complex. Zerbadiah appears out of thin air several feet in front and to the left of him and motions for Dmitri to follow. He'll show Dmitri the cell Elizabetta was kept in.

One curt nod is all he gives the demon, but Dmitri keeps Zerbadiah in sight as they navigate the maze of dark tunnels to an open cell door. Dmitri can already smell Elizabetta's scent—his heart sinks—and he pushes past the demon to step inside. The barren room contains a cot and nothing else. The strong lingering scent of his mate suggests that she was kept here for an extended period of time and only recently left. *Elizabetta, where are you? The sorcerer is on the run ... how much of a head start do they have?* Some of the others have gathered in the hallway behind him, but he doesn't pay them much attention. He rakes a hand through his hair twice as he tries to force himself to think.

No one says a word when Dmitri folds the cot and tucks it under his arm. Nafurael appears with Vladimir, and Dmitri agrees to leave the underground facility and search the mansion with them. The estate was abandoned in a hurry. Lights and TVs are on throughout the house, and dressers and closets appear untouched—obviously they never took the time to pack before leaving. The angel and demon confirm that only three resided in this house, the sorcerer, the prince, and the mystery woman, but they find nothing that reveals the identity of the woman or what her relationship is to the two men. When they move to investigate the outbuildings, they find them similarly abandoned in haste. One outbuilding seems to have housed servants, but it too is empty and the residents gone. An exhaustive search of Guillermo's estate provides no clues as to where he may have fled with Elizabetta and the others, but they do find a mutaport—confirmation and proof of their foes' escape.

"Where do we go from here?" Dmitri looks at each of his companions. The most disconcerting aspect for him is that neither the angel nor demon can detect whether Guillermo's entourage included demons. There's no way to confirm if he is using evil beings, or if he's simply calling upon dark magic. That means Dmitri's team has no idea the extent of what they'll face. *If we find him.*

Despair settles into Dmitri's bones as defeat pummels him into submission. For the first time in his long, unnatural life, he considers that Elizabetta may be lost to him for good.

The defeated look on Matt's face mirrors what Dmitri is feeling, and his heart sinks even lower when the mongrel says, "We need to return to Venice ... regroup. We'll have to start our search all over again."

## CHAPTER 31: ELIZABETTA

# Hide-and-Seek

Although Elizabetta is physically alone in her cell, she's not alone in her head. It's abnormal, creepy, and wrong on levels that shouldn't even exist. Unlike the unity spell, which left her able to hide inside the witch's mind, whatever magic Dahliorn cast seems to have split her consciousness. Now she can feel herself and Ramira in both hers and the witch's heads.

A few hours pass before Elizabetta figures out that she can choose which brain to be active in—her own or Ramira's—though she keeps that detail to herself as she experiments with moving between the two. The sensation is bizarre. It's as if she's aware that her mind is sleeping in one while it's awake in the other, and to shift back and forth she must wake one while she puts the other to sleep. She can see one potential advantage: it will be the closest they'll come to being alone in their own heads, providing one is asleep while the other is awake.

The quasi-alone time doesn't last long. Elizabetta's

experimenting catches the witch's attention, and an hour later Ramira figures out how to move between them too. The mistake Elizabetta made was in not realizing that their individual essences are like steel balls present in both minds—with one major twist. An active presence warms the ball, while inactivity cools it. She's certain that's what alerted Ramira to her movements. So far Elizabetta hasn't figured out how to be busy or dormant in both minds simultaneously, and the shift in heat occurs each time she jumps from hers to the witch's brain. Now that Ramira's caught on, the damn witch won't leave her alone and is intent on being wherever Elizabetta's presence is active.

«You can run, but you'll never get away from me.» Ramira's mocking tone follows Elizabetta from one mind to the other. «I told you that I own you now.»

Everything in her is screaming to retort or find a way to attack, but she's trying to give Dahliorn the benefit of the doubt even though meekness has never been one of her traits. *If I find out this was a trap all along, I will fight back with everything I've got.* «Why can't you leave me alone?» She deliberately adds a whimper, which turns Ramira's tone hostile.

«I'm going to take full control of you, and then I'm going to use you like you used me to kill that vampire in New York.»

«What vampire? I don't know what you're talking about!» *Time to sell a load of crap.* «One moment I was at Machu Picchu, and the next I was waking up on the ground with you in my head. I don't even understand why I'm here or what your twisted uncle did to me.»

Silence. Elizabetta begins to believe her BS song and dance worked, but then Ramira says, «My uncle didn't do anything to you. His pet freak put you here.»

Elizabetta tries to sound panicked, which isn't difficult—considering she's already unnerved by having the witch in her head and still doesn't know why Dahliorn betrayed her this way. Until she can get answers from him, she'll need to continue this charade with Ramira. «Why won't you explain what is going on here? I told you ten times already that I don't understand any of this.» *Jeez, I hope she's buying this drivel. This is flipping insane.*

Their conversation keeps going in circles until Elizabetta wants to strangle the worthless witch. *I need five minutes to myself. Is that too much to ask?* She makes the switch to Ramira's mind, but seconds later the witch joins her. For the next several minutes Elizabetta bounces back and forth, which only gives Ramira more practice at doing the same. «Argh! Stop following me. Leave me alone!»

She jumps back to her own mind as Ramira says, «That's not going to happen.»

Desperate to push the witch away, Elizabetta scrambles for any idea that may change Ramira's mind. She knows it's too soon to try any vampiric influence, and she dares not use the skills she learned under the unity spell to force the witch away. Dahliorn never explained what he meant by thought, mimic action, and deed, either, which prevents her from exploring options in this new shared reality. That, and her own brain won't stop mocking her with a twisted rendition of a Rolling Stones song; even fingers in her ears won't make it stop. *In flies a witch flirting with evil, screaming she owns me now. I say, hey! You! Get out of my head. Hey! You! Get out of my head.* Yeah, it doesn't work— she's going to end up in the loony bin. *That's it!* That's what she needs to do—drive Ramira crazy. But Elizabetta needs something better than the Stones, and she quickly replaces the lyrics with an old ditty.

Pleased with herself, she smiles. To give extra impact to what she's about to do, Elizabetta decides to use both her mental and physical voices. *She's really going to love me for this ... time to let her have it in stereo.* She clears her throat and begins singing, «Oh, yesterday upon the stairs I saw a witch, and she was not all there. She was not all there again today, oh, how I wish she'd go away. She's freaking nuts ... you bet ... she's freaking nuts.» Granted, it's a further variation of an old tune, but Elizabetta is confident that it should do the trick and drive the witch away.

For a long minute there is only stunned silence from Ramira, and then she starts shouting at Elizabetta to shut up. Smirking, Elizabetta repeats the ditty over and over— the more she sings it, the more upset the witch becomes.

«Stop it! Shut up, you stupid bitch!»

She ignores Ramira and continues looping the song until finally the witch gives up and goes back to sulk in her own head. Elizabetta sighs in relief and lies down on her cot to bask in the silence for an hour or so. But that measure of relaxation is elusive. Her thoughts keep drifting to Dahliorn, who has remained quiet since casting the spell. Ramira may intrude again at any moment too.

Still, Elizabetta needs answers, and she doesn't want to try a conversation with Dahliorn while the witch is chasing her around the crazy tree. «Dahliorn, we need to talk.»

«Yes, I know.» A sigh whispers through their link, and the sheridauk says, «We'll talk when Ramira goes to sleep, and I promise to answer all your questions and tell you everything I know. For now I can reassure you this was the best option, the only option to keep you safe.»

*All? Yeah, right, I'm not that stupid.* Elizabetta's mind whirls as she replays the words he spoke to Ramira right before he did the incantation putting her in this new hell. *Twisted truth and deliberate omissions, that's what he'll give me ... or so he thinks.* She's done playing his games. «Damn it, Dahliorn, no! I need answers now!»

The sheridauk pulls one of his typical stunts and ignores her. It boils her blood—everything is always on his terms, his way, what he wants or needs when he wants or needs it. *I'm sick of his shit.* Regardless of what she says to get Dahliorn to respond, he remains silent, and it forces Elizabetta to seek out Ramira—it's the only way she'll know when the witch goes to sleep, as the dark cell doesn't allow her to discern if it's day or night.

«Oh goodie, look who's come to visit me,» Ramira sneers before announcing Elizabetta's arrival to Guillermo. Doubtless it's to ensure he doesn't reveal critical information—at least not until he's certain Ramira has dominated her.

*Pluck a duck, it's dinnertime. Lucky me, this is going to be a long evening.*

But the sorcerer stiffens as he gives his niece a hard, scrutinizing glare. "Do as I've instructed, and don't relent until you have her total submission. We've lost enough time, and we need her to learn her place fast." He tosses his napkin onto his plate and storms out of the dining room.

Evidently he doesn't plan on staying in her presence; either he has a lot to hide, or he's afraid to engage her in conversation through the witch. *Interesting.* The witch makes a pathetic attempt at interrogation, and it's almost laughable; Elizabetta bites her insubstantial tongue to keep from showing her amusement.

«Did you make me fall down the stairs?» «Tell me where the Druzhina headquarters is.» «Where does that werewolf stay when he's in the US?» «How long were you there before I discovered you in my head?» «I order you to submit and tell me what I need to know!» «I know you killed Constance ... that actually helped us.»

The last comment freezes Elizabetta to the core, and when the witch describes the setbacks the queen's death has caused the vampire realm and the way the Druzhina has lost control, shame and guilt wrap her in layers of regret. She never expected the assassination to cause more problems or add to the unrest now tearing the world apart; she believed she was helping the Druzhina. *How much worse did I make everything?* Now, trapped in her bond with Ramira, there's no way she can mitigate the harm this has done. It's just one more regret on top of the others threatening to help Guillermo and Ramira destroy her life.

Ramira's shrill voice pulls her out of her dark thoughts. «Are you even listening to me?»

«Just leave me alone.» Until she talks with Dahliorn, she will not give the witch any cooperation or do anything that allows Ramira to think she's gaining control. That leaves one option: be the frightened, meek victim. The distaste of playing this role leaves a rancid flavor on her taste buds. *How much longer can I keep pretending to be confused and scared?*

For hours Ramira cajoles, taunts, and begs Elizabetta to cooperate, to tell her what she wants to know, and in response Elizabetta keeps dodging and feigning ignorance, confusion, and fear. The mental sparring leaves her exhaustted, and when the witch finally gives up and demands Elizabetta return to her own head for the night, she doesn't waste a second to leave.

Ramira says, «I'll come wake you tomorrow—you'd better have a change in attitude.»

It's about all she can muster to let the dig go and instead reach out for Dahliorn. *If he ignores me this time, I'm going to make his life hell. Only fair, right?* «The witch is leaving me alone for the rest of the night, or at least that's what she claimed. Is there any way for her to sneak in without me knowing it?»

«You'll always know if she's with you or not. I can't say the same for her, though.» The sheridauk's mood is lighter than usual—it heightens her suspicions and flat-out pisses her off.

She puts as much sting as she can into her words. «What the hell is that supposed to mean?»

«If she believes the unity spell failed, then she'll begin to associate your presence with your submission to the mirror bonding spell. There's a chance you may be able to tunnel into her mind through the unity connection, but it will take a conscious effort not to go through the bonding link. Regardless, you need to be very careful—the risks are higher now.»

Confused, Elizabetta asks him to explain, and the answer leaves her feeling more uncomfortable. According to the sheridauk, there's a slight chance Ramira may feel Elizabetta's entry into her mind through the unity spell, and if she does, it will allow the witch an opportunity to claim control—not just temporary dominance. «How do I fight back if that happens? Unlike in New York, I can't leave her mind without her following me now. And what did you mean when you told the demented sorcerer we're tied by thought, mimic action, and deed?»

«When you're both in the same mind, you can communicate your thoughts, as you've already discovered. Mimic action means what happens to one affects you both— mortal wounds included. If one of you experiences something that results in joy, anger, pleasure, or pain, the other will share that emotion. The best example would be to imagine Ramira kills one of your friends. Because you're in her head when it happens, it would leave you feeling euphoria, triumph, and joy foremost, and fear and grief to a lesser extent.»

Elizabetta's stomach plummets through the floor at the image of the witch hurting Dmitri or Matt—the notion that she'd find pleasure or satisfaction in their pain builds an unease she's never known before. She questions what would happen after she returned to her own mind, and Dahliorn's answer makes her feel even worse. He claims that in her mind the emotions would flip and leave her conflicted. But Ramira would experience the same, which means that the mental and emotional conflict would eventually drive them both insane unless one of them achieved dominancy or control.

*So one of us forces her feelings onto the other, or it destroys both our minds? Great, perfect ... son of a bitch.* Elizabetta has had her mind wiped, her life stolen and restored, and she's been kidnapped. But this ... it's too much. The idea of her and Ramira being crazy and tied to each other until they die is unfathomable. Abhorrent.

Elizabetta knows it will be nearly impossible to sleep after learning this. If Ramira keeps after her all day and she spends every night training, the inevitable will happen— she'll become too exhausted to remain careful. «How does this help us, assuming you're not secretly trying to destroy me?»

Shock tinges his reply. «I'd never harm you. Why would you think that I—»

«I remember very well what you said to Ramira before you cast the mirror bond, and why you were willing to take the risk. It's quite clear where your loyalty lies.»

A long, awkward silence settles between them, and Elizabetta wonders if he's trying to craft another clever fae not-quite-a-lie. «Ah,» the sheridauk says, «I understand your anger toward me now. It seems we must start this where it all began: with Guillermo's threat to redo the unity spell.»

Elizabetta says very little as Dahliorn swears that the mirror bonding was the only way to prevent a permanent union with the witch. He promises it will provide cover for Elizabetta to continue her efforts to take over Ramira's mind, and eventually will allow her to sever the link with

Ramira so he can fully return Elizabetta to her own body someday—once they kill Guillermo and find their freedom.

Everything he says affirms what he's told her in the past, but it's what he's not saying or explaining that leaves her wary of his true motivation and intentions. «So tell me, then, where does that leave Ramira as this goes down and we kill the sorcerer?»

«I don't understand your question. That hasn't changed—the outcome for her will be the same as it was before.»

«You've never defined exactly what her outcome is supposed to be. Do you realize the risk she'll be if we leave her alive? Even I have more doubt than hope that there is anything redeemable about her.»

«Yes, and that's why her outcome has not changed.» His voice carries a hint of confusion, or perhaps evasiveness—Elizabetta isn't sure which.

«Just stop it. Knock it off. I mean, come on, Dahliorn—I heard what you said to her.»

His tone turns brusque. «There's no deception in what I'm saying, little dove.»

Elizabetta gives a rueful laugh. *Does he really think I'm that dumb?* «No, of course not, just evasive enough that it's the same damn thing. Did you really think I'd overlook you pledging your undying love and loyalty to that witch-hare right before you planted a kiss to seal the deal? And stop calling me 'little dove'. My name is Elizabetta.»

Elizabetta expects a defensive comeback, a denial, or even some twisted variation of the truth from the sheridauk, but she isn't prepared for his reaction—he laughs. He actually sends a boisterous laugh through their link, and it takes him a couple of failed tries to compose himself somewhat. Even then there is an undertone of mirth in his reply. «I would never offer those sentiments to Ramira. It was my misguided attempt to assure you—you were so afraid, and I had no time to prepare you. And that kiss conveyed no affection but was the only way I could get close enough to sneak in the second spell to protect you.»

Her jaw drops, leaving her mouth agape. She can hardly believe how sneaky and underhanded he is, and she's not sure whether to feel impressed or more frightened of him. «Second spell?»

Dahliorn clarifies that though the sorcerer can't read the fae language well, he understands it when it's spoken. To shield the first protection layer that altered the outcome of the original unity spell, Dahliorn had to cast another that reinforced it while adding a second level of protection for the bonding spell. There was only one way to do that nonverbally—a fast-acting potion in powder form. «I coated a clear disk with it—the kiss to her forehead allowed me to press it to her neck. The disk was absorbed through her skin almost instantly, putting the second shield in place before I finished casting the mirror bonding spell.»

*He has to be telling the truth—fae can't lie. Oh shit, this is humiliating.* «Uh ... I'm sorry, Dahliorn.» She wishes there were more she could say, but after what she just accused him of it seems lame to simply say she was wrong. «I ... I'm—»

«It's all right.» The sheridauk says he understands, but Elizabetta hopes he won't hold her accusations against her nonetheless.

## CHAPTER 32: DMITRI

# Good and Bad Developments

Upon arriving back in Venice, Dmitri's first action is to stow Elizabetta's cot in his quarters—he finds comfort in her scent and will use it to help stay focused, to not lose control. He doesn't linger long, though, since Matt is waiting near the door and the others are expecting them in the ballroom to discuss their next step. Dmitri longs to put all of this behind them, but ever since Elizabetta was taken from him, very little has gone smoothly or right. *That needs to change.*

As he enters the ornate room, it strikes him how different it looks now compared with when Shashenka was alive. The plush chairs still line the walls, but the long mahogany conference table in the middle of the room gives it a businesslike atmosphere—nothing like during the debauchery and macabre events it held before. Dmitri looks at the others already seated and mentally checks the list of those present: nine Druzhinas, a fae, two pixies, an angel, a demon, Maria, Matt, Sally, and Antonio. Then he notices

Teresina sitting by herself in a chair along the wall. "What is she doing here?" *Has Justin changed his mind about executing her?*

Justin meets Dmitri's gaze. "I asked her to come. We're mated now, and I'd like to resume my duties as a Druzhina. I also want to propose we add her to our ranks—she's ready to join us. We could use her skills." Justin details resources she has around the globe; he believes her unique abilities and contacts will help them find Guillermo and increase their chances of rescuing Elizabetta. But then he adds, "She did a good job—"

Dmitri's scowl cuts him off. *Good enough to be a traitor.* He understands his friend's supportive behavior may be driven by a mate bond, and he moves in front of the two, searching for the telltale signs of a mating. The matching ring of color around their irises ... deep violet. The marks ... half-moon shapes that would make a full moon if they were put together like a puzzle. Dmitri rubs his hand over the mark on the back of his own neck—his half of a teardrop shape that perfectly matches the opposite of Elizabetta's mark. Sometimes, regardless of how much one wishes things were different, there is no denying the truth. *They are mates.*

He doesn't want to lose time on this matter, but he opens the request for debate, knowing the Druzhinas deserve a say—he won't make a unilateral decision. For several minutes the Druzhinas weigh the pros and cons of adding her to their ranks. As far as Dmitri is concerned, yes, her trustworthiness is a huge issue. Although there were extenuating circumstances, this doesn't remove the fact that she did betray them, and that her actions contributed to Sofia's death and Elizabetta's capture. The Druzhinas are split equally—four against and four for her inclusion in their ranks—giving Dmitri the deciding vote. As the Druzhina's leader and their king, he knows decisions aren't easy and that some will not be well received, but it's tougher when it involves making decisions that affect his friends' lives and impacts their future.

He's about to offer his opinion against Teresina, when Nafurael says, "I know this is your decision to make, but we can help you make the right one."

"How so?" Dmitri raises an eyebrow as Nafurael motions between Zerbadiah and himself. Neither angel nor demon has given him reason to distrust them, and both have proven themselves to be an asset in his efforts to find Guillermo and Elizabetta. He trusts their judgment to be fair—they don't have a vested interest in this outcome.

Zerbadiah says, "We can read her true intentions and motivations, much the same as we were able to sense your mate's status and condition."

Justin looks hopeful and meets Dmitri's gaze with silent pleading. *Damn it.* He's made so many wrong decisions, and this is one he must get right. Dmitri looks from his friend to the rogue to the two celestial beings—the latter seem to be waiting for his approval. *I can give Justin that much—he's been a valuable friend.* "Go ahead and do what you need."

"Teresina, will you come here?" Nafurael says as he and the demon turn their chairs away from the table. She swallows hard and wipes her hands on her slacks before she approaches them. When Nafurael explains that they will touch her, she gulps again but nods her consent.

Zerbadiah places a hand on her head as Nafurael places his over her heart. A long minute swells the silence in the room while everyone watches and waits. A small measure of shame fills Dmitri when he realizes that a part of him hopes they will find something that warrants him refusing Justin's request.

Zerbadiah is the first to speak. "There is no ulterior motive or hidden agenda in her mind, not even on the subconscious level. I detect no magic or evil possessing or influencing her."

"I concur." Nafurael nods. "She has made mistakes and bad choices, as many do, but she's true in her desire to do right by others. Her betrayal of you wounded her deeply and has left its mark upon her soul. She wishes to redeem herself."

Dmitri nods—it's settled. "Cast your vote, Druzhinas." The earlier split is gone, and the decision is unanimous— all, including Dmitri, favor adding the rogue to their ranks. *I have to trust we've made the right choice.* He asks Maria to conjure a chair next to Justin, and when the chair materializes, he gives the rogue a polite smile. "Please sit, Teresina, and welcome to our ranks. We'll take your blood oath at the end of this meeting."

There is no denying that she will be an asset, one that Dmitri plans to use to her full extent. She'll need to redeem herself first, though, and the echo of betrayal can ring a long time—sometimes it resounds forever.

Dmitri's jaw clenches at the reminder of another piece of unfinished business, Milo Kohler. While he was willing to show mercy to the rogue, Milo deserves none. *I don't need anyone to tell me what's in that maggot's heart.* He announces that it's time to execute Milo; he assures the others that his bloodlust is under control and that he will not be cruel in carrying out the deed. This time he's met with support. The others agree that there's no reason to delay the execution, and Dmitri selects those who will witness it.

Dmitri, Maria, Matt, and Vladimir head to the wine cellar to deal with the condemned vampire. Milo's head snaps up when Dmitri opens the door—dread fills the vampire's eyes. A low growl from Matt is a reminder that he was there too, the night Milo duped them into changing him and sent them into Guillermo's trap. Hate and disgust fill Dmitri, but although he feels no pity for the man, he will honor his word not to be cruel.

"Milo Kohler, you were sentenced to final death because of the treachery you committed in manipulating us to turn you while knowing you were sending us to be captured and killed. The day of your execution has arrived. Do you have any final words?"

Milo swallows hard; his eyes flash in fear and then narrow with hatred. "Go to hell—you'll eventually get yours. You have no idea what Guillermo is about to unleash on this world, and it will be your downfall."

Dmitri steps forward and draws his dagger out of its sheath. "Explain yourself!"

"I'm dead either way—do what you came to do." Milo shrugs with indifference and averts his gaze. *I doubt he knows, or he'd be using the knowledge to stay alive a little longer.*

The others standing behind Dmitri remain quiet—it's his decision when to act—and he looks back, meeting their supportive nods. The doomed vampire closes his eyes as his body trembles. Dmitri doesn't hesitate; he steps forward and decapitates Milo with two quick swipes of the dagger's blade. He places the head on the floor, takes the torch Vladimir is holding, and sets the severed head on fire. Within moments Milo's body is reduced to ash, and Maria uses the obliterate spell to remove all traces of the dead vampire.

*I should have ended him before I ever turned him.*

It almost amazes Dmitri how quickly the plan for the new search comes together; there's a higher energy level to those around him now. *I'm not the only one ready to do something, finally.* Teresina and Justin will talk with some of her contacts in the hopes of obtaining new information on the sorcerer. Maria will visit the Orde de Maxia to see if they have any leads and to provide the council with an update. Even the Seelinarans step forward to help—Zerbadiah and Nafurael are returning to Guillermo's estate to recover a few of the sorcerer's personal items. The celestial team will use them to learn more about Guillermo and perhaps discover where he went.

The three-pronged start gives Dmitri the first sliver of hope he's had in days. Two of the teams leave immediately, but he and Maria need to select details for the report she will give to the council. After they finish, Dmitri starts to leave the room, but she announces a personal request: she wants to take Matt with her.

While he still has some concerns about the two, he knows separation will be just as distracting if they're worrying about one another. But this is also an opportunity for him—a peace offering to make up for his earlier behavior. Dmitri fights to hide a smile as he gives his approval.

Since there is little to be done until the others return, the rest of the Druzhinas address the escalating conflict in the human realm. They need to do what they can to influence world leaders to pull back from the brink of war. Vladimir and Anna will approach the superpower nations while Victoria and Stephan and Katherine and Kees go to the UN and NATO respectively and attempt to persuade the delegates and representatives there to seek peace. The last thing Dmitri needs as a new king is the complication of a global war, and he's hopeful the Druzhinas will succeed in their efforts. The calm in the werewolf realm, along with the stabilization of the vampire realm—now that Constance's death is behind them—should help lessen the madness of the humans.

Once more this will leave a smaller core group waiting at La Perfezione to manage, plan, and evaluate the issues they are handling. Dmitri resigns himself to being patient once more, but Elizabetta is never far from his mind, and her absence keeps the bloodlust lurking beneath the surface.

The first to return to La Perfezione are Nafurael and Zerbadiah, who found the sorcerer's wand hidden in a dresser in the unknown woman's room. The wand also holds remnants of Elizabetta's essence, though they're not sure why. It raised their curiosity enough that they decided to bring back items belonging to all three—Guillermo, the woman, and the fae prince. There's a slight chance that they may be able to find the sorcerer using the traces left by the woman and the prince. *They need to figure out if he's our enemy or not. I need to know if he's a threat to my wife.* Unlike the quick assessments they made of Elizabetta and Teresina, this time they will "go deeper," as they term it, to find the answers they seek. Dmitri hopes those answers include more than just telltale signs of Elizabetta and her condition.

Another night passes before Maria and Matt return, but their discontented moods and sullen faces grate on Dmitri and elevate his concerns. Maria claims the maxian supreme council is no closer to finding Guillermo than they have been for centuries. A collection team was sent to Rathlin Island, where more of the sorcerer's possessions were gathered to aid their efforts, but none are hopeful that they'll locate Guillermo anytime soon. Maria says, "Getting the council to do even that much was difficult. They're more concerned about moving our people underground and the looming potential for war."

"I think it's more accurate to say they've gone beyond shelving the search—they're mothballing it." Anger radiates in Matt's words and confirms what Dmitri feared might happen. For centuries the maxians have put their people above everything else in the world, even though their magic allows them better odds of survival than those of any other realm. *The more I have to interact with them, the less I like and trust them.* Somehow Dmitri doubts Jacques would have stood by the cowardly choices they've made since his death.

The maxians should be helping the Druzhina in their efforts to prevent world war; it is one of their own, after all, who is causing most of the problems. If the world explodes into pandemonium thanks to Guillermo, it may be impossible to stop the humans from launching a war and in turn will greatly hinder Dmitri's ability to save Elizabetta. Worse, he is certain that the sorcerer will destroy her once he has no further need of her—and the maxians will be culpable.

The ache in his heart burns more painfully at the thought that it may already be too late—that the world's instability may be what dooms them—but regardless, he knows he must be realistic about what they're facing. *I will not give up. We have to do more to stop those intent on destroying this world, and along with it mio amore.*

Returning to his quarters, Dmitri ignores Sally's presence as he stares at the cot and reflects on the many times he lost Elizabetta—and how he may possibly lose her for good now. Unlike the moments he wanted to end his life due to the torture he endured, this time he won't make pathetic attempts to follow her if she dies. He will demand Vladimir give him the honor of final death and reunite him with his mate.

A month after the botched raid on Guillermo's estate, they are no closer to finding answers. Zerbadiah and Nafurael are frustrated by the sheer volume of information they're trying to sort through; Guillermo's presence has touched so many countries around the world that they can't tell if he's keeping his entourage on the run or whether he's meddling in human realm events on his own. Both angel and demon remain confident that they'll find a lead eventually, but neither can predict when that will happen.

Even the Druzhinas struggle in their missions to quell the unrest around the world. They report that the strife and disagreement among nations is escalating, and there aren't enough Druzhinas with access to key people to influence the humans and turn their governments away from their push for war. *Shit, this does not bode well for any of us.* The only Druzhinas seeing any measure of success are Justin and Teresina; her sources are providing leads to humans and supernaturals who have had contact with the sorcerer in the past. Unfortunately their progress is hindered by the wide-ranging locations of those leads—this will keep Justin and Teresina traveling around the world. And none of the Druzhinas have stumbled across one clue leading to Guillermo or Elizabetta's whereabouts. What Dmitri once hoped would be a fast rescue has morphed into so much more—at the least, three lives are on the line, and if they fail, three other lives will join them. Most have a direct interest and a stake in the outcome now, and it's weighing everyone down. Even Liathera and Tavorell's antics no longer divert Dmitri's attention—if anything, their threats to dust him anger him more.

Still, the thought nags at him that perhaps it is one way to numb himself and prevent him from unleashing his deadly wrath. Deciding to seek Milnea's advice—he doesn't trust the pixies to answer his questions—Dmitri waits until all the others have turned in for the day and then slips out of his room two hours after sunrise. Sally is supposed to be watching him, but she fell asleep, and he's content to let her rest. As he steps into the hall he sees Maria quietly open Matt's bedroom door and sneak inside. *Interesting. Why are they hiding their relationship?*

Pushing his curiosity aside, Dmitri locates the elemental fae in the library—she's become fascinated with Earth books and has moved from history books and a few classic works of literature to more modern novels to read for pleasure. Fantasy books are her favorite, especially stories about the fae. Some tales are so ludicrous that she laughs all the way through them, and others she recognizes as the handiwork of a preternatural being with actual knowledge of Seelinara.

"Your majesty." She inclines her head in greeting as Dmitri approaches. "What happened to your watcher?"

"My babysitter fell asleep." Dmitri draws a deep breath and chooses to be honest about the purpose of his visit. He quickly mulls over the best way to word his inquiry—he doesn't want to alarm her. "You know I'm struggling against the bloodlust. Tavorell and Liathera are hounding me to permit one of them to use their pixie dust on me. Is it something that will help, or is there too much risk?"

Milnea laughs, and her blue eyes sparkle with amusement. "It would certainly distract you and put you in a joyous mood for however long you stayed under it. The problem is that you can't remain that way—there are risks to being exposed too long—and you may feel worse once it's removed."

"So you are recommending that I not try it?"

"Not at all. You need to understand the risk and consequences if you choose to use it. But if you do accept their offer, make sure you give them a time when you want it removed. Pixies love watching someone under their thrall, and they are prone to leaving it in place too long." She smiles at him.

Dmitri nods and thanks her before returning to his room. If nothing else, the pixie dust is an option if something doesn't give soon in their search for Elizabetta. While he's not looking forward to embarrassing himself under a dusting, he can't ignore that it may be a better option than killing one of his friends if the dark evil he's capable of wins control.

He's still considering it a few days later when Matt leaves to attend to his businesses in the States. It isn't totally unexpected when Maria announces she's going with him; it's apparent they've become quite close. But how close? While Dmitri has let go of some of his suspicions about their loyalty, he can't shake his curiosity over their behavior. They seem to find a lot of excuses to go away together, like now.

Sally and the fae do all they can to keep him encouraged, but after Matt leaves, their efforts begin failing, and Dmitri is afraid to admit that to any of them. *Two more days, he'll be back in two more days.* He chuckles ruefully when he realizes that thought has become his mantra so he doesn't lose control. It frightens him how dependent he's become on Matt's friendship to keep him grounded and sane. More disconcerting is Dmitri's need of the wolf; even in all his centuries of friendship with Vladimir, he's never felt this type of pull.

Then an idea sparks, one he can't ignore. Vladimir is his maker—Dmitri took his blood—and Vladimir has never denied the want of their kinship. *Matt had my blood.* Although he is not the werewolf's maker, it may have created the same type of bond.

When Matt returns, Dmitri gives him a day to settle in again and then seeks him out; his curiosity won't allow him to leave it alone. The two men go to the office, which is well away from the others, to talk. "Before you left, I saw Maria enter your bedroom when most everyone was sleeping. Was the meeting personal or business?"

The mongrel's eyes widen, and he looks guilty, but Dmitri isn't sure why. While he doubts that either Matt or Maria would betray him, it's still a risk he must rule out. Matt remains quiet, but Dmitri pushes for an answer. "If it's personal, I don't need the details. But if it's related to anything we're dealing with and you two are working on it behind my back or keeping it a secret, I need to know what you're hiding."

Matt starts to chuckle and swipes a hand over his mouth and chin. "My time behind closed doors with Maria is personal."

*How personal?* Dmitri doesn't pry further, at least for now, in part because he'd have a hard time explaining his own feelings for the mongrel to anyone else. If he's being honest with himself, he has to accept that his and Matt's connection as good friends started before their possible blood bond. *Oh, moyata svyetlina, I think I understand your attachment to the mongrel now—I can't let him go from my life either. I'm addicted to a werewolf's kinship.* Elizabetta will never let him live it down, if she ever finds out. He takes another deep breath and smiles at Matt—perhaps Dmitri doesn't need pixie dust after all. *If he keeps me in check, I won't risk making a fool of myself.*

## CHAPTER 33: ELIZABETTA

# Learning on the Fly

Over the next few nights Elizabetta practices slipping into Ramira's mind when the witch is asleep. On the surface the mirror bonding will make it seem as if she's cowering, even becoming submissive to the witch, but instead she will try planting a few specific commands, using her vampiric ability to influence Ramira's mind.

In the meantime, Dahliorn will help Elizabetta learn how to focus her brain to tunnel in and carry out multiple interactions, which—if she can master it—will eventually allow her to use part of her mind to maintain the façade of Ramira's dominance, while in fact Elizabetta will be slowly taking complete control of the witch through the unity spell.

*This is going to be the deadliest game of hide-and-seek I've ever played.*

The difficulty isn't getting in and out unnoticed, it's coming up with the best suggestion or command; she must be careful that whatever she chooses doesn't catch Guillermo's attention if Ramira complies. In the course of a week the witch follows Elizabetta's suggestions to scratch non-stop, ignore an untied shoelace, cut her shoulder-length hair into a messy pixie cut, not complain, and not rely on others to remind her to follow the training schedule. Each success convinces Elizabetta to try something more daring—something risky—to see if Ramira will pull it off without her uncle noticing. One such test sends the witch sneaking into the mad sorcerer's quarters to snatch and hide his wand, which she does with glee.

Dahliorn seems so pleased with Elizabetta's accomplishments that it emboldens her to try multiple complex commands. The seventh night is when Elizabetta decides it's time for the ultimate test. It's been months since she last fed, and she wants to plant a two-part command: first, for Ramira to ask Dahliorn to take blood to Elizabetta, and second, for the witch to come along to dine with Elizabetta herself.

Immediately the sheridauk rejects her plan.

«Oh, come on, Dahliorn, this is perfect.»

«I will bring you blood if you need it,» he says. «This is too risky without wiping her memory of the event.»

«Then let me try removing it ... it will be a trifecta of success if I can get her to do both those tasks and then forget them.» Elizabetta is tired of taking baby steps—she'd rather push the training along so they can make an attempt to escape or kill Guillermo. *I've been here way too long already. I need to get home to Dmitri.*

Dahliorn won't budge—he insists the odds are too great that Elizabetta will expose herself through the unity connection, and that a momentary revelation is all Ramira will need to take control. Their argument abruptly stops when the sheridauk says in a panicked rush, «There's been a breach—»

«What are—» She startles as the sorcerer blasts her door off its hinges and slaps the immobility spell on her the moment he steps into her cell.

*What is going on here?* Guillermo jerks her shirt up, places a silver belt—similar to the one Dahliorn wears—around her waist, and mutters another incantation. "Don't try to resist. Your strengths are blocked." Guillermo releases the immobility spell, grabs her by the arm, and races into the corridor, dragging her with haste up to the mansion and over to the mutaport.

Dahliorn, Ramira, Michio, Sir, and several caretakers and servants are pouring into the room. The sorcerer shoves Elizabetta aside and rips his shirt off at the same moment he picks up an EPM and straps it onto his back. He doesn't take the time to put the shirt back on but instead shouts for everyone to link their arms or hands together. The sorcerer grabs Elizabetta by the elbow—Dahliorn's hand is clamped on her shoulder—and gives the quick chant that activates the device. There's a flash of bright light, and before Elizabetta can blink the white spots from her eyes, the entire group is transported somewhere that is pitch black.

*What the—where the hell are we?* A light comes on, and she looks around the room; it's a twenty-five-by-twenty-five-foot concrete box with no windows or doors. Guillermo's rage-filled eyes pierce her with an unspoken accusation before he turns to Dahliorn. "I've blocked her strengths, but that doesn't mean she won't try to use her skills. You are to keep her under control until I return."

The sheridauk dips his head, but before he looks up, Guillermo is gone. Excited murmurs ripple through the group. It doesn't take long for Elizabetta to figure out what just happened: the wards protecting the sorcerer's estate have been breached, and it's believed at least one of the intruders went straight for the underground facility. *Dmitri ... Matt? It had to be them—they finally came for me!* Her heart leaps with joy but then constricts in despair when she realizes how close they were to rescuing her. The sorcerer clearly had an escape plan all along.

«Are we still on the estate?» She looks at Dahliorn—it feels strange to see him face to face when they're silently talking. Ramira steps in front of Elizabetta, blocking her view of the sheridauk and delaying his answer. The witch places her hands on her hips, drumming her fingers in agitation, as a hostile look settles into her smug facial expression.

He says, «No» at the same moment Ramira says aloud, "Don't give us any trouble, or you'll find out that belt you're wearing can punish you." Her lips curl into a smirk. "I hear it can be quite painful, isn't it, Dahliorn?"

"Yes." His gaze shifts to the floor as he tells Elizabetta, «We're in a safe room, but I'm not sure where—there's at least one on every continent. When Guillermo comes back, he'll take us to one of his other estates.»

Elizabetta knows she can't keep looking at Dahliorn or it will raise suspicion, but neither does she want to show

Ramira how much contempt she has for the impotent witch. *Yes, because I'm so meek and mild. I wonder if that twisted sorcerer really did subdue my strength?* She deliberately looks at each person in the room, trying to project nervousness by fidgeting and hugging herself, but she says to Dahliorn, «It sounds as if you've done this before.»

«More times than I can recall. It's why the maxians have never been able to stop him.» Dahliorn pulls her toward a wall and says aloud, "Sit down, this could take a while."

She notices that his spoken voice is unlike the caring tone of his mental voice—he sounds brusque and cold—and she suspects he's also putting up a front for those around them. There are a dozen questions she'd like to ask him privately, but she realizes that it will seem strange if she is too quiet. *I have to act the part of a scared victim ... don't they whine and ask a lot of questions?* "Where are we? What's going on?" She doesn't care if anyone answers. Once more she forces a fearful inflection into her words, although she'd much rather assert her authority as a Druzhina and demand answers.

"It's none of your business. The only thing you need to know is that you will do what you're told." Ramira's superior and haughty attitude about propels Elizabetta into action, but she contents herself with glaring at the witch—by the looks the others are giving her, they clearly expect some level of resistance.

Maybe she's been playing it too safe. "Whatever you and your sick excuse for an uncle think you're doing, I'm not going to just roll over and bow to your every whim." *Even without my strength, I bet I could kick her ass in a fight—*

*boy, would I love to do that.*

Ramira makes the mistake of stepping forward and slaping Elizabetta across the cheek. Without thinking it through, she punches the stupid witch in the face, causing her to stumble back a few steps. *Damn, they weren't lying about my strength—that hit should have knocked her on her ass or across the room.* The witch scrambles forward and lunges for her, but Dahliorn steps in front of Elizabetta and grabs Ramira by the arms. "Your uncle will return any moment. Do you think he'll be happy to see you losing control and being pushed around by this vampire?"

Before Ramira can answer, Guillermo returns in a pulse of light. "Link up," he commands, and everyone rushes to comply; Dahliorn obviously wasn't kidding about doing this often.

Elizabetta is still processing his sudden arrival when she's whisked away again, this time to another mansion. It's daytime here, but she has no idea if it's morning or afternoon, or where in the world they are. The most she can speculate is that they may be somewhere in the Pacific Ocean, as the decor and what little she sees out of a nearby window suggest a tropical location.

The sheridauk glances at her and seems to understand her confusion. «We're at Delap-Uliga-Djarrit, on the Majuro Atoll of the Marshall Islands.» When her brows draw together, he adds, «In the Pacific Ocean, about twelve time zones from Rathlin Island.»

*How in the world will Dmitri ever find me here?* She still isn't certain where they are—it wasn't a known place to her before the first failed rebellion, and Dmitri's programming of her mind didn't include this information. There's no way for her to know if this estate offers any chance of escape. *I may as well be marooned on a deserted island.*

The evil sorcerer orders Dahliorn to take her to a room on the second floor and to stand guard until he comes up to seal her inside. *No dungeon or cells here? Maybe his mutant spiders missed the transport ... God, I hope Dmitri and Matt are killing those things.* Elizabetta notices that Ramira follows them but enters a room next to the one Dahliorn opens for her. *Great ... at least we aren't roommates.* She's about to ask questions about this estate when the sheridauk announces that Guillermo is approaching the room. Hiding her disappointment, she hopes they'll talk later. Having a conversation face to face is a rare luxury for them.

Several minutes pass after the sorcerer and Dahliorn leave, and when Elizabetta doesn't hear any more sounds from the hallway beyond her room, she places a hand on the doorknob, expecting it to be untouchable, as her cell was. To her surprise, she finds it unlocked. But when she opens the door she discovers it's another Xi'an-style magic block-ade. *Shit, un-flipping-real.*

Elizabetta glances across the room, toward the sliding glass door and the balcony outside. Disregarding the mid-day sun, she races over to it, slides it open, and sticks her arm through the opening. *What the—* Without a second thought she dashes forward and leaps to clear the railing. Her body slams into an invisible obstacle and bounces back into the open doorway, landing with a thud. The burning sensation of direct exposure to the sun has her scrambling to her feet and pulling the curtain closed.

*Should have known I wouldn't get that lucky.*

Over the next few days Elizabetta settles into her new room. The daily routine here is the same as they had in Ireland, the only difference being the witch's constant efforts to force her into submission while Elizabetta pretends to be worn down and on the verge of capitulation. If Elizabetta thought the witch was annoying before, now she finds her intolerable—Ramira never stops hounding her.

The two adversaries have one mutual agreement—each remains in her own head at night when the witch is sleeping. At least that's what Ramira believes. For now that serves Elizabetta's purposes, but eventually she'll need unfettered access under the guise of submission to prevent the witch from becoming alarmed or suspicious if she discovers Elizabetta in her head in the middle of the night.

When Dahliorn feels assured that Elizabetta's submissive attitude has bolstered Ramira's confidence enough, he begins Elizabetta's new training—she must learn how to keep her mind active in both bodies while simultaneously controlling the unity and mirror bonding spells. The sheridauk believes this will allow her the best opportunity to avoid detection, in particular if she can lure Ramira into her mind and keep her busy while she rummages around in the witch's head.

The lessons are intense—Elizabetta equates it to using the subconscious while dividing the conscious part of her brain in two at the same time—and the training allows just two to three hours of sleep for Elizabetta and Dahliorn each night. *This is multitasking on steroids.* It stuns her when Dahliorn confirms that is exactly what he's trying to teach her, and he isn't sure if she'll ever accomplish it, let alone master it. He explains it's a trait that only a few fae possess—he's never heard of a human, vampire, or other species developing the skill. *Great, nothing like giving me the freaking impossible.* This time he can't cast a spell to help, as the magic needed is beyond what his restrictions allow. Failure is the constant result as she tries again and again, night after night, and she too begins to believe it will never work.

Even more discouraging is the blatant reminder of how critical it is for her to quickly perfect this ability. Ramira is walking past one of the many TVs that are always on, when a breaking news alert causes the witch to stop and watch. The human realm turmoil has hit its flash point, and over half the world's militarized countries are launching attacks by land, sea, and air. Every time Elizabetta is within sight or sound of a TV, her stomach twists into a giant knot. Her thoughts go more and more to her friends. She has no idea where in the world they are or if they're safe—and whether this will prevent them from searching for her. *That evil piece of shit did it—he's unleashed global anarchy and started World War III.* Somehow she has to stop him, but she'll need absolute control over Ramira to attempt it.

To that end, when it looks as if progress is hopeless, Elizabetta pushes for Dahliorn to agree to her earlier suggestion, the blood dinner trifecta. They argue over her idea for days, but her persistence finally pays off. Dahliorn relents on one condition: she must practice memory manipulation when Ramira is awake. The biggest hurdle Elizabetta will face is avoiding detection of what she's doing in Ramira's mind, though her presence won't alarm the witch—Ramira typically demands it as she goes about her day.

The night finally arrives when both she and the sheridauk believe she's ready to plant the suggestion. Elizabetta slips into Ramira's head, gives the command, and retreats without the witch ever knowing she was there. The next morning Ramira pops into Elizabetta's mind and summons Elizabetta to join her, but instead of going to the dining room, the witch pauses at a window to watch the sunrise.

«I can feel your hunger,» Ramira says. «Will you cooperate with me if I bring you blood?»

This isn't something Elizabetta bargained for, and she's cautious with her reply. «What do you need my cooperation on?»

«Stop fighting me—fully submit. If you do that, I will ensure you don't starve. Refuse, and I won't allow you to feed until you accept my dominance over you.»

*Just what I need, another hurdle, let alone one that may trip me up.* Dahliorn encourages Elizabetta to accept the terms, but she isn't comfortable giving up that much control. «What if she uses it to discover the unity bond?» she says to Dahliorn.

«The risk is slight, and if you can perfect your skills at manipulating her memory, influencing her, and planting new suggestions or memories as needed, then the only thing she'll have is a false belief that you've submitted to her.»

Dahliorn sounds so confident that Elizabetta gives the witch her reluctant agreement. Ramira turns away from the window and goes to find Dahliorn. When she whispers her request, his head dips—a common response when he's accepting an order from one of the Sanchezes—and he asks her to meet him outside of Elizabetta's room after dinner, as he needs time to collect the blood. The witch reminds him of the peril they face if either is caught. *I'm beginning to wonder if this was such a great idea.*

The hours drag by, only adding to the tension between Elizabetta and Ramira. The witch repeatedly demands Elizabetta's submission, which she won't give until she's fed. After dinner Ramira begins pacing the hall outside the bedrooms—she seems so eager that Elizabetta considers backing out. Then Dahliorn arrives, leaving her speechless. In the sheridauk's hands are two silk orbs. *Shit, Guillermo's mutant creatures are here.*

It's the push she needs to stay the course and follow through. The moment her bedroom door opens, Elizabetta unleashes her vampiric influence and gives one final suggestion, a last-minute condition, before returning to her own mind—she wants Ramira to drink at least a sip of blood without getting sick. She gives the command out of spite for the way the witch is trying to force her into submission. *At least my ability to influence is still there.*

Ramira lifts one sack to her own lips. "To new alliances. Cheers!"

Elizabetta drinks from her silk pouch, never taking her focus off the witch. To her surprise, Ramira takes more than a sip—she drinks every drop, licks her lips, and asks for a bit more. Elizabetta waits for the puking to start, but the witch doesn't show any sign of her usual nausea. *Why isn't she getting sick this time?*

The sheridauk moves in front of Ramira and studies her face, rubbing his jawline and chin as he watches her down the viscous liquid. «I don't know how you did it, but this may be beyond influence or bonding. She's acting like you have control.»

Excitement bursts through Elizabetta—her mouth gapes as her eyes widen at the sight before her, but she quickly veils the reaction. *That would be huge!* «How can we make sure? What do I do now?»

«Let's not push our luck—stick to our original plan and start wiping her memories of your command and her actions. We don't need her vomiting blood afterward.»

Somewhat reluctantly Elizabetta slips into Ramira's mind, claiming she wants to thank her privately for the blood. While the witch prattles on about their changed relationship, Elizabetta brings up the virtual console and searches for the memory threads. One by one she removes or blocks them from being stored or remembered. Dahliorn leads Ramira out of the bedroom to return the witch to her own room, and once Ramira is there, Elizabetta wipes that final memory and then retreats to her own head. She has a lot to think about; the possibility that there may still be a chance to control the witch without the dual consciousness skill gives her new hope.

Her lips curl into a grin. *I'll bet you think you have me right where you want me, you psycho sorcerer. Mark my words, I am coming for you.*

## CHAPTER 34: DMITRI

# Hit and Run

The moment Dmitri feared arrives in a violent fashion—diplomatic efforts by the humans are failing at an alarming rate, and both the UN and NATO are preparing to vote whether to launch the war. Dmitri recalls the Druzhinas to Venice. The last thing he needs is for them to be scattered around the world if bombs start dropping; he's fought in a few wars and seen more fighting over the centuries than he cares to remember. But his memories drift back over the catastrophic results of the first two world wars, and the possibility that a new global war will be worse than anything they've seen before sends a chill down Dmitri's spine. Guillermo doubtless will help the humans destroy most of their kind and a large part of this world.

In response to the growing unrest, the maxian supreme council summons Dmitri; he knows what is coming and doesn't want to hear that they told him so. Still, there's no way to avoid the meeting, and when Maria and Matt offer to go with him, he is grateful. The wizard notifies the council to send someone with an EPM. Within moments Henri arrives—Dmitri wonders if he's the council's main remote transporter—and whisks them back to the catacombs under Paris. The council members are seated and waiting for them. There are no spectators this time. The somber and angry faces greeting them make the cavern feel oppressive, stifling the air.

High Witch O'Mordha doesn't hesitate to address them. "We warned you, Mr. Markov. While you mostly succeeded in stabilizing the vampire and werewolf realms, you've failed miserably at managing the humans."

The high witch recognizes too late that she should have spoken with more care; Dmitri's claws are out, and his fangs nick his lip as he tries to suppress a hiss. The bloodlust has noticeable tremors coursing through his body. Maria places a hand on his arm. "Let me address them."

He gives her a curt nod, and she says, "You are wrong to lay all the blame on *King* Markov's shoulders. He's done the best he can with the resources available. You share equally in the pending debacle, as you've been more concerned with protecting the maxians and their realm than following through to help stop this nightmare."

The council members gasp at Maria's audacity, but the wizard continues her tirade. "One of our own is most responsible, and your suspension of the search to find Guillermo Sanchez has allowed that sorcerer to bring this upon the world. High Warlock Jacques Boucher would be ashamed of the leadership this council has shown since his death!"

"We will not tolerate your behavior, Miss D'Arcy." High

Witch O'Mordha's nostrils flare, and her eyes angrily rake over the three of them. "You will treat the supreme council with the respect it is due, or we will strip you of your powers."

"She's a member of my coven—"

"She's my mate, you will not—"

*Mate?* Dmitri glances to the right and sees Matt's canines lengthen—the wolf's body is on the brink of shifting. He places a hand on Matt's shoulder as Maria grabs the wolf's partially transformed hand. Matt tells him to go first, and Dmitri says, "Maria is a member of my coven. If you harm or punish her, you will invite war with my realm." He nods at Matt to signal it's his turn.

"You are threatening my mate. The werewolf realm will ally with the vampires if you touch her. She's spoken the truth, but your kind is too self-centered to admit your failure."

The council members look taken aback—Dmitri is certain they never expected this turn of events. *Neither did I. Is Matt bluffing?* The look on the mongrel's face seems to suggest he's dead serious.

If indeed true, it explains some of their recent behavior. *But why hide it?* In some ways the thought troubles Dmitri, but he'll protect their secret for now. Werewolves only live two to three centuries, while maxians can survive for millennia. He wonders how Maria will handle that and if she'll choose to follow the wolf to his grave. Dmitri doesn't want to think about losing these two friends, or what it will mean for him and Elizabetta when that time comes.

Dmitri's penetrating gaze freezes O'Mordha—she

doesn't even blink. Raw power carries in his voice. "We have no wish to fight you, but war is coming, and unless we work together to stop the human leaders from making this mistake, all realms will suffer."

Dmitri's words have enough impact on their own, but what happens next is the exclamation point. The high witch is about to reply when the ground jolts and several booming thumps shake the cavern's walls and floor. *They've launched their bombs. We're too late.* He doesn't wait for the stunned council members to react, but shouts at Henri, "Get us out of here—now!"

Without waiting for permission or orders, the warlock activates the EPM, and in an instant they arrive in Venice. Maria implores Henri to stay—he's their only resource for quick maxian transport, and if they're to stop the chaos the humans have unleashed, they will need his help. They race for the ballroom, Henri trailing after them, and find the Druzhinas, including Justin and Teresina, waiting for them along with the Seelinarans. There's no need to explain what has happened; they've already seen the flashes of light against the night sky, coming from the direction of Rome. Their exceptional hearing catches the whistling of more missiles flying over Venice.

Dmitri's primary concern is survivable shelter, since the villa may not keep them safe if the humans attack the city. Milnea says, "Maria, Nafurael, Zerbadiah, and I can place wards to protect it."

"Is that even possible, witchy-poo?" Matt's worried gaze darts toward the wizard.

She rolls her eyes, looking insulted. "Yes, *mo shíorghrá.*"

"We'll glamour it to match its surroundings if every-thing else is damaged in this area," Milnea says without hesitation, but it's the certitude in her tone that convinces Dmitri to give his consent.

For a brief moment his thoughts flicker to the home he and Elizabetta own in the Cannaregio District. It's selfish, but Dmitri can't allow harm to come to it—the home is the last place they knew peace and were completely happy. "Can you protect and glamour two locations at once?"

Nafurael says, "It can be done."

That's all Dmitri needs to hear. *At least I won't lose these ties to Elizabetta.*

The world is rocked on its heels as more countries enter the fight. News becomes sporadic—too many power plants and news facilities are being targeted—but the information that does trickle in indicates that all the warring countries, major and minor, have engaged in battle. The humans are in an all-out panic. A growing refugee crisis is straining the situation even more, and it brings a complete halt to Dmitri's search for Elizabetta. He can only hope that Guillermo is keeping her safe.

When the bombing of Venice starts, Dmitri has Henri transport him and Matt to the coven and pack headquarters around and near the city. He intends to take in as many as they can for protection—something of their species must survive. The Seelinarans may have no choice but to ride it out; the safety of the veils is unknown. If they can get through, Dmitri will petition the Unseelie king for help, as without it they might never stop Guillermo or find the king's son.

Zerbadiah and Tavorell volunteer to return to Seelinara and inform King Altheron of the developments. Much to Dmitri's relief, they return just a few hours later with a contingent of royal warriors—including four of King Altheron's personal sheridauk guards. This uniting of all the other realms—with the exception of the maxians, who refuse to do anything but hide—bolsters Dmitri's hope that he might bring an end to Guillermo yet. *And save Elizabetta. I hope we're not too late.*

Between the extra vampires and werewolves now being sheltered at La Perfezione, and the arrival of twenty fae soldiers, they are running out of room to house everyone at the villa. Dmitri chooses to lead by example and suggests they start with his quarters—he wants his suite divided, with a bedroom added for Matt. Sally follows his example and offers to share her room with Maria, Milnea, and the two pixies. Soon others are doing likewise, and the Druzhinas move into remodeled rooms that will hold two couples each. Other rooms, such as the various cubicula, are turned into barracks with bunk beds to house the single vampires, werewolves, and fae soldiers.

Dmitri can't help marveling at the solidarity amid chaos, and the respect the different species are showing each other. Everyone is making sacrifices to survive the war and doing what they can to help Dmitri put a stop to it. *Only in Venice ...*

They're in the middle of working on a new plan when a courier delivers a message to Teresina with the news that one of her contacts has word on Guillermo's whereabouts.

Liathera claps her hands together—Tavorell's excitement matches hers, and he recommends a double whammy of pixie dust. She gives a jubilant squeal and says, "It's about time—I'd love to dust that monster and watch him enjoy himself to death."

"We still have to find him before you can unleash double trouble, so take a chill pill, you two." Matt's grin is met with their scowls and wiggling backsides. "Don't even think it—you're not pixie-alizing my furry ass."

Dmitri clears his throat to cut off their banter. "Teresina, how reliable is this source?"

"I've never had a problem with him, and he's usually good on his word."

Looking down at the message again, Dmitri weighs his options—this is not a time for rash decisions—and finally decides he'll send a scouting party to verify the validity of the information. To the displeasure of some who just want in on any action, his team consists of himself, Matt, Maria, Henri, Zerbadiah, the pixies, two sheridauk guards, Alexander, Vladimir, and Anna. He doesn't want to take too large a group and tip off Guillermo to their presence, but at the same time he needs the right team members to fight the sorcerer if necessary, and to possibly rescue Elizabetta if she's with Guillermo's entourage.

When Dmitri's reconnaissance team is ready, they link together, and Henri transports them to their destination—a beach on a tropical island. It's daylight here, and the sun won't set for another few hours, which gives those who can go into the sunlight enough time to clandestinely check for wards and traps. The vampires will have to wait under the sun barrier Maria erected upon their arrival. Dmitri expects it will be a tense few hours until dark.

Then an hour before twilight Henri appears within the barrier, startling the vampires with his unexpected arrival. "Link together—we must go now!"

No one questions the urgent command, and a split second later they are under the cover of a magical shade in a tropical clearing, where the rest of Dmitri's team is waiting. He takes a moment to look at each one and notices some of them are injured. "What happened?"

Zerbadiah confirms it was a trap. "The sorcerer wasn't here, but one of his minions was, along with the woman and two other men. They ambushed us the moment we arrived and engaged us in battle."

"I suspect the two men may be maxians," Maria says. "They seemed untouchable, as if they were protected by personal wards, but they fought like trained killers." The wizard describes one man as an Asian with remarkable martial arts skills and the other as a soldier or fighter well trained in hand-to-hand combat. "Zerbadiah killed the soldier, but the Asian escaped."

Matt growls. "Baby vamp wasn't here, but unfortunately the stories of big hairy-assed spiders are true."

*Same one that attacked Vladimir, or are there several of these creatures?* Dmitri cringes when he hears the spider impaled a sheridauk's chest with its fangs. Matt then tangled with the creature, and his side was slashed open by one of the spider's fangs. The only non-spider injury is Liathera's. Her wing was nicked by a samurai sword when she dive-bombed the Asian to shove Tavorell out of the way.

"It was hiding," Matt says. "The mystery woman started to fight the fae and was on the losing end of it when the gargantuan spider came out of nowhere to defend her. It had the sheridauk on the ground so fast it was unbelievable. I lunged at it, but it took a swipe at me, grabbed the woman, and ran off." He looks down at his side. "I have a bad case of fang envy now."

When Dmitri frowns, the wolf points a finger at him. "Don't give me that look. If you saw the size, you'd be envious too."

Dmitri glances around at his team. It's obvious to him the scouting mission is a bust; he doesn't want to return to La Perfezione but fears they don't have a choice. "We'll have to go back to Venice and wait for another lead."

To his surprise, the demon advises against it. "I have the flavor of their essences now and can track them wherever they go in this world." Zerbadiah's comment is not boastful; he sounds as if he has done this many times before. "It won't be fast, it may take a few hours, but I will locate them."

*Hours is better than days.* "Maria?" The wizard is still performing mending spells on the three injured, but she assures Dmitri that they will all be able to fight within the hour—even the sheridauk, who, she explains, has a faster healing ability than vampires or werewolves.

While they recover, Vladimir recommends they retrieve the rest of the Druzhinas and two more sheridauk guards, or at the least Nafurael and Milnea. Dmitri agrees. He dispatches Henri to bring those Vladimir suggested, but leaves the fae selection to Milnea, Nafurael, and the Unseelie royal guard.

Once the warlock departs, Dmitri questions Matt further about their encounter. It surprises him to learn that the woman may be no more than an ordinary human—she used no magic, and Matt reports her fighting skills are poor to mediocre. Vladimir speculates that may be why she chose to attack him from behind at Jacques Boucher's home, and she may have taken the high warlock in the same manner. But he suspects the spider was the reason she succeeded in decapitating Jacques.

The spider is still the biggest mystery. Zerbadiah is bothered by the magic residue on the beast; there are multiple layers of magic, but the giant arachnid doesn't carry the scent that the demon has noticed on smaller spiders he's encountered. He isn't sure what it is other than not natural, and such an admission by a being who has undoubtedly seen evil Dmitri can't even imagine is chilling.

"Is it possible for a demon to mask their appearance that way?" Alexander stares at Zerbadiah as if there might be some deception on his part too. Dmitri can't fault him for asking; he was thinking the same thing.

One of the sheridauk guards says, "Fae, angels, and demons can only glamour themselves in a shape that matches their own. I've heard of no demon that looks like that spider."

"So what is it, then?" Anna's voice has a tinge of fear— she almost lost Vladimir to the mutant beast—and it's something Dmitri's only heard in rare instances during their long friendship.

Zerbadiah shakes his head. "The smell is wrong; the

layers of magic are too tangled to get a true understanding of the purpose of their cast. If there are more of these creatures at the sorcerer's command, we will need King Altheron to send more troops."

*We could really use maxian help.* Dmitri's confidence plunges into uncertainty, his anger building at the maxians' arrogance in treating others as beneath them while flaunting their powers—even as they hide until someone else brings peace to the world. He's still seething over it when Henri returns with the others.

It doesn't take long to brief the new arrivals, and it's disheartening to hear the angel and the other fae confirm Zerbadiah's suspicions. *How do we go up against something like this? What does it mean for Elizabetta's safety?* If it weren't for the constant reassurances from the demon and angel that she's alive, defeat would consume him until nothing but bloodlust was left.

Then Zerbadiah shoots to his feet, startling many a-round him—some draw weapons and others scan wildly for a threat. "Do you know of a place called Roswell?"

"New Mexico?" Matt looks puzzled for a moment, then laughs. "Of course, where else would gargantuan spiders come from but outer space? They're on vacation at a world-famous alien hotspot."

Several Druzhinas laugh at his comment, and even Dmitri sees the mongrel's humor in that location. He shakes his head and drags a hand through his hair before he gives Henri the order to transport them. There's at least some good about the enemy choosing that area of the United States—by now it's dark, and there have been no reports of recent fighting in the area.

When they arrive just outside of Roswell, the demon attempts to pinpoint the location of their quarry—it's still just the three of them, apparently. A trenchant moment of silent communication passes between Zerbadiah and Nafurael. Without a word the angel shoots up into the night sky, and the demon chases after him in mist form.

*What the hell?* Everyone starts talking at once, but before they quiet down the angel and demon return, confirming that their three foes are northwest of Roswell in the middle of the open countryside. Neither detects any sign that the sorcerer is nearby, and from what they can tell, the spider is wounded. The woman seems insane, Nafurael says—they describe her as arguing with herself. The Asian man is the only one alert and on guard.

Dmitri sucks in a deep breath. "I want the man and woman captured alive if at all possible—this may be our best chance to find out where Guillermo has taken Elizabetta. As to the spider ... kill it."

*This will be over soon. Amore, ti amo e non smetterò mai di amarti.*

## CHAPTER 35: ELIZABETTA

# The Nightmare Begins

Elizabetta resumes her lessons with Dahliorn, but her progress is miserably slow despite her success with the blood dinner. The sheridauk insists that she continue planting suggestions and wiping memories—he claims she needs to be faster, more adept at doing them simultaneously, before she can risk splitting her active mind and working from her virtual console to take control of Ramira. It becomes a daily argument between Elizabetta and Dahliorn—she keeps pushing for more, and he refuses to introduce her to the steps she'll need to perform multiple tasks at once. The routine is so boring and predictable that they finish each lesson within an hour, and both are getting almost a full night's sleep.

During the day Ramira continues her pattern of training, arguing with her uncle, and haranguing Elizabetta while asserting her "dominance." As Ramira drones on yet again about her demand for submission, Elizabetta wants to growl. «Dahliorn, if you don't show me how to take over this poor excuse for a witch soon, I swear I'm going to lose it.» Of course, he ignores Elizabetta. *My complaints probably sound as pathetic as Ramira's.*

The impotent witch isn't content to be a control freak in her own mind; she gradually pushes Elizabetta to give her control of both minds. «Nice try, wrong again, Ramira! Submission has nothing to do with control. You can go to hell if you think I'm going to allow you to completely take over my mind and body.»

The witch whines, «Then you're not really submitting, are you? You promised to give me dominance ... you lied. If you don't give in, it will be years before I allow you to feed again.»

*God, I hate this bitch.* The daily squabbles are driving Elizabetta insane. She's become the witch's favorite verbal sparring partner, so much so that there are fewer disagreements between Guillermo and Ramira. Elizabetta doesn't know if the psycho sorcerer hasn't noticed or if he's not mentioning it as a way to avoid reminding his niece that she's slipping and not showing her usual bitchiness.

Every day over breakfast or dinner, Guillermo verifies Ramira's progress by testing Elizabetta's submissive state. To her total humiliation, the few times they've allowed her out of her room, Elizabetta has been forced to do demeaning acts to prove Ramira's superior position. She's crawled on her hands and knees, barking like a dog, and played dress-up Barbie when Ramira insisted Elizabetta give the witch a makeover. She's been made to strip and walk naked through the mansion—she can still see the deep shade of red Dahliorn turned when he saw her that day.

Other commands have angered her—being forced to pelt the cook with raw eggs, spar with and deliberately lose to Ramira, and clean every bathroom in the mansion with a toothbrush and a small piece of rag.

For weeks, each day starts out like every other day before it. Elizabetta wakes to Ramira's shrill voice in her head, the witch making demands and being a general pain in the backside. Then there's a small amount of bickering between the witch and Guillermo over breakfast before Ramira goes to work out with her trainers. From there it's shower, eat, bicker some more, and read the worst books in existence before falling asleep.

But one afternoon, when Ramira is in the middle of a stealth exercise with Sir, one of Guillermo's servants interrupts to relay the message that the witch must report in haste to her uncle's study. Ramira doesn't hide her nervousness, not that Elizabetta can blame her—the mad sorcerer is unpredictable, and there's no way to know why he's disrupted her schedule.

*I've done nothing wrong, and it can't be more intruders—the servant wasn't upset.* Every path of speculation leads her to the same two conclusions: the war or another bullshit mission. But Ramira hasn't been sent anywhere since the war blew up into the conflagration now devastating the planet. *It's the war, has to be.*

Even though the war is still new by any standard, some smaller and weaker countries have already collapsed, and the superpower nations seem to have no interest in peace. Even their location in the Marshall Islands isn't immune. Elizabetta has periodically felt the reverberations of strafing fire and missile impact, though Guillermo laughs maniacally whenever the attacks come close to his estate—its wards and protections prevent anything from damaging the property.

Ramira stomps toward the house, but the self-important witch insists on taking a shower before reporting as ordered. Elizabetta checks in with Dahliorn while the witch is getting dressed. «Do you have any idea why that scumsucker needs his little tyrant of a niece?»

«No, but the trainers and I have also been summoned. I'm about to enter the study now.»

The last part is a polite way of telling Elizabetta to shut up. *I don't know how he's survived centuries in this freak show, or how he's even remained sane.*

Ramira is the last to arrive for the meeting, and Guillermo once more berates his niece when she enters. *Dear old uncle is pissed—again.* The witch sits in a huff and pouts as the sorcerer glares at her, and again Elizabetta considers the risk involved in telling the witch some of Guillermo's secrets—the most important being his death wish for his niece. If she could figure out a way around revealing that she has been in Ramira the whole time, she'd do it. *But how can I explain the things I've learned or seen, like her hidden and altered memories?* She keeps these thoughts to herself, though, especially from Dahliorn. *He'd have a total conniption fit.*

Ramira's shrieks bring Elizabetta's attention back to what is going on around her. "I'm not ready, Uncle! This is suicide, pure madness ... if you want to kill me, then why don't you just give your freakish pet the order to do it?"

*What have I missed here while daydreaming?* The fear radiating through Ramira is palpable, and it's enough to send Elizabetta's pulse pounding. If the witch is this freaked out, whatever it is can't be good.

The sorcerer's tone is filled with icy hostility. "I told you that you're not going alone. If the Druzhina and the new vampire king take the bait, they'll send a small squad to verify the authenticity of the information. I doubt there will be more than two or three Druzhinas, and between you and the others it will take little effort to wipe them out and send our message to the vampire realm."

*We already have a new king? I wonder what schmuck they gave the power and title to this time. Sure hope I don't have to force Ramira to take out another poor excuse for a vampire ruler.*

"We have human governments doing exactly what we want. The maxians are in hiding and will not help anyone but themselves, and the werewolves still aren't concerned about issues beyond their territories." Guillermo's chest rises and falls in rapid breaths, and Elizabetta doesn't know if it's due to anger or to excitement over his plans coming together. "The time has come to bring down the vampire realm, starting with a few of their Druzhinas."

Ramira whines, "But what if they do send more than a few? How do you expect me to get out of there alive?"

The sorcerer turns a scorching glare on the witch. "We're not arguing this point any further! You are leaving in ten minutes. I suggest you pack—we don't know how long this assignment will take, and given the turmoil around the world, it could take the vampires anywhere from a few days to a couple of weeks to reach the location you're going to."

When the witch keeps sitting there, Guillermo shouts, "I said, go. Now!"

Ramira storms out of the room, huffing, screaming, and lashing out every step of the way to her quarters. She rips paintings off the walls, upsets furniture, throws vases and porcelain figurines, and kicks a hole in her door before she opens it.

«That's real mature.»

«Shut up!» Ramira screams as she rips another painting off the wall.

*I've never seen such a spoiled-ass bitch in my life. Good grief.* It takes Elizabetta all she has to keep her mouth shut and not tell the brat exactly what she thinks of her. Instead Elizabetta turns her attention to Dahliorn. «Where's he sending us?»

«You were there. Weren't you listening?» Dahliorn's question isn't condescending—there's a hint of confusion to his words.

She rolls her imaginary eyes. «I was tuned out ... I can only take so much of Ramira on a good day, and today has most definitely not been one of those.»

«You're going to an uninhabited atoll near the Line Islands in the middle of the Pacific Ocean. Michio will operate the EPM to get you there and back.»

«What do you mean, 'you,' and why aren't you going to guard the witch?»

There's a long, pregnant pause before he responds. «There will be plenty of protection for Ramira—don't worry, little dove, you will be safe.»

She doesn't find that very reassuring, and once more she notices that his answer is vague enough to imply many different things. *Damn fae secrecy and creative truth-telling.* But she knows he won't say more and that it's useless to try to get him to reveal what he's determined to hide. The only thing she can do is watch Ramira have a tizzy fit; clothes, gear, boots, and shoes are tossed about the room and stuffed angrily into her suitcase. *This is going to be a long trip.* When the witch finally slams her case shut, she latches it, drags it into the hall, and pitches it down the staircase. At the bottom of the stairs Ramira picks it up and slams it into the floor a few more times as she screeches with guttural sounds. *A very long trip.*

As the witch enters the parlor, Elizabetta notices that Sir is also packed and waiting beside Michio. Guillermo follows Ramira into the room and gives the group their final instructions. "If the vampires do as I predict, you should be home within a short period of time. If they send more than you can handle in one confrontation, then you are to take out as many as you can and go to the second set of coordinates on your list. If you fail there, you better think of a good way to lure them to the next location, because I will not tolerate you returning here empty-handed."

The two men acknowledge his orders, but Ramira lets out another huff. The sorcerer's fingers sizzle with magic—a clear threat. "I mean it, Ramira. You are to kill all but one and bring that one here alive. Don't come home until you can do that, or I will punish you."

Ramira whines, "But what if—"

"I expect you to succeed on this mission, even if it takes you a few months." Guillermo flexes his fingers as the energy pulses between each digit. Unadulterated contempt pours from each word he spits at his niece. "I have a lot of work to do to keep the war on track, and I can't afford your childish distractions. Do as you've been told for once in your life!" With that, the sorcerer storms out of the room.

Michio clears his throat and asks if everyone is ready to go. The witch stomps over to him and grabs his arm. "We. Don't. Have. A. Choice."

It's dark when they arrive on the atoll, and Dahliorn was right about it being uninhabited—there are no signs of civilization at all. They're in a clearing of some sort that is surrounded by palm trees and plants. But the mostly level ground free of shrubs, rocks, and trees creates advantageous conditions for the Druzhinas. Elizabetta is confident that they can face Ramira, Michio, and Sir without difficulty here.

A sense of trepidation whispers that regardless of how this ends, she will suffer loss. There's no way for her to know which Druzhinas will be sent, and she would never choose any of their lives over another's. Aside from the risk that one of her friends or even Dmitri could be injured or killed, there's a stronger possibility she herself won't survive the coming confrontation. Ramira doesn't stand a chance against well-trained and seasoned killers, and in a fight the Druzhinas will not hesitate to kill an enemy. *If she dies, I die.* Sorrow for all she'll lose and leave behind sinks her into despair.

The silence is broken by a flash of white light and the

sudden appearance of not three, but six individuals—Matt and Maria are a welcome sight. She doesn't recognize the maxian who transported them, or the other three ... men. *Who are they?* She's not sure what they are either, other than not human. The big guy next to Matt points in her direction, and she can feel Ramira's body tremble. The witch whispers, "Perhaps we should run. We're going to get slaughtered."

Michio scowls at her. "Today we fight!"

*Where are the Druzhinas? Dmitri? Are they coming after dark?* Elizabetta watches with pride as Matt motions for his compatriots to form the fighting arc intended to flank opponents if necessary—he has adapted so well to Druzhina-style defense and offense. *I hope Dmitri taught him other fighting techniques as well.* Elizabetta's heart aches. If Matt and Maria find out they were a direct cause of her death, they will never forgive themselves. She must hope that Guillermo will destroy her body and not deliver it to inflict a psychological blow against those she loves. Her mind flickers to the question Dmitri asked so long ago ... she still doesn't know if she's ready to meet her destiny. *Maybe no one is ever really ready to face their last breath, their final moment.*

Ramira wipes her palms on her cargo pants before she draws her sword. For a moment Elizabetta thinks she may have to help the witch swallow the lump frozen in her throat. The roar of Ramira's heartbeat pulses in her ears— Elizabetta tries to stick her illusory fingers into her imaginary ears to drown out the noise. It doesn't work.

Matt's team will be upon them in seconds. Michio

reminds Ramira to take a fighting stance, and the space between the foes shrinks with each step Elizabetta's friends take. Her own heart picks up the pace. *This will all be over soon.* Through Ramira's eyes she watches as Matt sheds his clothing—he will shift to fight—and she recalls how quickly his sharp teeth can tear through a vampire's neck. If he's the one to take down Ramira, it will be a fast death. At his side Maria readies a green bolt of energy, and then the big guy next to Matt suddenly changes into something so hideous that Ramira's body sways, and Elizabetta suspects she's on the verge of passing out. *What the hell is that thing? It looks like a freaking devil.* Without a word spoken between them, Matt lunges forward as Maria throws the first bolt, and the devil turns into red mist.

Between a blink and a breath, Ramira is already floundering; her balance is off, she lunges when she should feint, and the way she's flailing her sword around is a neon sign announcing she's ready to have her ass handed to her. She's fighting—if it can even be called that—one of the unknown men. Elizabetta knows the witch doesn't stand a chance, and relief washes through her—it won't be one of her friends burdened with the guilt of her death.

Unlike the woman she's trapped inside, Elizabetta is no coward. She squares her insubstantial shoulders, straightens her back, and prepares for the deathblow that should come any second. *Dmitri ... I will miss you, amore. Ti amo e non smetterò mai di amarti.*

But then to Elizabetta's horror, the man attacking Ramira is knocked to the ground by Guillermo's mutant spider—it seemingly came out of nowhere again. *Oh, give me a friggin' break!* The creature stabs the man in the chest with his fangs—a horrified scream contorts the man's face as his hands scrabble to dislodge the creature. A second later her favorite wolf rushes in and hits the spider in the side. Matt's canine teeth rip a hole in the spider's cephalothorax, halfway between its eyes and abdomen. *Go, Matt, go! I love that crazy werewolf.* Her excitement doesn't last. The spider pivots to roll as Matt's body sails over the top of it, and at least one of its fangs slices Matt's side. *Oh my God, let him be all right!* The wolf lets out a pained whimper as he rolls and clambers to his feet. Elizabetta's eyes dart between the wolf and spider; she's never felt so terrified for Matt before, and she contemplates using Ramira to save him—even if it does trap her forever.

The spider raises its front legs, its fangs poised to strike, then steps back toward Ramira. *Damn it! That monster is going to protect her. I wish Dahliorn were here—irrefutable proof these creatures must die.* Matt is favoring his wounded side and backing away too. As long as the distance continues growing between them, Elizabetta will wait to act; there's still a chance someone else may end Ramira and the spider.

Ramira, being the coward she is, ducks down beneath the spider, looking for her other two comrades. The devil, in a half-mist, half-solid form, and one of the other unknown men are tearing Sir's body to pieces. The witch almost throws up at the sight. *Yeah, and she's going to be the big, bad killer of vampires.* Michio is yelling and running toward her, ducking just in time to miss one of Maria's energy blasts. But then Elizabetta notices something else—

two very tiny creatures buzzing and flying erratically near Michio's face. From this distance she can't tell what they are, but it's clear the martial artist is trying to defend himself against them. She sees his sword arc and slice at the larger buglike thing, but the smaller one hurtles down, pushing the other out of the way. Michio's sword hits the second creature, and it tumbles out of the air and disappears in the grass.

Michio, still in the follow-through of the sword's swing, starts the EPM activation as he closes the final paces between himself and the spider and Ramira. Ramira wraps her arms around the spider's leg at the same moment Michio grabs another leg, and in a quick burst of light they transport to a new location—what appears to be a desert environment.

Ramira dashes out from under the spider and spins around to take in their surroundings. Obviously they're in the middle of nowhere, but Elizabetta doubts any of them will reveal where in the world this is. All she knows is that wherever they are, it's nighttime. *God, where is Dahliorn?*

The witch's gaze shifts to the spider, which is folding its legs and lowering its body to the ground, giving Elizabetta her first good view of its injuries. She can see that Matt tore a large chunk of flesh out of the spider's side. *I hope that's a fatal wound.* Michio approaches the creature, intones an incantation, and spreads a poultice over the injury—he apologizes that it's the best he can do, given their circumstances.

Ramira sits on a boulder nearby, and Elizabetta can sense her conflicted feelings. Against Dahliorn's earlier advice, she taps into the witch's active thoughts. Ramira wants the spider dead, but doesn't. She yearns to defy her uncle but craves his praise more. *I'll never figure her out.* Elizabetta lets go of the energy strand, grateful Ramira never noticed the intrusion. Instead the witch wraps her arms around her sides and mutters, "We're going to die ... we can't survive against the vampires and their allies."

*Better late than never to wake the hell up.* Elizabetta says, «You're right—you won't survive. Your insane uncle has sent you on a suicide mission, and you have two choices.»

For once the witch doesn't come back with a hateful or arrogant remark; she sounds almost defeated as she continues speaking aloud. "What are they?"

Elizabetta considers for a moment whether to answer the question. *Dahliorn can kiss my ass. This may be my best opportunity to subvert the witch.* «You can either continue doing your uncle's bidding and end up dead, or you can seek the Druzhina's help and bring an end to Guillermo. It's your choice to live or die.»

That comment reawakens the witch's hatred, which bubbles forth in a swell of venom and acid. "I should have known you'd come up with a solution that involves my uncle being dead. Do me a favor and don't give me any more advice—you're just proving yourself another stupid vampire."

Elizabetta tries to convince Ramira that her advice isn't a trick, it's the truth, but there's no changing the witch's mind. *I'm doubting an entrenching tool could dig deep enough to find her real memories. Guillermo's done one helluva number on her.*

They're still debating when Michio returns and lays out his plan. By his estimation, it could take the spider a week to fully mend and be ready to fight again; Michio will provide magical cover as needed, but they will otherwise remain here to recoup, giving the spider time enough to heal. Afterward they'll go to Guillermo's second attack site, and Michio will use the redecrystapiezo to make arrangements with the sorcerer's contact to lure the vampires to the next confrontation.

*How long will it take for the Druzhinas to realize they are being baited?* After the failed attack, Elizabetta knows that the Druzhinas will hit them harder the next time— there will be more, maybe their entire force. If that happens, Michio, Ramira, and the spider will meet their end.

*So will I.*

## CHAPTER 36: ELIZABETTA

# The Horror of Truths

The sun is several hours from rising, and Ramira, curled up against the spider's side, is still asleep. Elizabetta doesn't know for sure where Michio is, only that he's on guard duty for the night—he insists they remain vigilant. If the witch were in a deeper sleep, Elizabetta would attempt to use the unity connection to boost her vampiric influence and convince Ramira to give up, but the less-than-ideal sleeping arrangement has the witch hovering just below consciousness.

Elizabetta can't shut her mind down, and her thoughts are scattered between the sorrow of knowing she'll never be in Dmitri's arms again, and her friendships with Matt and Dahliorn. Meeting these men, she believes, has been more than dumb luck—each man arrived in her life at a critical time, and that can't be coincidence. Now she's on the cusp of losing everyone who matters to her. *If the witch would just surrender, we'd all have a chance to get our lives back.* She and Dmitri have come through so much together, and she relishes the fact that he was at her side when they destroyed Shashenka. A smile breaks over her insubstantial face as her thoughts drift to Matt—he's been an incredible friend, steadfast at her side since the day they met. It's still hard for her to believe how lucky she was the day Matt found her in Yellowstone.

In some ways Dahliorn's also been there for her, although it's not the same. She has too many questions about his loyalty to her and his commitment to ending or even getting away from the sorcerer. The sheridauk has moments when he seems as solid as Matt, and he has certainly given her hope and comfort, but it's the instances when he does something that stifles their progress that cause her the greatest concern. Over the last few months she's also seen a frightening side to him that keeps her distrust alive. *Is it a mistake to have so much faith in him? Will he ever be ready to take down Guillermo?*

Her thoughts are still whirling when Michio runs toward them, whisper-shouting for Ramira to wake up. Somehow Matt's team has found them already, and they are about to attack. *How did that crazy wolf find us so fast, make a deal with the devil?* Ramira jumps to her feet. "Transport us out of here!"

Michio shakes his head no. "There are more of them, and if they can find us this fast, then we're not safe anywhere. We make our final stand here." He seems to understand the fright pulsing through Ramira, and in a solemn but pride-filled tone he says, "I'm sorry it has come to this, Ramira, but remember that there is nothing more honorable than dying a warrior's death."

Ramira doesn't have a chance to respond—her attention is drawn to the fighters moving toward them from all sides. The witch's eyes dart wildly as she turns in a circle, and Elizabetta's would bug out of her head if she were in her own body. There are twenty on Matt's side now, and Dmitri is leading them. *What an incredible sight! Oh Dmitri, amore ...* She inwardly smiles as her heart breaks; at least she is able to look upon his face one last time. Then her focus shifts to those around them and rocks her back on her illusory heels; maxians, werewolves, and the Druzhinas she expected, but they are accompanied by others she never knew existed before. *Is that an angel? Who are those men? Great, the devil is back. We are going to be beyond fubar by the time they get done with us.*

Dmitri takes the lead, and Ramira's gaze locks on him as she pulls the sword into fighting position. The strength vibrating off him enhances the determination and hatred in his eyes—Elizabetta basks in the thrill and attraction of watching him in battle, but ... *I've already seen this.* The dream she had, where she saw him come at her in much the same way. Then she realizes that he's coming for Ramira, and her heart shatters more than it already has—it will be at his hands that she'll die. *I hope he never finds out—it will destroy him. Ti amo, amore. Do what you must.*

The battle begins, but Elizabetta knows it will be over before it ever really starts. The spider runs away when it catches sight of its approaching foes. *Didn't expect that—a coward just like Ramira.* She can hear Michio scream—he's already in trouble and likely will be dead within seconds.

The devil and angel flank Dmitri, Matt, and Maria; the

others to either side complete the formidable Druzhina fighting arc. It's the assortment of fighters that makes it a baffling but glorious sight. Still, Ramira is stupid enough to accept Dmitri's challenge, and he closes the gap, his dagger poised to strike. *Go for the heart, amore—make it quick.*

Those with Dmitri keep their distance as he tests Ramira's fighting skills. At first Elizabetta's surprised that he's not moving faster for the kill. Then she recognizes the malevolence in his eyes. *Does he intend to draw Ramira's death out to satiate his need for revenge?* Ramira foolishly thinks she has a chance and makes bold attempts to inflict an injury on Dmitri. He deflects her easily and slices her with the dagger each time she moves within his reach. *Death by a thousand cuts—is that how this is going to go down?*

Then without warning the spider reappears and pounces, landing in front of Ramira and pushing Dmitri away. Elizabetta's heart leaps with anticipation—Guillermo's mutant pet is finally going to die. The angel and devil rush forward, flanking Dmitri. Maria lobs a white ball of magic at the spider—it's a direct hit, and the creature stumbles back. Ramira dodges to the right and out of the way of the staggering creature. Taking advantage of the opening caused by the spider's movement, Dmitri rushes forward, grabs Ramira, and races several paces away from the mutant creature. His action catches the witch by surprise, and she drops her sword to push against his chest in a feeble attempt to escape. Elizabetta looks over Dmitri's shoulder—the spider is attempting to get on its feet, but she's not too concerned. Her friends and the others will kill it soon.

An enraged scream draws her focus to Ramira—the bitch is savagely biting Dmitri's shoulder. He jerks back and repositions the dagger to stab the witch in the heart. Ramira's eyes widen, and Elizabetta realizes that he's done playing; when his arm thrusts forward, the blade of the dagger will deliver a mortal blow. He's about to make the move when a horrible chattering sound comes from the spider, and Dmitri spins and leaps behind Ramira, capturing her around the waist and bringing the dagger against her throat. Then the impossible happens, and Elizabetta feels as if her sanity has finally buckled under the weight of all she's been through—she cannot believe what is happening in front of her.

The spider rises to its full height, the air shimmers around it, and its body begins to shift. A second later she sees a naked man, and he's shouting, "Don't—you'll kill Elizabetta."

*Dahliorn? What ... how?* Elizabetta can feel her illusory eyes blink and blink, trying to absorb and process what she sees through Ramira's vision. She feels as if she'll be sick. His words echo in her mind: "abomination," "not the only victim."

Dmitri presses the blade harder against Ramira's throat, and the sharp edge sends blood dripping from the cut—it's not deep, but it stings. Dahliorn puts his hands up in the air and takes a step forward. The gaping wound in his side— the same side as the spider's injury—is still seeping. His gaze darts to Ramira, and Elizabetta can see shame, embarrassment, and even an apology move through his expression. "The witch has Elizabetta inside her mind. They're tied, and injuries inflicted are shared by both. If you kill her, Elizabetta will die."

Ramira relaxes a little when the blade pulls away from her throat, giving some space between her neck and the dagger. One of the unknown men runs toward Dahliorn and falls on his knee, head bowed. "My prince, we are here to rescue you."

*What the hell is going on here? Prince? Dahliorn is the hideous spider? What the fu—*

Three other men and a woman, the angel, and the devil move forward and join the first man on their knees. Murmurs of "Your majesty," "My prince," and "It's good to find you alive," become a chorus of reverence for the naked man before them. The woman then says, "Why do you not clothe yourself, my lord?"

Dahliorn looks down and touches the silver belt at his waist. "A sorcerer has restricted my powers and altered my natural state."

Elizabetta is still trying to wrap her head around this turn of events; there's so much she understands now. Dahliorn's revulsion and his reluctance to kill the spider. *I begged him to kill himself. Why didn't he tell me?* The times he was sent with Ramira, but the spider always showed up to bail her out of trouble. *Did Guillermo know he held a prince from the fae world?* She wonders why he never revealed his royal status. Then she looks at those still on their knees in front of him, and it hits her like a sledgehammer—they are fae. He is no longer alone.

## CHAPTER 37: DMITRI

# The Clock is Ticking

Dmitri barely notices when Milnea conjures a long cloak and steps forward to wrap it around the man's naked body. *This is their prince? This is King Altheron's son?* If he is their prince and he's telling the truth, that Elizabetta is somehow inside this woman—the prince called her a witch—he can't risk further harm, or worse, chance killing Elizabetta. Dmitri withdraws the blade from the woman's throat and whispers, "*Amore*, are you in there? Can you hear me?"

The witch cackles. Dmitri doesn't know what to make of her response. He looks at the prince and pushes Ramira forward.

Milnea says, "My prince, this is King Markov, leader of the vampire realm."

Dmitri grimaces at the reminder of his kingship. "Care to tell me your name?" The months of frustration carry in his tone—he'll be damned if he's going to address this fae by title.

"Dahliorn."

A hand comes out from under the cloak, but Dmitri hesitates to shake it. He's afraid to let go of the woman in his arms. *Where is Elizabetta's body, if she is indeed inside this woman?* The surrealism of the moment has him caught up in a mix of elation, fear, confusion, and doubt—he's not sure how to respond or what to say.

Matt's head ping-pongs between the woman and the prince, and he echoes Dmitri's unspoken questions. "What do you mean, Eliza is inside her? What the hell happened to her body?"

Dahliorn turns his head to the side. "And you are?"

"Matt Wolfe." The werewolf gives the prince a hard glare and folds his arms over his bare chest. "Where is she? And who is this woman?" He nods toward the witch in Dmitri's arms.

The fae starts to lower his hand, but Dmitri reaches forward and shakes it. He needs to set aside his fears for Elizabetta in order to learn what the prince knows about her captivity. Dmitri still doesn't quite understand where she is, or how she can possibly be inside the witch, but this fae prince is the closest he's come to finding her so far. "Tell us what you know—I need to get my wife back." Instinct tells him the time for rescuing her just became a lot shorter.

Nafurael and Zerbadiah come forward and offer to take the witch, who shrinks away, tightly pressing against Dmitri's chest. Milnea assures Dmitri that the other two will not harm the woman, Ramira—the prince finally reveals her name—or his wife, but they will make sure the witch can't use her magic to escape. The prince shakes his head, and Dmitri feels still more confused when Dahliorn tells the others that Ramira is powerless. *She's an enigma we need to understand.* When the angel reaches for the woman, Dmitri slowly allows him to take her.

To his left, the witch's cohort lies dead. Maria is already preparing an obliterate spell to get rid of the remains, but Dahliorn stops her. "He is a descendant of Sengchou, Batuo's disciple from the Shaolin Temple, and he deserves a warrior's burial. Like me, he had no choice but to serve the sorcerer." Even though Dmitri never knew the man, he can't deny the respect he feels; to have lived such a long life enslaved by Guillermo, yet never lose honor or the goodness of his soul is remarkable. It had to have been the man's training—Dmitri knows that Batuo's disciples created the Shaolinquan fighting style, one of the first martial art forms. He nods in agreement. Dahliorn calls two of the sheridauks over and instructs them on how to handle the body for a Buddhist burial.

Maria puts the EPM the man was wearing into her pack, since Henri can't touch two of them or both will activate. With her tasks finished, she moves to Matt's side, handing him a pair of jeans. After he pulls them on she slips her hand into his. Dmitri wonders if he'll ever feel Elizabetta's touch again. He looks closer at the witch. *What if she's the nearest I ever come to being with my wife again? Is amore's body a husk, an empty shell?* His heart constricts at the thought, and he tries to push it aside. If that is all that is left of her, what does it mean for them? Would he have to let her go, or is it possible for him to find a way to win the witch's affections and keep at least that much of Elizabetta with him always?

Upon their return to La Perfezione Dmitri asks Milnea to create a barrier around the witch. Maria conjures clothing for Dahliorn and then seating for everyone, and the sheridauk prince receives Dmitri's permission to begin his report.

Dmitri's heart drops into his stomach as the sheridauk describes his centuries of captivity—the control that Guillermo holds over him even now—but his stomach plummets through the ground when the prince details the spells cast against Elizabetta. *I'm grateful he protected her, but if the Seelinarans can't find a way to break the dark magic ...* The thought that it may take the sorcerer's death to free her fills him with dread.

After Dahliorn finishes his tale, Dmitri moves over to the barrier surrounding Ramira and stares at her, hoping, needing to see some reflection of his wife in her eyes. Nothing but hatred pours out of the brown eyes staring back at him. *Can amore see me? Hear me?* Dmitri tunes out what the prince is saying—his own thoughts swirl and tangle into a mess. He doesn't know if this witch will help or hinder their efforts to free Elizabetta, but the longer he studies the witch, the more uncomfortable and angry she seems to become. Her arms are crossed, and she paces like a caged tiger.

A slight smile parts his lips when he recalls Dahliorn's claim that the witch and Elizabetta can communicate—he knows how persistent and stubborn his wife can be. *I'll lay odds she's threatened this woman with everything she can think of as she tries to claw her way out of this nightmare.*

*I'd rip the witch to shreds if I thought it would free her.* A part of him needs to feel Elizabetta again, and without thinking Dmitri places his palm against the invisible barrier. He whispers, not knowing if she can hear him, "*Moyata svyetlina ...* come back to me."

## CHAPTER 38: ELIZABETTA

# Reality Warps Again

"Ramira? I know Elizabetta can hear me. Will you relay what she says or not?" Desperation tinges Dmitri's voice, and anger lights his eyes.

Ramira glares at Dmitri—Elizabetta can tell by the way her view of the outside world is suddenly narrowed—but it's Elizabetta the witch chooses to acknowledge. «He can go to hell. I'm not helping any of you!»

«Just friggin' answer him already, even if you're only going to say no.» Elizabetta tries to put a good dose of vampiric influence into her tone as she adds the underlying command to her words. *I'd love to lift her hand and punch her in the face with it.*

«You can go to hell too.» Ramira's emotions are too strong—she brushed off Elizabetta's attempt more easily than she should have. The witch adds, «You made an agreement with me—you submitted. I won't allow them to take you from me.»

*Allow them? Does she think she can dictate her terms to*

*them?* The witch flinches when Dmitri strikes the invisible barrier with his fist. Elizabetta wants to hold him, reassure him that everything is going to be okay, but she knows it may never be okay again.

Dmitri leans his head against the shield. "*Amore ...* I will do all I can to bring you back." He looks up, and his elongated fangs and narrowed eyes are meant for the witch—Elizabetta knows it. "Mark my words, witch, I will free my wife!"

Elizabetta tries to focus her gaze on Dmitri, but Ramira's eyes keep darting elsewhere. It's a clear sign of her rising panic—and her hatred for her captors. «Make them stay away from me! You're all dead when my uncle finds out what's going on here. Do you hear me? You're dead!»

Ramira continues screeching at her, but Elizabetta's mind is too numb to process her own thoughts and listen to the witch too. Even turning away from the outside world doesn't block the distractions so she can think. Then the trembling of Ramira's body gains her attention, and she pivots her focus to see what has the witch upset now. Elizabetta notices for the first time that Ramira is standing still, her gaze transfixed by the three men now standing outside of Ramira's cage. *Rage, fear?* They're trying to question her, reassure her, or get her to respond. *Dmitri ... Matt. God, I've missed seeing their faces.*

A sad illusory smile parts her lips as she looks from one to the other. Dmitri's enraged eyes are filled with an underlying sadness, and his voice is saturated with equal parts of fear, hope, and barely contained anger. *Bloodlust. How much longer can he hold it together?* It rips her heart out to see him this way, especially not knowing if she'll ever be free to return to him. Even though her body is hundreds of miles away, she'd gladly take her final breath if she could feel his arms around her just one more time. *Ti amo e non smetterò mai di amarti.*

Matt seems frustrated, dejected—she knows that look. He uses it when he thinks he's messed up big-time and doesn't know how to go back and fix things. There's nothing he could have done differently, and she'll never blame him for what happened to her. In many ways he's done far more for her than she's ever been able to do for him. Elizabetta cherishes their friendship in ways he'll never know. Her heart clenches at the hollow, distant thought that always lingers at the back of her brain: unlike Dmitri, Matt won't live forever. She'll never be ready to let him go.

Then there's Dahliorn ... he's promising he will help save her, answering the other two men's questions, and trying to elicit a response from her so he can reassure both men that she's all right. *I am the furthest thing from all right. I am all wrong ... just one more of Guillermo's abominations. You know all about that, don't you?*

Every encounter she's had with the sheridauk since she was taken captive replays in her mind. Like tumblers on a lock, so many little things slide into place and make sense— comments Ramira made, and the way Dahliorn obscured the truth every time their conversations drifted to the spider. The underlying sadness and resignation that came through him whenever they talked. *I missed something. This can't be real ... it doesn't seem right.* All those months of fearing mutant spiders, begging Dahliorn to help her kill them ... only to find out there is just one spider, and it is him. Dahliorn—Unseelie prince of the fae.

She actually cheered Matt on when he wounded the sheridauk, and she injured him herself when he helped Ramira kill Jacques. The witch never blacked out in the high warlock's garden; it was her, she was the one who stabbed him and collapsed his lung. Guilt settles like a one-ton weight crushing every cell of her body. Elizabetta can't clear her head enough to understand why, even after all she subjected the sheridauk to, he actually saved her life to-night, and that of all crazy possibilities it was Dmitri he saved her from. *Total mind job ... I need to reconcile all of this.*

Worse, even with this turn of events, they're nowhere near safe. Guillermo still has control of both of them through the silver belts strapped to their bodies, and these restraints can deliver punishment or even death. That thought brings her back to the present.

The sheridauk doesn't seem able to hold eye contact. Elizabetta can hear in his silent pleading that he feels ashamed and is worried that he's lost her friendship. All of his fae not-quite-a-lie answers now smack of deceit and betrayal, and he's clearly regretting it. *How am I supposed to feel?* She's numb, hollow ... empty where he's concerned.

Elizabetta wants to return to her own body and shut her mind down for a while, but it's not possible now that she's bound to Ramira—there's no escaping the witch. She needs to regain her sense of balance and understanding. She hopes at least Dahliorn can put her to sleep. *Will he refuse if I ask?* Her illusory head is pounding—she's unable to take much more. She finally reaches out to him. «I'm not ready to talk to you. I don't even know what to say ... Tell Dmitri I love him—I know he will find a way to save me. Let Matt know I love him too for always being there for me. But as to you ... I may never figure it out, and I can't think anymore right now ... Sleep, I need sleep. If you know of a way to do it, just put me to sleep.»

Dahliorn's eyes pulse between his normal dark green and a lighter shade. He places a hand on the barrier. For a dozen long breaths, Elizabetta stares at his hand before looking back at his face. A part of her wants to reach out to him, but she doesn't know how to do that until her world turns right side up again.

The sheridauk draws a ragged breath. «Your messages will be relayed. I never meant to hurt you—I am sorry, and when you are ready I will seek your forgiveness, peace-bringer." When she doesn't respond, he looks down at the floor. «Sleep now, little dove.»

Everything starts to turn black, and Elizabetta breathes out a mental sigh of relief as her mind shuts down and she begins to drift off to dream. *Peace-bringer ...* She brushed off Dahliorn every time he brought that up. Now it seems to be an epiphany; it's the first thing to make sense to her since this whole crazy odyssey began. *I wonder if the fates knew what they were doing when they selected me?* Then it hits her—she's not the key, she's the catalyst. If anything, the whole prophecy is about them.

She takes a moment to look at the men who have been so important to her life, each in their own way. *Dmitri. Matt. Dahliorn.* Good, fair men worthy of leading their people.

She'll lay odds that her role in all of this was designed to bring them together. She smiles to herself. *Something tells me I'll have a lot of work to do to keep them together too—once they figure out how to save me.*

*Coming Spring-Summer 2017 ...*

*Redemption*
Book Four of the *Nights of Shadow* series

But before *Redemption* arrives, we will cross over
into another corner of the
*Nights of Shadow* world and meet
Nate and Rafe Redhawk
in
*Flight*
Book One of the new *Rise of the Thunderbirds* series!

Read on for an excerpt from *Flight ...*

# RISE OF THE THUNDERBIRDS—*FLIGHT*

## *Excerpt*

"Rafe!" Nate hollers from downstairs, and I can hear the stress in his voice. Something isn't right. Without a second thought I run out of the room and leap down the steps, skipping two at a time, Ina hot on my tail.

Both Nate and Jo have their wings out and are facing something that shouldn't even be in this world. I skid to a stop next to them, my wings bursting through my shirt, and out of the corner of my eye I see Ina do the same. "What the—"

"Don't know. That crazy demon just waltzed in here like he owned the place, dragging that woman with him. He waved me away and said I can't see them, as if he were some kind of Star Wars Jedi. But it's pretty fucking clear we can all see them."

Nate isn't exaggerating. There really is a huge reddish demon with gnarled, pointed teeth and a crown of horns circling his head just standing there. And he's massive—the living room has ten-foot ceilings, and if they were eight, he'd have to stoop to fit.

The brunette he's holding against her will is struggling to get free, but I don't think she's all there, because she's arguing with herself. It seems part of her wants the demon and the other part doesn't. Then she yells, "He's not what he seems. Zerbadiah won't hurt you—believe it or not, he's a good guy." Before any of us can reply, the woman adds, "No, he'll kill us all. You have to destroy him. Save me!" It's almost as if she read my mind.

"I don't want to hurt any of you. Just stay calm, and everything will be okay," the demon says as he adjusts his grip on the crazy lady, who is still writhing wildly.

Okay, this is beyond weird, and I can see right now the gal will be of no help; she's either possessed or too divided over her feelings for the grotesque beast. Without taking my eyes off the demon, I say as quietly as possible, "Well, bro? Any bright ideas, or are we just going to wing it?"

Nate says, "Real fucking funny."

Now in all fairness, I was going for cliché and didn't mean to toss out the pun. "Hum a few bars and fake it?" This isn't what I expected after all those centuries waiting to become a thunderbird. I thought we'd be battling Earth-type bad guys.

"Not helping, bro," Nate growls through clenched teeth.

Jo takes a half step forward and glares at the beast. "What are you doing here, and what do you want?"

I should have seen that coming, considering the hellcat she is.

The demon says, "I won't hurt you. I'm here with Matt."

Unable to contain it, I let out a snort. I knew there was

something really off about our boss, but I'll admit that I didn't see this coming.

"If we can just sit tight"—the demon inches toward the couch, pulling the lady along with him—"he and some of the others will be up to the house soon and can answer your questions."

"There's more of you here?" Ina's voice pitches up in terror, and I can't say I blame her. One of these demons is more than enough.

"What made you think we couldn't see you?" Nate's glare is intimidating, but I'm not sure it's going to be enough against this monster. I have no idea if even the four of us can take on a demon and win.

The demon shrugs. "I expected you to be humans, not thunderbirds." An aha look crosses his face, and he whispers in the crazy woman's ear, "The lost thunderbirds ... the last element of the peace-bringer prophecy."

My eyebrows shoot upward. I heard what he said, and Nate likely did too, but it's the demon's recognition of us as thunderbirds that I find unsettling. "What does being human got to do with anything, and how do you know what we are?"

Okay, I'll admit it; it was probably a stupid question, considering what I'm talking to, and there's no ignoring that our wings are on full display.

The front door opens, and in walks Matt and some tall, pale-looking dude with dark hair and eyes. Doubtless the looks on their faces mirror my own—shock, mistrust, defensiveness. They're ready to fight. I watch as my boss does a quick assessment of the four of us and then the demon holding the brunette, and he gives a sideways glance to his pale friend. Then Matt moves between us and the demon, holding his hands out as if to keep our two sides separated. "Whoa!"

In the next instant his eyes seem different, with the green in his hazel eyes almost glowing. But it's what happens to his nose and mouth that's the most disturbing. The former seems to resemble the start of a canine or bear snout, and the latter fills with long, deadly fangs. His words come out in a growl as he looks at the demon. "I thought you said they wouldn't see you?"

Okay, now I know for certain there's something strange about the man, but I'm not sure what he is or why he's in league with a demon. I don't think any of us know what to do, because we're just standing our ground in a defensive posture.

The demon's red eyes bore right through us. "You didn't tell me your hired hands were thunderbirds."

I swear I'm going to suffer an aneurysm if we don't start getting answers here.

The pale one steps closer to the demon. His lip curls and his eyes narrow as he looks at the confused woman in the demon's arms, but just as quickly a sappy, lovestruck expression settles on his face, and I'm thinking he and the woman may make a good couple—they're both fucking nuts. I get the sense that he'd fight to the death to save the gal, but if that's the case, why isn't he attacking the demon? The power rolling off the pale freak would make a grown man piss his pants.

"Thunder-what?" Matt's head spins toward us. "Rafe,

Nate, you want to tell me what's going on here? And include what the hell you are."

"What the hell are we? Fuck, man, what the hell are you?" Nate's fists clench.

Matt growls. "Nate, I've warned you before, that word won't be tolerated in front of women! You better check that shit and answer my question. Now!"

For a moment he somewhat sounds like our friendly boss, or at least the one we know. If he were going to hurt us, wouldn't he have done so months ago? But when I think back, I realize this was behind his inside jokes and strange humor. Like he really got off on knowing he was something other than human while those around him were ignorant. It kind of pisses me off, but it also tells me he's not a threat if we can come to terms here. I step forward and try to keep my voice level and calm. "It seems we all have some explaining to do."

# Playlist for Nights of Shadow—Chaos

The songs in this playlist fit the themes and scenes of *Nights of Shadow—Chaos*, and some are specific to Dmitri, Elizabetta/Eliza, and Matt. They helped inspire me during the writing of *Chaos*; hopefully they will also help you enjoy a deeper emotional connection to the story and its characters.

YouTube: http://tinyurl.com/o8hceoj

1) "Black Roses" by Candice Night [Eliza's anthem]
2) "My Silver Lining" by First Aid Kit [Dmitri's anthem]
3) "Blaze Of Glory" by Jon Bon Jovi [Dmitri and Matt fighting side by side]
4) "Welcome to the Jungle" by Guns N' Roses [Dmitri and Matt on Seelinara]
5) "Bitch" by Meredith Brooks [Elizabetta's determination to fight back]
6) "Devils & Dust" by Bruce Springsteen [Dmitri's fear and struggle with bloodlust]
7) "Fighter" by Christina Aguilera [Elizabetta's willingness to sacrifice herself and protect others]
8) "Bad to the Bone" by George Thorogood & the Destroyers [Dmitri at leadership contest]
9) "Window of Opportunity" by White Island [Elizabetta seizes the moment to kill Constance]
10) "The Reason" by Hoobastank [The deepening love between Matt and Maria]
11) "He Who Walks Alone" by Orchid [Dmitri's continuing struggle]
12) "Lullaby" by Nickelback [Elizabetta trying to reach out to Dmitri through Ramira]

# Acknowledgments

To my readers, I humbly thank you for buying this book. Please consider writing a review for this story wherever it was purchased online. I want to hear your thoughts about Eliza, Dmitri, Matt, the Druzhinas, and Maria. Shashenka's time has come to an end, but Guillermo is the first to rise to take his place. What do you think will become of the shadow realm world now? Let me know what made you laugh or cry or made you angry, but most importantly, whether you enjoyed the story.

Special thanks to my beta reader team—Sandy, Tim, Abe, Elaine, Ruth, Tony, Rachel, Henry, and Mark. Your critical and complimentary input, along with your enthusiasm and encouragement, helped make the final version of this story possible.

My heartfelt thanks goes to my family, for putting up with me when I'm in serious writing mode and for all the times you have pushed me to follow this dream. I couldn't have done this without you.

Lastly, I again want to thank my editor, Christina M. Frey of Page Two Editing, for all of her diligent and hard work; she catches all of my tongue-in-cheek humor and double entendres. I came to you with the desire to put my best work out there, and I believe you have succeeded in helping me accomplish that goal once more. As always, it has been a pleasure working with you.

# About the Author

Lianne Miller grew up in the mountains of southwestern Montana, about two hundred miles northwest of Bozeman. She now lives on the high plains in the northeastern part of the state, where she runs a horse ranch with her husband and an extended family member.

From riding horses to driving a semitruck and owning a small business, Lianne has worn many hats and labels, and she often claims to be a jack-of-all-trades and master of none. Now many of her days are spent writing and bringing to life the stories she began creating while raising her children. Lianne's books delve into judgment, tolerance, prejudice, and acceptance—challenges in both the human and the paranormal worlds. *Nights of Shadow* was her debut series, and next spring she will release the first book in her crossover series, *Rise of the Thunderbirds*.

For news about Lianne's stories and characters or to sign up for email alerts, visit her online world:

Website: www.liannemiller.com
Blog: http://apps.liannemiller.com/Blog
Facebook: www.facebook.com/MillerLianne
Twitter: https://twitter.com/_LianneMiller
YouTube Channel: http://tinyurl.com/owrvqhh